MAGE FORETOLD

Book 7 of "Circles of Light"

I0680473

*For Michele
and in memory of her Teka*

*With love to John and Ben
as always*

MAGE FORETOLD

Book 7 of "Circles of Light"

———————

E M Sinclair

Mage Foretold – Book 7 of *Circles of Light*
First published 2015

Typeset by John Owen Smith

Cover photo by B Melville

Published by Murrell Press

© E M Sinclair 2015

E M Sinclair can be contacted via the **Circles of Light** Facebook page.

ISBN 978-09554135-7-5

Printed by CreateSpace

Chapter One

Tilliat Kranch pressed herself even tighter into the angle of the two half-tumbled walls and silently cursed her stupidity. It had been crazy enough to come to the Citadel but unbelievably careless to stay so long. Dusk fell early in the winter but seafog had darkened the whole day and now the fog had thickened even more. The streets were dangerous in normal daylight but with the rapidly advancing nightfall, and the fog distorting every sound, Tilliat knew she could be in serious trouble. The guttural voices which had sent her into the shell of this building sounded again, louder. Booted feet scuffled and thumped on the cobblestones.

'We meetin' Vert tonight again?'

'Nah, we can do better on our own. He's nothing but gas and wind.'

''E stuck that merchant good though,' the first speaker cackled.

'And then sent us straight into a militia band afterwards,' the second voice snarled back.

Tilliat heard a slap and the first voice spoke again, whining now.

'Watcha mean Pen?'

'Vert told us to go down Lime Street didn't he? But where'd he go? Opposite direction. Reckon he done a deal with the militia.'

The voices faded but Tilliat didn't move immediately. Her ears strained to hear the slightest sounds but there was only the murky silence. She frowned. She would have to make a move and risk the alleyways back to the Traders District. She drew a deep breath and rose from her hiding place.

It took far too long before Tilliat finally reached the door to her house: twice she'd had to wait in shadows to let gangs tramp past and once she'd detoured a vicious brawl involving twenty men or more. She hurried up the four steps and the door swung open as she reached it. A hand gripped her arm, pulled her inside, and the scolding began even as the door was slammed shut. The elderly man swung down two sturdy bars across the door then snatched up his crutches which he'd leant against the wall.

'Where in all the hells have you been child? We've been worried sick.'

He glared at Tilliat but she understood his fury truly stemmed from his terror that she might have been caught, out in the dangerous streets. She stepped close and put her arms round his waist.

'I know. I was really stupid Pakal. I forgot the fog was so bad.'

Tilliat moved back and looked up into his angry face. His expression softened slightly and he shook his head.

'Well, brace yourself for Jomah's welcome girl, she is in a rare temper.'

Tilliat led the way along the hall and pushed open the door at the end. Lamps lit the large kitchen and their light sparkled back from copper pans and bowls set on a great dresser along a side wall. A short, plump woman was bent over, taking a tray from the oven beside the fire. She glanced up before setting the tray on the long wooden table, then threw down the cloth she'd used and put her hands on her hips.

Jomah's tirade lasted some time during which she still managed to carve the roast meat, serve vegetables and sauces, without a single fumble or pause. A slice of fruit pie was pushed in front of Tilliat in a sudden silence. Pakal took the opportunity to remark:

'Trader Pearl called to see you just after the midday bell.'

Tilliat glanced across the table at the old man. 'Uncle Davin? Did he say why?'

'No lass, but he's worried about something that's for sure. He said he'll call again tomorrow morning.'

Tilliat nodded then laid aside her spoon. 'We've known trouble would come. I'll send a message to Skala first thing.' She studied the two familiar faces with a sudden ache in her heart. 'Papa's been gone five years come spring – you know he'd have got word to us somehow, if he'd been able. And you know we planned for me to leave if things got – difficult – here.'

Jomah pushed her chair back, clattered dishes together and piled them in the sink, her mouth set in a grim line. Pakal rubbed his hands over his face and gave a gusting sigh.

'I feel so useless with these cursed legs. It should be me coming with you.'

'Oh yes?' Tilliat snapped back. 'You think Jomah would let you come off with me, wandering gods know where. Your place is here – that was decided before Papa – disappeared – and you know it. You have to keep the business running for us.'

She got to her feet, trying desperately to ignore the brightness in the eyes of this couple so dear to her. 'Uncle Davin will not have good news tomorrow I'm sure. I'll come down for a hot drink later.'

She swung away from the table, through the door and up the stairs. 'Gods, this is going to be hard,' she muttered as she reached the sanctuary of her own rooms two floors above the kitchen.

Three streets away, lights blazed from the solid plainness of the Traders Guild Hall. A reception was being held for the Chancellor and his officials, various investors and bankers, as well as a few members of government. The main hall where the reception was taking place was a large space but modestly decorated and furnished: no point in openly displaying to any greedy officials the vast wealth which the Traders preferred to keep to themselves.

A tall thin man wearing trousers of dark blue wool tucked into blue leather boots, stood near one of several alcoves inset along one wall of the hall. His paler blue shirt bore the insignia of the Traders Guild Council on the left shoulder. He held a goblet near his face but was drinking very little, his dark eyes casually observing the crowd of guests.

Another man emerged from the throng, similarly clothed but his garments were a soft grey rather than blue. He wandered towards the tall man and raised his own goblet in salutation.

'Another message from the Citadel, Belk. It's all happening too fast.'

The tall man tilted his head slightly. 'And too soon, Pearl, much too soon.'

Trader Pearl laughed, as though Trader Belk had made a jest, and murmured: 'Tilliat Kranch must either leave the city or we must give her safety here.'

Trader Belk bowed politely as two gaudily robed Chancellery officials passed close by. 'We must speak of this once all this nonsense is over,' he replied, then stifled a groan. 'Gods help me, he's heading this way.'

Trader Pearl gave a genuine grin. 'The joys of leadership Master Trader,' he said, backing away as Chancellor Kanack arrived with five underlings all enveloped in an overpowering cloud of strong and costly perfumes.

To Davin Pearl the evening seemed endless. He, like his fellow Traders, male and female, mingled with their guests, answered incredibly inane questions and nodded humbly when told how he could run his businesses more profitably. Serving men removed some of the younger guests who had succumbed to too much alcohol and passed them on to guardsmen to be loaded into various carriages.

Davin Pearl noted that Chancellor Kanack had dismissed his juniors and was discussing something intently with Master Trader Pirus Belk. If he'd been a gambling man he would have wagered that their conversation focused on Trader Kranch's multiple business concerns and his prolonged absence from the city. Oh yes, thought Davin, poor Tilliat must leave, and very soon.

At last the Chancellor moved towards the great outer doorway and Traders bowed polite farewells. Once the most important guest had departed, the rest quickly followed suit. When the doors were closed, Traders nodded to each other, some leaving through the inner doors, some gathering in small groups to exchange information garnered from the evening's guests.

Master Trader Belk raised his voice as he made his way to a door at the furthest end of the hall. 'Ladies and gentlemen, thank you all for your support tonight – and your patient endurance! I will meet with you tomorrow at midday.'

Davin Pearl smiled as a woman joined him to cross the hall in Belk's wake. 'I noticed you avoiding our good Chancellor – only because I was watching. I don't think it was too obvious.'

Mahza Chern gave an unladylike snort. 'Bloody man. Thinks he has the most intelligent mind in the land and that he is irresistible to every woman no matter their age. Odious beast.'

Pearl held the door open for her and grinned. 'No need to be polite my dear, you don't like him much then?'

Mahza glared up at him as she passed. She wasted no breath on a reply, the stairs being many, and steep, and her age, regrettably, catching up with her ability to climb them. Davin Pearl made no further comment until they reached the seventh landing. Mahza halted for a moment and Pearl waited patiently until she was ready to continue to the only door on this level.

Lamplight shone softly on wood so dark it seemed it was stained with midnight itself but as Davin lifted the latch, other lamps from the room within caused a profusion of intricate carvings to show in brief relief. Pirus Belk sat in a deep armchair beside a blazing fire. He gestured them to sit near him. While Mahza Chern sank gratefully into the chair opposite, Davin Pearl moved to a side table and poured wine into two goblets. He handed one to Mahza as he took the remaining chair.

'Kanack is about to try for Stevro Kranch's investments and holdings,' Belk announced without preamble.

'I still don't understand why,' complained Mahza. 'Other Traders have been in similar situations as Stevro and then reappeared after long absences. Neither the Chancellor nor anyone else has made a grab for their businesses before. Stevro had a broad base for his trade. What have I not been told Pirus?'

The Master Trader drained his own goblet and set it on a small table beside his chair. He rubbed his temples and leaned back with his eyes closed for a moment.

'Stevro Kranch had many contacts .'

Mahza grunted. 'We all have many contacts Pirus – it's how traders actually trade, remember?'

There was a brief silence broken by the sudden snap and hiss of a log splitting on the fire. Mahza pushed herself upright and stared at the man opposite her. 'Contacts? Gods, what has he got into? The primary tenet of our Guild is that we have no political affiliations or ambitions. Tell me Kranch hasn't got involved with any of the factions?'

'None of the factions here in Kelshan, no,' Belk replied.

Mahza's mouth dropped open and she stared first at Belk, then Pearl, and back to Belk. 'But there is war in the eastern provinces,' she began.

'And a strong leadership has arisen amongst the clans at long last,' Pearl interrupted her.

'The clans? And they're looking this way?' Mahza's whisper was barely audible.

'Look at the histories. How have we, in our civilised wisdom, treated the clans for a thousand years and more? Of course they are looking this way. They have always been divided: so many small independent clans, bickering among themselves, but recently, they have united under one leader.' Pirus sighed. 'And I'm sure I can guess the message you received from the Citadel tonight Pearl?'

'I'm sure you can Master. Within the week this city will be in turmoil. The factions have reached boiling point.'

'And thus the carnage will begin,' Pirus finished for him.

Mahza Chern paled. 'I thought we had longer,' she muttered.

'We always hope such things my dear, but that is why I called a meeting for tomorrow. I will give all Traders of the Guild the choice of getting to their homes or bringing their families here.' Pirus smiled sadly. 'There are supplies within this building to last us all for a good while, and the whole structure has been inspected and reinforced over the last five years. For just such an event as we now face.'

Davin said nothing, thinking briefly of the massive extensions that had been discreetly dug over a period of many more years, far below the Traders Guild Hall.

Mahza cleared her throat. 'Maybe it won't be as – violent – as we imagine?'

'My dear Mahza,' Pirus's tone was gentle. 'It will be a blood letting as bad if not worse than when the Imperators were overthrown. How long have the gangs ruled the streets at night? And they are increasingly bold in daylight this last year. No my dear old friend, it will be bad, very bad.'

Mahza Chern set her goblet aside and pushed herself to her feet, suddenly looking every one of her eighty-three years. 'I'll leave you two now I think. There are letters I must write.' She moved to the door, turned with her hand on the latch. 'How many of our belongings can we take down to the haven Pirus?'

Pirus rose and went to her, his arm across her shoulders. 'You

10

will have a room about half the size of your present quarters – you will not be too cramped.'

She closed her eyes and allowed herself to lean against him for a moment. Then she straightened. 'I'll write my letters and start sorting my things then.'

The two men sat in silence until Pirus leaned forward in his chair and pushed another log onto the fire.

'Are we ready for this?' Davin asked softly.

'Is anyone ever ready for this,' Pirus retorted. 'It will be called civil disturbances to start with, but once news gets out of Kelshan, the other cities will think "oh what a good idea," and civil disturbance will become civil war.' He met Davin's steady gaze. 'And weak though our rulers think the nations of Tarran and Jerrad may be and far enough south though they are, both those countries have their eyes very closely upon us here in Kelshan.'

Davin nodded: he too had his informants.

'Stevro Kranch was hoping to find a way to the Isles of Vremilia, but those lands remain in their chosen isolation as far as I know.' Pirus stared into the fire. 'The small principalities will probably try to stay independent, closing their borders like clam shells, but the dependencies close to the clan lands in the north will join whoever looks to be the winning side.'

'And you still think Tilliat should travel to the south?' Davin asked. He tried to make his tone casual but this was a point he had long been troubled over.

Pirus chuckled and glanced across at him. 'Of course not. North then east is the route she must take although there will be false trails suggesting she has gone south.'

Davin couldn't help an audible sigh of relief escaping. Pirus raised his brows at the sound. Davin spread his hands, palms up.

'I've always known Tilliat was – special. Since Stevro brought her back as a tiny girl. He said her mother died soon after the babe was born and he had not wanted to leave her in the care of the mother's clan. So he waited until she'd grown enough to travel with him.' Davin studied the Master Trader carefully. 'Is she Stevro's true child?'

Pirus hesitated for too long. 'I don't honestly know if he fathered her or not,' he admitted at last. 'But I do know – as well

11

as you – that she has received an education and training far beyond that needed by any other child.'

'She is a child no longer,' Davin pointed out. 'She was eighteen this last summer.'

Pirus nodded. 'I believe Stevro would have taken her from this city two or even three years ago had he been here to do so. Unfortunately, he neither told me all of it, nor even half, and I have found nothing among his papers. Obviously he believed he would be returning from his trading journey to the eastern provinces but no word has ever reached us either from him or about him.'

'He always told me he had wed a clan woman from the furthest north east, but he never specified which clan,' said Davin.

'Nor to me, and he left absolutely nothing here. Are there papers at his own house, would you know? I never felt right asking Tilliat, and as for Pakal and Jomah, if they do know anything they'll take it to their graves.'

Davin stretched his legs out and crossed his ankles. 'Pakal wasn't with Stevro on that trip. He was mending from the accident that took the use of his legs. And I have never traced any other wagon drivers or guards who worked for Stevro that year.'

Pirus grunted. 'Me neither. And believe me, I've tried.'

Silence fell and then Davin changed the subject. 'How will the Bench of Governors end do you think?'

Pirus gave a bitter laugh. 'Taris will possibly survive but I would guess all eight of the others will be dead within days.' He waved a hand around his room. 'Nearly all my papers and books are down in the haven. Will you stay with us Davin, or try to get clear?'

Davin Pearl rose to his feet. 'I'm still undecided Master. I wonder should I travel with Tilliat Kranch? I'll knock on Skala Vek's door on my way down and talk with him.'

Pirus remained silent and Davin Pearl moved to the door. 'I told Skala that you should go with them if you offered. It will be perilous if you go, but just as perilous staying here.' The Master Trader gave a tired grin. 'Goodnight Trader Pearl. I will see you at midday tomorrow.'

Davin Pearl made his way down past two landings then strode along the length of the third, ignoring the doors regularly spaced on each side of the passageway. At the furthest end he stopped and rapped his knuckles lightly on a dark panel set into a lighter coloured door. A voice called for him to enter and, lifting the latch, Pearl went into the room.

As usual when visiting Skala Vek, he was startled by the emptiness of the apartment. A fire in the hearth had burned down to a thick bed of glowing embers and one lamp was lit on a shelf above the fire. A man sat cross-legged on a rug, his head turned to watch Pearl over his shoulder.

'I trust I am not disturbing you Skala, I know it's very late to visit.'

'No, Davin Pearl. Many things disturb me but you are not one. Please, sit if you wish.'

Davin settled on the rug beside Skala Vek and grimaced.

'I wish you had a few items of furniture here, such as a chair or two, and I also wish you could refrain from portentous comments. I've just survived the Chancellor's reception and my brain can cope with no more.'

Skala Vek's mouth twitched slightly. 'You have my sympathy. Did you need my shoulder to weep on?'

Davin laughed aloud. 'I will forgo that, but I do deeply appreciate the offer.'

Skala Vek watched him, his eyes the pale blue of a winter sky but warm in the lamp and firelight, when more often they seemed like ice.

Davin took a breath. 'I would travel with you when you leave with Tilliat Kranch,' he said softly.

Skala's pale gaze moved from Davin's face to the embers of the fire. 'I would be glad of your company,' he admitted, looking back into the Trader's eyes. 'You had to freely offer to come though. On this journey there will be no changing of minds you understand.'

A chill prickled down Davin's spine. He'd known travelling would be difficult – gods, getting out of the city would be fraught enough. But something in Skala's tone warned him of dangers he could not yet imagine.

'I'm going to the Kranch house tomorrow morning. Tilliat

was out when I visited today.'

'Tell her to prepare to leave in two more days Davin. I have horses here in the Guild stables, but if it seems inadvisable to try to ride out, there are more at the inn beyond the north gate. It is not the best season for travelling of course, and winter hangs on longer further north – where we will be going.'

The two men sat for a while, unspeaking, both thinking of the prospective journey.

Skala Vek was young, barely twenty-five, lean and fit, his black hair held back in a short tail by a plain silver clasp. He was said to be full blood clan, but he looked more like the Kelshanite people than a clansman. His blue eyes would be considered most rare among the clans and his face was thinner, his nose straight rather than a hooked beak.

Davin had made a point, years ago, of checking into Skala Vek's past. It proved exceedingly obscured, but Davin was fairly confident that Vek came from the Black Claw clan, although he had never discovered why or how the boy had suddenly appeared at the Traders Guild Hall.

Fifteen years past, Pirus Belk had become the Master Trader and so no longer undertook trading missions, busying himself with the unending details of administration. He had taken the ten year old boy under his protection with no comment to anyone, and now, fifteen years later, Davin Pearl was still unsure in what exact way Skala Vek earned his keep. He did know that Vek was a dangerous man – one glance into those cold eyes told anyone that fact.

Davin climbed to his feet, unable to stifle a wince. He used Skala's shoulder to heave himself upright and headed for the door.

'Should I perhaps suggest Tilliat comes here sooner?' he asked.

Skala considered the question. 'Yes. Pakal and Jomah are both named per Kranch and they have the right to shelter here. I think Tilliat would prefer to know they are as safe as possible. Yes.' Skala Vek rose as well. 'They can spend tomorrow packing the most necessary things. It will keep them all occupied before we leave.'

Davin nodded and let himself out. He heard the soft snick of bolts sliding in the door behind him and then made his way back to the stairwell. He climbed back up to the floor below Belk's solitary quarters and entered his own apartment. The single candle he'd left burning hours before was guttering and he quickly lit several more and set them around the main room. He looked around.

Most of his books and papers had gone down to the haven days ago. A wooden chest stood by the unlit fire, half filled with oddments which he couldn't bear to part with. That would go down tomorrow. He rubbed his hand over his grey, bristle cut hair and thanked all the gods he no longer had a family to worry over. Was that why you've offered to join this mad expedition, he asked himself.

He'd had a wife and three children once upon a time. They had died of a plague while he was away, trading in the far south. They had been dead nearly a full year before he'd learned of it. And that was twenty two years ago. Davin Pearl had never even considered taking another wife, and now here he was, over fifty years old and not one of his blood remained in this world. There were a few Traders who would mourn briefly if he was suddenly to die, but nobody would miss him with the pain he still felt for his lost family.

He went to a cupboard and took out a bottle. Pouring a good measure into a crystal glass, he gulped half of it down without pause. He topped his glass up then firmly replaced the stopper in the bottle, the bottle in the cupboard, and turned back to the room. Knowing he would sleep little if at all tonight, Davin Pearl continued to sort out and pack his possessions.

Chapter Two

Lying in bed in one of the several guest apartments in the Traders Guild Hall, Tilliat tried to get to sleep. Skala Vek wanted them to leave before dawn, although it was nearly impossible to tell when dawn might arrive when the city was shrouded in winter sea fog.

The last two days had passed in a blur of activity: crating up most of their possessions in the Kranch house and taking the crates down to the hiding place beyond the cellar pantry. She and Pakal and Jomah had arrived at the Hall after midday, Pakal driving the small wagon through streets filled with aimless crowds. Jomah sat up front with Pakal while Tilliat huddled under the wagon's cover. She watched between Jomah and Pakal's shoulders as the wagon crept slowly through the streets.

The people didn't seem to be going about their various businesses and Tilliat saw very few children among them. The playground outside a school they drove past was empty, the door and windows of the building heavily shuttered and barred. It seemed strangely quiet when there were so many people thronging the streets but Tilliat only realised the crowds were all heading towards the great Citadel as Pakal drove them through the gates of Traders Hall.

There was a palpable sense of relief when they heard the heavy gates close behind them and the dull thud of the iron bars locking into place. Trader guards and servants unloaded their wagon and ushered them into the great Hall. When one guard made to lead Tilliat one way and another guard indicated a different direction to Pakal and Jomah, Tilliat baulked.

Davin Pearl was, fortuitously, entering the Hall at that moment and hurried to join her.

'Don't worry my dear, you can visit them later and reassure yourself as to their comfort, but the Master specifically asked that you be brought to him as soon as you arrived.'

Tilliat looked at the two Kranch retainers. Pakal looked

16

exhausted and Jomah white with worry, but Jomah nodded.

'Go along with you. Just don't forget to come and say farewell.'

Tilliat followed the guard up unending flights of stairs to a room she'd never visited before. The guard rapped his knuckles against the black wood and when a voice within called to enter, the guard lifted the latch and stepped back. Tilliat walked inside, the guard closing the door quietly at her back. Master Trader Pirus Belk rose from a desk set against a wall and below a narrow window. He bowed.

'I am relieved to see you Tilliat Kranch. Please, be seated.'

Tilliat turned over in her bed yet again. She had hoped against hope that Master Belk would have information for her, even the miracle of a letter left in his keeping by her father five years before. But all that Master Belk spoke of were things she'd long known. She listened so carefully to every word but there was nothing new to be learned, nothing at all.

At least lying awake meant there were no dreams to plague her. Dreams that had begun soon after her father left Kelshan City for what turned out to be the last time. They had been occasional dreams at first, extraordinarily vivid, but then they were gone like morning mist as soon as she woke. Slowly over the seasons, the dreams increased in frequency and also in violence, dreams which left her drenched in cold sweat and shivering with dread.

Then, just before her eighteenth birthday she had faced the dreams, had refused to let herself surge back to the waking world. And what she learned and felt from the dreams since then had filled her with a different kind of fear. This fear was no longer for herself but for her world, for everyone in it. As the uneasiness grew in the city, so did the urgency of Tilliat's dreams. She knew she should ask someone to help her decipher these almost-visions, but was unable to fix on just who. If her father was here – but he wasn't; so she'd taken to searching the Citadel library for any single hint that might match with what she saw in her head.

Tilliat had been on some trading journeys with her father, both north and south, although they were short journeys – three turns of the moon at most. But she recognised nothing that appeared in

17

her dreams. Needle-thin spires – whether of natural rock or somehow made by human contrivance, dark forested mountains, vast plains and stretches of water bluer than any she'd ever seen.

Those dreams made her ache with curiosity but it was the other dreams that made her ache with fear. She saw a face, very pale, an almost perfect oval with eyes slanted sharply upward at the outer corners, above cheekbones like cliffs. The thin mouth was pressed straight and the dark eyes stared directly at her. She saw the face from a much lower position and knew that she was kneeling, her arms extended sideways and held by manacles.

Sometimes Tilliat was able to force herself awake after only a few lashes to her back, but other nights she endured a seemingly endless time and would finally wake with her face wet with tears and her back and shoulders ablaze with pain. These fearsome dreams grew gradually more frequent and she was now enduring them with only four or five nights between them.

She turned over yet again. Perhaps this journey would cast the dreams from her. The rap on her door roused her from what felt like barely a few moments sleep, but she called for Skala Vek to enter. It was indeed the clansman and as Tilliat pushed herself up in the bed, she heard a rattling against the shuttered window and shivered.

Skala grinned. 'Sleet and hail, but it will turn to snow by midday. Hurry now Tilliat, I'll see you downstairs.'

The only people Tilliat saw when she, Davin Pearl and Skala Vek left the Traders Guild Hall were maids sweeping the lower passageways, one of the kitchen staff who provided bowls of porridge and mugs of tea, and two stablemen.

Tilliat had rarely ridden a horse and was perched nervously on the back of what seemed to her to be an extraordinarily tall dark brown creature. Her apprehension was forgotten when a stableman swung open the outer door and Skala, holding a leading rope to her horse, tugged her forward.

It was still more dark than light but the wind hurled grains of sleet into her face with a viciousness and iciness that made her gasp. Davin Pearl rode up beside her, leaning across from his saddle.

'The weather's keeping the streets clear at least but I fear it will take the whole morning for us to reach the inn Skala wants us to get to.'

Tilliat peered through already ice-crusted lashes and saw Davin's grin with some disbelief. The trader seemed to be enjoying himself. After only the first few paces, Tilliat concentrated solely on staying on her horse and forcing herself to tense and relax various muscle groups. Despite this action, she was appalled to realise how rapidly her legs lost all sensation and how insidiously the rest of her body followed suit.

She had prided herself on her physical fitness. Her father had engaged tutors to teach her many different forms of combat – Skala Vek had been the hardest taskmaster – but she had followed every instruction and practised every discipline from her tenth year. Here she was, virtually immobilised, on top of a horse within only a scant few miles of the city. She gritted her teeth, bowed her head against the raging wind, and endured.

Tilliat was quite unaware when Skala led her horse off the road and inside a stable attached to Red Feather Inn. She blinked to see Skala's face looking up at her.

'Can you get down?' he asked.

She realised there was no wind knifing into her body, no ice particles stinging her face.

'Of course I can,' she croaked indignantly, only to find that none of her limbs seemed inclined to obey her orders.

Skala muttered something and reached up to her. Tilliat remembered no more until her eyes opened again and she saw she was in a small bedroom. She turned her head slightly to see a fire blazing cheerily in a hearth to her left. She felt a heavy tiredness throughout her body but as she tried to raise herself higher on her pillows, she groaned. The inside of her thighs and knees were stabbed with fire.

The door opened and Skala Vek came in carrying a laden tray which he placed on a table to the side of the fire. He brought a bowl of soup and a hunk of bread across to Tilliat. She sat straighter and took the food from him. Skala sat carefully on the edge of the bed.

'I'm afraid we can only stay here until the morning,' he said quietly. 'You should have told us that the cold was troubling you so badly. We'll lose time – it is dark already so we can travel no more today, but we must move tomorrow.'

She swallowed a piece of bread and nodded but before she could speak, Skala went on.

'There is some salve you can rub into your legs and bandages to wrap around them. The sleet has stopped and the wind is lessening but the snow is falling heavily. You understand Tilliat? We cannot stay here beyond the morning?'

'Why will no one explain why I have to go to Gulat?' Tilliat asked sharply. 'My father said the time might come when we would go there and since he – disappeared – Uncle Davin and Pakal and Jomah talked of it more and more. All I've managed to learn of the place is that it is one of the independent cities where any races may meet freely to trade. But why must I go there?'

Skala's icy eyes met her grey ones briefly then he looked towards the fire.

'I will confess that I have long believed it was foolish to keep you in ignorance, even before Stevro vanished. But it was always his sternest command.'

Again those wintry blue eyes glanced at her and away. He gave a short humourless laugh. 'And now is most certainly not the time or the place.'

Tilliat stared at him. 'You mean you know about all this stuff?' She waved the bread at him.

'Tilliat, I know some of this "stuff" as you put it. Not enough, certainly not all. But there are others who know much more and they are seeking you. We have to avoid them. There is one in Gulat who will give us further instructions. The journey will not end in Gulat, in fact you could consider Gulat to be only the start.'

Tilliat's fingers tightened on the bowl: it would be enormously satisfying to hurl it across the room. But she didn't. 'Who do we have to find in Gulat?' she asked Skala.

'A woman in the precious gems district. The wife of one of the most senior jewellers in fact.'

'Her name?'

Skala shook his head slowly. 'Not yet Tilliat. The risk is too great.' He stood up, taking the bowl from her hand. He passed her a small clay pot. 'Salve,' he said. 'Try to relax and be ready for an early start again. Davin and I are in the adjoining room – no one can come in here without coming through our room.'

Tilliat stayed as she was for a few moments then wearily pushed back the covers. She winced as she saw the redness on her inner thighs and the broken skin at the sides of her knees. She unstoppered the pot and sniffed the contents cautiously. She dug a finger into the paste and touched it to her leg – at least it didn't sting.

In spite of a general lethargy, Tilliat had slept all afternoon and did not feel at all sleepy now. She saw her backpack on the chair across the room and a roll of white linen beside it. She fetched both back to the bed and carefully wrapped the soft linen around her legs. Digging in her pack, she found a thin pair of woollen leggings which she put on over the bandages. She leaned back on the pillows and watched the flames blazing in the hearth.

A woman, in Gulat. Tilliat could make no sense of the little Skala had divulged. She sighed. Why had her father been so secretive? He had talked often of his many business deals and of trading contracts but he had never, ever, given any reason why it was so important that "one day" they would have to go to Gulat. It was at least twenty days travel for a trading caravan to reach Gulat, and that was in good weather with a sufficiency of armed guards as escort.

Tilliat had never contemplated having to make the trip in weather which was more winter than spring and with only two companions. And why oh why Gulat? It was the northern-most of the independent cities. There were two, widely separated, on the central plains and four more southwards and at least another four in the far east.

The clans lived mostly to the north but only a few lived as far north as Gulat. From the occasional comments from Skala over the years, she had concluded that his clan dwelt in the east but nowhere near as north as Gulat. Tilliat had never heard Davin Pearl mention Gulat, and he had entertained her childhood with endless tales of his trading journeys.

She closed her eyes, the fire making red shapes against her eyelids, and tried to find the stillness within which one of her tutors had insisted was an essential exercise to be practised daily. She ignored the twinge of guilt that crept into her mind. She hadn't practised the art of stillness for a very long time, but she began to regulate her breathing and seek that quietness now.

21

It seemed no time had passed when Tilliat became aware of movement in the next room and she presumed Davin and Skala were readying themselves for the day. She drew on her trousers, two shirts and a fur lined jerkin and was tugging on her boots when the door opened. Skala nodded approval at her apparent readiness.

'We'll have a good breakfast before we start,' he said. 'And the snow has stopped for now so we can perhaps make up some time.'

When they stepped out of the back door of the inn the air slapped Tilliat's face with its chill but at least there was no sleet or snow falling. Skala put a sheepskin cover on Tilliat's saddle and made her stand on a crate to ease herself aboard her horse. The skin of her thighs seemed to crack and tear but she was able to keep her expression blank and even managed a slight smile. Thirteen days were to pass with her having no memory from this particular moment.

When finally she regained some awareness, she was lying wrapped in blankets so tightly swaddled that she was unable to move. It felt as though her eyes were sealed together and she couldn't free a hand to rub them clear. Eventually she could see a blurry line of torn lashes. A fire smouldered right in front of her and someone was lying opposite – Davin Pearl she realised when a snuffling snore came from him.

'It's awake!'

Her head ached appallingly but she tried to look for the source of the voice. She appeared to be in a cave or a building of rough hewn stone. Tilliat gave up trying to see, the flickering embers jabbed through her eyelids, poking at her headache.

'It's a she, stupid, you know that.'

Tilliat groaned. It sounded like a voice in a dream but she was sure she was awake right now.

'How are we supposed to get her out when she's – well – what is she Toomay? Is she sick or what?'

'I think she's sick, but she's full of strange medicine too.'

'So what are we going to do?'

'Shut up and let me think.'

'Who are you?' Tilliat thought irritably.

22

When there was no further comment she forced her eyes open as much as she could. Davin still lay snoring, the fire still flickered and there was no sign of Skala Vek. She was lying on her side but she tried to twist her head up a little to look further around. She rolled onto her back, which sent needles of pain searing through her head. Gritting her teeth, she looked but saw no one else nearby.

Relaxing her neck muscles, her gaze moved up towards the ceiling. She blinked. Two faces seemed to shimmer on a ledge, shadowed high above her.

'Can you hear us then?'

That was the second voice Tilliat decided but she could only think 'yes' because she truly didn't believe those faces were real. Both faces were similar in size to a horse's head but much more slender. They had brilliant eyes which seemed to shiver with fluctuating colours. And these faces were undoubtedly scaled. Tilliat groaned and let her eyes close again. The second voice whispered deep within her mind.

'Someone comes. Remember, we are near and we are watching. Beware.'

Tilliat groaned again. She was surely ill, brain-fevered or just crazy. Someone touched her shoulder and she forced her eyes open again. Skala Vek stared down at her, his face impassive.

'Can you hear me Tilliat?'

She blinked and tried to speak but her mouth was so dry, her tongue so swollen and stiff.

'You are ill but I don't know why or what the cause may be.'

He held a tin mug against her lips, lifting her shoulders slightly. Water trickled into her mouth. She tried to gulp more but Skala moved the mug away.

'Slowly, Tilliat, slowly. You have kept nothing down these last four days.'

He allowed a little more water to dribble into her mouth while she heard a whispery echo in her mind: 'Beware.'

Tilliat must have slept yet again because she roused to the awareness of her face being wiped with a warm damp cloth. Thankfully she found her blankets had been pushed away and her limbs were free. Gently the cloth cleared her eyes of the stickiness she'd experienced before.

'Oh Tilliat, I've been so worried. Skala seems not to know what ails you and I've certainly never seen the like of this.'

The cloth was removed and Davin Pearl's face floated before her, furrowed with worry. Tilliat tried to sit up and Davin helped her, propping her against the wall. He reached towards the fire and brought a mug to her lips. Not water this time but tea with a faintly bitter tang which seemed to clean her whole mouth. Tilliat was horrified at the thinness of her hands and how exhausted she felt merely trying to hold the mug herself. Davin sat cross-legged beside her.

'What has happened my dear?' he whispered after a glance over his shoulder. 'You were not feverish but it was as though you had became an empty shell. Tilliat just didn't seem to be there – we were simply carrying your body along. Could it be a spell do you think?'

Tilliat nearly laughed but didn't when she saw the concern on the trader's face. And as he looked at her, she saw fear deep in his eyes.

'I remember nothing,' she said, then coughed to clear her throat and lifted the mug in a shaking hand. 'Nothing,' she repeated. 'How long has it been?'

Davin shook his head. 'It is fourteen days since we left the inn, fifteen since we left the city.'

He took the mug from her and refilled it from the kettle beside the fire. He shrugged.

'I wanted to turn back but Skala said we must keep on for Gulat.' He lowered his voice even further. 'I confess I am afraid my dear. Skala Vek has always been distant, but his attitude is all wrong. I – '

'So you are awake at last.' Skala appeared from some distance beyond the fire. His pale gaze scanned Tilliat's face then flicked briefly to Davin Pearl. Tilliat also looked at the trader but his head was bent over her mug of tea, then he was turning away to the fire.

'I think she may be recovered enough to try a little food, Skala,' Davin remarked, his tone sounding wrong even to Tilliat's confused mind.

But Skala's attention was focused on Tilliat. 'You feel better?'

Did he sound surprised? No. Skala's usual tone was quietly unemphatic – he spoke as usual Tilliat decided. 'I don't remember being unwell,' she said, her voice sounding rusty to her own ears. 'I recall leaving that inn – and then nothing until a few moments ago when Uncle Davin was washing my face.'

Davin looked across to her and she smiled at him, her face feeling a little less stiff. Skala continued to study her then got to his feet.

'We are barely halfway to Gulat. We have had to stop too often but that cannot be helped I suppose. It is already midday now, we'll move on in the morning.'

He moved away, picking up a leather pail. 'I'll fetch more water.'

Tilliat had learnt never, ever, to expect any sympathy from Skala Vek but still she felt a pang of resentment. She had no idea what had caused this strange illness but she surely hadn't wished it on herself.

'Take food only from this one beside you.'

Tilliat froze.

The whisper in her head repeated: 'Take food only from this one beside you. Beware.'

She realised Davin had spoken to her. 'Sorry Uncle Davin, what did you say?'

'I asked if you thought you might manage some travel bread with this broth. Perhaps it's better if you just try the broth though – we've not managed to get any solid food into you all this time.'

He came to sit beside her and offered a spoon while he held the bowl in front of her.

'I am truly concerned Tilliat,' Davin murmured as she spooned up the broth. 'Skala has something going on which I have come to fear is not to our benefit. More specifically, not to *your* benefit.'

Tilliat leaned her head back against the wall, her stomach full after only half the bowl of broth. Footsteps sounded and Davin urged her to try to finish the food.

'Beware.'

Tilliat glanced at the trader. Had he said that, or was it the whisper inside her head? Skala appeared and Tilliat was aware of a difference in the atmosphere between the three of them. She felt alert and not the slightest bit unwell.

'What is this place?' she asked.

Skala continued to sort through a pack, leaving Davin to reply.

'We're already quite high in the Belvar Hills.' He smiled at her. 'Nearly mountains rather than hills to an elderly trader such as I. Fortunately Skala knew there were caves in the area and we reached here around dusk yesterday.'

Tilliat wondered just how exactly Skala knew of caves or anything else about this region. As far as she knew, he had been on very few journeys since appearing in the city of Kelshan fifteen years ago. The silence deepened.

'Are we as far north as we need to be yet?' she asked.

Davin gave Skala a quick glance. 'Probably a little further north in fact, but Skala found signs of clan movements several days ago. He thought it best that we continue north until we're mostly beyond their territories for sure.'

Tilliat tried to recall which clans lived in which areas, but failed. The clans kept to themselves since the great rising against the Imperators a thousand years ago. They trusted none of the lowland people and tolerated occasional visits by very few trusted traders.

But surely there couldn't be any real danger from them, could there? There were no tales that she could remember of any murderous attacks on travellers in recent times. She knew the clans would likely rise again if Kelshan was in turmoil, and that seemed more than likely from the deterioration of civil order in the last year or two. But they would hardly kill innocent travellers out of hand now. Would they?

Chapter Three

Instead of being weak beyond belief, Tilliat was astonished to discover that she was as fit as she'd ever been. Her legs were no longer sore, she seemed able to move with the horse's rhythm and she was fully alert to the world about her. True, she'd lost a lot of weight during those many days of unconsciousness. Since she'd woken two days ago in the cave, she'd ridden between Skala Vek and Davin Pearl, strung out along narrow trails threading always upward and always northward.

The ground was still snow-covered and the frost was sharp during the nights but the sun was surprisingly warm in the clear air. They had halted only briefly to rest the horses at midday today and Skala gave Davin directions to where he wished them to halt for the night. He told them he was going to check their back trail because he suspected they were being followed. Davin and Tilliat stepped into their saddles and took the ropes of the spare horses between them.

'Are we being followed?' Tilliat asked.

Davin shrugged. 'If we are, I do not know by whom. I know that there must be some secret connected with you Tilliat, but who wants to catch you is beyond my reasoning.'

Unfortunately, with the trail so narrow and mindful of Skala Vek's warning that sound carried too easily in these altitudes, the two rode on with no more conversation. The sun was half hidden by a shoulder of the mountain to their left when Davin drew rein. The trail widened and a group of tent pines clustered against the western wall of the gully they'd entered half a mile back. Tilliat helped Davin unload the horses and rub them down.

'You learn fast my dear,' Davin told her. He broke the ice that hid a rustling water course and let the horses drink before pulling aside the downswept branches of one of the trees.

Tilliat peered over his shoulder, astounded at the space beneath the tree.

'Tent pine,' she said.

Davin grinned. 'They don't like to grow much lower than this but they're very useful for travellers.'

He hobbled the horses, gave them feed bags of grain and then collected the packs. He ducked under the branches of the next tree, causing snow to cascade onto Tilliat's back as she followed him. It took a few moments for her eyes to adjust to the darker greenish light beneath the branches. She saw Davin kneeling beside a small circle of stones.

'People use tent pines for shelter in the Barrier Range far south,' he told her. 'I've some kindling in my pack but can you find some wood outside? Whatever you do, don't break any fresh wood though.'

Tilliat was about to make a pert reply but Davin had lit a small lamp and she saw by his expression that he was definitely not joking. She went out to search for wood, pondering the fact that she would never have suspected Davin Pearl of being as superstitious as he clearly was.

She had a large collection of broken branches and slabs of bark and was turning back to their tree when something glimmered just ahead of her. She straightened and in the fast fading light, stared at the low bank of snow-mounded bushes against the rocky wall. She saw the long scaled face, pale blue she thought but it was difficult to be sure in the poor light. The head rose and she saw wings furled against a sturdy body, not as large as a horse but close enough in size to make her retreat a pace.

'We thought you were travelling too far north but perhaps it is for the best.'

The words formed in Tilliat's mind and the creature's eyes shimmered with colours like a dark opal her father had once shown her.

'I spoke to you before – I am named Toomay.'

There was a hint of impatience in his tone but Tilliat was totally unable to make any response.

'The one with you now is trustworthy, but not the other – never the other. We will tell you when to take another route.'

The creature shrank back behind the bushes and was gone from Tilliat's sight. Completely bemused, Tilliat hurried to the

28

tree where Davin was making their camp.

'Oh well done Tilliat,' he said when she dropped the wood beside him. 'Are you well though? You're pale as snow again. Sit, sit. I'll make some tea as soon as the fire is going well.'

Davin chattered while he built the fire and fetched water to fill the kettle, giving Tilliat a chance to push her vision – for surely that's what it had been? – to the back of her mind. Before she was forced to make any reply to Davin, Skala Vek came through the branches. There was a strange light in his icy eyes which dulled after a few moments. Maybe she'd imagined that as well, Tilliat thought: her imagination certainly seemed to working wildly these days.

Davin set out three bowls before looking at Skala.

'Well?' he asked. 'Are we being followed?'

'Not anymore.' Skala gave a brief smile which sent chills down Tilliat's spine. 'Five clansmen will hunt no more.'

Skala squatted beside the fire. Tilliat and Davin's eyes met across Skala's bent head then they both stared into the flames as Skala was apparently doing. Skala had never been a great talker but this evening Tilliat and Davin Pearl found they had very little to say either. Tilliat couldn't eat much of the stew Davin made, preferring to sip mugs of tea. She pulled her bed roll from her pack and prepared for the night.

Skala produced a narrow bottle. He measured three drops into Tilliat's mug which she'd left close to the fire. He saw her watching and he smiled.

'A tonic Tilliat. I gave it to you whilst you were so ill. I believe it kept you alive.'

Behind Skala, Davin's expression was blank but his eyes showed deep alarm. Tilliat smiled weakly.

'How kind of you Skala,' she managed as he passed the mug across to her. She raised it to her lips, tipping it so that the liquid touched her mouth. Putting the mug carefully by her blankets, she settled herself down.

Skala was still watching her so she grasped the mug and pretended to drink again. Skala nodded, apparently satisfied. He spoke quietly to Davin Pearl and helped himself to another bowl of stew. Tilliat moved the mug to the other side of her bed roll and turned so her back was to the fire. Scraping carefully at the packed earth beneath her, she tipped the tea out of the mug. Had Skala been keeping her unconscious with whatever concoction was in that bottle? She closed her eyes and spoke a name in her mind.

'Toomay.'

'I hear you.'

'I don't understand any of this – I mean you, and your friend. What are you anyway? Why are you here? What is Skala Vek doing?'

There was a considerable pause. 'I am Toomay. My companion is my cousin, Kezia. We are of the Dragon Kin. Skala Vek was – changed – as a small child. His orders, which are only now seeping into his mind – were to seek you out.'

Tilliat's mind spun at the words. 'And who am I that Dragon Kin appear? Skala Vek has known me since I was but twelve or so. Why has it taken so long for him to try to – what? Kill me? Is that what he plans. And I don't believe in Dragons.'

The other voice seemed to splutter in her mind.

'Whether you believe in Dragons or no, we exist.' A pause. 'We have only just realised the one called Vek was sent in search of you. But it is not simple to explain. Ideas, plans, orders, were set in his mind long ago, and only gradually are those orders coming to his awareness. My cousin is seeking advice on this while I remain with you.'

Tilliat considered the creature's words. (Dragon? Surely not.) And realised he hadn't answered her first question.

'Why must he seek me?' she thought.

But there was no reply.

Toomay settled halfway up the trunk of another tent pine and considered what he had learned directly of this human female, and the little he'd been told before being sent on this mission. His nostrils twitched in annoyance at the thought of Kezia being chosen to partner him. He had serious doubts about her intelligence and strongly suspected she'd been chosen only because her mother was one of the most senior of the Elder Council.

Both he and Kezia were young to be entrusted with the task of finding this female. They had been barely ten years old when the great trouble came upon the Elder Council. Eighteen years had passed since then and Toomay still didn't know the full story. All he understood was that Elder Zehara had sworn an oath to a great queen of the humans. This queen had spoken with Elder Zehara only once in the flesh but many times in dreams. But an oath had been given, and it appeared that now the time had come to fulfil the terms of that oath.

Toomay kept part of his mind watchful of the female who now slept under an adjacent pine while he considered the whole problem. His chin rested on a higher branch, his tail wrapped securely round another. He was disturbed that the male called Skala Vek had spoken of Gulat. Why was he determined to take the female there?

Toomay knew Gulat as a place to be totally avoided and so he would somehow have to get the female away from the Skala creature within the next few days. He considered the other male. He had probed his mind, with caution, and found only genuine concern for the female and a growing apprehension towards the Skala. The female had called him – what? Toomay closed his eyes in concentration. "Uncle." That was his name, and she had a fondness for him, so Toomay must include him in his plans to escape Skala Vek.

He rippled his wings gently and stretched his spine round the tree trunk. He hoped Kezia would return soon with specific instructions. The situation was far more complicated than he'd anticipated, and he feared he really wasn't going to be able to cope for too long. This was the furthest he had ever been from the Dragon Realm and he had only known humans who were permitted to live within that Realm.

Toomay was disconcerted by the harshness of the mind tones he'd picked up from the huge numbers of wild humans who lived beyond the Realm's boundaries. Young Dragons were not encouraged to visit the strange buildings in the centre of the Realm until they were at least seven years old and well grounded in Dragon lore and tradition. Then, groups of youngsters met one or two of the human mages, usually Pauson or Farrina.

Pauson was much beloved by the Dragon children: he told the most amazing and exciting stories. Farrina was loved for her magical tricks – flowers, strange animals and fish, conjured of

31

weird colours and sparkling flakes of light. Only when the young Dragons were comfortable in the presence of these two mages were they occasionally allowed to meet others, always carefully supervised by an adult Dragon. Toomay had grown surprisingly close to a younger female mage, Layna, daughter of Pauson.

Curled high in a tent pine, Toomay thought of Layna and wished he could talk to her right now. He'd believed he knew quite a lot more about how humans thought from spending so much time in Layna's company. But he admitted to himself that, as he'd been taught, over and over, wild humans outside the Dragon Realm were very, very different from those within it.

Toomay confirmed that the female and Uncle were safely asleep, that the Skala male was wide awake, and he sighed. This was to have been a good adventure but he felt there was an increasing foreboding about the whole situation.

The next two days saw Skala Vek leading Tilliat Kranch and Davin Pearl ever northward. The weather stayed clear and dry. Despite their distance north, the snow was thawing fast and the air smelled of new life. On the third afternoon from the camp under the tent pines, Skala Vek halted, and pointed to a line of high peaks directly ahead. Great mountains soared to the sky, their shoulders still hidden under shawls of snow, their heads wreathed in cloud.

Skala dismounted and led the way to a group of boulders.

'We'll stay here tonight. Tomorrow I'll go alone for a while. There should be a trail east then we turn south straight to Gulat.' A smile flashed briefly across his face then he turned away to see to the horses.

Davin had spoken little in the last two days. Mornings and evenings Skala had insisted on adding drops of his "tonic" to Tilliat's drinks. It had taken considerable ingenuity for Tilliat to dump those drinks without Skala or Davin noticing what she was doing. She became almost silent and Skala seemed to approve. Tilliat guessed that whatever drug he was giving her would make her acquiescent and thus she behaved.

Tilliat knew Davin was desperately worried now, but Skala was with them constantly these two days and nights and she dared not risk speaking to the trader. This night though, Skala left them and walked off alone, still towards the north. Davin Pearl, busy making their supper, watched until Skala disappeared in the growing twilight.

'Tilliat – are you well? Child, I grow more fearful each day,' Davin began.

Tilliat didn't move from her position, slumped on her bed roll against a rock.

'Hush Uncle. I'm not drinking whatever it is he gives me.' She glanced across at the trader. 'A voice has been speaking, in my head.'

Davin stared at her and Tilliat wilted, staring down at her hands.

'I know it sounds crazy and maybe I am, but the voice says he's – someone called Toomay. He told me not to trust Skala, that he had been looking for me and that you and I have to get away from Skala soon.'

She gave Davin another quick look and saw Skala reappear further along the trail.

'Shh, he's back.'

'I'm with you Tilliat, crazy or not,' Davin murmured.

Skala Vek was cheerful as he sat by the fire that evening, and, by his usual standards, almost chatty. Tilliat leaned back against her rock, eyes half closed, and listened as Skala talked. He spoke about the wonders of Gulat, how superior the buildings were to those of Kelshan. Davin Pearl offered Skala more tea.

'How is it that you know all this?' he asked casually. 'I've known traders who have visited the eastern free cities and one who journeyed south, but I know of none who visited Gulat.'

Skala hesitated. 'Stevro Kranch visited Gulat.'

'Did he?' Davin asked in surprise.

'Well of course he did. It's where he met Tilliat's mother and where Tilliat was born.'

Tilliat bit her lip. Her father had never told her that. Yes, he had mentioned Gulat, but she had always had the impression that he was repeating things he'd heard of the city, not telling about it as though he had actually been there himself. Tilliat turned away and curled up in her blankets, but not without Skala Vek kindly placing a mug of hot tea beside her.

'Make sure you drink it before you sleep,' he said gently.

Tilliat couldn't bring herself to reply. Once Davin and Skala had also settled for the night, she called Toomay's name in her mind.

'I know. I have been listening,' Toomay replied at once. 'My cousin Kezia is here and we are working out a plan to separate you from the Skala. When you hear my voice, you and Uncle must move immediately as I direct you. Will you do that – without hesitation? Will you trust?'

Tilliat felt a coldness settle around her back. 'Yes, I will.'

The next morning Skala's good mood seemed to have evaporated. He was in a hurry to break camp and get them moving. He led them on a twisting trail between boulders which looked to have been rolled down from the higher slopes in some giant's game. A few withered bushes clung to patches of snow-mottled earth along the way but they showed no sign of greening yet. The sun was hazy by midday, clouds thickening from the south.

They stopped by a narrow spill of water which rushed down from somewhere above. While Davin and Tilliat let the horses drink, Skala scrambled onto a rock, staring back the way they'd come. Tilliat's heart began to thump when Skala cursed and slithered back down to the trail.

'Smoke,' he said, grabbing his horse's reins and swinging into the saddle. 'Keep to this trail. I'll catch up with you.'

He was scarcely out of sight when Toomay spoke.

'Come,' he said.

Tilliat looked up and guessed by Davin's expression that he had heard the word in his mind too. Davin pushed the lead rope of one horse into Tilliat's hand, snatched the other two and climbed onto his horse. Tilliat glanced back and saw smoke rising maybe a mile or more down the trail.

'Follow now, swiftly.' Toomay's words rang in both Tilliat's and Davin's minds. Turning forward again, Tilliat saw Davin's face, shocked, disbelieving and pale. And beyond Davin was Toomay.

He hovered a little higher than their heads and seemed to be of no colour and all colours. His eyes glittered at them before he turned, wings sweeping gently.

'Hurry. Kezia has caused the fire to distract that one. We can

34

hide a little further.'

Davin glanced at Tilliat, shrugged and kicked his horse forward, dragging the others on their lead rope. Tilliat followed, her mouth dry and her heart hammering against her ribs. The trail twisted and turned and her left shoulder felt pulled from its socket when the horse she led suddenly baulked. She clenched her jaw and tugged harder at the rope.

A grating noise sounded and when Tilliat rode round yet another bend, she saw a dark gap in the rock face which rose before her. Davin rode straight into it and disappeared.

'Hurry!'

Tilliat dug her heels into the horse's sides and followed him. A crunching screech and sudden darkness told Tilliat that rock had somehow moved and closed the way behind them. Blackness was absolute. She could hear her own breath rasping from her mouth, the clack of hooves moving restlessly on the stone floor and apprehensive snorts from the horses. Before panic took hold, three globes of light appeared, floating above them all.

The dim glow slowly brightened until Tilliat and Davin could see as clearly as in full daylight. They were in a narrow corridor of rock, the roof half as high again as they were on horseback. There was no sign of a crack in the wall behind them: it appeared to be seamless stone. In front of them the floor sloped upwards quite sharply. Toomay stood at the top of the rise and Tilliat and Davin Pearl studied him carefully.

He was undeniably a Dragon, but not like the two huge Dragon statues which stood in the first courtyard of Kelshan's Citadel. His scaled body was as long as a horse's body. A narrow, elegant head was lifted on a slender neck an arms length above that body. His legs were surprisingly short, making him less tall than the horses. Leathery wings were furled close to his back and his tail stretched down the sloping stone. Toomay returned the stares of Tilliat and Davin, his large eyes reflecting the light from the three mage globes in splinters of gold, crimson, green and blue.

Layna had taught him how to conjure the lights and he felt rather smug at his success now. To be honest, he also felt quite relieved that he'd managed it at all.

'You should get off your animals now,' he said, in the

35

humans' minds. 'There is no need to worry about them. I have calmed them and they will follow us with no trouble, but the stone grows lower in places and you may bang your heads.'

Toomay moved further up the stone ramp and Davin and Tilliat slid down from their mounts. Side by side they followed the Dragon up and round a curve to the left. The mage globes wafted above them and the five horses plodded steadily at their heels. Tilliat saw that Toomay's head on its long neck was higher than either her or Davin, but his back only reached her chin.

He moved ahead of them in a smooth sinuous motion. He had delicate, leaf shaped ears which swivelled forward and back as he walked and his tail, as long again as his body, tapered to a narrow point. Toomay's wings were tight against his back and sides and Tilliat saw large curved claws on their edges, similar but smaller than the four claws on each of his feet.

'What about your friend?' Tilliat asked as they walked steadily in the Dragon's wake. She spoke aloud but Toomay's answer came in their minds.

'Kezia is a cousin, not a friend.' Toomay's tone was irritable.

Tilliat and Davin exchanged glances.

'Kezia will fly on, over these hills and meet us later. We will be perhaps three days below ground. You may not like it but it is safest,' Toomay continued, his mind voice slightly mollified. 'Kezia was sent with me to seek you out because her mother is high in the Elder Council.' He looked back over his shoulder briefly. 'She is not very intelligent, so that is the only reason I can think of for sending her with me.'

Davin was suddenly convulsed with a fit of coughing while Tilliat bit her lip, hard, to stop a grin. There was no mistaking the disgruntled feeling behind Toomay's words.

They walked for a long time until they heard the sound of water dripping ahead of them. Both Tilliat and Davin were glad when Toomay told them they would rest beside a small pool which they were now approaching. Riding boots were not ideal for walking far, the two humans had discovered by now. They found the water trickling into the pool was cold and fresh with a very faint mineral tang to it, and the horses drank eagerly.

Davin took some dried food from a pack and shared it with Tilliat. They gave the horses a little grain but only loosened girths rather than unloading them. Toomay politely refused Davin's offer of food but his lip curled in a way which suggested dried fruit and nuts was an incomprehensible idea of sustenance.

'You can rest for a while,' Toomay told them. 'I will wake you when it is time to go on.'

He settled himself on one side of the small pool and the mage globes faded to a faint glimmer. Toomay curled like an enormous cat, his tail wrapping him closely. Tilliat, rolled in her blankets, watched the Dragon's eyes close and was astonished to note the fringe of long silver lashes lining each large eye. Her own eyes closed and she fell into the deep sleep of mental and physical exhaustion without sparing a thought of where Skala Vek might be. And, for the first time since leaving Traders Hall in Kelshan, Tilliat dreamed.

She saw again the pale, sharply angled face, the hard dark eyes, the brows drawn tight in anger. And she heard the words this man spoke as she knelt manacled before him. Even in the dream she knew he spoke in a language unknown to her, and yet she understood him.

'You have until the next moon rises. Your pleas of ignorance and inability, as I have told you again and again, are unworthy of your line. You *will* reveal your powers to me and to your people. Time runs short.'

And then the lashes started again over her back and shoulders. Tilliat began to scream.

Chapter Four

Tilliat woke to find someone shaking her, hard. She fought against the hands grasping her arms even as her eyes flew open. Over Davin Pearl's shoulder she saw the Dragon standing, his wings half raised and his eyes flashing with alarm. For a moment she thought it was blood making her hands slick against Davin's and causing the tickle down her spine and sides, then realised it was only sweat. From trying to fight him off, her hands grabbed the trader's arms with relief. She began to shiver and Davin pulled up a blanket, wrapping his arm round her shoulders. Tilliat spoke quite calmly, her gaze locked to the Dragon's.

'It was the usual dream Uncle.' Then she frowned. 'But the man in the dream spoke this time, words I could hear. But the boy doesn't know what the man is demanding of him.'

The mage globes had brightened and the Dragon was closer than he had yet come to them. Now, he settled beside them, studying Tilliat's face. She looked confused.

'I always thought it was me being whipped, but it isn't. It is a boy.'

Breath hissed from Toomay's nostrils and his ears shot straight upwards, quivering gently.

'You dream of being whipped?' Davin asked, his worried expression unchanged. 'But who would whip you child? And why? Do you know this man you see?'

Tilliat pulled the blanket closer around her. 'I see the same man each time. He stands in front of me and I am tied somehow. I am kneeling, with my arms stretched and tied to the sides. The lashes come from someone behind me.' She looked from Davin to Toomay and back. 'I thought it was me but it isn't. Who is being beaten like that, and why should I dream of such things? It always feels so real, but it can't be, can it Uncle?'

'You didn't believe I was speaking in your mind,' Toomay observed. 'If you have had the same dreams for a long time, then

I doubt they are merely dreams.' His tone grew frustrated. 'I was not warned of this, although perhaps the Elders did not know of it. You and Uncle must get to the Realm much more swiftly than I'd thought.'

Toomay tilted his head and peered closely at Tilliat, his breath warm on her face.

'Do you wish to sleep again, or shall we travel on?'

Tilliat shuddered at the idea of going back to that dream again. 'Let's go on.'

Again they walked, until Tilliat was dizzy with tiredness and kept upright only by holding on to her horse's saddle. Davin asked Toomay if they should rest just as the globes of light revealed a widening of the passageway. Tilliat dropped to the stone floor while Davin led the horses, one at a time, to a narrow gutter of rock through which water seeped slowly.

'I will watch her thoughts Uncle. You should sleep now.'

Davin was a little surprised to be addressed as Uncle but too tired to do more than nod. He dropped a blanket over Tilliat, wrapped another round himself and was asleep in a heartbeat.

Toomay was seriously worried. It would take another day to walk to the exit of this cave system where he had arranged to meet Kezia. While there was great safety here, the thick rock above them meant he could not send thoughts either to Kezia or attempt the much more distant contact with the Realm. He could not receive messages any more than send them, and he was concerned whether Kezia had followed his instructions properly.

Toomay let the humans sleep as long as he thought wise, and he was relieved that Tilliat slept dreamlessly. He roused them and encouraged them to eat something before urging them on the way. Davin had noticed many tunnels leading off from the one they walked, but Toomay had no hesitation in the direction he led them. Again he kept them moving until Tilliat was staggering and Davin's face was grey with weariness before letting them halt.

Both humans collapsed on their blankets and slept, but only for a short while. Toomay nudged Davin Pearl with his long nose.

'Uncle, awake! She begins to dream again! Rouse her quickly!'

Davin groaned, desperate for more sleep then snapped fully awake as Toomay's words registered. He rolled over and reached for Tilliat, shaking her like he had before. But this time Tilliat was rigid in his grip although her eyes were open and staring. Davin turned to Toomay.

'I don't think she's really awake. Can you not call to her mind?'

Toomay shifted his weight from one front foot to the other and back. 'I've tried. But the dream has her fast in its snares.'

'Snares?' Davin slapped Tilliat's cheek and shook her again.

Words suddenly sputtered from Tilliat's mouth, words in a tongue Davin had never heard. It wasn't Tilliat's voice that spoke either: it was deeper toned and harsh. She suddenly gasped and sucked in air as if she had been suffocated. Her eyes lost their glassy stare and sweat beaded her face. Davin held a flask of water to her lips and she swallowed greedily.

'The same dream?' he asked, wiping sweat from her forehead with a corner of a blanket.

'No. The boy was alone. His back is so badly torn he can scarcely move. An old man came in, trying to tend him. I think he cares for him but he is very afraid. I could only feel the pain.' She hesitated. 'And despair and grief. He can only feel those now: pain, despair and grief. He's in a room bare but for a bed. No windows except very high near the ceiling, and one door. He was thinking of the man who shouts.'

'And you have no idea who this man might be?' Davin asked her.

Tilliat shook her head. 'He is – an important man I think. Perhaps a council man in the city.'

Davin nodded to show he followed her thought.

'He is not the boy's father – I'm sure of that. The old man who tries to look after the boy is small – my size maybe – and very frightened. The boy is *not* frightened.'

Tilliat's face suddenly paled even further. 'He wants it over. He *wants* to die rather than go on like this.'

The only sound was that of one of the horses scraping a hoof against the stone floor.

'Can you picture the man in your mind that I may see him?' Toomay asked eventually.

Tilliat frowned in concentration. She had no sense of Toomay inside her mind but he must have seen the picture she formed. Tilliat and Davin Pearl watched in astonishment. If Dragons could hop then that is what Toomay did. He was clearly much agitated as he bounced back and forth before calming himself with great effort.

'We must go on. I am sorry if it tires you, but speed is essential. The animals can carry you in a while – the roof gets higher again when we near the exit place. I hope Kezia is there.'

His eyes flashed with colours, reminding Tilliat again of the opal her father had once shown her.

'Surely Kezia will be waiting for you won't she? It must be easier and quicker to fly the distance we have walked?' Tilliat asked.

Toomay blinked. 'You do not understand how Time works. It is – different – down here.'

Davin gaped but before he could ask anything, Toomay whirled away from them and began marching down the endless corridor of rock. The horses obediently plodded behind him. Davin and Tilliat grabbed their blankets, stuffing them into their packs, and hurried after.

In the Dragon Realm, on a ledge high on the cliffs to the north of the settlement the humans had been permitted to build within the Realm's bounds, an old Dragon lay. He reclined at the entrance to a shallow cave, basking in the first warm sunlight of the year. Snow covered the slopes around and above and still blanketed the trees on lower ground. But on his ledge Thorn enjoyed the brightness and warmth. He stretched his black wings and groaned with pleasure then rested his head on his front feet. No one would interrupt him here unless it was on a matter of desperate urgency, and he needed some time to himself.

He rarely came here in the winter: most of the Dragons, the older ones especially, stayed at lower levels and often gathered around the hot pools in the east of the Realm. Thorn's tail twitched. He closed his eyes. But it was no good, he wouldn't sleep although he was enjoying the sun on his scales and slowly warming his old bones. The thought of Toomay kept niggling at him.

41

Toomay was a many-times-great grandson, and he was dear to Thorn. He had been furious to find that members of the Elder Council had seen fit to send Toomay in search of the human girl child without consulting him or Zehara. And he could scarcely believe that they'd sent Kezia with him. In Thorn's considered opinion, Kezia should have been trodden on when she was an infant. This fate befell a very few Dragon children in each generation but of course, Kezia had blood kin within the Elder Council and, against Thorn's better judgement, she had been permitted to live.

Both he and Zehara had been away; Zehara consulting with the humans in their settlement, Thorn himself visiting Dragons on the eastern shores. The Council had been called in haste, with many Elders absent, and Bellia and Terak had hurried the decision through to send the two young Dragons westwards.

Thorn's skin rippled down his spine and he snarled, giving vent to his annoyance. He had made his disapproval clear on his return yesterday and Zehara had supported him fully. But the damage was done. Zehara was as concerned as he was about both Toomay's task and the sending of the unstable fool Kezia as his partner. Thorn snarled again, louder, rising to his feet and stalking round the narrow ledge before reclining again. But his pleasure in the day's warmth was gone.

His eyes half closed but his mind searched westward, seeking the mind of Toomay.

Tilliat and Davin were hardly aware when they emerged from their time under rock. Both were on their horses, Tilliat asleep in the saddle and Davin only awake because the wind was suddenly fresh and sharp against his face. He looked blearily around for the Dragon but saw no sign of him. The trader half fell from his horse and staggered to Tilliat, who roused enough to help him get herself down. They both sat helplessly where they landed, the horses dropping their heads to tear at the scant grasses underfoot.

Tilliat rubbed the back of her neck which ached from the position her head had been in for too long – her chin had dropped to her chest gods knew how long ago. She winced as the vertebra cracked, and tilted her head far back, staring at the evening sky. She blinked and stared harder. She nudged Davin and he followed her gaze. At first, they both thought it was a hunting bird, spiralling high overhead. But it lost height rapidly, becoming much larger, until it was clearly the Dragon Toomay. He landed with a smooth grace and folded his wings close to his back and sides and paced towards them.

Both humans already recognised the flashing change of colours within Toomay's eyes as a sign the Dragon was disturbed.

'I can feel no trace of Kezia and I should be able to within this distance. And it is still too far from the Realm for me to reach anyone there.'

He came to a standstill in front of the two humans and gave a gusting sigh. 'Rest once more and then we must travel on. At least you can go faster from here.'

Davin and Tilliat needed no further encouragement and slept almost immediately. Toomay watched over them as the sky darkened then prickled with starlight. His responsibility was to this human female, but he was tempted to go back and seek out Kezia. If only his many-times-great grandfather had been at the Council meeting which had ordered Toomay and Kezia on this journey.

Toomay's mind constantly searched the area around, finding only the signs of small animals, insects and sleeping birds. If only humans were not so frail – they needed food and sleep so very often. He found these halts a great trial of his patience.

Dawn was the faintest hint in the sky when Tilliat's dreams began. Toomay prodded Davin with his nose and then pushed at Tilliat's shoulder.

'Wake!' he called to her mind. 'Flee the world of dream!'

Tilliat woke with tears pouring down her face, but she would say nothing of what this dream had shown her.

Toomay glanced at the sky: still too dark for the humans to guide the horses safely. He sent a thought to Davin's mind, suggesting the trader make a small fire to heat water for the drinks humans seemed to find so comforting. Davin nodded and set about the chore while Toomay continued to watch Tilliat. He was quite unable to break into the dreams the female experienced. Those who used speech mind to mind learned early not to impose on any other creature's mind without that creature's consent.

Toomay spoke to the minds of these two humans on the very

surface level of their awareness. He had tried to share the dreams – which he should have been able to do quite easily, although it would be seen as a serious breach of propriety by his seniors in the Realm. The dreams were impossible for Toomay to penetrate. He thought back through his early lessons and could recall no one telling him that dreams could be encased like this female's. It was almost as though the dream had floated into her mind in a bubble to which only she had access. Toomay had learned how to block his mind against any threat but this was not the same thing at all. He watched the female but made no attempt to touch her thoughts.

Tears still fell down Tilliat's cheeks but she was totally unaware of them. This dream had told her something. The man who shouted and ordered the floggings wanted something which the boy could not provide. The boy was not being stubborn, not being difficult. He was completely ignorant of what was being demanded of him. She had dreamed of the boy when he himself was asleep and learned a little more of him from his unconscious mind.

It was jumbled: odd pictures of when he was a tiny boy, standing in a garden where the flowers were taller than he was. Another scene had flashed before her. The boy was older, gazing out over the bluest stretch of water she'd ever seen. All the pictures felt as if they were seen and experienced by Tilliat herself. She was looking through his eyes, his memories. And she wept because in these odd little glimpses of his life she felt a happiness mixed with a touch of loneliness. She knew, how she couldn't begin to guess, but she knew he was unaware of the loneliness at those moments. He was fully aware of it now though.

Davin Pearl brought her a mug of tea and she took it gratefully, wrapping her hands around its warmth. The boy was asleep, dreaming of long ago, and she hoped he would remain so for a good while. The tears dried on Tilliat's face and she drank the last of her tea. Davin Pearl had been checking the horses while Toomay lay silently beside Tilliat. Now he tightened the girths of the two horses they'd been riding, and waited.

Toomay hesitated, then carefully moved closer to Tilliat and pushed his nose under her arm until she looked at him in surprise.

Her arm was across the Dragon's neck and his face nearly on her knees, one eye staring into hers.

'Is the boy so sad?' The words whispered in Tilliat's mind and she managed a shaky smile.

'It was just me that was sad this time,' she replied aloud. 'He was dreaming of when he was small, before the bad things began.'

Toomay let his chin rest on Tilliat's knees and the whisper in her mind was even fainter. 'I believe his name may be Tetsura. Tetsura A Serissama. I cannot be sure, I do not know enough. I am sad for him too.'

Tilliat was stunned. She moved her arm from the Dragon's neck and put a hand on each side of his long face, looking deep into his strange eyes.

'Tetsura? If I said the name in the dream, would he hear me do you think?'

'I don't know. I don't know how *you* can hear *him*.' Silver eyelashes rested against palest blue scales on Toomay's cheeks then lifted again. 'We *must* get to the Realm quickly Tilliat. You should speak with Thorn and Zehara, perhaps with some of the humans too.'

Davin Pearl joined them and squatted beside Tilliat.

'The horses are ready and it's light enough to see the trail,' he said. He reached a tentative hand to the Dragon's neck and let his fingers trail over the scales.

Toomay pushed himself up and studied the sky. 'I will fly low most of the time but I will need to check every now and then from much higher. For Kezia and also to make sure your way is clear.'

Tilliat and Davin collected the spare horses, climbed into their saddles and waited. Toomay lifted easily with a few powerful strokes of his wings. Davin indicated Tilliat should lead the way and she knew he intended to protect her back. For the first time in days her thoughts turned to Skala Vek. Where was he? Where was the other Dragon? She recalled Toomay saying Kezia had caused a fire to distract Skala and tempt him back down the trail.

How did Dragons make fire, she wondered. She thought of the old children's tales, of Dragons spouting fire over Kelshan's Citadel and across the land during the great wars following the removal of the Imperators. Tilliat found herself glancing up at the Dragon flying of her. Could he spit fire? Well, only a short while ago, she had scoffed at the very idea of Dragons being real creatures, so why not fire breathing as well?

Her horse stumbled and she grabbed a handful of mane to steady herself. The sky directly in front was much lighter, a line of glaring gold was widening over the dark horizon.

Toomay held them to a steady pace until the sun was fully risen then he moved faster. The riders below him urged the horses to a canter, the trail staying fairly level and straight for much of the morning. The sun was high in a clear blue sky when Toomay settled to the ground.

'Your animals tire,' he said. 'They are suffering from their time below the hills.'

The slow speed was extremely frustrating to the Dragon but he allowed no hint of it to colour his mind voice. He led them on through the afternoon and halted as the sun behind them sank into crimson pillows.

Toomay left them to set up their small camp. Tilliat was tired but Davin Pearl was close to exhaustion. Tilliat made him lie down while she saw to the horses and then lit a small fire. Davin massaged his left shoulder.

'I wonder if we'd be wiser to let the spare horses go,' he suggested. 'We could probably move faster without them.'

Tilliat added thicker chunks of bark she'd gathered to the fire and put the battered kettle over the flames.

'He kept them calm when we were in those caves, or tunnels, or wherever we were,' she said. 'I think he wants us to bring them with us.'

Davin pushed himself up to a sitting position. And groaned. 'I ache everywhere, Tilliat. You'd have been better with a younger, fitter trader accompanying you.'

She glanced at him and actually grinned. 'Someone like Skala Vek perhaps?'

Davin frowned. 'I wonder where he is? Could he be on our trail?'

Tilliat shrugged. 'I'm sure Toomay's keeping watch for him. I just wonder where this Realm of his is and what we'll find there. I've never heard of such a place. You know Uncle, every now and then I think this must all be a dream – or a nightmare.'

'What about your other dreams?' Davin asked quietly.

Before Tilliat could answer, there was a rustling sound and Toomay landed a short distance from the fire. He folded his wings to his body and the two humans realised the rustling sound came from the movement of those leathery wings. He paced towards the fire, dropped two scrawny rabbits, and edged back a little.

'Better nourishment,' he explained.

After gods knew how long with no fresh meat, Davin ignored his aching bones and immediately moved to skin and gut the Dragon's gifts. When he was about to drop the pieces into the pot Tilliat had filled with water, he paused.

'Would you like some of this Toomay?' he asked.

'Thank you for the offer.' Toomay sounded surprised. 'I find humans ruin good fresh meat with their burning and steaming. And I have already fed,' he added.

Waiting for the meat to cook, Davin asked the question that had bothered him all day.

'How long were we underground Toomay? You said Time was different there – what did you mean?'

Toomay regarded the trader for a moment then gave one of the sighs they were getting used to.

'It would have taken you more than twelve days to travel this far above ground. We took three days to move that distance.'

Davin waited politely but when Toomay seemed to have said all he intended, the trader pressed him again.

'How can Time be different?'

Toomay shifted where he lay. 'I understand we have difficulty explaining this concept even to the human mages in their settlement within our Realm. Only a few seem able to understand.'

Davin snorted. 'So you think there's no chance a simple trader could follow the idea?'

Toomay flickered his eyelashes and Tilliat hid a smile.

'The simplest example would be to suppose you were in pain. The pain lasts for one day but while you experience it, it seems to be for many days. If you are having a really pleasant day, it seems to pass in the blink of an eye. So Time may appear to slow down or speed up.'

The Dragon regarded them, apparently awaiting a response. Davin and Tilliat nodded.

'Those examples are only seemings – it *seems* Time has moved at different speeds. We know how to alter Time in reality. And I have no intention of even trying to explain that,' Toomay ended hurriedly, closing his eyes to indicate the conversation was ended.

The two humans settled by the fire, their stomachs full of warm food for the first time for days, and both fell asleep at once.

Toomay waited a while, then opened his eyes. He felt sorry for these frail humans. Fancy having to cover yourself with different wrappings to keep warm, then uncover yourself to cool down. And they smelled rather strong he noticed. He paid close attention to Tilliat's mind, wary of her suffering more dreams, but part of his own mind sped ever eastwards, calling, calling, for Thorn.

Chapter Five

For three more days Toomay led the humans on, bearing slightly north of east. When they stopped that evening, Tilliat was tense: she had not dreamed again but suspected she would tonight. It was just a faint prickle at the back of her brain, but she was positive that was what it heralded. They had travelled among higher ridges these last days and there was more snow lying than when they'd first emerged from the tunnels.

Toomay had just settled beyond the camp fire when he sprang to his feet, wings half raised. Davin Pearl turned in a circle, a long knife in his hand that Tilliat hadn't even noticed he carried. Then the Dragon relaxed, his eyes sparkling. Another Dragon landed gently beside Toomay and the humans could only stare.

This new Dragon was black, and nearly twice Toomay's size. His eyes raked both humans before turning on Toomay. It was clear the Dragons were speaking to each other but Tilliat and Davin heard nothing. Cautiously they sat back on their blankets and waited. At last both Dragons reclined close to each other, the huge black Dragon's body partly curved around Toomay.

'Will you go and look for Kezia sir?' Tilliat asked aloud.

A deep rumble came from the new Dragon. 'We have no such names child. I am Thorn, and Elder of our Realm. And no, I will not seek her. I have much to discuss with Toomay now. You should sleep and I will help escort you tomorrow.'

His mind voice was much lower toned than Toomay's and reverberated in Tilliat and Davin's minds. They concluded, rightly, that Thorn had no intention of saying more to them at the moment so they rolled into their blankets and soon slept.

A slender moon moved slowly across the sky while Toomay told Thorn everything that had happened. When his account was finished Thorn remained silent, deep in private thoughts. A movement beyond the male human's sleeping form caught his attention. He blinked.

'Hunt well, little brother.' He sent the message gently into the mind of the fox that stood there, surveying the small camp.

The fox still wore his white winter coat but brown patches were starting to show on his shoulders and ears. He lifted his nose and tested the air.

'It is long since I've seen your kind here,' he replied. His mind voice was whispery with a gruff undertone.

'There are troubles in the world, little brother. Walk with care.'

The fox vanished into the darkness. Thorn moved a little: Toomay slept. The humans had no idea how tired the young Dragon was but Thorn had seen his fatigue at once. He considered the quickest route back to the Realm but was interrupted by Tilliat's sudden thrashing. Thorn moved quickly to her side, trying to wake her mind but was aghast to find the girl's consciousness barred from any access.

He prodded her but to no effect. The male, Uncle, was rousing, crawling to the girl's twisting body.

'Wake her Uncle. Wake her swiftly. I cannot breach her mind.'

'I'm trying but she's not here. Look!' Davin held Tilliat's shoulder and shook her like a dog with a rat. His other hand slapped once across her face, then again. It took longer than on any other occasion for Tilliat to return from the dream that held her in thrall. She stared wildly at Davin then covered her face with her hands.

'Can you tell us of it child?' Thorn's voice was quiet in both their minds.

Tilliat shook her head. 'Not yet. Please. I'll tell you later – in the light.'

Thorn glanced at the sky. 'Unless you need more sleep, we can begin our journey soon.'

'Yes,' Tilliat agreed. 'I want this travelling finished with.'

Somehow, she'd got the idea that when they reached this mysterious Realm, the dreams would cease and all would be explained as something utterly straightforward. Tilliat staggered as she got to her feet, and went to help Davin with the horses. He suggested she stir up the embers of the fire and prepare them a hot drink before they set off.

Thorn roused Toomay. The young Dragon was ashamed he had slept so deeply but Thorn told him briskly that he had needed the rest. Once more they rode from earliest dawn, when the sky trailed delicate lavender and pink fingers through the lingering clouds, until midday.

'Can you speak to us now child?' Thorn asked, while Davin retrieved some of the few remaining supplies from a pack.

Before Tilliat could answer, Toomay stiffened, his nostrils wide as he sniffed. He swivelled, staring at Tilliat.

'Blood.'

Tilliat had slumped onto a small boulder and she looked up as both Dragons and Davin Pearl stared at her in alarm. Davin knelt beside her and took her hand. He started to speak, changed his mind, and looked down at the hand he held. Blood oozed from the cuff of her sleeve. Very gently, he reached to unfasten the buttons and eased the coat back off her shoulders, his breath hissing between his teeth.

Next, he removed the fur lined jerkin but as he did so he realised it was heavy with blood. The dark shirt was also soaked and now Tilliat began to shudder. When Davin peeled the shirt away, Toomay wailed aloud and Thorn moved closer, eyes blazing with angry colours of crimson and gold.

'A fire,' Davin choked out. 'I must have warm water to clean her.'

'Fill the pan you use for your cooking and put it here,' Thorn ordered.

Davin scrambled for their cooking pot and filled it with ice from a frozen streamlet whose course ran across their trail. Thorn didn't appear to do anything, but steam started to rise from the pot. Davin pulled out clothes from his own pack until he decided one shirt was still clean enough to use for this.

Carefully, he wiped Tilliat's shoulders and back until her skin was mostly clean and they could see the narrow crisscrossing of lines, some still sluggishly oozing dark blood. Davin sat back on his heels and met Thorn's still angry eyes.

'She dreams of this,' he whispered. 'But now it is real.'

Thorn focussed on the girl's back. Davin Pearl had travelled widely and had seen healers at work in many places in this vast land, but he had never seen such as this. A glow began to form

51

between Tilliat's shoulder blades, a silvery glow. It spread right across her back, over her shoulders and upper arms. The glow thickened and brightened, obscuring her skin while it pulsed gently then faded away.

It vanished, leaving Tilliat's skin unbroken but marked with silver lines where each bleeding cut had been. Davin wrapped a blanket round Tilliat who now seemed drowsy, almost unaware of what had happened. Thorn's voice murmured to him.

'She will sleep for a while. Then we must move. I have many things to do.'

The black Dragon moved away while Davin pulled out a bed roll and urged Tilliat to lie down. He sat at her side, trying to think. So many strange things were happening – his fears regarding Skala Vek, his terror for Tilliat's tortuous dreams and now, the powers the black Dragon could wield. Toomay lay along Tilliat's other side, his gaze on her white face.

'Who could do such a thing Uncle?' he asked.

Davin only shook his head.

Wings flapping caused Davin to look round. Three large black crows were perched on a boulder, shuffling ragged feathers into a semblance of order. He was astonished to hear other voices in his mind.

'Thorn lets you hear,' Toomay told him.

'I thank you for responding to my call.' Thorn's tone was grave.

'We are glad to help the Dragon kin when we are able. What message do you wish us to carry and where to?'

Davin couldn't work out which of the three crows had spoken but the mind voice was melodic, gentle, not at all what he might have expected.

'I would ask that two of you seek out this human male.' A picture of Skala Vek filled their minds. 'I wish to know exactly where he is but do not approach him. If you can spare the time, I would that you follow him. I also ask that one of you travel with speed to the Realm. Seek out Zehara and tell her we are on our way but our problems are much greater than we feared.'

The crows bobbed and fidgeted, clattering their horny beaks.

'We will do as you ask, and gladly. We have felt trouble on the winds, bad trouble. We think you know of this and we would

52

have you understand the feathered kindred are ready and willing to help in any way we can.'

Thorn lowered his head for two heartbeats. 'The Dragon kin are honoured by your offer.'

More bobbing and beak clacking. 'We have had news from the human lands where the sun sets. There are great clashes between different groups, fires burn in many of the gathering places where the humans live. Much food.' Davin Pearl swallowed hard, imagining bodies lying upon battlefields, covered with a heaving mass of black feathered crows and ravens, and other carrion feeders lurking close by.

The three crows glanced at the trader and he feared they may have felt his sudden revulsion. He concentrated hard on feeling grateful that they were offering their help in these dreadful times. The crows lifted into the air, one flying fast to the east, the other two more slowly, to the west. Thorn paced back and forth. He came to a halt by Tilliat's head.

'We will go on. I will change Time so that we reach the Realm's border soon after nightfall.'

Toomay gasped but Thorn ignored the young Dragon.

'Leave whatever you deem unnecessary Uncle, the less your animals have to carry, the swifter our travel. You will need to tie the girl on to her animal to ensure she stays safe. We will not stop until we are within the Realm. Now I must prepare.'

Davin sorted through the packs on the spare horses. He found, with disbelief, that most were stuffed with stones and rags. The packs he'd used on one horse alone held dried food supplies. Toomay remained by Tilliat, watching Davin Pearl.

'These hold nothing,' Davin muttered eventually.

'Who packed them?' Toomay asked.

Davin grunted. 'Skala Vek of course. Toomay, you seemed – bothered – when Thorn said he would speed our journey.'

Toomay's eyes glittered and his wings rattled against his scaled back. 'It is very dangerous, so we are taught. I didn't know any Dragon could still actually work the magic.'

'Will it harm us? I mean Tilliat – she is too thin since Skala Vek made her ill or whatever it was he did to her. And now this, with her back. She has little strength I think. I will lead all the horses – Tilliat can only cope with her own.'

'I will calm them as I did before. It is a simple magic.'

'You said Time changed in those caves,' Davin frowned. 'How could that be if you don't know how to do that?'

Toomay's eyes flashed and his ears flicked in Thorn's direction. 'The spell is fixed within the stone.'

'You mean anyone who got in there would move faster?'

Toomay snorted. 'How do you imagine anyone could get in there without knowing how to open the way? I was taught to recognise signs of gateways and how they may be opened and closed. No humans do, I am quite sure.'

Davin piled the useless bags he'd taken from the horses between some rocks set back from the trail. Then he began to sort through the clothes and possessions he'd pulled from his own pack when looking for something relatively clean to tend Tilliat's back. When he'd repacked what he wanted to take he searched Tilliat's bag for another shirt or jerkin.

He woke her and helped her dress but she was dozy, barely aware of what he was doing. The now load free horses had perked up. Toomay took a pace towards them. They calmed and merely stood, watching the Dragon.

'Do you speak to their minds?' Davin asked curiously.

'Not as I do to you. They are animals that live in groups so they have a sort of group mind – not as intelligent as wolves for instance. Wolves have pack minds but also individual minds.'

Davin wished he hadn't asked. He tightened the girths of the two horses he and Tilliat rode then pulled her carefully to her feet.

'Tie her,' Thorn told him.

Davin used rope he'd carried in his saddle bag and looped it round Tilliat's wrists, fastening it to the saddle horn. He hoped it was neither too tight nor too loose and felt guilty at tying her at all. But she still seemed to scarcely notice what was happening and the trader wondered if Thorn had done something to keep her docile.

'Tilliat, you will follow close behind me child.' Thorn's voice crooned to her.

Tilliat opened her eyes and looked at the black Dragon. She yawned, then nodded. Thorn regarded Davin Pearl.

'Follow,' he repeated. 'Take no notice of anything you might see. Think only of staying on your animal, close to the child.'

54

It was midday but Davin Pearl had the sensation of the sky darkening to twilight. He blinked and shook his head. Thorn appeared to float barely a man's height above the ground in front of Tilliat and the light around them was definitely dimming. Tilliat could never remember that time, but Davin Pearl had nightmares for a long while afterwards.

The landscape became ashen and he thought it – wavered. Nothing seemed solid except his own horse between his knees. The surroundings grew darker still and for a disbelieving moment, Davin thought he saw a half moon from the corner of his eyes. He had absolutely no idea how long they'd been in this weird world, which surely was not his usual world. But he became increasingly exhausted, as if he'd really been riding endlessly.

He saw Tilliat slumped awkwardly over her horse's neck and was glad he had obeyed Thorn's order to tie her to the saddle. Davin's eyes were heavy and gritty when he saw the horizon paling faintly. Suddenly his whole body tingled: it wasn't painful exactly but it was uncomfortable. The horses felt it too and for the first time, they protested with snorts and jinking. The spare horses were running behind Davin and he sincerely hoped Toomay, at the very rear, was able to control their minds and keep them calm.

The tingling sensation intensified until it did become painful and then they were out of this ashy half world. Davin found himself gasping for breath and trembling with strain. The spare horses came to a standstill, their sides heaving and foam flecked, their eyes rolling wildly.

Davin suspected his legs would not yet support him if he dismounted so he urged his horse alongside Tilliat's. The girl was still lying forwards on her mount's neck but her face was towards Davin. She was either asleep or unconscious and still as pale as the snow. Davin sent a heartfelt prayer to every god he'd ever heard of that she would be safe. He doubted he'd be of any help to her now.

Toomay rushed past them and Davin watched him approach the huge black Dragon. Could things get worse, he thought when he saw Thorn lying on snow covered rocks. The shine of the dark scales had dimmed to a murky grey and the Dragon's head was

55

on the ground, his eyes closed.

'Do not fear Uncle,' Thorn's voice was faint inside Davin's mind. 'I will recover.'

Davin kicked his feet free of the stirrups and stretched his trembling legs. Before risking descending to the ground, he took in their surroundings. It looked disappointingly like the same country through which they'd been riding forever, but he guessed by that odd tingling barrier they'd passed through, they must be in Thorn's Realm.

Davin Pearl got Tilliat off her horse but was not able to rouse her. He left her in her bed roll and was searching for something to make a fire when a bugling call rang out from high above. He watched a Dragon spiral down to settle beside Thorn and Toomay. Lavender eyes studied him briefly then turned to Thorn. Toomay backed away and paced towards Davin, pausing only to sniff Tilliat's face as he passed her.

'I am greatly relieved Zehara is here Uncle,' the young Dragon said. 'Thorn used far too much of his strength twisting Time for so long. But we are home now. We are safe.'

High in the Phoenix Palace, many miles from Thorn's Realm, a man sat at a window, gazing out at a grey and angry sea. His face was impassive although he was alone. Inwardly he seethed as furiously as the waters far below. Hikmat was the Regent of this kingdom and had been for seventeen years.

The Queen died giving premature birth to a son, the heir to the Phoenix Throne. The King, Tetso, had been away and his Queen was already sealed in a magnificent coffin by the time he returned ten days later. The baby was tiny, desperately frail, for he had been born too soon. Physicians and healers and nurses worked frantically to keep him alive.

When the King at last reached his palace, Hikmat prostrated himself, tears flowing freely, as he reported the untimely death of Queen Naila and the fragile health of the newborn Prince. Tetso was aware, even through his harrowing grief, of his First Minister's own despair. He knew Hikmat tried to spare him any trivial matters of state in the days that followed, unobtrusively distracting other ministers who prolonged their visits of sympathy and did the most menial tasks to give his King the privacy he craved.

For a year, Hikmat served the Phoenix Throne in this manner, dividing his time between his Lord and the baby Prince. Then the King grew ill. Intermittent bouts of sickness, dizziness, lasting only a day or two at first. The most renowned physicians pronounced it was one thing, then another, but whatever, it was nothing serious. They concluded it was a low fever the King had contracted during his progress through the Kingdom prior to his Queen's death. Somehow during that year the King had turned away from the healers, and he now refused them admittance when he was ill.

Prince Tetsura began to thrive halfway through that first year before his father's illnesses. King Tetso was greatly pleased with Hikmat's devoted attention to both himself and his heir. On the first anniversary of the child's birth, Tetso named Hikmat Highest Minister, and ruled that, in the unlikely event of the King's premature death, Hikmat would rule as Regent.

Several people, although unfortunately none of the King's physicians, noted just how soon after these announcements King Tetso succumbed more frequently to the mysterious fevers and sicknesses. Hikmat summoned physicians from across the Kingdom but the King's illness became almost constant and much more debilitating.

King Tetso could use magic but he had never been as powerful as his Queen, who was also his cousin. Magic was in their blood, and *must* be in the blood of any who would sit on the Phoenix Throne. As the Prince's second birth anniversary approached, King Tetso collapsed at a council meeting and died, in agony, two days later.

He was genuinely mourned by most in his Kingdom – high and low classes alike, but there was no panic or arguments over the succession. Wasn't there a healthy little Prince, in the Palace nursery? Hadn't King Tetso appointed his High Minister and devoted friend Hikmat to be Regent until the Prince came of age? The Phoenix Kingdom had no King or Queen, true, but it had a Crown Prince and a powerful Regent. So things went on much as before.

No one really noticed the taxes going up. It was a very slight increase at first, but it was an increase, year upon year. Insidious

57

rumours led to the people slowly shunning the help of healers, preferring mundane physicians. Mage born teachers found themselves unemployable. Hikmat couldn't care less what the ordinary people of the Kingdom thought of him or his rule. All the senior posts of administration were held by men loyal to him, loyal through greed, blackmail, or fear, it made no difference.

For the last five years, Hikmat's energies had been concentrated on the heir, Prince Tetsura. The boy's mage powers should have manifested when he reached puberty. But they had not. Hikmat had always cultivated the boy's affection. He had played with him when he was a small child, taken him travelling through the Kingdom cities, and seemed Tetsura's dearest friend. When Tetsura failed to show any ability with the smallest magics, Hikmat consoled him and suggested he was still young. He must practice diligently and surely his powers would be revealed.

Hikmat had made sure there were no blood relatives left alive during Tetsura's early childhood but now he scoured the familial records and found an elderly uncle on the Queen's side of the family who had survived Hikmat's scourge. He was brought to the palace to try to train the Prince in the magical arts. He was no more successful than anyone else had been. Last year, after the Prince had passed the seventeenth anniversary of his birth, Hikmat's patience vanished.

He held the Prince confined in two small rooms deep within the Palace, allowed only the old manservant Vilad to attend him, and began a regime of bullying. At first, he shouted at the Prince, then kept him without food for days at a time. In less than a moon's turn, Tetsura would be eighteen years old. On that day he would appear before his people and give a spectacular display of magic for their delighted entertainment and to prove his indisputable right to the Phoenix Throne.

Hikmat's face remained impassive, but his hands tightened into fists. There were so few days left before the Day of Presentation. Having discouraged healers and mage born from admitting their powers during the years of Tetsura's childhood, Hikmat found himself in a serious quandary. He had formulated a new ritual and ceremonial for the Presentation but his plans needed polishing and he doubted he had enough time. Hikmat regretted flogging Tetsura but he'd found he rather enjoyed the boy's cries of pain and the blood – . Well, he'd always liked to see blood welling from human bodies, and to see it pour from the sacred person of the heir to the Phoenix Throne was more pleasurable than he would have guessed.

Hikmat decided he would have time to get the boy healed ready for him to perform his part in the new ritual. He had already sent for cattle, pigs and fowl to be brought to the city. He would give the people a magnificent feast. Barrels of wine and ale were on their way by road and by ship, but he would have to announce the change of plans within the next day or two. Let the people gossip and worry at the alteration of ancient custom, then enjoy a day and night of feasting and drunkenness.

The governors of the larger islands in the Kingdom would be arriving. With them at his shoulder, along with his docile councillors and administrators, he was sure they would present a confident solidarity to the populace when Tetsura was Presented. Hikmat rose to his feet, his oval face smooth and calm. He would visit Tetsura in the morning and would be kind and avuncular – his old way of dealing with the boy. He glanced once more at the angry ocean and smiled, thinking of seasick governors.

The last time he'd flogged the Prince his enjoyment had been halted. Tetsura looked up at him, just before he'd slumped unconscious between the manacles. Hikmat had the eerie feeling that someone else had glared out at him from Tetsura's face. Nonsense of course. Hikmat made his way down the curving stairs to his private study, his mind already busy with his many plans.

The boy's manservant Vilad would remain as sole carer until Tetsura was well healed. Vilad had no tongue so he could tell no tales. It was the only reason Hikmat had left the old man alive this long.

Chapter Six

Davin Pearl must have slept for when he opened his eyes next the sun was again high in the sky. He shivered. Obviously he'd dozed off sitting at Tilliat's side and while he had wrapped her securely in her bed roll, he had not done the same for himself. Toomay still lay alongside Tilliat.

'Zehara keeps her sleeping,' he said. 'Thorn sleeps too.'

Davin looked about. The country appeared little different but presumably they were now in the Dragon Realm. He groaned as he stretched his aching back and hoped they'd soon find shelter and warmth. Toomay caught Davin's eye.

'There is a gateway close by,' he began.

Davin closed his eyes. 'You mean more tunnels? More riding?'

Toomay glared. 'A tunnel yes, not far. It will take us down to the second plateau. It is warmer there and provisions are always left ready for travellers. It is the only gateway we have shown humans.'

Davin knew he should show some appreciation for Toomay's news but he couldn't summon the energy. Unlike Tilliat, Trader Pearl did not believe that all their troubles would be over once they reached this Realm. But maybe there could be some explanation, some reason why Tilliat attracted this unwelcome attention. He watched some small birds flittering past in a jerky flight and remembered the crows. They'd said there were battles in the western lands. He hoped Pirus Belk, Mahzda Chern and other old friends were still safe within the fortified Traders Hall. They already seemed to belong to another life, he might have been away a year rather than less than thirty days.

The new Dragon had drawn closer without Davin noticing. Her scales shimmered through all the hues of purple, lavender, palest violet and silver. Different shades flickered in her large eyes, which now stared into Davin Pearl's.

'I am Zehara, Uncle, and you will soon be able to rest.'

Was she reading his thoughts, Davin wondered, even as he gave an awkward bow. He heard the unsettling sound of a gurgle of laughter within his mind.

'Thorn will wake shortly. It was dangerous beyond belief to use the Time magic when he was already weary, but he is strong. When he rouses, we will move on. I will carry the girl child.'

Toomay pushed up on his front feet and stared at the other Dragon in plain disbelief. She ignored him but for an irritable twitch of her ears.

'You may ride or walk, as you choose Uncle. Toomay will once more soothe your animals.'

'Why do you insist we bring the horses?' Davin asked crossly. 'And why do you all call me Uncle?'

'These animals are greatly desired by the humans in our Realm. We've never really understood why as they don't travel far. They seem to like riding them about. We call you Uncle because that is your name.'

Zehara moved away, conversation ended.

Davin realised his mouth was open and closed it with a snap that rattled his teeth. Toomay peered at him, clearly worried.

'Uncle *is* your name. I heard Tilliat name you thus,' He moved from foot to foot and his mind voice sank to a whisper. 'It's not a rude name is it? Surely Tilliat is greatly fond of you – she wouldn't be rude.'

Davin was torn between annoyance and amusement. Amusement won.

'No Toomay. Uncle is a very special name to me.'

Toomay's relief swamped through Davin and the trader managed a weary smile. 'My name is also Davin Pearl, and I am a trader.'

Confusion promptly followed relief and Toomay settled down to continue watching Tilliat. 'I am surprised Zehara will carry her,' he said in a too obvious change of subject.

Davin nodded. 'How will she carry her? Tilliat is scarcely aware of anything. How will she hold on?'

'You will lay her on my back,' Zehara said, making Davin jump.

Gods, but these Dragons could move quietly for such large

creatures.

'I can control her easily, she will not fall. Thorn is not recovered enough to use any magic at all. So Toomay will open the way and keep your animals obedient. We are ready now.'

Lavender eyes regarded Toomay steadily and he hurried across to a blank rock face.

'Lift her gently Uncle. I fear many poisons have been put into her body which we must deal with as soon as we can.'

Davin lifted Tilliat free of her blanket and with a little effort, placed her face down on Zehara's broad back.

'Magic will hold her. Fear not Uncle.'

Hastily Davin snatched up the bed roll, shoved it behind his saddle and struggled onto his horse. There was no screeching, grating sound this time. The rock in front of Toomay simply shivered and was gone. Toomay stepped aside. Thorn paced to the opening and entered. Zehara rose to drift a slight distance above the ground and floated behind Thorn, Tilliat unaware and unmoving as if she was in her own bed.

Entering after Zehara, and hearing the hooves of the other horses clatter behind him, Davin found they were in a much narrower tunnel or passageway than they'd travelled before. And it sloped quite sharply downwards. It was a surprisingly short ride. Daylight showed and then Davin was outside again, his horse walking on much more luxuriant grass than he would have thought possible. He looked about him with interest. Rock towered around and behind him but ahead, the land stretched wide and smooth.

Thorn was pacing away along the sheltering cliffside. Davin wondered if he should gather the horses and rig lead ropes again, but Toomay told him not to bother.

'The animals need rest as much as you Uncle. Only a little further and there is one of your shelters. Zehara has decided two humans must be summoned, they need to be here.'

'Why?' Davin demanded. 'Why can't we just rest for a day or two before we have to meet these people?'

Toomay's strange multi coloured eyes regarded the trader for a moment.

'Zehara says Pauson must come. He is old in human ways of measuring age and someone usually accompanies him if he rides out.'

Davin followed the Dragons on, round a slight curve and saw a low stone building, single storied with a sharply pitched roof and a fenced paddock close by. The grass was starred with tiny bright flowers. He tilted his head back and stared up at the cliffs. He couldn't estimate the height: it was too much. He couldn't believe they'd descended a sloping passage that far in the time. The sun had scarcely moved past midday, which was the time he'd guessed before they began their descent.

He dismounted and opened the gate to the paddock. The other horses followed him in and after removing the saddles on his and Tilliat's mounts he left them, hock deep in the lush grass. Davin swayed, tiredness thudding down on him like a wagonload of timber. Toomay and Thorn were watching.

'Come Uncle. Lift Tilliat from Zehara's back and take her inside.'

Davin did as Thorn told him, stumbling over a low stone step before the door. He lifted the latch awkwardly, Tilliat's head lolling away from his shoulder as he did so. The door, wider than a normal door, swung open. Davin blinked in the sudden gloom. Then he made out the details of the simply furnished room. Two beds took up one end, a rough table was set against the wall by the door. Windows on that same wall were shuttered. A fire was laid in the hearth opposite and a stack of logs was piled at the side.

At the opposite end to the beds were cupboards, presumably holding basic necessities – pots, plates, dried foods, but Davin's tiredness was suddenly overwhelming. He turned to his left, towards the beds, and laid Tilliat on one of them. He knew he should check the covers for dampness but he was just too weary. Without removing any of his own clothes, not even his boots, he dropped onto the other bed and was lost to sleep.

When Davin woke he was disoriented, with no idea of where he was or what time of day it might be. He sat up, a quilt tangled round him, and Toomay's head lifted level with his.

'You are well Uncle?'

Davin cleared his throat and unwound his covers. He looked towards the other bed.

'She still sleeps. Zehara says Pauson approaches and he has

Zeltan with him which is good.'

The names meant nothing. For the moment only one thing mattered: getting a fire lit, water boiled and tea made to clear his mouth of its foulness. Davin saw his and Tilliat's packs close by.

'I brought them in for you,' Toomay told him, a touch smugly. 'There is a well at the corner of this shelter.'

Davin patted Toomay's head before he realised what he was doing and made for the door. It seemed to be early morning by the height of the sun and Thorn lay half curled, his tail securely wrapped round himself. Zehara was nowhere to be seen. Along the side of the house Davin found the well and hauled up a bucketful of water. He splashed some over his head and face and gasped at its iciness.

'A mug of tea and I might be human again,' he said to Toomay as he re-entered the house and knelt to light the fire. He glanced at the Dragon. 'What's wrong?' he asked in alarm.

Toomay's eyes flashed and churned in a myriad of agitated colours.

'You are not human now?'

'Um. It was just a nonsense remark. I was still half asleep, not feeling too bright – you know.'

Toomay calmed. 'You have strange sayings.' His eyelashes fluttered. 'You patted my head.'

Davin busied himself filling the kettle from his pail of water and hooking it on an iron bar, ready to swing it over the fire. Before he'd managed to come up with a suitable reply, Toomay spoke again.

'It was rather pleasant. You can do it again if you like.'

Davin bit the inside of his cheek, struggling to keep his expression solemn. He reached out a hand and gently patted Toomay between his ears. Thankfully, they heard Zehara's bugling call and both hurried out to see her land in front of the house.

'Pauson and Zeltan approach. Have you eaten yet Uncle?'

'I was just making tea, but I've not even looked in the cupboards yet.'

'No matter. Zeltan will prepare food.'

The Dragon reclined in the grass by the door. 'I have told Pauson of Tilliat's condition and he has many herbs with him to clear her body of poison.'

Davin thought that sounded ominously unpleasant but he said nothing. He went back to the fire, finding the water at last hot enough for his desperately desired tea. He was finishing his first mugful when he heard the sound of hooves cantering towards the house. Hastily refilling his mug he wandered to the door. Two men were dismounting, one young, the other old.

The younger man unloaded both horses then turned them in to the paddock. The older man came straight towards the house. He halted beside Zehara, looking up at Davin. His hair was white, tied back in a tail. His face was deeply lined, oval in shape with white eyebrows slanting up at the outer edges over dark brown eyes. Those eyes were friendly, as was the smile he gave Davin.

'I am truly glad to see you – Uncle.' His smile widened. 'Names can be difficult,' he murmured. 'I am Pauson. I am mage and healer.'

'Pleased to meet you,' Davin answered. He raised his mug. 'I've just made tea if you'd like some. And I am Davin Pearl, Trader of Kelshan,' he added quietly as he led Pauson within.

Pauson gave him a grin. 'The Dragon kindred have one name only. They are confused by the varieties of human names. They mean no offence.'

Davin smiled back, pouring tea for the newcomer. He hadn't been aware of how much he'd missed talking to someone normally.

'I know, but it was a little disconcerting to be called Uncle all the time.'

Pauson moved to the end of the room and stared down at Tilliat. Davin joined him. The girl's face was thinner than it should be, her cheek bones sharp edges below her closed eyes. Her dark hair was lank but still showed faint hints of reds and gold within the darkness. Pauson sighed and turned back to the fire.

'She looks so like her mother,' he whispered, staring into the flames.

Davin would have questioned him, but at that moment the other man entered. His features resembled those of Pauson although he was much younger and his hair a dark nut brown. Pauson smiled.

'This is Zeltan. He is the grandson of my sister, and I raised him after she and his parents – died.'

Davin gave a slight bow which Zeltan returned but concentrated on Pauson.

'You said Tilliat looks like her mother. You actually know her mother? Where is she? What is this all about?' The trader didn't care if he sounded rude.

Pauson laid a hand on Davin's arm. 'Let's have a little stroll.' He grimaced. 'I'd just as soon not sit down for a while. My old bones don't take kindly to the sort of ride we've just had.'

Zeltan was delving in the cupboards along the end of the room.

'Zehara said you haven't eaten. I'll fix a meal while you talk.'

Davin followed Pauson from the house. The old man ambled towards the paddock, leaned against the top rail and watched the horses grazing.

'Do you know anything of these lands Trader Pearl?' he asked quietly.

Davin shrugged. 'Very little. Trade has been discouraged for as long as I know of. I had no idea there was a Dragon Realm. Or Dragons for that matter.'

'Is that all?'

Davin frowned, leaning on the rail beside Pauson. 'There are said to be clan folk along the coast further east. They fish and hunt seals for fur. Beyond that are supposedly the Isles of Vremilia.' He regarded Pauson curiously. 'Is that what you mean?'

Pauson's smile was sad. 'Partly. Vremilia used to be a much visited group of islands. The people were renowned for their superb craftsmanship in all things beautiful. Art, woodwork, metal work, and also in their great learning. The kings of Vremilia withdrew after the Imperator wars threatened their lands. They have had little if any contact with these lands for a thousand years. Life in the Isles continued as always, they had never had a great regard for your people. So they isolated themselves totally and life in the Isles of Vremilia continued to be good.'

Pauson sighed and moved away from the fence, walking into the open meadowland before the house.

'Twenty-five years ago a king died, and his only son took the throne. The son was a weak man but he married a strong woman, a princess of his own bloodline.'

Pauson stopped, turning to face Davin Pearl. 'The queen became pregnant. There was great rejoicing for they had been married over five years with no sign of a child. She gave birth to twins, and died immediately after.'

Pauson drew a shuddering breath and Davin saw the old man's eyes fill with tears.

'Twin births were – are – anathema to Vremilians. One twin was taken from the birth chamber and hidden away. It was announced that the surviving child was the only child. That child was fragile. For the first half year his life hung by a thread but he began to thrive. He was proclaimed as the heir and his father's devoted friend was named Regent should one be needed. The king died, most unexpectedly, before the child's second anniversary.'

Tears began to roll down the wrinkled cheeks. 'I had three sisters. One of those sisters bore a daughter. That daughter was the queen who died.' Pauson's voice took on an angry edge. 'I said she died. She was murdered. When a female mage is pregnant, she must refrain from using her powers for fear of harming the unborn child. So she was defenceless in all ways. Another of my sisters was a seer such as had been unheard of for generations. She foresaw all these events and warned our niece, but although my niece knew all this, she also knew that a child of hers was absolutely necessary, to Vremilia and to the wider world.'

Pauson clutched Davin's arm. 'The son born to my niece is eighteen years old in less than a moon's turn, and he has no magic. His name is Tetsura A Serissama, and the twin whose existence is still unknown in Vremilia is Tilliat A Serissama.'

Davin's mind went blank for several heartbeats, then one thought popped into his head. 'Stevro Kranch. Did he know all this? And Tilliat had her eighteenth birthday at the end of last summer.'

'Stevro Kranch was a brave man and true. He knew it all. We decided to say the child was older so she might be overlooked by any who might seek her. She too will be eighteen soon.'

'Where is Stevro?' Davin asked, trying to comprehend this

Stevro whom he'd never have guessed to be involved in such plots and schemes.

'Dead,' Pauson said. 'There is a small group whose mages somehow learned part of the events I have spoken of. They suspect Tilliat is, or will be, a mage of vast power, but they don't know her real history. We think another seer, like my sister, foresaw these days and that seer told mages who had very specific reasons for wanting such a child under their training and control.'

Davin scrubbed his hands over his face, stubble rasping as he did so. How long since he had had a real wash or a shave? The mundane thought flashed through his mind and was gone.

'If Tilliat is the baby of this queen, how did she get here from Vremilia?' He shook his head, trying to absorb all this new information.

'Zehara brought her.'

Davin groaned. A Dragon flew gods knew how far across open sea and flew back with a newborn baby.

At that moment, Zeltan called from the door of the house. He had made a meal – fresh food too, as Davin's nose told him. They sat at the table and Davin ate until he could manage not another bite. Toomay was still lying near the beds but when the humans had finished their meal, he paced to the door.

'We shall walk now Uncle.'

Davin started to object to any sort of exercise right now, but Toomay forestalled him.

'Pauson must cleanse the child's body. It is best if you are not here.'

Davin saw Zeltan was at the hearth and had many small packets and jars laid out beside him. Pauson had begun to sort through a leather satchel he wore across his chest. The trader swallowed, wishing he had not eaten so much after all.

'I'll leave you for a while then,' he said aloud.

Pauson glanced up and smiled gently. 'Take some kindling and a kettle. You can make yourself some tea. We won't be finished until the stars are in the sky I'm afraid.'

Davin paled, nodding rather than replying. He collected his old battered pan, a small sack of tea leaves and a mug, and followed Toomay from the house. He really didn't feel brave enough to stay to witness whatever horrors Pauson intended to inflict on Tilliat. He felt a twinge of guilt at so easily running out on her but not enough to stop him hurrying to catch up with Toomay.

He noticed Thorn was gone although Zehara was sprawled on an outcrop of rock, eyes closed, basking in the afternoon sun. Toomay led the way, keeping their backs to the immense cliffs towering behind them. The ground sloped unexpectedly and Davin realised the long sweep of grassland was a deceptive view from the house. To their left was a group of slender trees, not very tall but already thinly clothed in delicate leaves.

Toomay marched down the incline towards the trees and then reclined on the grass, turning his face up to the sun with a sigh of pleasure. Davin lowered himself by the Dragon's head.

'Do you know what they're doing?' he asked abruptly.

Long silver eyelashes lifted and Toomay met Davin's gaze. 'You don't want to know Uncle,' he said firmly. '*I* don't want to know. It is not nice but they will make sure that Tilliat remembers little or nothing of what they must do.' He rattled his wings. 'Why don't you look for wood for your fire?'

Davin glared at the Dragon who simply closed his eyes and rested his chin on his front feet. Although Davin would like nothing better than to lie back himself and digest his meal, he got to his feet and stomped closer to the trees. Ducking under trailing branches he nearly jumped out of his skin as a flock of tektek birds rose in shrieking panic.

'Are you alright Uncle?' Toomay's voice sounded sleepily in Davin's head.

'I'm fine,' Davin thought back.

He looked behind him and realised the drifting branches with their long fragile leaves already hid him from Toomay's view. He walked on, the leaves shushing softly around him. He reached a small space where the trees appeared to have formed a circle. In the centre was a round block of white stone, about as high as his waist. It had no markings on it but it was too perfectly shaped, too smooth, to be natural. Half this little clearing was in shadow but Davin sat on the sunny side, away from the stone. Although there were no marks on that stone, Davin had no desire to annoy any local gods who might regard it as sacred to them.

He lay back, wishing he had his pipe but that was long since lost. Reluctantly he began to go over Pauson's explanations. Pauson said Stevro Kranch was dead. Where, how and why were the questions he'd like answers to on that subject. Davin had to admit that Pauson's story of Tilliat's origins was too fantastical not to be true. Surely no one could invent such a tale.

His mind skittered over the idea of a Dragon flying over the ocean with a tiny baby on her back. Someone must have been holding that baby. Pauson? The name of the other child had sent chills down Davin's back. Tetsura was the name Toomay had given them regarding the boy in Tilliat's nightmares. He didn't understand what Pauson meant when he'd said twins were anathema to Vremilians.

Twin births were not unusual in any of the lands Davin Pearl had traded in so he found Pauson's comment most puzzling. From the little he knew of healers or other mage born, their powers began to appear at puberty. As far as he knew, no such signs had developed in Tilliat. When he was in Kelshan which, over the last five years since Stevro Kranch's disappearance, was more frequently than in previous times, Davin had spent a lot of time at the Kranch house.

He liked Jomah and Pakal and he believed they would have mentioned anything about the girl that might have caused them concern. But no such things had been spoken of. Skala Vek. *Was* he of the Black Claw clan? The shape of his face, the set of his eyes, were similar to Pauson and Zeltan rather than the clans Davin had encountered.

Pauson had spoken of a group of mages who wanted to get hold of a mage as powerful as Tilliat was prophesied as being. Who could they be? Where were they based? Kelshan's government had no mage born councillors. The mage born were tolerated – after all, mage healers were amazingly successful in treating all manner of hurts and illnesses. But since the great wars when the last Imperator was overthrown, no mage was permitted to hold high office.

Davin racked his memory for the reason for that particular decree but could recall nothing. Davin believed Pirus Belk's words, when he'd said he did not know the reason why Tilliat was important, only that she was. But Stevro must have told him *something*. The old Master Trader knew Tilliat had to leave

Kelshan but Davin believed Pirus knew no more than he himself had.

A buzzing noise made him open his eyes. He turned his head and watched a solitary fat bee lurch drunkenly over a group of tiny yellow flowers half hidden in the grass. Listening to the steady drone, Davin fell asleep.

Chapter Seven

When Davin Pearl woke, the sky was growing dark. He'd heard the faintest sound of running water when he'd first come among the trees and now he stumbled back to collect his pan. It only took a brief search to find where a narrow streamlet wound through the little grove, some pieces of fallen twigs and bark, and then he returned to Toomay. They sat together watching the stars thicken across the bowl of the sky until a moon, just past half full, drifted into sight over the trees.

Human and Dragon sat comfortably in each other's company, needing no conversation as both had plenty to think about. Davin poked at the fire which was down to embers and wondered whether to try to find more wood, when Toomay stirred.

'It is done Uncle. We can return. Tilliat will sleep until dawn and Pauson will decide then if she is fully clear of the poisons Skala had given her.'

Davin was already stamping out the last of his fire. Toomay paced close to the trader who rested a hand on the Dragon's back. They climbed the slope and lights shone from the window on the right of the house and out of the door. Davin felt a slight shiver ripple the scales on Toomay's long back but the Dragon kept walking.

Zeltan came to the doorway, wiping his hands on a towel. Davin saw the young man's face was pale and drawn but he offered the trader a smile.

'It is over. Pauson sleeps,' he said, gesturing to the beds in the shadowed half of the room.

Davin noticed a strongly astringent smell, not unpleasant, and he saw the stone floor was damp as if freshly washed. Zeltan followed the trader's gaze and grimaced.

'Cleansing is never a pleasant thing, and it taxed Pauson more than he'd thought it would.'

Davin looked at him in query. Zeltan shrugged, tossing the

towel aside and sinking onto a chair at the table.

'Pauson didn't expect more than the physical poison, but it had been spelled. And by a mage of some strength. That is what exhausted him. The mage who did this, caused Tilliat to fight anyone who attempted to tamper with the spell.'

Davin was growing increasingly alarmed.

'Does that mean someone – this mage or whoever – would know if the spell was countered? Or even where Tilliat is now?'

Zeltan was overtaken by an enormous yawn. 'Pauson didn't believe so, but he was too tired for long explanations – he more or less collapsed. I just put him to bed. We'll have to use bed rolls tonight.'

Davin fetched his bedding and spread it on the floor near the fire. Toomay settled at his back. Surprisingly, Davin Pearl slept almost at once, waking just before dawn to see Zeltan asleep at the table, head on folded arms. He felt Toomay's solid body still against his back.

'Are you awake?' he thought.

'Yes Uncle.'

'Did you understand what Zeltan said, about spelled poison?'

'No Uncle.'

Davin sighed.

'I'm sorry Uncle. Perhaps I can learn more but it is not a subject we study. It is something humans seem to use a lot.'

Davin sat up, pleased to find he had few aches even after a night on a stone floor. He scratched his chin and felt the stubble. He decided he'd let his beard grow: shaving was one chore too many for now. He stirred the embers of the fire and carefully placed a couple of thinner logs on top. Then he went out to the well, hauled up a pailful of water, splashed his head and face and only then saw that Toomay had followed him. Toomay's long face tilted to one side.

'Now you are a human again?'

Davin heard the shy amusement in the Dragon's mind voice and he laughed.

'That's right my friend,' he agreed, blotting his face with his sleeve.

Toomay's eyes whirled and sparkled in the growing light of dawn.

'Friend, Uncle?' he asked.

Davin paused. He'd begun to realise just how young this Dragon was and how inexperienced in interaction with humans. He stroked the side of Toomay's face.

'I'd like to think you were my friend,' he said aloud.

Toomay lowered his head and pressed his brow against Davin's chest.

'I will be your friend Uncle.'

There was something in the Dragon's tone Davin couldn't decipher but then the moment passed.

Re-entering the house, Davin found Pauson fastening a clean shirt. The old man turned towards him and smiled.

'Tilliat will wake soon.' His smile faded. 'It will be a long morning I suspect, but she must know it all before we move from here.'

Pauson was correct. By midday, Davin felt exhausted. His heart bled for Tilliat as she listened, at first without comment. They were all outside, sitting on the grass, as Pauson spoke steadily on. Both Zehara and Thorn reclined nearby and although both had their eyes closed, Davin knew they were listening carefully.

When Pauson stopped speaking, Tilliat began asking questions. She was most agitated by the suggestion that Stevro Kranch had not been her father. Davin understood what Pauson apparently did not. Tilliat was truly upset over the news about Stevro. But she was nagging at it like a dog with a bone simply because she was reeling at the other information. Davin watched her, his back propped against Toomay's side, and waited. Finally she pushed herself to her feet.

'I don't know what you've done to me, who you are, or what you want of me. But I don't believe any of this.'

And she ran.

Zeltan got to his feet but Davin held up his hand.

'Leave her,' he said. 'I'll seek her in a while. Just leave her.'

Toomay had lifted off the ground and was gaining height. 'I will watch her Uncle, then I can tell you where she is.'

'I had not expected this reaction,' Pauson began.

'And exactly what *did* you expect? You don't know the girl and yet you come out with these bizarre tales and think she will just sit here and say "how lovely"?' Davin also got to his feet, suddenly furious. 'I'll bring her back when she feels she wants to come. And I suggest you let her talk as she chooses. Do not try and lecture her again.'

He walked unhurriedly in the direction he and Toomay had gone yesterday.

'She is among the trees,' Toomay said in his mind. 'I think she will walk through them to the other side. It isn't a very great area.'

Standing at the edge of the incline, Davin saw the little grove of trees and wandered down, choosing to skirt it rather than pass beneath the branches today. He walked some way beyond those trees, noticing the view widened and deepened. What had Toomay said? They were going down to the second plateau? Clearly the land here was still considerably higher than what lay in front of him.

He gazed out at the panorama and realised why it seemed strange. It was all wild land, no cultivated fields, no single chimney or roofline. There were only ragged clumps of woodland, open meadows between, and the glitter of water whether of streams, rivers, lakes or ponds, Davin couldn't guess. A movement caught his eye and he squinted. A small herd of deer were suddenly running into the cover of trees, but he couldn't see what might have spooked them. A high pitched scream above him made him glance up. He saw two eagles circling lazily but definitely in the direction of the deer.

Davin walked on a little further and saw Tilliat sprawled on the grass to his left. Toomay lay some distance beyond her, apparently admiring the view. Davin didn't pause. He walked to the girl's side, sat down and rested one hand lightly on her back. She rolled over, grey eyes blinking at him, then sat up.

'Had they told you all that Uncle Davin?'

'Some of it my dear, some of it.'

Tilliat wrapped her arms round her drawn up legs and rested her chin on her knees.

'It's true,' she said, her tone flat.

Davin raised a brow.

'It *feels* true, especially about the boy. Did you know about my – Stevro?'

Davin sighed. 'I spoke of this to Master Belk, before we left Kelshan. He admitted he had doubts that you were truly the child of Stevro Kranch and I have often wondered the same myself. I'm not sure why Stevro left no message for you, or any information with Pirus for us to use in the event of his death.'

'Perhaps he wasn't expecting to die.'

Davin met her gaze. 'I suspect he was. I fear he had news that alarmed him and sent him off on that last journey. I also suspect it was a very cleverly laid trap to lure him away.'

Tilliat's eyes were enormous in her too pale, too thin face.

'But no matter what happened to him, he didn't tell them anything. I would surely have been attacked long ago.'

Davin nodded. He waited a heartbeat. 'Master Trader Belk had watchers everywhere Tilliat. I know of at least seven people who were – disposed of. On his orders. They had enquired too closely about Stevro Kranch's daughter.'

'I *was* his daughter.'

Davin held out a hand towards her. 'Help an old man up Tilliat.'

When they stood together he put his hands on her shoulders.

'Stevro Kranch was a very fine father, and he adored you. *You* Tilliat, not whoever Pauson says you might be.' He felt the girl's shoulders tighten and her chin came up.

'I have a few questions for that old man,' she began then let out a squeak of surprise.

Toomay's head was just above her shoulder, his eyes glowing silvery blue. 'I didn't mean to startle you. I am Uncle's friend. I would be yours too.'

Tilliat glanced quickly at Davin who wore a bemused expression.

'I would count your friendship a great honour. I will be as good a friend to you as I possibly can.'

Both humans felt a wave of something like warmth, affection, trust – it was difficult to define. Tilliat realised she was walking with the Dragon Toomay on her left side and Davin Pearl on her right. She had an eerie feeling that their positions were not accidental, were somehow inevitable. And permanent.

They approached the house, Tilliat aware for the first time how very high the cliffs towered in a wall which stretched in both directions as far as she could see. Zehara was not in sight but Thorn was stretched on the grass by the house. Zeltan worked on the horses in the paddock, not raising his head when Tilliat, Davin and Toomay arrived. Tilliat halted by Thorn. He opened his eyes and lifted his head.

'You are well child?' His voice was deep honey in their minds.

'I am well, thank you. I am ready to hear what you think I must do.'

Thorn's eyes whirled. 'I will not tell you what you must do.' He sounded indignant. 'Pauson will speak with you but it is not for Dragonkind to order human lives.'

Pauson emerged from the house. 'There is tea fresh made, if you wish,' he remarked mildly.

Davin smiled and went inside. Pauson sat on the doorstep and waited until Davin emerged with two mugs. He handed one to Tilliat and sat beside her. Tilliat took a cautious sip, her hands wrapped around the mug's warmth.

'How do you know my father is dead?' she asked abruptly.

'We are still able to contact a trusted group in Vremilia,' Pauson started.

'No,' Tilliat interrupted. 'I do not want to hear of your king. I want to know of my father.' She stared straight into Pauson's eyes and waited.

Pauson kept his expression calm but Davin had the feeling the old man found Tilliat's attitude somewhat irritating: he had a lot to learn yet. Pauson set his tea down and opened the leather satchel that he appeared to wear constantly. He withdrew a small pouch, untied the fastenings and pulled out a chain.

Tilliat took a breath. She recognised the object that Pauson now let swing free from the chain. It was the black opal Stevro had shown her only once, many years ago. She had thought he had sold it, but apparently not.

'I gave Stevro Kranch this stone. It was spelled to resonate between us but to be used only at direst need.' Pauson weighed the chain and stone in his palm then passed it to Tilliat. 'It is of no use now, merely a bauble.'

Tilliat clenched her fist around the chain. A tingle throbbed through the bones of her hand and radiated up her arm but she gave no indication of her surprise.

'May I keep this?' she asked.

Pauson shrugged. 'Of course. Stevro warned me through the spelled stone there was danger closing in and that he was leaving you in Kelshan and he would make for Gulat. He was sure Gulat held answers but he died before he got there.'

'And you know this – how?'

'I found him.' Zeltan had joined them and stood leaning against the wall. 'I had met him a few times so I recognised him.' He hesitated. 'He was barely alive. His captors surely thought they'd left him dead. He could never recover from such wounds.' Zeltan straightened and looked directly into Tilliat's eyes. 'He asked me to ease his path. I did.'

Davin Pearl thought he would burst with pride when Tilliat replied with complete calm.

'I thank you for that kindness Zeltan.'

Davin was trying to watch both Zeltan and Pauson and was sure he saw surprise, quickly concealed, on the old man's face, while the younger man looked only relieved.

'There is not time to get you to Vremilia to take the throne on your eighteenth anniversary – that is only twelve days away. But we can get messages through, warning of your coming. Then plans made long since will be implemented.'

Tilliat stretched her legs out in front of her. 'And my brother?'

'Will die.' Pauson spoke in a matter of fact tone.

'He will not.' Tilliat replied in exactly the same way.

'But he must. Twins are cursed in Vremilian society. *You* are the one with the magic.' Pauson was quite agitated while Tilliat appeared utterly calm.

'How do you know?' she asked. 'I have never been aware of having a talent which could be due to magic.'

'But of course you have magic – the dreams you have experienced indicate you have farseeing powers. I, with other adepts, will train you and you will soon come into your full strength.'

'So might my brother surely? Perhaps *he* is the one who

78

forced the dreams upon *me*.'

Pauson sprang to his feet and began to pace back and forth.

'This is nonsense. *You* are the one foretold, *not* the boy. There was no clue that Naila was carrying two babies.'

'No? I would imagine she must have known. Midwives in Kelshan could always tell if a woman carried twins, and you said this queen, my mother, was a powerful mage. I do not believe she did not know there were two children within her.'

Pauson glared at her, then continued his pacing. 'The boy has at least given you the years to grow. Perhaps that is why he was born at all.'

Davin risked a glance at Tilliat. Her face showed no emotion but he recognised the storminess in the grey eyes from the few disagreements he'd had with her down the years.

'He will *not* die by any order of yours, old man.'

Pauson stared at her, his face slowly flushing a dark angry red. 'He *must* die. Twins are evil.'

Tilliat stood up, pulling Davin up with her.

'Very well. I am apparently a twin. Therefore, by your logic, I must be evil. We part company old man, but I will know if you try to harm my brother.' She turned away and faced Zeltan. 'I would know more of my father's end.'

Zeltan shot a nervous glance at Pauson, inclined his head and moved towards the paddock. Tilliat strode after him, escorted again by Toomay and Davin Pearl. Odd, she thought, it did feel as if they were escorting her, but how could she think she needed an escort? Protection perhaps, but escort? Surely she was still suffering delusions from whatever toxins Skala Vek had put in her system. Or maybe Pauson, she added grimly.

Zeltan was leaning on the rail fence when Tilliat reached him.

'Pauson sent me to find Stevro,' he said without prompting. 'He told me where he thought he was – about twenty miles north west of Gulat. I have small magical talent. In fact, all I can do is find things. Or people.' He paused. 'I would honestly rather not tell you what was done to Stevro. He suffered most harshly and he was near death when I found him. He described those who had held him prisoner but he was mostly concerned for you. He asked me to give you the opal he wore.'

'He wore?' Tilliat interrupted. 'I never saw him wear it.'

'It was around his neck. I was surprised to see it because the gold chain alone would be worth coin to the men who had captured him. They were common armsmen he said, but ordered by two other men, who didn't touch him although they were the ones who questioned him. And told the thugs what to do to him when he refused to speak.'

Zeltan stood away from the fence and rolled his shoulders. 'His injuries were terrible Tilliat. I do not believe I could have spoken as coherently as he did through such pain. I buried him beneath a great holly tree, a distance from where he died. I could not bring him back here.'

'You have my deepest gratitude for being with my father, in time to hear his words and,' her voice wobbled then firmed. 'I am truly thankful that he died with a friend beside him.' She drew a long shuddering breath and exhaled slowly. 'You are Vremilian?'

Zeltan nodded. 'I was brought here when I was five, with a group of mageborn escaping the repressions that had begun against all born with magic. The Dragonkind gave us refuge here.'

'Do you believe this nonsense, about twins being evil?'

Zeltan looked uncomfortable. 'I have been taught this, but I cannot see how it is right.'

'Do you agree with Pauson? That I should go to Vremilia?'

Zeltan faced Tilliat. 'And kill your brother? No. But things are very wrong there. Tetsura is merely Hikmat's puppet. I know of your dreams. I believe Tetsura is in danger of being killed by Hikmat unless he proves he has magic. If he cannot do so, then his only hope of living is to obey Hikmat in all things. Pauson says Hikmat will reorganise the Presentation ceremony to hide Tetsura's inability to use magic.'

Zeltan spread his hands in a helpless gesture. 'If you wish Tetsura to live, perhaps you should dream to him, tell him to obey Hikmat. For now.'

Tilliat looked startled. Dream to the boy? How, by all the gods, did you go about doing any such thing? Zeltan was waiting for a response. Tilliat turned her back on the horses in the paddock and stared out over the plateau.

'I would appreciate your help Zeltan. There are many things I need to know of Vremilia, and of those who killed my father. I'd like some time, to regain my fitness and to decide what I will do. Perhaps the Dragonkind will allow us to make camp somewhere so I could do this?'

She turned to Toomay. 'Is this possible?'

Toomay's eyes remained calm, a smooth pearly blue. 'Thorn suggests a place to the north. It is near his own special retreat but he says you would be welcome.'

Tilliat hid her surprise. 'That is extremely generous of him. And you Zeltan, will you come with Davin and me for a few days?'

Davin tried to remember what Pauson had told him. He'd said Zeltan was the grandson of one of his sisters hadn't he? So he must be a close cousin to Tilliat. The silence had extended for several heartbeats before Zeltan answered and clearly his thoughts had followed the same line as Davin's.

'Our grandmothers were sisters to Pauson and Pauson raised me when we came here. But I have had doubts about his opinions. He and other elders have not changed in the years of exile while I and several others of the younger generation have concerns. The elders have had no open contact with the government of Vremilia for over twenty years. I find it hard to believe a small group of us could even sail back there, let alone overthrow a government and then rule what has now become a land and people unknown to us.

'So yes, I will come with you, that we may talk of these things. We are the ones who will have to follow Pauson's plans and probably be swiftly killed for our troubles.' He finished with a grin and a shrug.

Tilliat managed a smile back. 'Will you be in trouble with Pauson if you come with us for a few days?'

'I expect so, but then he'll think I can be his eyes and ears and will report everything to him when I return.'

'And will you?'

Zeltan tilted his head to one side. 'That depends entirely on what we talk of and what conclusions either of us reach.'

'Fair enough. Can we leave now?'

'I'll saddle the horses. I think I know where Thorn suggested we go. It will take a day or so but I think time is not so pressing now.'

Zeltan went off towards the house for the saddles and Pauson immediately followed him inside.

'I'd better get our packs,' Davin muttered. 'I don't intend to get into conversation with the old man. I'll wager he's scorching the ears off that lad right now.' He touched Tilliat's arm lightly. 'You all right child?'

She reached up and kissed his cheek. 'My head is spinning with all of this. I am *very* glad you are with me Uncle.' She glanced aside as Toomay moved closer. 'And I am very glad to have you as my friend Toomay.'

There was that wash of warmth through their minds again and then Toomay sank back onto the grass.

'I'll fetch the packs. Let's hope Pauson doesn't turn me into something disgusting.'

Tilliat snorted but Toomay's eyes flashed suddenly. 'He wouldn't do anything like that. It is not allowed.'

Davin looked thoughtful. 'Not allowed? That must mean he could if he chose. I think I'll be very polite.' He wandered towards the house, obviously not relishing an encounter with an annoyed mage.

'You will like the place Thorn offers,' Toomay remarked.

Tilliat stroked the smaller scales between the Dragon's ears. 'You know it?'

'Oh yes. I have been there many times, only when invited of course.'

'Oh of course. Does he invite many there?'

'I don't believe so. I know Zehara goes there but I know of no others. I am of his blood you know. He has always been very kind.'

Tilliat smiled. 'Well I'm sure it isn't hard to be kind to you. You seem kind to me.'

Toomay shifted his weight from one front foot to the other. 'Oh I'm not kind at all. I get very cross, especially with those like Kezia. She and her friends always try to get me into trouble and they say very untrue things about me to the teaching Dragons.'

'How old are you Toomay?'

'I am twenty eight years,' he told her shyly.

She stared. 'Twenty eight? How long do you have lessons?' Then she corrected herself. 'When will you be considered an adult?'

'When I have passed seventy years.'

Tilliat remembered to close her mouth. She cleared her throat. 'May I ask how old Thorn is?'

Toomay's eyes sparkled with pride. 'He has passed one thousand five hundred years. That was two years ago. We had a great celebration because he is the oldest of us all.'

Tilliat tried to assimilate the information Toomay had just given her. 'Did Pauson and his friends celebrate with you?'

'Of course not.' Toomay was shocked at the suggestion. 'They know very little of us, although they think they know all.'

Tilliat laid her cheek against Toomay's long face. Oh yes, they had a great deal to discuss in the next few days.

Chapter Eight

While the others readied the horses and swung into their saddles, Pauson remained in the house. Even when they rode past the doorway there was no sign of him. Toomay flew above to indicate their direction and very quickly they were out of sight of the small stone house. There was no trail to follow but the ground was clear and open. The great wall of cliff was to their left for a while, and to the right was the wide vista of the lower land.

They rode in silence, all three slowly relaxing from the tensions that had held them. Small slender trees appeared, hazily green with new leaf and the darkness of conifers began to form an unending barrier. Approaching this forest, they saw there was little undergrowth and the trees were far bigger than they'd first assumed. Davin drew rein and craned his head back.

'I've never seen the like,' he marvelled.

'These trees were all across the northern lands when Thorn was a child. Humans destroyed nearly all beyond this Realm.' Toomay sounded regretful.

Davin and Tilliat stared at the huge trunks in awe. Those trunks soared, bare of branches, many man heights upwards until great thick boughs began to extend out from them. Each tree commanded considerable space around it and there was no difficulty riding among them. A woodpecker drummed rapidly from somewhere close by and a gaily coloured bird screeched furiously before dashing in front of Zeltan's horse. The horse snorted and side stepped indignantly but quickly steadied.

Tilliat breathed deep of a sharp resin scented air and felt at real peace for the first time since leaving Kelshan. She was quite content to ride through these gigantic trees. She was absolutely confident in Davin's presence and although the Dragon Toomay was not in sight, she was aware of his nearness in a tiny corner of her mind. Tilliat had no clear cut opinion of Zeltan as yet. He seemed reasonable, open to debate. But he had grown up under the influence of Pauson. She had no doubts about Pauson. He was set in his ways and impervious to argument. Tilliat had felt his mind push against hers when she'd argued with him. It was a feeling similar to when the Dragons communicated with her, but with a different edge to it. She wasn't sure how she'd pushed him out of her head, but she had.

They rode on, occasionally passing through open glades made when one of the giant trees had crashed to the earth, probably because of age, or winter storms. In those glades grass flourished along with herbs and small flowers just breaking into colour. Toomay was reclining in one such clearing and suggested they make camp. There was only necessary chat that night, all three trying to sort out the various chunks of information they'd absorbed of late. There was a chill in the air as they settled to sleep, but it wasn't really cold.

Tilliat stared up at the circle of sky edged by the huge fir trees. Stars winked and flickered and she wondered what they were. No one had ever been able to give her a satisfactory explanation as to what stars were. Something else flickered, but it was inside her mind – a silvery shimmer. Tilliat breathed steadily and pictured the boy the last time she'd dreamed of him. She felt a gentle tug and then a jolt.

The grey eyes staring into hers were a mirror image of her own. Somehow she had found him and he was awake. His mouth opened but she spoke to his mind.

'Keep silent. No one must know of this. Are there mages close by?'

The boy's eyes widened then his mouth twisted in a wry smile. 'There are no mages in these lands now. Who *are* you? How are you here? Am I dreaming?'

'It will take too long to explain all now, but you are not dreaming. I don't think. I am your sister, born your twin. I have only learned this recently myself. Listen. There is a man called Hikmat?'

The boy nodded and frowned.

'You must do whatever he tells you. Be obedient in all things. For now. I will reach you again Tetsura.'

'Wait. *Wait*! What is your name? How can we be twins –

twins are destroyed at birth?'

'My name is Tilliat Kranch, and obviously we weren't.'

She saw the boy lift his hand, then she fell into a spiral of silver and became aware of stars above her again. She started to move and stifled a moan as her head pounded with pain. Something pressed against her side and Toomay's head loomed over her, crowned with stars.

'You did well,' he whispered in her mind. 'Sleep. I will show you some plants to chew if your head still feels bad in the morning. Sleep my friend.'

Tilliat woke to new daylight and Davin Pearl squatting beside her, a mug of tea held towards her. His smile faded as she cautiously sat up. Her head felt heavy and dull but wasn't hurting too badly.

'Did you dream again my dear? You look as if you barely slept.'

Toomay shifted against her and Tilliat forced a smile.

'Perhaps I slept too heavily. I'm fine.'

She saw Zeltan leading the horses over to them.

'You should have woken me sooner.' Tilliat made herself crawl out of her blankets and get to her feet. For a moment the world tilted and her stomach lurched. She breathed deeply for a few heartbeats, aware of Toomay's solid body against her. Zeltan halted in front of her and handed one set of reins to Davin Pearl.

'Are you fit to ride Tilliat?'

'Do I look that bad?' Tilliat asked, as lightly as she could.

'Yes. You have black circles round your eyes and you are far too pale. Perhaps Pauson didn't cleanse all the badness from your body after all.'

Tilliat narrowed her eyes. 'I'm quite sure he did.'

She tipped away the dregs of her tea, gave the mug to Davin and began to roll her bedding. They rode at a steady canter for much of the morning, between the massive trees, and halted to water the horses in yet another clearing around midday.

'We will soon be out of the Old Woods,' Toomay informed them when they set off again. 'Then it is but a short distance to Thorn's retreat.'

It was as the Dragon said. Tilliat looked over her shoulder as they emerged from among the trees. Something moved on the trunk of one tree to the right, but although she stared, she could make nothing out. Probably a squirrel or a bird. They seemed to have approached the rearing cliff wall that encircled this Realm, but looking southwards they could see for miles.

Lines of hills rolled across from east to west, wave after wave vanishing into a hazy distance. Some looked rocky and bare, others were blanketed in trees but Tilliat didn't think they were the same kinds of huge trees as the ones they'd just ridden through. She realised she'd been thinking of this Dragon Realm as a sort of overlarge quarry, like ones she'd seen to the south of Kelshan City. But now she was aware that it was indeed a considerably larger place.

Zeltan turned his horse in a circle. 'We are not where I thought we would be.' He sounded puzzled.

'Very few know how to reach Thorn's special place.'

Tilliat looked carefully at Toomay. His remark seemed casual, but his eyes suggested he was rather pleased with himself. They rode on, the ground dipping and rising slightly. Toomay led them, bearing to the south. He flew low until they reached a river, not wide, but definitely not one of the many little rushing streams they'd seen previously. Then, the Dragon suddenly lifted high and moved north, following the river upstream. The three riders followed. The river banks became steeper and when they passed a cluster of willows they saw the river vanished under the foot of the cliff. Toomay was perched above them on a much higher ledge.

'You can let your animals loose. I can command them back to you whenever you wish. There is a good cave in here.'

Tilliat dismounted and dumped her saddle on the ground, keeping a watchful eye on Toomay. He had said he was twenty eight years old, but he was displaying the glee of a much younger human. He glided down from the ledge and paced towards three large birch trees which grew close to the cliff wall. Their branches were still only thinly clothed in palest green but Tilliat could see blackness behind them. Curious now, she heaved her saddle onto her shoulder and followed the Dragon.

The sinuous pale body disappeared into the dark and Tilliat paused at the threshold, blinking. Then a light globe popped into existence and she saw Toomay moving up a slope of stone to the left. Following him she saw black water to the right, reflecting back the glimmer of the mage light. The globe hovered although Toomay had already disappeared. Tilliat heard Davin and Zeltan clattering in behind her. She shifted the weight of the saddle and climbed after Toomay.

He was reclined against a wall, his eyes blazing with delight. Tilliat could only stare in surprise at the long room stretching before her with daylight coming through narrow vertical cracks in the wall above Toomay. There was a tumbled heap of blankets against the opposite wall. A box held various pots and dishes, which appeared to have been thrown in haphazard fashion rather than packed tidily. Tilliat leaned her saddle against the wall and shrugged out of her pack straps.

'There must be others who visit here,' she said.

She knelt and rummaged through the blankets. 'These are all dry – they cannot have been here long Toomay.'

'You would have to ask Thorn about that.'

'I will.'

Zeltan dropped his gear on the floor and went to the further inside corner. He'd seen what Tilliat hadn't noticed: a hearth with a tube of stone rising up through the roof.

'I will hunt' he announced. 'You should find firewood.'

Davin nodded. 'You stay here,' the trader told Tilliat. 'You still look too tired. I won't be long.'

He followed Zeltan out of the room. Tilliat moved slowly round the walls and found something Zeltan had missed. The rock on the far wall had something like a fold in it and roughly hewn steps led upwards. She glanced at Toomay. He watched her but said nothing. Her eyes were accustomed to the dimmer light now and she could see quite well. Tilliat climbed the stairs and discovered more rooms. The place was a honeycomb of rooms, large and small. The ones at the front of the cliff all had cracks where daylight could enter. The rooms further back were dark and Tilliat didn't enter.

There seemed no end to them. After a while Tilliat decided she should go back down in case Davin had returned. Her foot hit something and she squinted in the gloom. She found two objects, one a shallow stone bowl and the other a pear shaped lump of rock. She put both in her jacket pocket and retraced her steps to the lower room. Toomay was where she'd left him but she felt he was somehow pleased, whether with her or something entirely different she couldn't guess. Tilliat pulled a blanket from the pile, folded it and sat cross legged beside Toomay.

'I thought Thorn might have been here already,' she said, retrieving her finds from her pocket.

'He had things to do. What have you there?'

The Dragon's head dipped to peer more closely at what Tilliat held.

'I don't know. I nearly trod on them in one of the rooms above.'

She held out the shallow bowl. 'It is surely too small for food. Perhaps it could be for spices?' She held it up and saw a simple zigzag design incised around the outer edge.

'It was a lamp.'

'A lamp?' Tilliat laughed. 'It is much too small.'

Toomay said no more and Tilliat turned the bowl over and over in her hands. There was a small rough patch on the base but she couldn't work out what it might be. She let it fall into her lap and studied the other stone. The fatter end fitted comfortably in her palm and the tapered end she saw was chipped down both sides in a series of semicircles.

'It was a tool, for chopping.'

Tilliat looked into Toomay's eyes. She ran a finger down the chipped edge and jumped in surprise. Blood beaded on the pad of her index finger – the stone was much sharper than she would have imagined.

'Who uses such a tool?' she asked, sucking her finger.

'Ancient Ones.'

Before Tilliat could ask more, Davin entered, his arms full of wood. He smiled at Tilliat. 'You look a bit better already,' he said.

He began to lay a fire. He bent and peered up the pipe.

'How long since this was used Toomay?'

'A long time.'

Davin grinned. 'Let's hope it isn't blocked or we'll be smoked out.'

'It is quite clear.' Toomay's mind tone was placid.

'So we'll blame you if we choke,' Davin smiled.

Toomay's eyes flashed briefly: he was finding human humour was often difficult to decipher.

But the kindling caught quickly and no smoke billowed back into Davin's face. Zeltan returned with four fish which he'd cleaned by the riverside and handed over to Davin. The fresh fish was delicious and when it was eaten they all sprawled comfortably on blankets heaped on top of their bed rolls. Toomay had wandered outside when Davin began cooking the fish, his nostrils twitching at the smell.

The sky beyond the window cracks was dark before the Dragon came silently back. Once again he settled alongside Tilliat. Davin began to snore softly and Zeltan rolled onto his side, his back to the fire and Tilliat. The fire gave enough light for Tilliat to see the rough texture of the wall where it folded and hid the stairs. A silvery shape shimmered by that fold and had vanished by the time she'd blinked.

'I've seen that before,' she spoke to Toomay's mind.

'Yes. It is a Shadow.'

Tilliat twisted to peer up at Toomay's face. 'You know much more, don't you?'

'You must wait for Thorn.'

Tilliat thought quickly. 'But not Zehara.'

Toomay took his time before answering her. 'No. Not Zehara. Only Thorn.'

'And you I think. You know far, far more than you admit.'

He lowered his head until his chin rested on her chest, his eyes so close they looked enormous pools of blue pearl.

'Thorn is on his way here. He has been beyond the Realm, seeking information on this group of mages close by Gulat, who set Skala Vek on your trail.'

Tilliat sighed. 'Should I try to reach Tetsura tonight?'

Again there was a pause while Toomay considered. 'It would be easier from here perhaps but I think you must ...'

'Wait for Thorn,' Tilliat finished for him. She reached up to stroke his face and then turned on her side to sleep.

Light was poking pale fingers into the room next day when Tilliat woke. Davin and Zeltan still slept so she rose quietly and crept out, down the slope of stone and out into a fresh clear morning. She walked along the bank until its incline decreased.

She knelt at the water's edge and scooped a handful of water to her mouth. It was so cold it made her teeth ache but she scooped up more to splash over her face. Gasping she pulled a scarf from her pocket and blotted the water away, her skin tingling and goose bumps rising all over.

Tilliat wasn't surprised to find Toomay had joined her and was watching.

'Uncle says that makes him human again. Does it do the same for you?'

Tilliat laughed. 'It wakes me up for certain.' She stretched her arms over her head, palms together, and then began one of her exercise routines. After a very few heartbeats she stopped and groaned. Every bone and muscle was making its presence known. How long since she'd exercised? Far too long. Toomay's expression was quizzical.

'I'll try again, later, when the sun is warmer.' She thought for a moment. 'I'll be right back.'

She went back inside and found the two men still sleeping. Tilliat took her pack and tiptoed out again. Sorting through her clothes, Tilliat cringed at the filthy state of most of them. She set to washing shirts and underclothes, watched by a very interested Dragon.

By the time Zeltan and Davin Pearl emerged, Tilliat had spread her clothes over some bushes to dry.

'Good thinking.' Davin went back for his own pack. When he came out again a bugling cry rang overhead and Thorn descended in a lazy spiralling curve. Toomay flattened himself, reminding Tilliat and Davin irresistibly of a puppy hoping to ingratiate himself. Thorn leaned low and rested his brow for a moment against Toomay's. Toomay sat up, his eyes sparkling with pleasure. Thorn's gaze moved over the humans and they felt a ripple of amusement from the huge Dragon. Davin and Zeltan knelt at the water's edge, wet garments spread around them.

'I shall rest briefly. I have flown far and fast. When you have finished – playing with the water – we shall begin our discussions.' He reclined elegantly in the early sunshine and closed his eyes.

Tilliat felt an urge to shriek with laughter at the expressions on the men's faces but she spun away from them. 'I'll just walk a little way,' she managed and trotted hurriedly downstream.

With Toomay pacing at her left side, she came to a low outcrop of rock. Glancing back, she could see Davin and Zeltan still beside the water, the Dragon Thorn lying like a patch of midnight on the grass between them and the cliff. The sun was at its height when Toomay nudged his shoulder against Tilliat.

'They are ready.'

The humans sat facing Thorn, Toomay's sturdy side providing Tilliat with a convenient back rest. Thorn's eyes flashed then steadied to a smoky gleam.

'Long ago we Dragonkind lived in the islands you now call Vremilia. Humans came and they treated us as enemies. We have little if any interest in humans, but we tried, on many occasions, to communicate with them. Their mages were puny compared to the power of magic we can command of course.'

Thorn studied each human in turn.

'There were some among us who wanted to exterminate the human interlopers. It would have been a fairly simple task.'

Tilliat shivered. The quiet, unemphatic voice in her mind was speaking the truth and the idea that a human population could be wiped out "fairly easily" indicated vast powers indeed.

'We left the islands and found this Realm. It was wild land, empty of humans, so we made barriers to secure the whole region and settled here. Well, about half of us did. The others decided to travel further and either find a land for themselves or return here.'

Thorn paused. He sighed. 'We heard no more from them. We decided we would keep ourselves secluded here. Humans long ago were different from the ones we've encountered since our days after leaving our islands. Your kind want to kill anything that lives, apparently just because you can. We do not understand this. The barrier we set around this Realm is twofold. It gives an illusion of an impassable mountain range to those approaching and it gives warning to all of us if any human persists in exploring and inadvertently breaches the barrier. Sometimes, younger Dragons attempt the long flight back to the islands.'

He glared at Toomay who sat up and glared back.

'I have *never* done that,' he said indignantly.

Thorn grunted. 'Perhaps not. But I know some still think it's a good adventure. The thing to always remember is that there is no such thing as a good adventure. I went, once only. Zehara had made the journey several times. She said there was one island where she was made welcome and treated like an honoured guest.'

Every scale on Thorn's huge body seemed to bristle with irritation. 'Be that as it may, Zehara continued to visit that island and that is where she met Pauson and his niece, your mother. No one knows, not I nor Pauson, what they spoke of together. That last time when Zehara returned here, she was severely disturbed over something. She has never visited that island again, or any other as far as I know.'

'Then how was I brought here?' Tilliat couldn't help but interrupt. 'I thought Zehara carried me here somehow.'

Thorn looked at the sky then found the view deeply fascinating. 'She did not bring you. But she said she swore a great oath concerning you. Unfortunately Zehara has never seen fit to tell any of us just what that oath entailed. You must understand that Dragonkind rarely see any point to making such promises: we speak truth to each other, so if I say I will help you, it will be so. To make an oath of the immensity Zehara has always implied, would be extraordinary. She may decide to tell you more Tilliat, but I wouldn't count on that thought. This oath implicates all of us. Those of us who are Elders in our Council were greatly perturbed that Zehara would catch us all in this web of mystery. And angry, I do not deny.'

'Do you know of Pauson's plans to return me to Vremilia, kill my brother and become the ruler there?'

'Yes.'

'And do you approve of this plan? Does Zehara?'

Tilliat saw Zeltan flick a glance in her direction but couldn't read his expression. Again Thorn took his time to reply.

'My personal thought is that Pauson is very wrong. I also fear that Zehara is not of sound mind. There have been signs, throughout her life – she is younger than I by perhaps four hundred years – which have suggested an instability which has always bothered me.'

'So what am I supposed to do? The country I have left is at

war from the little I have heard, and my brother is in danger of being murdered in the islands. I am a trader's daughter. I have never felt anything which might be taken as magical talent. Why am I here?'

Tilliat felt a wave of warm affection smooth her troubled mind.

'Unless we know of Zehara's oath or your mother's prophecy there is little I can advise you child.'

'I'm sure Zehara has told Pauson more,' Zeltan said abruptly. 'He has begun to say something then stopped himself so I think he must know more. But, I will admit to you, that Pauson worries me more than I have said. He has been obsessed with getting Tilliat here and he means it utterly when he says Tetsura must die. If Tilliat has no magic can you not farspeak the boy, Thorn, and warn him of the dangers he faces?'

Tilliat felt a twinge of guilt that she had not admitted being able to somehow dream to Tetsura and by the flash of colour in Thorn's eyes she suspected he was well aware of what she'd done.

'I cannot,' Thorn replied gravely.

Zeltan leaped to his feet and began to pace. 'There are too few of us here: seven near my age who were brought from Vremilia, and seven who were born here. Thirty adults came, eleven of those already elderly. Pauson plans to take control of Vremilia through Tilliat but it cannot be done. It simply cannot be done.'

Tilliat stared at him in disbelief. 'You have around forty people and Pauson intends you to invade another land?'

Zeltan grimaced. 'Seven adults have died and five of the children are under fourteen years of age.'

'Oh it sounds a better and better idea by the heartbeat. Unless Pauson or others among you are mages with powers beyond belief?'

'They are not,' Thorn stated before Zeltan could comment.

Zeltan frowned. 'I thought Pauson was a very powerful mage?'

Thorn's laugh rang through their minds. 'Unlike humans, Dragons are not encouraged to boast. I would expect a Dragon child, much younger than Toomay, to be able to neutralise any magic which Pauson might cast at them.'

Chapter Nine

Tetsura was stunned. The girl who had appeared, right before his eyes, looked exactly like him. She had said they were twins, a fact she had only recently learned. He leaned against the balcony, staring over the city of Garjetka. He didn't see the needle thin towers and spires, the domes glittering in the sunlight which also sparkled over the blue waters of the harbour. All he saw was the face of Tilliat Kranch and wondered just where she was.

Immediately after he'd seen her and heard her voice inside his head, he had studied his own face in a mirror. The eyes were the same, the nose, the mouth, the cheekbones. Tetsura had sat on his bed in complete shock. His back was healing and although Hikmat had not visited him for two days, he had been moved back to his own apartments. He still had no servants attending him other than the old man Vilad, but food was brought to him by the usual stewards. The first, an older woman, had bowed deeply when she'd seen him.

'Are you recovering from your fever my lord?'

So that was how Hikmat had explained Tetsura's seclusion.

'Slowly, thank you,' he'd replied.

The steward had smiled and departed.

Tilliat and her news that they were twins filled his thoughts. How could he ever find out the truth of this? The silk gown he wore chaffed at his back and Tetsura moved restlessly back inside his bedroom. He lifted a statue set on a table close to his bed, a smile lifting his lips. He ran his hand over the delicately worked gold. He stroked a finger down the face of the dragon and put the statue back in its place of honour. There was a much larger statue of a Phoenix on a shelf opposite his bed but he'd never liked it, preferring the gold dragon. It had been given to him on the first anniversary of his birth by a lord from one of the outer islands, and he'd adored it, refusing to sleep unless it was close at hand.

Tetsura sighed and sat on the edge of his bed. Who would

know any details of his birth now? Had his father known it had been a double delivery? He considered the idea and concluded that Tetso could not have known. Hikmat had given him all the King's journals and notebooks when he was eleven and he had pored over them, desperate to feel closer to the man who had fathered him.

Tetsura had read the writings many times and while the script was exquisite, the content was boringly mundane. Tetsura had realised his father was a vain man, not very intelligent, and had made not one mention of his Queen. There were few enough notes about the Crown Prince but Tetsura had never found any writing concerning his mother. He had asked Hikmat about only once or twice. Hikmat had told him she was beautiful, a powerful mage. The second time he'd asked, Hikmat had said perhaps it was for the best that she'd died giving birth to Tetsura in the light of how his father had taken against the mage born.

Tetsura recalled asking Hikmat why, if mage born were undesirable people, it was so important that *he* should be proficient in magic. Hikmat had changed the subject and Tetsura still had no idea why he had been so badly beaten to try to force out magical talent which Hikmat clearly hated. Tetsura tried to ease his sore back and shoulders. The sky beyond the balcony was streaked with fire, crimson, gold and orange fingers clawing across the darkening blue.

The outer door of his apartment clicked and a moment later Vilad came in silently as always. He gave Tetsura a quick glance and set about lighting the lamps. Tetsura frowned. Vilad had always been here, always been his body servant. Could he know anything of Tetsura's birth? How long ago had Vilad been made mute?

'Vilad,' he said suddenly.

The old man turned and bowed.

'Were you here when I was born?'

Tetsura was watching Vilad carefully and his heart thumped in his chest when he saw something flicker deep in the man's eyes. Vilad nodded then waved a hand in a backward motion.

'Before I was born?'

Vilad nodded again and spread the fingers of one hand.

'You worked here five years before I was born?'

Vilad shook his head. He pointed at Tetsura, then moved his hands in front of him, indicating a womanly shape. Tetsura frowned. Vilad disappeared into the next room, a room Tetsura used for study and increasingly, for dealing with matters of government. He came back with a narrow scroll which he handed to Tetsura. Tetsura unrolled it and found it was a map of the archipelago which constituted the Phoenix Kingdom of Vremilia. Vilad jabbed a finger at a small island, the northernmost of the group and the most western.

'Rashken?' Tetsura asked.

Vilad nodded vigorously.

Then it dawned on Tetsura. Rashken was the home island of his mother, Queen .

'You were servant to my mother?' he whispered.

The old man's eyes filled with tears and he shook his head. He took Tetsura's hand and held it gently. Tetsura thought hard.

'You were her friend.'

Tears spilled over and ran down the lines of the man's wrinkled face.

'I always thought you lost your tongue as a punishment.' Tetsura stared at the old man.

Vilad shook his head and shrugged, offering a shaky smile.

A knock at the outer door told of the arrival of Tetsura's evening meal and Vilad turned to attend to it.

'Vilad. Was I born a twin?' Tetsura asked softly.

Vilad turned to look back at the Crown Prince of the Phoenix Throne, his face lit by a radiant smile.

On another balcony high in the Phoenix Palace complex, Regent Hikmat stared at the sunset colours blazing over the sky. He used the splendid apartments which had once belonged to the Phoenix King, Tetso, in the eastern tower. He had respectfully kept to his own modest quarters for nearly two years after the king's death, then he had moved in. By then of course, the few men who might have objected to his temerity were no longer able to voice their opinion, being in their graves.

The last two days had been exhausting. He had announced the changes to the rituals for the Presentation Ceremonies in ten days time. As he had anticipated, there had been the greatest consternation from the priests of the Phoenix Temple. Hikmat held on to his temper, but it had been a close thing. The fools had ranted on, and on, about tradition, about the unchanging forms of the ceremonies, about continuity. Hikmat had needed every particle of his patience and his persuasiveness. He had finally convinced them with the argument that Tetsura was the first new king for over twenty years and, as such, he should represent innovation and change.

If Hikmat was honest with himself he knew that statement had stopped their protests but had started new worries as to what he might be implying by "change". He knew he would face questions about that in the next days. Hikmat entered his sitting room and pulled a bell rope. A servant appeared instantly, bowing low and remaining in that position until the Lord Regent spoke.

'It is early but I will eat now. I have appointments later and I will not wish to be disturbed.'

The servant bowed again and backed out of Hikmat's presence. The Commander of the Phoenix Guards was visiting the Regent this evening and for the first time, Hikmat felt a certain wariness to the encounter. Anjit was the closest person to Hikmat: certainly not a friend, but Hikmat had believed Anjit understood his aims and intentions for the future of this Kingdom. Hikmat had also thought Anjit was supporting him in the certainty that he would remain as Commander of the Phoenix Guard with total control over all military matters.

That included the policing of the civilian population and control of the judicial systems. But during the meetings with various officials as well as the priests, Hikmat had been concerned at Anjit's silence. Anjit made only occasional comments in any such meetings, but during these last two days Anjit had sat in complete silence. Hikmat at first thought Anjit found the hysterical scenes boring and a waste of his time. The Regent gradually realised Anjit was listening, very closely, to every single word.

When the meetings finished earlier that evening, Anjit had approached Hikmat. He asked to call on the Regent, privately, and although this was far from being an unusual request, Hikmat's senses were alerted to something different in Anjit's demeanour. Hikmat had survived as King Tetso's devoted friend by his ability to be aware of everything around him, and of everyone's opinion of him. A few unfortunates had commented on this almost *magical* ability which had incurred Hikmat's instant reprisals. After his meal Hikmat tried to work on some papers involving the demolition of shacks and shanties on the west side of the main docks. He wished the pathetic Councillors still in supposed control of such things knew just how complicated the paperwork was. It all had to appear legal and righteous: the fact that he was the one who would profit from redevelopment must be well buried.

A bell chimed softly in the entry to the apartment. Hikmat covered the papers on his desk with two leather bound volumes of Phoenix Kingdom land and building laws and left his study for the sitting room. A servant was closing the door behind the stocky figure of the Commander of the Phoenix Guards. Anjit stood ramrod straight, left hand on his sword hilt, right palm over his heart.

'Lord Regent.'

'Commander. May I offer refreshment? Please, be at ease.'

Hikmat lifted a crystal decanter as he spoke, filling one of several goblets set on a gold tray. Anjit removed the plumed helmet he wore to mark his rank and placed it on a stand beside the door.

'Thank you my lord.'

'Join me.' Hikmat indicated a chair, handed Anjit a goblet of wine and took another chair opposite the Commander.

Hikmat sipped his drink and waited. Anjit took only a sip of his own wine then sat staring into the dark red liquid before meeting Hikmat's gaze.

'My lord, I have ordered two outlying garrisons into the city. They will come discreetly of course, but I would feel much happier knowing the complement of armsmen is considerably increased at present.'

'You anticipate civil disorder at the Presentation?'

'Your plan to begin the festivities two days before Presentation can do two things my lord. Yes, the populace will no doubt overeat and overdrink and accept your new formalities. It will also provide ideal cover for the most determined troublemakers.'

Anjit paused. It was clear to Hikmat that the Commander was choosing his words with care.

'I am expecting a considerable increase in robberies – of both businesses and private houses. But more than that, it has come to my notice there is a large group who have moved into the city over the last half year.' Anjit stared straight into Hikmat's eyes. 'My lord, it is a group of mage born and I have been quite unable to infiltrate them.'

Hikmat sat frozen in his chair. This development had never crossed his mind. Anjit nodded.

'The mage born have found a way over the last twenty years, of concealing the fact of their abilities. Again, I have no idea how that might be managed. The Phoenix priests test every newborn but none have been identified as possessing talent. I checked, my lord. It was thirteen years since a child was recorded as mage born and consequently destroyed.'

'So the priests are actively protecting the mage born?' Hikmat sounded calm but his eyes were icy.

Anjit shrugged. He stared down at the goblet in his hand and absently swirled the wine. 'Some of them surely must be. The problem lies in the fact that these islands have always had magic and the people who can work that magic. I fear that no matter what you do to suppress the mage born my lord, the majority of the people would prefer that magic was available when needed.'

'Names. Do you have any names of the leaders of this – rebellion?'

The Commander looked startled. 'Rebellion my lord?'

'Oh yes indeed Commander. Any who choose to oppose laws issued from the Phoenix Throne are rebels. And will be dealt with accordingly.'

Anjit kept his eyes on his wine. The laws prohibiting magic had been issued by the Regent, not the Phoenix Throne. Or was the Regent finally admitting that he indeed intended to take that Throne for himself? Commander Anjit of the Phoenix Guards looked the Regent straight in the eyes. And he lied.

'I have been unable to name any of this group my lord, but rumours of its existence are growing more general.'

The inn at the corner of two narrow streets near the docks was bursting at the seams. The Sea Slug was renowned for its food, its ale and its girls. Two merchant ships had docked this morning and the crews had made straight for the Slug. The songs had progressed from ballads and sea shanties to generally bawdy and the girls were beginning to flag. The owner of the inn was Deng. He was a short, plumpish man with a deceptively genial countenance. His wife Saima was half a head taller than Deng and quite astonishingly beautiful. While Deng had charge of the ales, wines and spirits and maintained a strict discipline among his customers, Saima took care of the food and the girls.

Already this evening Deng had thrown five sailors out of the bar with orders not to return for ten days. He'd also thrown out two local apprentices who had deliberately goaded the sailors into a brawl. They thought their tricks had gone unnoticed but they were young and had yet to learn just how sharp eyed Master Deng was. They were told not to return for a full year. Deng couldn't abide unruly behaviour, hated violent brawls and had an unerring knack with a hefty cudgel he kept behind his counter. He used the cudgel to emphasise his points when expelling bad mannered customers from the bar.

The demand for food had at last eased and the cooks were slumped around the kitchen. The bar staff on the other hand, were working frantically to appease the thirst of the customers. Saima was in the private sitting room upstairs, trying to persuade two of her girls that they could surely summon the energy to satisfy just a few more clients. But the girls had really had enough of rough handling by increasingly drunken sailors and would agree to only one more each.

Saima promised they could have hot baths and a day of pampering tomorrow. Well, until sunset anyway. The girls went back to their rooms and Saima rubbed her temples. No one would guess she had a raging headache, except Deng. She squared her shoulders, prayed closing time would come swiftly and returned to the bar room.

At last the bells in the guard towers across the city rang out, the signal for all drinking places to close their doors. Deng sent his wife straight to their rooms and he oversaw the tidying up and washing of tankards and the departure of most of the staff.

Finally he made a large pot of Saima's special tea, arranged a tray and took it upstairs. Saima was lying on their bed, a cloth across her eyes and forehead. She removed the cloth and smiled while Deng poured her a cup of tea.

'Why is the pain so bad recently my dearest? I hate to see you suffer so.'

'Something is happening, but I cannot farsee. And the poor boy in the Palace is in pain.'

Deng had undressed and now he was burrowing into a voluminous nightshirt. Saima held the bedclothes open for him to climb in beside her.

'There is a meeting tomorrow,' she murmured. 'Perhaps one of the others will know more by now. You know several of us have had worsening headaches. I think it must mean the girl is much closer than we believed.'

'You will be careful tomorrow my dove. There are more people coming in to the city by the day and we have no idea who are informers.'

Saima set her empty cup aside and turned the lamp low. 'You know we take all the precautions we can.'

Deng's voice was a mere breath in her ear. 'Does Pauson have the girl, do you think?'

'That devil has been after her for years. If he gets her and convinces her to work with him then we are all doomed. Now sleep, my heart. Dawn will arrive all too quickly.'

The following afternoon, Saima kissed Deng goodbye and left the inn, walking away from the docks towards the centre of the city. The narrow streets were thronged with local people bustling about their business and also with gawping country folk who'd come in from distant villages to enjoy the forthcoming celebrations. She cut through Flower Street, where shop after shop frothed with petalled cushions, trumpets and flaring daisies and the mingled scents made her light-headed.

Along the street where carpet weavers clattered at their great looms and into the dressmakers' quarter. Saima dawdled, studying displays first on one side of the street then the other. She would normally be able to pick out a follower by using her talent but the constant headache had dulled that ability. Having worked her way to the end of the street Saima turned back and strode boldly into a small shop that specialised in intricate embroidery work.

She nodded to the two middle aged women who were working at a long table tracing out a complicated design on the full skirt of a brilliant scarlet gown. Saima ducked past a heavy curtain at the back of the shop. Immediately to her left was a door, half hidden under cloaks and jackets. The latch and hinges were well oiled. The door opened easily and silently and Saima passed quickly through, closing it behind her. She went down a steep flight of stairs to another door at the bottom which opened as she reached it.

'Welcome child.' The elderly man who stood there smiled and embraced Saima before closing the door again. He waved a hand towards the door and Saima knew fresh wards had been set.

The cellar they stood in was cosy. There was a curtain blocking a further area where Nabil and Addi slept. There was another exit hidden through there, Saima knew, but she hoped they would never need to use it. A tiny old lady sat in a rocking chair, her feet tucked under her. Saima bent to kiss the parchment skinned cheek.

'How are you Addi?'

'Same as ever child, except for the added joys of an aching head.'

Saima grimaced with sympathy. 'Am I imagining it or is it really getting worse?'

The old woman snorted. 'It got worse but now it's steadied again.'

'Meaning?'

'The girl has been travelling towards the coast of the Kelshanite lands. Now she's stopped somewhere.'

Nabil handed the women mugs of tea, generously laced with willow bark. Saima sat on a stool beside Addi.

'Is she with Pauson?'

Addi leaned her head back against the high back of her chair. 'Youki was here earlier. She dreamed the night before last and saw Pauson. He was angry. The girl had left, with the Dragon Thorn.'

Saima leaned forward. 'She rejected him? Surely, that is a

good sign?'

'We don't know what plan Pauson might have laid to deal with such an event.' Suddenly Addi cackled. 'What a blow to that pompous fool's pride it must have been, to have the girl spurn him! My brother should have been drowned at birth. He would have been if only he hadn't been born before any of us girls.'

Saima kept silent. Addi so rarely spoke of her two dead sisters and even less often mentioned the fact of who her brother was. Saima knew the story. Pauson had fled Vremilia believing all three of his sisters were dead and most of their children dead with them. There were whispers about him but Addi never spoke explicitly about him or his actions. When his name *was* mentioned, Addi was utterly contemptuous and dismissive. Saima waited to be sure Addi had said all she intended.

'Did Youki see the girl?'

Addi frowned. 'No. Everything we've learnt of that child indicated either no talent or a very late blooming of talent. We know the poor boy has no ability but I suspect something has now stirred the girl awake.'

'Are you sure the boy has no talent?' Saima asked.

Addi shot her a quick glance from under white brows. 'Why would you ask that? It is well known Tetsura has no magic.'

Saima shrugged. 'No one has ever got near him to check him. Perhaps he could be late developing them as it seems is the case with the girl.'

'Enough of this. I will mention your suggestion to the others, but I think there is small likelihood of the Prince having mage powers. Now, have you heard that our beloved Regent has increased the guards within the city?'

Saima was alarmed. 'I hadn't heard of that. Why?'

'He was told there is a large group of mage born gathering here.'

'He was told? By whom?'

Addi cackled again and smiled, shaking his head at her. 'By us of course.'

'Us?' Saima asked faintly. 'Has he got our names? The names of any of us?'

'No, no. We can't be that helpful! But apparently our dear

Regent was greatly shaken to learn of a large number of mage born still alive in these islands.'

'Who would betray us?'

'Oh child, you disappoint me. Can you think of anything else which would agitate Hikmat more than that snippet of information? We need him off balance for the next nine days and for the full turning of the next moon. The situation will be resolved, one way or another, within that time span.'

'How did Hikmat learn of mage born? Did you arrange for an informant through the guards?'

'Oh we managed rather better than that. If we had done it through some street rumourmonger it could have taken far too long for someone to decide it *might* be important enough to pass it higher.'

Saima stared from Addi to Nabil and back. Addi sighed and stretched a hand to brush Saima's beautiful smooth cheek.

'We have a daughter.'

Saima nodded. 'Zinab.'

Very quietly, Nabil joined the conversation. 'Zinab is a twin.'

Saima sat in silence, her mind racing to make sense of what she'd just heard. Finally she managed to find her voice. 'But Zinab and I are much of an age. Did she know?' Something else struck her. 'Did the twin die? How did you hide it all?'

'The twin lives,' Nabil spoke so softly Saima had to strain to hear his words.

'But where is she? Did you send her away? Well of course you must have. But does Zinab know? How could she have kept such a secret when we were children?'

'So many questions dear Saima.' Addi's faded grey eyes looked down the years of memory and she smiled gently. 'Zinab's twin went to live in Pahook, with Nabil's cousin. And the twin was a boy Saima.'

'A boy,' Saima whispered in wonder.

'And yes, Zinab knew from the earliest days. She is powerful in magic. She knew, and kept silent. She spent the hottest part of each summer in the country. With her brother.' Addi touched Saima's cheek again. 'Her brother, our son, is Anjit, Commander of the Phoenix Guard.'

Chapter Ten

Zeltan killed a small deer and Davin found herbs, a few tender new onions, and cooked a wonderful supper. As before, Davin and Zeltan quickly fell asleep. Toomay guided Tilliat out of the cave. The sky was ablaze with stars and she saw the huge bulk of the Dragon Thorn pacing away along the river. The water gleamed dark with occasional flashes where a star was reflected. Thorn finally reclined on the grass and his gaze settled on Tilliat.

'What do you fear Tilliat Kranch?'

Tilliat considered the question for some time, walking a circle around Toomay who lay opposite Thorn. Eventually she sat cross-legged, leaning against Toomay's shoulder.

'Being helpless I think. Being held in a cage of any sort and unable to get out, or to get anyone to hear me. Do you understand? Like when we travelled with Skala Vek. Occasionally I was aware and yet unable to speak to Uncle Davin or to move, or anything. If it is in my power, I will never be under another's control, helpless and voiceless.'

'And what would you wish for?'

Again Tilliat took time considering her reply. 'Somewhere safe,' she said finally. She glanced over her shoulder at the shadowy mass of the cliff then back at Thorn. Her teeth gleamed white in a quick grin. 'I'd quite like a place like those caves. They feel safe, comforting.'

Thorn gave his rumble of amusement. 'Many others have found sanctuary within that place child.'

'Who?' she asked instantly.

Thorn stretched a wing out to the side then furled it close to his back.

'Many humans, and ones who came before humans. They are known as the Ancient Ones. Dragons knew them long, long ago. We watched them change into creatures such as you but they understood the land, and time, as you do not. They made the

106

lamp and the axe you found.'

'Those were left for me to find weren't they? Who put them there?'

Now it was Thorn's turn to hesitate. Before he spoke a silver shimmer drifted above his back, then others to each side of him. They were like blurred smudges barely blocking the starlight as they moved. Tilliat felt no alarm when one of them wavered towards her and something dropped into her lap. She found a circle of cold metal which gleamed a dull pewter in the faint light. She held it up and it slipped in her fingers, sliding onto her left thumb. Tilliat stared. It fitted snugly and she saw a black spiralling curve cut into the silver.

'You will hear us better now.'

The voice was little more than a whisper in her mind but Tilliat suddenly knew it belonged to one of the shimmering figures in front of her, but she addressed her questions to Thorn.

'Who are these creatures and why have I been given this ring?'

'You could ask them directly but I admit they have a rather short way of conversing. We can hear them much more clearly than you I think.' Thorn sighed.

'I have had over a thousand years to prepare to explain this to the one who would come, and it still seems to be difficult.'

Toomay pressed slightly against Tilliat's back and she guessed he wanted to hear this new tale.

'There were great wars at that time, and strange monsters had been loosed all across the lands. It was when an Imperator called – oh my, what was his name? Jemin! That was the one. He fought and won a great victory but he was helped by a most powerful mage. She was very young. Her name was Tika.'

Tilliat frowned. Did he mean a woman she'd read of in the histories, called Theeka?

'Her soul was joined to the soul of a very young Dragon called Farn. This is how they were when I saw them.'

Thorn sent a picture to Tilliat's mind and she gasped. A brilliant blue Dragon drifted down from a clear sky, a small figure perched between his enormous wings. His face was long, like Thorn's and Toomay's, but his body shape was quite different. When he landed, the girl on his back slid to the earth and Tilliat saw a wild mop of black curls and eyes greener than any emerald

107

she'd ever seen. Those eyes were surrounded by silver rather than normal white and gave an impression of strangeness, of difference. Another Dragon landed, and another, both much larger even than the blue. Thorn took up his story, leaving the pictures in Tilliat's mind.

'The golden one was named Kija and the crimson one was Brin. Kija was mother to Farn. They had chosen to fly across these lands after the countryside was quiet once more under Jemin's rule. They knew of our Dragonkind and had decided to visit us before going to their own Realm. I was young then you understand and was not involved in their meetings with our Elders, but the young one, Farn, asked me to show them some of our Realm. He and Tika were devoted to each other.'

Tilliat could hear the puzzlement in Thorn's tone: he still found it strange apparently that a Dragon and a human made such a pair.

'I brought them here. It was a favourite place of mine even then. The human girl went into the caves with Farn and myself. She touched the walls and she knew of the Ancient Ones. The rocks spoke to her.' Thorn sounded awed even now.

'We stayed here that night and she spoke of the future. She said the Imperators blood was weak and they would be overthrown. She told me of these days, of two children born together and separated within heartbeats. This Tika said both children must survive or this world would fall into chaos worse than what she and her friends had just fought through.'

Thorn paused and the picture of the blue Dragon intensified in their minds.

'See his neck, that terrible scar. He fought and nearly died but the human child found her magic and she healed him.'

Both Thorn and Toomay shuddered at the thought of what such a wound must have been like to endure.

'This child told me many things which you do not need to know now. But she spoke of the islands called Vremilia where we once dwelt, and she said that was where you and your brother would first draw breath. She knew that you would be brought here to grow. But she did not know if you would or should go there later, she seemed to think your path lay through the lands you know, in Kelshan, while your brother must work in the islands. Tika left that ring and spoke with Shadows for some considerable time. The Shadows knew you were coming, knew who you were and they put out the lamp, the axe and this ring. I have no idea where they have kept the ring all these many years.'

Thorn looked carefully round at the haze of slender shapes.

'Shadows are most powerful child and if they answer to your command, be *very* cautious as to exactly what you command them to do.'

'But what can they do?' Tilliat asked.

'Hide,' replied the whispery voice.

Tilliat saw Thorn lurch to his feet and stare in all directions. 'Where are you child?'

She felt Toomay's body shivering against her back. She held out the hand with the ring, and she couldn't see it.

'Let me be seen,' she thought.

'Show,' replied the whisper.

Thorn's face loomed towards her, his nose against hers, his great eyes flashing frantically. Tilliat laughed and laid her hand against his cheek.

Aloud she said: 'Hide,' and immediately Shadows engulfed her. 'Show,' and she reappeared.

Thorn sat back on his haunches, his eyes still indicating a high level of disquiet.

'I wonder what else they can do?'

'Kill.' The whisper sounded hopeful.

'No,' Tilliat said in alarm.

'What?' Thorn demanded.

'They said they can kill. I wonder how they could do that. Do you know Thorn?'

'No I don't. And I'd much rather not.' The old Dragon sounded thoroughly rattled.

Tilliat turned the ring on her thumb. 'Thorn, I've read many of the old histories and I recognise the name of the Imperator Jemin. He fought his half sister, Veranta. She had very nearly ruined the capital city, which was called Kelshan then as it is now. From all the texts, Jemin restored the city to a successful, safe place to live and work. He had only daughters. One of them succeeded him and only just managed to keep things running as her father had done. Her name was Rika. Her son, Jerror, was a drunken idiot although the histories are more polite. Businesses collapsed and the Imperator system was ended. A council of nine was elected and that means of government has carried on – until now.'

Tilliat regarded her strange audience: two Dragons and an uncertain number of silver Shadows.

'There are two statues within the entry courtyard of the Citadel. One huge Dragon and a smaller Dragon with a rider. Their names are said to be Keecha, the large Dragon; the smaller Dragon has no name but the rider was said to be a mage called Theeka. They are the ones you met aren't they?'

'I would guess so child. Humans have short lives and even shorter memories. They often change names or words. The islands where once Dragonkind lived are called Vremilia now. We called them Fremala.'

Tilliat sat and thought. She was learning so many things so quickly she felt she needed time to try to make sense of at least some of this information.

'Is there a hurry Thorn? I know you said Tetsura will be eighteen soon, and I suppose so will I. Is the date urgent? Must something be done by then?'

Before Thorn could reply, the whisperer did so. 'Nine days and one full moon turn. Must finish.'

'Must finish *what*?' Tilliat cried in frustration. 'Will my brother know whatever it is he has to do? How can I get a message to him?'

'Take.'

'You can take a message?'

'Message. You.'

Thorn's eyes flashed in alarm but Tilliat was intrigued. 'Could Tetsura hear you, if you took word?'

The silence extended. 'Mages. Some hear.'

Tilliat looked at Thorn, waiting for his opinion.

'Pauson says the one who rules Vremilia now has had all mage borns killed. Babies are checked, at every birth through the islands, and any with the gift are murdered.'

'Many live. Hidden.'

Tilliat suspected the Shadow's truncated version of conversation could well become deeply annoying but she ignored

110

it for now.

'But how long would it take you to get there and then find a mage? Or my brother. It is several days sailing from this land I believe.'

'Your heartbeat.'

Tilliat gaped.

'Take you. Hide. Show. Talk.'

Tilliat didn't let herself think too seriously about such an action. She stood up.

'Do it,' she said.

She was plunged into complete darkness but before she could panic the whisper spoke to her. 'Not see. Make sick.'

She had no sensation of movement but also no awareness of any ground beneath her feet. Then suddenly there was solidity underfoot and a smooth wall at her back.

'See,' she murmured in her mind.

A narrow strip cleared in front of her eyes and she saw she was in a bed chamber. There was no one present but an open door let lamplight shine in from another room. Watching, she saw a small wisp of black shadow drift into the lamplight. She swallowed hard and wondered belatedly just what she might have got into. She heard a voice.

'What is it Vilad? There is no one here, do not fear.'

A very old man stood in the doorway.

'Show.'

The Shadows vanished, revealing Tilliat and the old man stared directly into her face. He dropped to his knees, tears streaming down his face, and reached out towards her. A chair scraped on the floor in the next room and a boy stood behind the old man.

'Tilliat,' he whispered.

Shivers ran all over Tilliat's body. It was an indescribably eerie feeling looking at Tetsura. It was like looking at herself, but the longer she stared the more she saw the little differences. Tetsura's face was unmistakeably male, although a male still changing from boy to man. His mouth was thinner than hers and there was a wariness about him which suggested a lack of confidence, an insecurity. Tilliat forced her gaze away and focused on the old man.

111

'Who are you?' she asked softly.

Tetsura cleared his throat. 'This is Vilad. He has always been my servant. He cannot speak but he knows of our birth.'

Tilliat moved to kneel in front of the old man and gently pulled his hands away from his face.

'Why can't he speak?'

The whisper came in her head. 'Speak mind. Mage.'

Vilad jumped and looked all around. Tetsura did the same.

'Vilad? Why can you not speak?' Tilliat repeated, but this time she thought the words.

The old man gave a gusting sigh and his hands turned to grip hers. Then she heard his voice in her mind.

'I chose to have my tongue removed.'

The colour drained from Tilliat's face.

'Five years before my beloved friend gave birth to you, I was silenced. A mute servant is no threat you see. So I was brought here to serve three years before your birth. I have served Tetsura since that day.'

A hand rested on Vilad's shoulder and tightened.

Tilliat glanced up. Tetsura's eyes swam with tears.

'I knew nothing of this until two days past.'

'I have little time here,' Tilliat said. 'I've been told there are mages here still. You have to contact them somehow.'

'I know several,' Vilad confirmed.

'Will we be able to talk like this, Vilad and I, when you are gone?' Tetsura asked.

'Will they?' Tilliat asked the Shadows.

'Yes. Boy wakes.'

Obviously neither Vilad nor Tetsura had heard that exchange.

'This magic stuff, it seems to be starting in both of us,' Tilliat told her brother.

'Few stay here,' interrupted the Shadow.

Tilliat groaned. She gave Vilad and Tetsura a hasty account of the Shadows who helpfully demonstrated their hide and show.

'Apparently some of them will stay here with you now.'

Tetsura gave an exclamation of surprise. He held his left hand out. A black ring circled his thumb but when he rubbed a finger over it, the blackness scattered into tiny specks, then returned to form a ring again. Tetsura eyed the ring dubiously.

'But how did you get here?' he asked.

Tilliat pointed at his ring then at the one she wore and shrugged. 'The Shadows brought me. I have to go back. I don't know what I'm supposed to do but I have to find out. You have to do something too. It has to be done before the next moon's full turn.' She got to her feet. 'I am glad to have seen you. Perhaps one day we will meet properly.'

Shadows closed round her before she'd finished speaking and when they released her, she was standing between Thorn and Toomay. Both Dragons rushed at her and sniffed her face. They were plainly upset by her disappearance and her popping back again. Tilliat found herself hugging both of them. It occurred to her that she would have laughed at the very idea of *hugging* Dragons such a short while ago, but already that life seemed to belong to someone else.

She looked up at the sky. The stars still blazed and didn't look to have changed position. So she really couldn't have been gone long. Tilliat drew in a long breath. She had a living, breathing brother. And for the first time, she wondered what kind of upbringing he'd had, what kind of life, which could have caused that wariness in his eyes.

Next day, in the city of Garjetka, Saima woke next to her husband and wondered what had changed. She lay for a while then realised her headache had gone. Deng snorted and woke himself up. He blinked, yawned, and struggled out of bed. Saima too peeled back the bedclothes and got up.

'No, no my dove. Stay here until I bring you some tea. Rest while you can. I can deal with the food merchants.'

She smiled, pulling her nightgown over her head and replacing it with a pale green robe.

'The headache has gone dearest. Quite gone.'

Deng gaped at her and Saima chuckled. Her husband always made her think of a dishevelled hen first thing in the mornings.

'Really?' he asked. 'Oh I'm so pleased.' Then he frowned. 'What might that mean, if you thought it was linked to either or both of those children?'

Saima was brushing her long hair, white strands gleaming among the dark. She tied it in one braid and made for the door.

But she froze there and saw Deng had also gone still, one trouser leg on, the other off.

'Addi,' Deng said a moment later.

Saima went back to the clothes cupboard and grabbed a shawl. 'I'll go and see what's wrong.'

She kissed Deng and turned again to the door. Deng caught her hand.

'Be careful. Please my darling. Addi is usually so strong in her sending, yet I could barely hear her.'

'I know. That's why I have to go. I'll be as swift as I can but you know I have to go.'

Deng reluctantly let his wife loose and finished getting dressed.

Saima abandoned any pretence at caution once she got outside of the Sea Slug's front doors. This morning she sped through Flower Street then cut down a winding alley and disturbed a ragged cat delving through a pile of rubbish. Saima turned right into a passage barely wider than her own shoulders and emerged into another alley. A door straight in front of her led into the backyard of the embroiderer's shop.

A ward prickled at her skin as she went through to the back entrance of the building. That door opened and one of the women who worked there smiled as Saima hurried in.

'Are they well? Both of them? I had a message from Addi which I couldn't make sense of.'

The woman spread her hands. 'I think so. They both *seem* as usual, although tired, as if they've not slept a wink. But they are calm. I don't believe it can be anything bad. I took them some breakfast but they eat so little now.'

Saima leaned in towards the woman and kissed her cheek. 'You are good to them Murra. We all appreciate your care.'

The woman blushed and flapped her hands. 'Oh who wouldn't love them both? They are dears and it is my great pleasure to help them.'

Saima kissed her again and went quickly on to the half hidden door that led down to the cellar rooms. As always, the door opened before she quite reached it and Nabil smiled a welcome. He hugged Saima much closer than usual and Saima's concern increased when she felt his frail body trembling. She saw Addi's tiny form curled in her rocking chair and noted the dark marks of exhaustion circling her eyes. But Addi smiled and held out a hand so thin it appeared to be a bundle of twigs covered with skin.

'Your headache has gone?' the old lady asked with a smile.

'It has indeed. And yours?'

Addi nodded. 'We had news last night. You were right after all dear Saima. The boy has power and is reaching for it. Just like the girl. Oh Saima, she was in the Palace last night. Physically here! Can you believe she might have such a gift!'

Saima could scarcely believe what she was hearing. Nabil brought mugs of tea, a rich fruity tang scenting the steam that rose from them. Addi leaned closer.

'Vilad came before dawn. He was with the Prince when the girl appeared in the bedchamber. Her name is Tilliat. Vilad suspects she is the cause for the magic to stir to life in the Prince.'

The room seemed to tilt while Saima tried to absorb what Addi was saying.

'The girl was in the Palace? But how is that possible Addi? We know of sending, illusions, dream walking, but you say she was here?'

'Yes. Her body was physically present. Vilad held her hands. She *was* there. No, I have no idea how she could work such a spell but she did. Of course, everyone's rattling their brains trying to work out how she did it.'

'Does Pauson know she can move herself through time and distance?' Saima asked.

Addi looked alarmed and frowned.

'I don't think he can. He would never have let her out of his sight,' answered Nabil.

'If she can move herself, bodily, I can't see how anyone could hold her,' retorted Saima.

A wicked smile lifted Addi's lips and she cackled. 'That's true enough. I wonder if the boy can do it too.'

Then she became serious again. 'Vilad brought much news. You know he never mindspeaks from within the Palace, just in case. Our beloved Regent has been beating the Prince badly for the last twenty days, in the belief he was deliberately hiding his abilities. Four days ago Vilad feared for the boy's life but then

Hikmat left him alone. That's when he announced the changes to the Presentation Ceremonies. Vilad told us Hikmat has no doubt that Tetsura has no magic.'

'And apparently he has.'

'Yes,' agreed Nabil. 'Vilad is not sure what Tetsura's strengths might be, it is too soon. But Tetsura knows Vilad chose to be close to him, chose the mutilation which made him beneath notice within the Palace.'

'And so does the girl Tilliat. She was there when Tetsura heard mindspeech for the first time.' Addi sighed. 'There is so much to ponder but no time. Now listen child. Nabil and I will be moving to the hidden city today. We must be with the majority of our people. We may have need of our combined strength. You and your sweet husband must remain in your inn until we call you. Unless of course you are in danger yourselves.

'Our son, of whom I told you, knows of you, and he also knows who and what Vilad is, and he has known for very many years. I tell you this because I understand you must have grave doubts about trusting the Commander of the Guards. But trust him you must Saima.'

Saima nodded slowly. 'To further the Dragon Prophecies I will do whatever you ask.'

'Good' said Addi with satisfaction. 'Now off with you. Poor Deng works hard enough without having your chores as well.'

Saima made her farewells, unsure when she'd see the old couple next, and headed back to the Sea Slug.

Captain Ras of the Phoenix Guards strode out of the Palace barracks. He looked smart as a new pin, belying the fact that he'd been up all night. He had checked five of the city barracks and in the process managed quiet exchanges with others who were of like mind to him. He planned no less than the downfall of Commander Anjit.

Ras was the son of a wealthy banker and had grown up with the firm belief that coin bought anything and anyone. To find it didn't buy him out of trouble within the ranks of the Guards had shocked him to the core. It wasn't his fault the girl had died after he'd beaten her. She hadn't pleased him, and as she was even less than a servant, why could he not punish her as he chose?

She'd come from a family in Flower Street and her mother had complained officially to the Commander.

Ras pointed out to the Commander that it was obvious the mother just wanted more coin out of him and he had not understood Anjit's reply.

'Is it possible, do you think, that she might want justice for her child?'

Ras hadn't believed the order was genuine until the first of ten stripes was laid across his naked back. He'd been given two days for his back to scab over and was then put under the recruiting sergeant and made to repeat the basic training course in every exhaustive detail, for a full moon. When he'd encountered the Commander afterwards, Anjit behaved as though the incident had never happened, but Ras believed it was all an act.

Captain Ras now made his way to the mess hall, well pleased with himself and what his fellow plotters had told him this night. He sat down to enjoy a most welcome breakfast. One of those he had spoken to, Sergeant Tag, was also enjoying her breakfast.

She was in a tavern in the east of the city and busily regaling her companion with the information Captain Ras had given her. The man across the table watched Tag finish a second heaped plate of food and wondered, not for the first time, just where exactly all that food could possibly be stored in the woman's tiny frame. Sergeant Tag pushed the plate away and sat back with a sigh of contentment.

'So what next?' she asked, stifling a belch.

'Oh I think the duty roster can be rearranged. At least five of those names have surely earned a posting to some of the Outward Isles, wouldn't you agree?'

Tag narrowed her eyes. 'You can be seriously devious sometimes. Have I mentioned that before?'

'You have indeed,' Commander Anjit agreed.

He tossed a couple of silver coins on the table, winked at the sergeant and strolled casually out of the tavern.

Sergeant Tag's laughter followed him into the street.

Chapter Eleven

Once she was back at the caves, Tilliat slept well, without dreams. Then she spent the first part of the next morning just strolling by the river. Toomay accompanied her. They returned to find Davin hopefully dangling a line in the river, closely observed by Thorn.

'Where's Zeltan?'

Davin squinted up at her. 'He's gone that way,' he pointed back to the forest of giant trees. 'Said he wanted to think. There's plenty of meat left for later.'

Tilliat sat next to the trader.

'I'm not going to the islands Uncle.'

Davin nodded calmly and waited.

'We have to go to Gulat. At least, I think so. I must find the people who have begun these troubles.'

Again Davin nodded. 'And do what exactly when we find them? Defeat them one at a time in single combat or – you have a plan?'

Tilliat laughed. 'No single combat I hope and I'm sorry but no plan either. Not yet.'

Davin looked at the old Dragon. 'Any ideas?'

Thorn huffed and said nothing.

'We will see Pauson as we leave. I think Toomay said the only way in or out of here was through that gateway place.'

Davin shivered at the thought of having to repeat that journey. Toomay shifted from foot to foot but made no comment. It was Thorn who spoke.

'There are other gateways known only to Dragonkind.'

'So you'd have to blindfold us,' Davin agreed gravely.

Both Dragons grew greatly alarmed.

'Blind you? By the great stars no! How could you think such a thing?'

Tilliat poked Davin, quite hard. 'He meant we could cover our eyes with a cloth, so we couldn't see,' she explained.

The Dragons calmed although a wave of disapproval emanated from Thorn.

'Will Zeltan come with us?' asked Davin.

Tilliat considered then she concentrated harder. 'Shadow?'

'Yes.'

'Is Zeltan worthy of trust?'

'Yes. But not for you.'

Tilliat clenched her teeth. The Shadow seemed to realise she needed a rather fuller answer.

'Zeltan serves Pauson.'

'No,' Tilliat said aloud. 'It will be only Uncle and me.'

Toomay became agitated and clearly some communication passed between him and Thorn. Finally the young Dragon settled beside Tilliat again. Thorn sighed.

'Toomay will travel with you.'

'Surely not? It would be too dangerous. What if he was seen?' Tilliat knew she would very much like Toomay's presence with them but the dangers would be far too great. Every hunter in the Kelshanite lands would jump at the chance to kill a Dragon.

'He can conceal himself well enough,' said Thorn. 'Only within a large gathering of humans, one of your big settlements, then he would keep apart from you physically at least.'

'I admit I would love to have Toomay's company but only if you are positive it won't put him in unfair danger Thorn.'

Thorn's eyes glowed silvery grey. 'He will travel with you.'

That didn't really answer the question but Tilliat decided to accept it.

'Shadow,' she asked once more, deep in her mind.

'Yes.'

'Do you know the city of Gulat?'

'Yes. Danger.'

'I know that,' she snapped and then closed her eyes, breathing deeply. 'Do you know what is happening there?'

'Yes. No.'

'*Which?*'

'Some.'

'Will there be any help for us?'

'See.'

Tilliat sensed a sudden vacancy within her thoughts. Had the Shadows dashed off, just like that, to find out what they could? She shook her head and then realised Davin was regarding her quizzically. She would have to do some explaining again.

'Thorn,' she said aloud. 'I'm going to tell Uncle about the Shadows and what happened last night. Will you warn me if Zeltan comes back?'

Thorn inclined his head then stretched himself out flat on the grass and closed his eyes.

It took some time to explain things to Davin Pearl and he was quite pale by the time she'd finished. He was about to speak but Thorn murmured that Zeltan would be in sight in moments. Zeltan sat down with Tilliat and Davin.

'Something bothers you?' Tilliat asked, as lightly as she could manage.

Zeltan hugged his knees to his chest. 'Yes. I have thought hard about your saying you would not go to Vremilia and claim the Phoenix throne. I believe you have reached that decision hastily because Pauson angered you and you are young. Pauson is old, and he is the wisest man in the world, so I'm afraid I will insist that you return to him under my escort.'

Trying to hang on to her temper, Tilliat heard the whisperer.

'Pauson stupid.'

Both Thorn and Toomay snorted and Tilliat found the urge to yell at Zeltan was transformed into a desire to laugh. She coughed.

'There is no hurry,' she said. 'It is getting late today.'

'Forgive me, but time is urgent. We will go tonight.'

Tilliat raised an eyebrow and stared all around.

'And the horses are – where exactly?'

Zeltan frowned. 'You can summon them can't you Thorn?'

Thorn opened his eyes. They shone with absolute innocence. 'I fear they have wandered far from here. It will take a day or two to find them and coax them this way again.'

Zeltan swore and stood up. 'Then summon them at once Thorn,' he ordered.

Tilliat felt anger rise again within her. How dare he speak to Thorn in such a manner? But Thorn spoke in Tilliat's and

Davin's minds.

'Be ready for Toomay to move you from our Realm tonight. I shall ensure Zeltan sleeps deeply.'

Davin cooked their supper and when Tilliat took the pots and dishes out to wash them in the river, Zeltan went with her. Her eyes glinted in the dusky light.

'Keeping watch on me now?'

Zeltan didn't smile. 'We are wasting precious time here. If you ran off it could take too long to find you again, even with my talent.'

Tilliat dried the dishes and took them back to the cave. She soon lay down and feigned sleep, knowing Davin was doing the same. Toomay spoke in her mind.

'It is time to go. Bring your things outside.'

Davin Pearl had heard the Dragon and he too rose, lifted his pack and crept after Tilliat. Thorn waited outside. He lowered his head until his broad brow rested against Tilliat's.

'I will help you as I can, but it will not be as much as I would wish child. Trust Toomay and trust the Shadows. May the stars bless you.'

Tilliat put her arms round his neck and hugged him. 'Thank you Thorn, for everything. Look after my safe place for me?'

She felt affection wash through their linked minds then Thorn touched his brow to Davin Pearl's and farewelled him. Toomay paced close to the old Dragon who twined his neck round the smaller Dragon's face and shoulders. Tilliat and Davin Pearl settled their packs securely as Toomay came over to them.

'Stand each side of me, close to my neck,' he told them.

They did as he asked.

'Put your arms across, and hold firm. Close your eyes.'

Davin Pearl never, *ever,* became accustomed to what the Dragonkind called gateways. The only good thing he could say about them was that they were quick. This first time, he held tightly to Toomay's shoulders. He felt nothing around him, not the movement of air nor ground under his boots. His eyes squeezed as tightly shut as he could manage: he had no desire whatsoever to know what might be happening around him. In one way Davin felt this experience went on forever but he was aware in fact that scarcely ten heartbeats had passed before sensation returned.

He opened his eyes and saw a river of stars pouring across the sky in front and above him. Then he groaned as his stomach caught up with him from across countless miles, and he sank to his knees. Davin was not pleased to find Toomay and Tilliat unbothered by their strange journey. In fact, he found Tilliat's excitement positively aggravating. He lay flat on grass which felt frosty and tried to calm his roiling stomach. He heard the murmur in his head which was Tilliat and Toomay talking and eventually he opened his eyes again. A long silvery shape bent over him and he yelped and sat up. Tilliat dropped beside him, her arm over his shoulders.

'Are you feeling better? Toomay says even some of the Dragonkind get sick using these gateways.'

Davin's mind boggled at the idea of a nauseous Dragon and he shook his head, pointing a shaking hand at the wisp of silver a few paces away.

'Sorry Uncle. I think he, or she, was just curious that you fell over like that after travelling.'

Davin muttered under his breath. Tilliat thought it was a string of oaths but prudently ignored them, helping him to his feet with no comment.

'Can you walk Uncle? The Shadow says there are two mages living nearby who may have information we can use.'

'Where are we exactly?' Davin croaked.

Tilliat turned him round. 'Look.'

He saw they were standing on a hillside, a few dark tree shapes were scattered round about but below and directly was a vast sea of lights.

'Gulat,' Tilliat informed him. 'We are about six miles outside the city walls.

Davin stared, unable to take in the size of the city. Tilliat tugged at his arm and pulled him round again.

'Uncle can you walk?' she asked him again. 'It isn't too far.'

'Lead on,' he told her, gritting his teeth against the pain in his head and his stomach.

Davin had no idea how long he staggered over rough uneven ground, sometimes under trees, sometimes under the starry sky. He held on to Tilliat and just kept going. A rectangle of light appeared and Davin crumpled at Tilliat's feet. A woman came running towards them and dropped beside Davin. A man followed her more slowly.

'Don't just stand there like a tree Pitzi Chay. Get the poor soul inside where I can see him properly.'

The man was huge. He bent and lifted Davin Pearl as though he was merely a baby. The man turned and retraced his steps to the house. The woman climbed to her feet and peered into Tilliat's face.

'Is he your father child?'

'No, my uncle.'

'Well he must be a crazy man to have you wandering around out here at this time of the night. Come in, come in.'

Tilliat called Toomay with her mind. 'Where are you Toomay?'

'Very close. Do not fear,' his tone was soothing.

The woman holding Tilliat's arm went rigid then forced herself on into the house. Once in the brighter lamplight she gave Tilliat a searching look before turning her attention to Davin, lying on a couch to the side of a hearth. The huge man handed Tilliat a cup of something steaming and gave her a slow, gentle smile.

'Sit down my dear, make yourself comfortable. I don't think your friend will be moving anytime soon.'

'He's my uncle.' Tilliat sat in a squashy old armchair.

'My name is Pitzi Chay and that is my wife Ty.' Pitzi sat opposite her and waited.

Tilliat thought frantically. What a fool she proved to be already! She hadn't considered what name might be safe to use.

'I'm Jomah,' she said, lifting the mug to her lips. She was surprised to find she was drinking a wonderful spicy broth. She glanced up when the woman left Davin's side and stood beside her.

'Your uncle is sick from a magical cause,' she said bluntly. 'You just said your name is Jomah. My talent says it is not your name. Who are you?'

'Shadow?'

'Yes.'

'Are these people safe?'

123

'Yes. If not, kill.'

Tilliat gulped and saw the woman had stiffened. 'What did you just do?' she demanded. 'Who are you?'

Tilliat raised her chin. 'My name is Tilliat Kranch.

There was a sudden ringing silence. The man leaned forward staring at her intently. Then his expression changed to one of wonder.

'It is. It *is* her, Ty.'

'Are you safe?' Toomay's voice murmured.

Both Pitzi and Ty stared. The man reached a massive hand to cover Tilliat's.

'Who mindspoke you then child? Is there another companion outside?'

Tilliat drew a deep breath. 'Yes. His name is Toomay and I would have him join me.'

The door opened suddenly, banging against the wall. Toomay's head was well below the lintel but his shoulders filled the doorway. He was clearly agitated. Tilliat glanced at the man, Pitzi who still held her hand and at his wife, and she did not let herself smile. Their mouths hung open in total disbelief when Toomay paced carefully inside the room. He lowered his head to sniff at Davin Pearl, then advanced to sit to the left of Tilliat's chair.

'Uncle sleeps. You are well.' He sniffed at the mug in Tilliat's free hand and his nostrils wrinkled.

It was the woman Ty who regained her power of speech first. 'Dragonkind in these lands once more! Where have you been all these years when we needed your help? And why are you here now?'

She held one hand to her throat, the other gripping her husband's shoulder.

Toomay studied them, his eyes calming to a pearly blue. 'I serve Tilliat.' His mind speech was clear to all.

'No.' Tilliat put her mug on the floor and slid her arm round Toomay's shoulder, her face resting against his long cheek. 'Toomay is my friend.'

Silence fell again for a few heartbeats more. Tilliat chose to break it.

'How did you know I am Tilliat Kranch?' she asked Pitzi.

124

'You said "it is her". But I have never been here before.'

The man rose and went to a corner of the room. He rummaged through a stack of papers, some clearly handwritten and some printed like the news sheets Tilliat read in Kelshan. He pulled a sheet out of the pile with a grunt of triumph. He handed it to Tilliat. The item concerning her was in the lower left corner. There was a small sketch of a girl's face which bore a passing resemblance to Tilliat but could equally as well be matched by dozens of other young girls. After she'd studied the sketch she read the words in blurred messy print alongside.

She read it through twice and still couldn't take it in. Toomay's chin rested on her shoulder.

'What is this?' he asked.

'These papers are sold or given away in most towns and cities, to let everyone know what's going on,' Tilliat explained. She pointed to the picture. 'That's meant to be me.'

Toomay peered closer, his breath warm on Tilliat's hand. 'It doesn't look like you,' he decided firmly.

'Hmm. But the writing here says Skala Vek is dead Toomay. My picture is shown because I am the one who apparently murdered him.'

Toomay's eyes flashed with darker colours. 'Why are such lies written on this paper? Does it say when the Vek died?'

The woman Ty answered his question. 'It was four days ago.'

Tilliat frowned. 'It says here Toomay, that he was tortured, beaten and then had his throat cut.'

Toomay hissed and shifted from foot to foot. 'Why do humans do these things?' he asked.

Tilliat stroked her hand along his jaw. 'Hush. Humans do that and worse my dear friend. Do you think perhaps you should go back to Thorn? This is not a world for you.'

Toomay's long neck twisted so he could stare closely into Tilliat's face. 'My place is wherever you are,' he said simply.

Tilliat pressed her cheek against the Dragon's, but made no reply. Ty sighed.

'We have heard talk from colleagues in the city about a mage travelling towards Gulat. No one knew your name until that paper came out.' She pursed her lips. Lifting a large covered dish from the table she put it in an oven beside the hearth. 'We knew something of that Skala Vek.'

Ty tossed aside the thick cloth she used for tending the oven and sat down next to her husband. Pitzi nodded.

'Many years back, when he was a boy of perhaps ten years. He is, was, the son of a mage, one of a group who control nearly all things in the city. Mostly their control is benign.'

Ty snorted but Pitzi continued. 'No Ty, mostly they *are* benign. There are a few others, in a smaller group who are not, and they go to great lengths to remain out of the public's eye. The leader of that inner group was Skala Vek's mother, the hardest, meanest bitch I've ever met.'

'And what is the intention of those mages?'

Ty stared into Tilliat's eyes. 'They want to disrupt utterly life in the western lands, so they can then go in, pick up the pieces and have total control over more people than Gulat offers them.'

Tilliat nodded. 'I have honestly no idea how I'm meant to do anything which, I'd guess, you and your friends have been trying to do for a long time already. But I know I have to try to put an end to this group, try to trace back where all their tentacles of powers might lead. I have been told I will be a powerful mage but no talent has manifested in me yet and it is late for such things to happen.'

Ty watched the Dragon Toomay. He seemed bothered by some of Tilliat's words.

'You disagree with this child Dragon Toomay?' she asked suddenly.

Toomay rattled his wings against his sides. 'She has mage powers already. But she has no idea how to use them,' he said, with a flutter of silver in Tilliat's direction.

'I have?'

'I hoped the Shadows would bring us to humans who could help you learn.'

Three people regarded the Dragon. He fidgeted but Davin Pearl roused before any more was said. Ty went to Davin's side and touched his forehead. The trader lay back, asleep once more.

'What have you done to Uncle Davin?' Tilliat asked.

Ty shrugged. 'Eased his head and belly. Sleep will restore him fully.'

'So can you help me reach my magic?'

126

Ty sat back by her husband. 'Will you let me touch your mind, to try to see if I can find a door or a key which I may be able to show you how to open?'

Tilliat considered. What options did she have? How *had* all this befallen her?

'Do what you wish, but Toomay will remain within my mind.'

'Lean back, close your eyes and relax. It won't hurt. You are used to the Dragon touching your mind – it will feel much the same.'

Tilliat did as she was told and immediately sensed a tiny push against her thoughts. Like when Pauson tried to use his mind to force her obedience to his wishes. Her instinct was to push back as she had done with him, but she remained passive. She heard a sharp intake of breath and her eyes snapped open. Ty had both hands over her mouth and her brown eyes seemed enormous as she stared at Tilliat.

'What is it? What's wrong?' Tilliat was alarmed. What could the woman have seen inside Tilliat's head?

'I don't know,' Ty faltered. Her previous ruddy complexion was drained to a muddy grey. 'I've never seen the like. There is so much there, a great web of power glowing throughout your brain. I have no idea how to begin to teach you anything at all.' She shook her head and Tilliat saw Ty was trembling. Pitzi's brows drew together in concern and he put an arm round his wife.

'What do you mean, a glowing web? That is not how magic reveals itself within a mage's mind.'

'I know that,' Ty snapped, her gaze resting on Tilliat. 'I can tell you a few things: how to protect yourself from other, intrusive minds, how to shield yourself so that your power is hidden. But teaching you magecraft is beyond me, and I would suspect there are none of our colleagues who would be able to either.'

Well, thought Tilliat, not much help here then. The whisper riffled through her mind.

'Woman teach you to shield. Magic comes anyway.'

'Who mindspoke you?' Pitzi asked sharply.

'Shadows,' Tilliat snarled back.

Pitzi and Ty both recoiled.

Oh gods, now what? Tilliat knew of gods and goddesses in Kelshan and across the Kelshanite lands, but she had to admit she

127

had never heard of Shadows before. These two people obviously had and their reaction didn't speak well of what they'd heard. Tilliat chose not to deal with that right now. Instead she asked how she could shield her mind from any other curious mages.

Pitzi and Ty exchanged a quick glance. Ty began to explain basic mind exercises which, oddly, reminded Tilliat of the precision of the physical exercises she'd been taught throughout her childhood. Pitzi listened for a while then wandered off and began setting the table and swinging pots over the fire. Toomay listened to Ty's words with great interest. How very strange humans were, he thought. They made something so simple and natural as magic into such a complicated puzzle.

After some time, Ty announced she would stop for now.

'I'll go over that and anything else I can think of again later,' she said.

'Aren't you going to check and see if I've got it right?'

'No.'

Toomay moved to the couch. 'Uncle wakes.'

There was a brief bustle while Ty made sure Davin felt recovered, if slightly wobbly. He was helped up to sit at the table as Pitzi began to put hot dishes out for the meal. Tilliat noted the sky was lightening beyond the window and thought it was strange to be eating supper at breakfast time. But her stomach was growling with hunger so she ate as heartily as the others. Pitzi made a large pot of tea and the four sat drinking quietly when they'd finished their food.

Pitzi gave Tilliat a wry smile. 'You said your name was Tilliat Kranch. It felt half true. Can you not tell us more? We will help you as we can but to trust you we have to believe that *you* can trust *us*.'

Tilliat felt she was virtually helpless in this place. Davin, Toomay and she herself were to pit themselves against an unknown number of mages who had already attempted her kidnap if not death through Skala Vek. Perhaps these two could help, and they had spoken of "colleagues". Tilliat conceded that she should take what assistance she could get right now.

'My father,' she began, then immediately and reluctantly corrected herself. 'The man who raised me and whom I consider fully my father, was a trader of Kelshan. His name was Stevro

Kranch, thus I am Tilliat Kranch. I've been having dreams for a long while, of places I do not recognise. My father left Kelshan five years ago. He was lured here I have lately discovered, and he was murdered.'

She faltered and Davin laid a hand over hers on the tabletop.

'Skala Vek worked for the Master of the Traders Guild in Kelshan but I cannot believe Master Belk knew anything of Skala's early life or what he planned. The city was in a state of turmoil when we left and Skala dosed me with some poisons which kept me nearly unconscious for many days.'

Silently, Toomay had come up to the table and his head poked over Tilliat's shoulder. 'She was very sick when I found her, north of here. We took her quickly towards the rising sun, where there is a safe place.'

Tilliat touched his cheek gently and resumed her account.

'There was a mage there who told me of my true history, and of a prophecy concerning my birth. He cleansed my body of the poisons Skala had given me and said a mage had also spelled the drugs. He said that mage was from Gulat. I thought about what I had learned and decided, prophecies or no, my feeling was that I must come here.' She shrugged. 'That's it.'

Ty and Pitzi had listened intently and now Pitzi smiled again.

'Not quite,' he said kindly. 'What was the prophecy you disagreed with and what is your true history?'

Tilliat flicked a glance at Davin and the trader tightened his fingers around hers. Toomay's chin pressed a little heavier on her shoulder. Tilliat lifted her chin.

'The mage told me I had been foretold. That I would become a powerful mage. He also told me I must return to my birth place, murder my brother and take his place.'

Pitzi held her gaze and whispered softly. 'Take your brother's place where Tilliat?'

She found her vision blurred with sudden tears. 'My brother and I were apparently born twins. I was brought away at once and very few knew I even existed. My brother is the Crown Prince of the Phoenix Throne in the Isles of Vremilia.'

129

Chapter Twelve

Hikmat was pleasantly surprised by Prince Tetsura's docility when he visited him the morning after his disquieting interview with Commander Anjit. He had no idea that Tetsura's calm demeanour was because of the enormous comfort he found in being able to use mindspeech. No matter where Vilad was in the Palace or the city, he was always within Tetsura's reach.

Hikmat noted the boy was moving stiffly still and felt a momentary regret at the viciousness of that last beating he had so enjoyed applying. They sat in Tetsura's sitting room, the glass doors to the balcony standing open and the pale blue curtains stirring slowly in the breeze. Hikmat explained the changes he had made to the Presentation Ceremonies and Tetsura nodded agreeably.

'I will send you the papers giving all the details and the two changed speeches you will make.'

'I have wondered sir, why my Lord Father took against the mage born so strongly when he and his wife, my Lady Mother, had those talents themselves?'

Tetsura spoke softly, his face showing innocence and only a passing interest. He saw the Regent's dark eyes harden although the man's body remained relaxed.

'They were freaks of nature my boy. People without these strange foibles became suspicious that they were being coerced in any dealings with such folk. They believed, rightly I think, that the mage born were cheating in any business transactions and so on. Her Majesty the Queen was said to be a visionary, seeing far future events in great detail. Such a gift had no purpose whatsoever of course. His Majesty the King could form illusions – pretty sparkling pictures which gave much pleasure to the public but again, was of no value to the Kingdom.

'Those who claimed other gifts, healing for example, were a danger to all. Ordinary folk believed magic would cure their ills and all it did was give them brief comfort. Far better they should ask a properly trained physician than one who said they could magic away their pains.'

This was the most Hikmat had ever said on these matters to Tetsura. The Prince politely hid a yawn behind his hand and saw the almost contemptuous look in Hikmat's eyes. Tetsura felt a surge of glee. For the first time in his life, he knew he had fooled the Regent.

'Well I must be off. There are still many details of your Presentation to be sorted out. I merely called by to ensure your improving health.'

Tetsura rose at the same moment and walked to the door with his guest. His glee had turned sour at the ease with which Hikmat referred to the beatings he had – personally – inflicted on Tetsura. It was almost as if Hikmat had convinced himself Tetsura had suffered a fever in truth. The door closed behind Regent Hikmat. Tetsura wandered back through his sitting room, out onto the balcony.

The city was busy by now and the Prince could hear the shouts of drovers, cries of street traders, the rumble of wheels on cobbled streets rising from beyond the Palace walls. Overhead, enormous sea birds screamed and squabbled, resembling scraps of white parchment as they drifted and wheeled against the blue sky. He heard the click of the inner door.

'Vilad?' he enquired in his mind.

'My lord.' The old man bowed.

'You heard the Regent?'

'I did my lord.'

'Do you know the real reason he tried to purge these Isles of all mage born?'

'He was afraid my lord. He has no magic himself and has never understood it. What he doesn't understand or like, he destroys.'

Tetsura nodded, looking over the Palace grounds to the distant walls.

'I wonder where she is?'

The old man touched the Prince's arm gently. 'Far away from here now my lord.' His mind was full of sorrow which Tetsura understood and shared.

'I thought perhaps you could try a stroll my lord. Just through the spice houses or the scented gardens?'

Tetsura looked sharply at the man.

'Already?' he whispered aloud. 'Someone will meet me?'

Vilad's eyes glinted with mischief and he shrugged. 'Maybe someone will be seeking a spice for a particular recipe my lord. Who knows?'

'Now?' The Prince's eagerness wrenched Vilad's heart.

'No my lord. When the sun passes its height.'

Tetsura tried to hide his disappointment at the delay, unsuccessfully to the eyes of the man who had served him since birth.

'I'll check the papers the Regent brought me – about the removal of the poor from the western docks.'

Vilad bowed and the Prince retreated to his study. It didn't take Tetsura long to read Hikmat's report and when he'd done so twice, he tossed it onto the table in disgust. Surely even Hikmat's tame advisors and councillors could see through the flimsy and implausible reasons for this destruction of poor folks' homes? And it took very little imagination to work out just who would buy up the land, rebuild and make an enormous profit.

By the time Tetsura had eaten a light meal and put on a thicker robe, Vilad was there, bowing low. Two servants were clearing the remnants of the Prince's meal when Tetsura acknowledged Vilad's arrival.

'Vilad,' he said aloud. 'I will walk a little, my fever seems much improved and I believe exercise will help it depart completely.'

Vilad bowed again and opened the door for his master. They made their way along a wide corridor to the head of a great sweep of stairs. Vilad walked half a pace behind Tetsura's right shoulder. Once outside they stood under a pillared walkway and several gardeners spotted the Prince and bowed. Tetsura crossed a gravelled path to speak to a couple who were setting barrowloads of small multi-coloured plants along the edges of all the paths. The gardeners were delighted to see the Prince. Word had spread of his illness and Tetsura was well liked among both indoor and outdoor servants.

He spent time asking about their families and their work

132

before strolling on towards a hedge of tightly curled dark green foliage. An arched space allowed them through the hedge to a section of both glass houses and sheltered open plots. This was where herbs, spices and the most delicate scented flowers were encouraged and nurtured. Tetsura had always worried that Hikmat's gaze would settle on these gardens which Queen Naila had caused to be made.

Naila had decreed that the city people could come and freely ask for the herbs and spices grown here. Several specialist gardeners working with these plants were always on duty, handing out what they could, depending on season and supply. Tetsura had fretted that Hikmat would cancel this arrangement. After all, it brought no profit other than the affection of the people and Hikmat had no interest in that.

Walking further into the enclosed area, they moved through patches of different perfumes. Tetsura loved this place and came here as often as he could. He'd learned a very great deal about the plants and their qualities. A short round man wearing brown trousers and a brown tunic came rushing from one of the three glass houses, his outstretched hands covered in soil. A wide smile split his face.

'My lord! My lord! We've been most concerned to hear of your fever. Are you recovered?'

He craned his head to peer at Tetsura's face and the smile became a frown.

'You look too pale – are you sure you should be about yet?'

A tall thin beanpole of a man walked jerkily in the first man's wake.

'For goodness sake Ori, His Highness is not a fool. If he was still unwell he would not be here. Welcome my lord, it is a pleasure to see you as always.'

'And you Kreeg and you Ori.' Tetsura clasped Ori's hands in spite of Kreeg's look of horror at the filthy state his colleague's hands were in.

Tetsura followed the two gardeners to their particular glass house and spent some time admiring the exotic and luxuriant display of flowers gathered from across all the islands of the Kingdom. Eventually Tetsura detached himself from Ori's exuberant explanations.

'I shall sit in the wicker house for a time my friends, and rest before I go back to work on the papers and reports which are far less fascinating than your gorgeous plants.'

Kreeg slapped Ori's broad shoulder. 'You see? All your chatter, after you said His Highness still looked frail.' He bowed to Tetsura. 'Of course my lord. Allow me to bring you fresh water and then you must rest quietly as long as you need.'

'Thank you, Vilad can bring the water and I will visit you again soon.'

Tetsura left the glass house and walked down a narrow grass path towards a corner of the dark hedge. Five cultivated willows grew in a curve across the corner and behind their pale drooping branches stood a tiny house. Vilad carried a plain wooden tray with a pewter jug and two clay goblets. The heat made condensation bead on the long neck of the jug and Tetsura regretted the thicker robe he'd put on for this outing. Vilad put the tray on a low table within the single room of the house and sat cross-legged on one of many cushions on the floor. The Prince loosened the sash at his waist and lowered himself gingerly, the scabs on his back pulling at his movement.

A darkening at the door caused Tetsura to look up sharply. A slender figure slipped inside, moving quickly behind Vilad. Thin hands reached to fold away the concealing shawl from the woman's head. The most exquisitely beautiful face regarded the Prince gravely. Tetsura stared back. Perhaps it was her eyes that instantly took the breath away, he thought. But no.

Eyes as blue as the ocean or the sky were unusual in these lands but they were set in a face of true beauty. Dark lashes framed those astonishing eyes but her hair, he now saw, was tied in a single braid which hung over her right shoulder and breast to her waist. He also saw the strands of ice white scattered through the black strands.

'Your Highness.' Her voice was low, musical. Most pleasing to the ear.

It took a moment for Tetsura to realise the woman's words had not come from her lips but directly to his mind. The lips he was staring at twitched into a slight smile and he gathered his wits.

'My lady,' he replied in his mind.

She chuckled. 'I am not a lady Your Highness. My husband

and I own the Sea Slug, an inn near the docks. I doubt you have ever visited the area.'

'Perhaps I could remedy that lapse after the Ceremonies?'

Vilad made the snuffling noise that was laughter for him. 'That might be a good idea,' he agreed in mindspeech. 'My lord, this is Saima. She, and many of the other mage born knew of your sister's approach. They all suffered headaches until the night she visited. So they are also aware of your awakening to magic. Saima will give you what instruction she can. Others will help as needed.'

'I asked Hikmat why he tried to kill all the mage born,' Tetsura began then stopped when he saw the delicate colour fade from Saima's oval face.

Vilad touched the Prince's arm. 'She and Deng lost three children to Hikmat's death squads.'

Before more could be said, Saima rose and moved close to Tetsura, a slight frown creasing the skin about her nose. She gently pushed aside the shoulder of Tetsura's robe and muttered something.

'Vilad told us you had been beaten but I hadn't realised how badly. I will help the healing a little but I dare not do a complete mending. I'm sure you are moving carefully – it would be noticed if you moved normally too suddenly.'

Even as she spoke Tetsura felt a warm itching across his shoulders and back. When Saima moved back to her previous place near Vilad, the Prince cautiously rolled his shoulders and stretched his spine. He sighed with relief when he felt his skin move without the sharp soreness he'd felt for too many days.

'Thank you,' he said simply.

Vilad poured water into the two goblets and stood up. 'I will wait outside. If anyone approaches I will indicate you are sleeping my lord.'

The sun was lower and the shadows long when Vilad re-entered the little house.

'We must go back my lord. We have been here much longer than is really wise but you can explain that you slept.'

Tetsura was astonished to see that so much time had sped by but then he saw Saima looked tired. Dark smudges lay under her eyes and he was instantly concerned.

135

'I'm so sorry Saima, you should have stopped earlier.'

She smiled. 'Your mind is so eager to learn my lord but your way of handling the magic is different to any others I've trained. Different, and quite difficult to penetrate.'

Vilad helped her to her feet and she swathed her head and face with her green shawl. She bowed.

'It has been an honour and pleasure to meet you Your Highness. Vilad will let me know when we can continue your lessons.'

'No my lady. It has been *my* honour and pleasure I assure you. I look forward to your next visit.' He grinned suddenly making Saima aware of how young he was. 'Perhaps I will call on you.'

She smiled back. 'That would be an excitement too far for our customers I suspect.' She nodded to Vilad and he plucked at Tetsura's sleeve and held out a hand towards the door.

'Will she be safe leaving here?' Tetsura thought.

'She can seem invisible should she so choose,' Vilad replied, his mind tone confident. 'But there will be no trouble for her now.'

'What about the guards at the gates?' Tetsura fretted.

'Sergeant Tag is on duty. She is a great friend to Saima, and indeed to many of us.'

'Do I know this sergeant?'

'You may have seen her around. She's very small, with red hair, and deadly with knives I understand. She denies she is mage born, resists any attempts to test her and, as she is so very nifty with a knife, none of us has felt inclined to insist. She is also a close comrade to Commander Anjit.'

Tetsura stopped in his tracks, horrified at that news. Vilad discreetly prodded him on towards the staircase leading up to the Prince's Tower.

'Had you truly not guessed my lord? Commander Anjit is himself mage born, and even more shocking to tell, he is a twin.'

Six miles outside of the city of Gulat, Tilliat slept for most of the morning. Davin Pearl was wide awake however and spent the time pleasantly enough with Pitzi Chay. Pitzi's wife Ty also slept, exhausted by being up all night with her unexpected guests, and working a minor healing on the trader. Mostly though she was tired by the very thought of the power in Tilliat Kranch's head. Power that was quite beyond her comprehension but she knew enough to know it was stirring to life within the girl. The idea of an untrained child possessing that much power scared Ty Chay nearly out of her wits, so she retreated into sleep.

Davin helped Pitzi bring in logs and offered to chop more from the dwindling pile at the northern wall of the house. The huge Pitzi grinned and clapped Davin on the back, nearly knocking the trader off his feet.

'Kind of you to offer, but Ty would have my hide if she caught you working up a sweat.'

He led the way into a barn close to the house and about the same size. Two donkeys and a large horse snuffled a welcome while hens scrabbled round Pitzi's feet. Pitzi set Davin searching for eggs while he turned the animals out into a small enclosure attached to the barn. Then he cleaned out the stalls. Pitzi talked while he worked, telling Davin the state of things within the city. Listening carefully, Davin learned that there was a repressive regime in control, led by Mahzu Vek, Skala's mother.

Mahzu's group was well hidden behind another council, one with much more agreeable public faces. Pitzi explained how trading was being gradually more restricted, with fewer outside traders being given permits to enter the city. The militia had been strengthened and the armsmen were recruited from the dregs of the population. Violence was common within the walls and escalating each year.

Many Gulatians had moved away, preferring to risk the world outside their city, even the wild clansmen or the barbaric Kelshanites far to the west than endure life here anymore.

'Will it be difficult for us, within Gulat?' Davin asked. 'I've been trying to think of a story to conceal who we are – not too difficult for a devious trader!'

Pitzi smiled but shook his head. 'No one has described *you*, only Tilliat. Ty can change her hair colour I expect and do other small things. You'll have to practice any false tales really hard to convince a mage, unless Tilliat can learn to shield you both. The militia usually have a mage at the gates – not highly gifted but good enough to spot false identities.' He emptied his loaded barrow onto the dung heap. 'You must know your way in Gulat.

137

At least some areas, so you just *might* have a chance to get out fast. You also need to know much more about the inner core who are under Mahzu Vek's thumb.'

Pitzi fell silent, staring over Davin's shoulder. Davin turned and smiled. Toomay paced with dignity round the side of the house, just as a grey cat sauntered towards the same corner from the other direction. Both creatures stopped and stared at each other, the cat fluffing out its fur to make it seem twice the size. Toomay's ears quivered forwards and his long head dipped slowly towards the cat. Davin was surprised to see Pitzi frown.

'What is it? They seem to be getting acquainted.'

'Exactly. They are mindspeaking.'

Davin was perplexed. 'Why wouldn't they?'

Pitzi gave a deep rumble of a laugh. 'We were not surprised that Dragonkind use mindspeech or have mage powers. We have never considered that animals might also be gifted.'

Davin shrugged. 'What's the difference? We're all animals of various kinds are we not?'

Pitzi studied the trader. 'That is true. So why has it never occurred to us?'

Toomay and the cat had clearly decided on a course of mutual respect and both joined the two men by the dung heap.

'Are you human again Uncle?' Toomay's voice held a teasing note.

Davin touched the Dragon's cheek and noticed his nostrils twitching.

'I am indeed. Let's move from here: beside a dung heap is not the best place for conversation.'

'Indeed,' Toomay agreed, moving rapidly away.

The two men followed but Davin stumbled. The cat had stretched up and hooked its front claws in the cloth of Davin's trousers at the knee.

'I would be carried – Uncle.'

Davin nearly fell over completely when he heard the soft female voice inside his head. 'Oh. Yes. Of course,' he said aloud.

Cautiously he lifted the cat and held her against his shoulder where claws sank into his shirt and a purr rose ever louder to his ear. 'Do you have a name?' he asked aloud.

Two answers came at once. From Pitzi: 'Dreesha.'

From the cat: 'Cloud.'

Pitzi's expression made Davin bite his lip. The cat's eyes had been closed while she purred her appreciation of Davin's care but now they opened. Shards of emerald glared at Pitzi.

'Never bothered to ask me, did you?'

The eyes closed again and the purr increased in volume. Davin glanced at Toomay and felt glee radiating from him. The trader left Pitzi, still stunned, and strode over to the Dragon.

'Is Tilliat awake yet?'

'Yes, but she is trying to learn more from Ty.' He sounded slightly disapproving.

'More about magic, or Gulat?'

'Magic. The magic is all *there* Uncle, she doesn't *need* teaching. And not by humans who truly don't understand her particular magic.'

'Perhaps we should just wait out here then?' Davin suggested. The last thing he wanted was to get in the way of two mages who, judging from a suddenly raised voice from within the house, were not in the best of moods. Changing direction, Davin walked at an angle to the house and found the trees that had seemed to surround the buildings had been thinned in one section.

The city sprawled before him, very different from the glittering pool it had appeared last night. Even from here the walls were forbidding. A thin layer of smoke floated above Gulat but Davin could see countless rooftops behind the walls and could only guess at the crowds of people crammed within. There was a gate to the left and already traffic, in the form of carts, wagons, riders and a mass of tiny figures walking, thronged the road to be slowly sucked into the city. It was strange Davin thought, to be aware of all those people and activities yet hear not a sound. The cat in his arms gave a massive yawn.

'I will join you in your travels I think,' she announced.

'But don't you belong here?' Davin asked in surprise.

Emerald eyes blazed up at him. 'Cats belong to no one. If I choose to go with you, then I will go.'

Davin could think of no argument and so stayed silent.

'I think that's a very good plan,' said Toomay. 'I can only keep in mindtouch once you enter that smelly place. It will be

139

good to know someone else is with you.'

Davin wondered exactly how much practical help a small cat could be but squelched the thought in case Toomay or Cloud were reading his mind. They were.

Toomay's eyes sparkled while Cloud spat rudely.

'You have no idea what I might do,' she said. 'Cats can go anywhere. You humans talk and talk and talk, never bothering if a cat is close by. All of us are just stupid animals to you.'

Davin stroked a finger down Cloud's spine and she half closed her eyes in pleasure.

'Why do mages not know that you use mindspeech?'

'None of them ever asked, or very few of them,' she amended.

'Who?'

'Dragonkind have many of what you call mages but there were some humans, long ago.'

'Tika.' Toomay sounded smug.

Cloud peered at the Dragon with some interest. 'Did you meet her?'

Toomay sputtered. 'I am still very young. My many times great grandfather saw her.'

'You must tell me the tale,' Cloud began but was interrupted by the harsh croaks of two crows.

Davin looked hard at them but accepted that he couldn't see any differences between them so he had no way of knowing if they were the two he'd seen before in the Dragon Realm. It turned out that one of them was. There was much head bobbing and beak clattering before one spoke in their minds.

'Greetings Dragon. And you Uncle. I flew far and saw much. Many dead humans.'

Davin felt slightly sick.

'Your news is for Thorn, within our Realm, but I can thank you for your assistance now.' Toomay inclined his head.

The crow shuffled his black feathers and strutted along the branch he was on. 'My brother stayed in those lands. He found a mate and they chose to stay where there was much food.'

Davin's stomach lurched.

'This beautiful one,' the crow bobbed towards his companion. 'She chose to come with me.' His mindvoice was suddenly coy. 'She had just suggested that we build a nest here when I saw you

140

and Uncle.'

The crow's head tilted to one side and a bright eye fixed on the cat in Davin's arms. He prudently remained on his branch. Davin felt the small body tense and tightened his grip on her a little.

'It is rare to see Dragons outside of the Realm,' the crow remarked.

'Uncle, and the girl Tilliat, must go into that city place and find the ones who disturb the world.'

The two crows chattered at each other, the new crow seeming greatly excited. The first crow turned back to Davin and Toomay.

'We can speak to others of the feathered ones if that might assist you?'

Davin was speechless. This all felt so utterly bizarre. He was a middle aged trader and suddenly he had a Dragon for a friend and crows and cats were talking in his head, offering help. He very much feared he might start whimpering.

Chapter Thirteen

It took a considerable effort for Tilliat to hold her temper in check. She was beginning to wonder whether Ty Chay was really trying to help her or trying to block the magic within Tilliat's mind. The magic was growing, Tilliat knew. There was a prickling sensation at the base of her skull, similar to how it felt before her dreams of Tetsura. But this was different, more like tendrils reaching up into her brain. Ty snapped another command at her and Tilliat closed her eyes, shutting the woman out.

'Shadow.'

'Yes.'

'Can you help me with this?'

'Yes. Away.'

Tilliat heard Ty gasp but when she opened her eyes she saw only blackness. For the briefest heartbeat she was aware of nothing underneath her feet, then the darkness disappeared and she found herself standing in the shelter of some trees. She breathed deeply.

'Shadow.'

'Yes.'

'Can you show me how to reach my magic and how to use it?'

'Some.'

Tilliat didn't let herself think about what could happen.

'Do it.'

She had braced herself for pain and there was none. She had no idea of how much time passed while she stood there. There was a blurred light before her eyes. Like Toomay's eyes, various colours emerged from a pale cloud. It slowly dispersed and Tilliat discovered her legs had given way at some point: she'd slid down with her back to the tree trunk and her head resting against rough bark.

'Shadow.'

'Yes.'

Tilliat stared. A silver figure stood in front of her. It was tall and etiolated, somewhat resembling a human in general shape but was most definitely not human.

'You see.'

'I can see you yes. Is that the magic?'

There was a lengthy pause. 'Maybe.'

'Do others see you?'

'No.'

'Oh.' Tilliat felt once again that conversation with a Shadow would continue to be frustrating whether she could see it or not. 'I don't feel any different.'

'Magic is there.'

'But how do I use it? Any of it?'

'Over there.'

Tilliat looked where the Shadow pointed with a wavery arm. A tree had fallen some distance away, its trunk as thick as Tilliat was tall.

'Lift.'

'How?'

'Think it.'

Tilliat scowled, stared at the tree trunk and willed it above the ground. She was appalled to see it lift as easily as if it was a twig. It kept rising until she hurriedly thought of it as it had been. It settled back to the ground with a slight thump.

'*That*'s magic? That's all there is to it?'

'Yes.'

'Oh my.'

'Unique.' The Shadow sounded – awed.

Tilliat needed time to assimilate what had happened. She sat gazing absently at the fallen tree.

'Toomay?'

'You are well?' Toomay's tone was gentle.

'Yes. What are you doing?'

'Talking with Uncle and Cloud. The woman came out and went to the man. She was very agitated. They are talking together.'

'Who is Cloud?'

'I am Cloud.' The feminine voice murmured in Tilliat's head. 'I am what you humans call a cat.'

Tilliat felt exhausted. 'And what do you call yourselves?'

'We are Kephi.'

Tilliat sighed. 'I look forward to meeting you Cloud of the Kephi. I will be at the house soon. Shadow?'

'Yes.'

'How am I supposed to do whatever I must in Gulat?'

'Kill all.' The Shadow's reply was hopeful.

Tilliat was caught between laughter and tears. Shadows seemed very attached to the idea of killing. She closed her eyes again and imagined a wall right around her. It wasn't difficult; one of her weapons instructors had taught her a similar exercise so she would focus only on what she meant to do in a fight. The shell enclosed her and she slid into the depths of her own mind, determined to find out all she could of what everyone else called magic.

Time passed and Tilliat only roused because the silver ring on her left thumb became achingly cold, burning to the bone. Her head ached and she felt sick.

'Shadow.'

'Yes.'

'Can you make me feel better, like Ty?'

'No.'

'Why not?'

'No magic.'

Tilliat digested that fact. 'Then how can you move me about or hide me?'

'Not magic.'

Tilliat groaned, rubbing her forehead.

'Dragon comes. Heal.'

Tilliat peered through the growing gloom and finally saw Toomay pacing almost daintily through the trees. He pressed his brow against Tilliat's when he reached her and the headache and vanished. As if by magic, she thought wryly. Toomay's laugh rolled through her mind.

'Uncle and Cloud are getting cold. They are just beyond these trees. The other two humans are – um – upset. They know something has happened.'

'The Shadow did something – '

'No,' the Shadow interrupted.

'Well I think I understand some of it but mostly I'll be guessing if magic needs doing any time soon.'

Toomay's eyes flashed with concern then calmed. 'You will know what to do.' His tone rang with a confidence Tilliat wished she could share. He led the way between the trees and Tilliat was surprised to see the back of the barn just ahead. The Shadows hadn't moved her far at all this time.

They walked round the side of the barn and nearly tripped over Davin Pearl. He was leaning against the wooden wall, a grey cat huddled close to his chest.

'Ah,' he said, straightening up. 'It's getting a touch chilly but we didn't feel like venturing in the house without you two. You all right child?'

Tilliat stretched up to kiss his cheek. 'Fine Uncle. And you must be Cloud?'

Green eyes glinted up at Tilliat. 'We've been waiting. Pitzi's not so bad but be cautious with Ty.'

Tilliat gave the cat a sharp look then nodded. 'Let's see if there's any food on offer, and then we can find out how far they can, or will, help us.'

Tilliat squared her shoulders and led the way to the house.

In a fortified building near the centre of Gulat, Mahzu Vek paced steadily round the outer edge of a circular hall. She, and several of her intimates, had felt a surge of power halfway through the afternoon. It had been brief, no one had been able to pinpoint the source. Mahzu had concluded it was not of great importance or interest. All who were aware of it, agreed it happened some distance outside the city walls. Such things occasionally happened when some uneducated peasant child came into mage powers. But the shock to them was usually so great, they burned out, quite literally, and thus a surge of escaping power roared through the surrounding area.

No, such a minor matter was forgotten almost as soon as it happened. What concerned Mahzu Vek was finding the girl. At least they now knew her name: Tilliat Kranch. Mahzu's position as undisputed leader had been oddly strengthened by the murder of her son Skala. The fact that Mahzu herself had ordered his death was known only to her. The armsmen who had carried out her order were now sadly deceased. Mahzu had sent them three kegs of the most expensive wine to celebrate their success. Of course, none of them had even considered the wine might have been enhanced with baneroot and when their bodies were discovered it was plain to all that serious overindulgence had caused their deaths.

Mahzu knew that Anat Fursh had his suspicions but he would find no proof. Anat Fursh was a powerful man. Unfortunately his basic intelligence was not very high. He had allowed others to become aware of his ambition to replace Mahzu Vek in due course and he could not see how that would make all wary of him. No one wanted to be connected with Anat Fursh or his plans. His magic was strong but he preferred to perform ostentatious spells and tricks which brought him a wide and appreciative audience. Unlike most mages of his strength, he had no interest in pursuing magic for the intellectual or practical furtherance of the general understanding of power.

Other mages within Mahzu's elite group all had particular subjects they studied in great depth. Mahzu Vek had only a few brief reports Skala had managed to send, giving the girl's name and a vague description of her appearance. He had been adamant she had no magical talent. Mahzu put little faith in that judgement. She had been horrified to find herself pregnant twenty five years ago, but Skala's father had promised her wealth and advancement within Gulat's mage council. She could now admit to herself she had been a fool to listen to him. But she still raged at her own stupidity.

To produce a child and then discover he had the barest minimum of talent was more galling than she could bear. His father had made the decision to send the boy to the city of Kelshan to await the appearance of the prophesied mage. Mahzu had little hope that the boy would be of any help at all but was delighted to have him far from her presence. Shortly after Skala's departure from Gulat, his father died. The death was a genuine accident, but Mahzu Vek saw it as a sign of her favour and superiority in the eyes of Reva, the god of Gulat.

Mahzu began pacing her third circuit of the hall. The prophecy was as convoluted and ambiguous as are all prophecies. The Mage Foretold would come from the east. Or perhaps from the west. She, (at least it was fairly positively stated the mage would be female,) would have a magic unseen for centuries and no mage alive would be able to teach her. *Where* was she? Several of Mahzu's mages had felt indications of power from both east *and* west. Mahzu pounded one fist into the palm of the other hand. It was so frustrating.

There was a discreet cough from the side door and Mahzu strove to appear calm.

'What is it Keril?'

'It is time for the evening rituals Mahzu.'

Mahzu Vek straightened her outer robe over her shoulders and joined Keril.

'I will visit Perra Koos straight afterwards. Arrange an escort please.'

Keril bowed. 'As you wish.'

'You will accompany me unless you are busy?'

The woman's hair swung around her face when she shook her head smiling. 'I am always happy to be with you Mahzu.'

The high priest who led the evening ritual in praise of Reva, god of death and rebirth, patron of Gulat, was a man Mahzu detested. She felt he had no true understanding of the mysteries of the god, an understanding that she of course had in abundance. The man was so very irritating Mahzu's mood was black by the time she left the temple precinct. She was appeased somewhat to find Keril Dwar waiting with six armsmen in the grey and black livery of the mage council guards. The guards came to attention and closed around Mahzu Vek and Keril Dwar. They set off at a brisk pace west from the temple, into a warren of paved streets and narrow alleys. The streets were lamplit, making the entrances to the alleys appear like dark mouths.

These alleys at night always worried Keril. They were shadow filled tunnels and even in daylight Keril never used them. She knew it was stupid of her but she was nonetheless convinced the shadows deep within the alleys moved and shifted to their own whim, not influenced by the sun or anything natural. She shivered as the escorting guards swung left, very close to one of those alley mouths.

'I am your servant Lord Reva, lend me strength,' she muttered under her breath.

It was nonsense she knew but the shadows seemed to withdraw.

They soon reached the solid wall of Perra Koos's home. There were no windows on the lower levels facing the street and when the iron door opened to admit them, it was to a small room lined with armsmen. The officer saluted, recognising Mahzu Vek and Keril Dwar.

'Apologies for inconvenience Lady Vek. Master Koos remains vigilant as to who enters his house.'

'I quite understand Captain. Master Koos is expecting us.'

'Of course.'

The Captain saluted again and opened an inner door to a narrow corridor. Two more armsmen guarded a door at the further end and flattened themselves to the side walls to allow the women to pass through into a sumptuous vestibule. Young girls bowed in front of them and took the visitors' outer robes. They offered slippers and bowed them on to a wide staircase.

Mahzu Vek always found Koos's house disconcertingly voluptuous. She had no idea how many exquisite servants he employed here and all the rooms were filled with rarities, paintings, carpets and furniture of stunning beauty. Yet Perra Koos appeared an austere man: he dressed plainly, although his clothes were of the finest cloth and cut, and he ate and drank frugally. He was obsessed with understanding the power and magic of Time and yet surrounded himself with such opulence. He was a paradox to a woman such as Mahzu Vek while he was astute enough to see through to her very core.

Perra Koos received his visitors in one of the upper rooms, one which was slightly more modest than the ones they'd passed through. He rose from a fireside chair as Mahzu and Keril entered. Perra Koos was fifty four years old, of average height but gaunt as a corpse. His hair, beard and skin were a similar shade of grey which made his dark blue eyes an arresting feature above the large beaked nose. He inclined his head in welcome but didn't smile – he rarely did – and indicated they take their seats.

Keril perched on the edge of a couch while Mahzu sank into the chair opposite Perra's. A servant offered tall glasses of golden wine and then withdrew. Perra Koos steepled long fingers against his chin.

'The evenings are still cold Mahzu. What has brought you to my house tonight?'

'The girl,' Mahzu replied instantly. 'We *have* to find her. And quickly.'

Perra's brows lifted. 'You really believe this is the Mage Foretold?'

'I do. Despite the confusions of the prophecy, it is possible to discern several alignments that are in place now. Rumours of the girl have increased enormously. Seers from several temples have confirmed that this is the time the Mage Foretold will appear among us.'

'But what do we honestly know of the mage who gave the first prophecy so long ago, or indeed of the mage who seemed to confirm it only twenty or so years past?'

'Theeka was the mage who originally spoke of the girl to come. She came from the west, but it is thought she was not a native of these lands. The more recent mage was named Zehara and it is believed she was from Vremilia.'

Perra Koos leaned back and crossed his legs. 'Vremilia has isolated itself too long. We heard rumours that all mageborn were being eliminated but we hear such things too infrequently. This Zehara. We do not even know if she is in these lands or if her prophecy was made through a dream link. Tura died almost immediately after she told of hearing Zehara. No one questioned her properly. And as far as I've managed to discover, she was not known for her mage talents. She was a priestess in one of the lesser temples – I forget which one – but certainly not a priestess of high repute.'

Mahzu waved her glass in dismissal. 'Many witnessed Tura's prophesying, not just the temple recorders who take down every word at such times. I believe Zehara used mindspeech to link with Tura.'

'Mindspeech? Over such a distance?' Perra was sceptical. Then he shook his head. 'This is irrelevant Mahzu. *If* the girl is near Gulat, *if* the girl is this Mage Foretold, surely she will make herself known to us?'

Mahzu set her empty glass aside and got to her feet. 'If she has been corrupted by Kelshanite mages she may have been told

149

to avoid us. I believe she is making her way to the east, to the coast. Maybe even to Vremilia. But we *must* get hold of her first and convince her to work for us.'

'*For* us?'

'I mean with us.'

'And what exactly do you think "we" will achieve with this powerful mage at our side?'

'The conquest of all the Kelshanite lands of course.' Mahzu's tone suggested Perra's question was barely worthy of comment.

Perra studied her tight face. He'd never heard her speak so openly of her ambitions and he wondered, not for the first time, about her grip on sanity. Keril Dwar had sat silently but now rose as Mahzu got out of her chair, standing with her hands loosely clasped in front of her but her eyes watchful.

'I will listen for any clues to this girl's whereabouts Mahzu and inform you of anything of interest.'

Mahzu Vek gave the briefest bow and made for the door which opened as she approached it. Perra Koos remained standing when the women had gone, staring into the fire.

This house was formidably protected. Koos reset particular wardings every few days. No one could penetrate these defences and yet he had an uneasy feeling tonight. He sat down again. He knew no one among the mage council had discovered what he had. He had been idly going through some of his uncle's journals four years ago and a brief sentence leaped at him from the page. The writing was nearly indecipherable. His uncle had never had a clear hand but at the age of one hundred and thirty one, as he had been when he'd written those words, the script was a spider's drunken scrawl.

"*Zehara is from the Realm of the Dragonkind.*"

Koos had heard of the mage Theeka before of course, in the many, and tedious, discussions of the ancient prophecy, but he'd never tried to trace her. No one ever spoke much of her, other than as coming perhaps from the far west at the time of the Imperators, but he recalled now a trader speaking of the Citadel of Kelshan. Koos stood up with a curse and strode from the room, making for a very private flight of stairs to his study and workrooms. Lights flared into life at a snap of his fingers.

Pushing chairs out of his way, Perra Koos worked along the

first wall of bookshelves. He cursed softly but constantly while he checked volume after volume. In the middle shelf of the third wall he found what he sought. He put the heavy book on the table and settled into a chair. The script was faded in places and written in a painfully cramped hand. Perra reached for his enlarging glass and bent closely over the first page. The curfew bell had long since rung out over the city before he found the reference he'd vaguely remembered.

"And within the first courtyard of the Imperator's magnificent Citadel, Jemin, the restored Imperator, caused statues to be set. People came from great distances to see the gloriously painted figures. On the left of the gateway stands the huge figure of the golden Dragon, Kija. Facing her is the smaller statue of her son, the blue Dragon Farn. On Farn's back rides the mage Tika, called daughter by Kija, most powerful of all, slayer of grotesque beasts who had been loosed upon the lands."

And that was all. Perra Koos cursed yet again. He closed the book, rubbed his aching eyes and sat back. That was what had tickled at his memory: Dragons. But Dragons were believed to be only mythological beasts. If they *were* real, and if they still existed, where was the "Realm of Dragonkind" his uncle had written of? Koos got stiffly to his feet and replaced the book on the shelf. He lifted a large flat case onto the table and untied the fastenings, revealing a collection of maps.

The dawn bell rang and Perra Koos straightened with a long groan. He stretched his back until the vertebrae popped. Leaving his study, he went to his bedroom, stripped off his clothes and stepped into his shower room. He let the water pound on him until his head began to clear, then dried himself, dressed and went down to the kitchen.

What no one outside of his house knew or would understand, was that Perra Koos lived very simply. His servants learned quickly to treat him as one of themselves in private and consequently many of them had been with him for years. He treated them as if they were his family and was a fair and generous master. Many of his servants had children who joined his service as soon as they were old enough. His cook put a heaped plate before him, sat watching him eat and scolded him severely for working too hard again. He was dismissed with a hug and made his way to the guards' quarters at the front of the house.

The men greeted him casually and he explained that he needed them on high alert for reasons he was not yet ready to give. Then Koos asked for four volunteers and led them into the Captain's office. He was pleased to see two of the men came originally from a mountainous area to the north east of Gulat. Perra described the exact region he wanted the men to check for him. He told them more than he might normally have revealed due to a nagging sense that there was an urgency to all this.

The two from the mountains nodded immediately – they recognised the land Perra Koos was describing.

'But sir, the terrain becomes impassable quite quickly just beyond the foothills.'

'That's what I need you to find out for sure Bar. I've seen some reports of various attempts to move north and east into that range. Men have told of feeling ill, becoming confused and having a desperate desire to get away from there. I will give you some medicines and I'll explain how and when you must take them. I hope they will keep you clear headed enough and able to move on to the point I'll show you on a map.'

The man nodded. 'Whatever you want sir. We'll get as far as we can.'

'Prepare for an early departure tomorrow. How long do you think it will take you to reach the foothills?'

The men glanced between themselves. 'Five or six days sir.'

It was the other mountain man, Chesan, who replied. 'We may make better time if the weather holds.'

'Good. I will see you later this afternoon and give you a map and fuller instructions. This is a matter of great urgency and secrecy, and I am placing my trust in you men. I do not think you will face danger, but there is always the possibility of that.'

Four faces grinned at him. 'It will be good to get out of the city sir. It's been a long winter cooped up.'

'Come to my study at the fifth bell and I will have your orders.'

Perra spent the rest of the day in his study, drawing a copy of part of a particular map he had pored over most of the night. He also spent a considerable amount of time considering what exactly he should tell the men he was sending on this probably mad hunt. Eventually he decided on a compromise. He would write a letter, containing the words he wanted relayed to a Dragon, should the men actually find a Dragon, and one who might understand their speech.

He would tell the men as much as he dared but he thought he would have to hold back about Dragons. He drafted letter after letter until he was satisfied enough with his words. He folded the paper carefully, sealing it with a large blob of crimson wax and impressing it with the crow emblem on his ring.

The fifth bell was tolling when there was a knock at his door. He called the men in and began his explanations. He noticed their expressions were serious immediately, intent on his every word. He knew these men; they had been in his employ for several years. One of them was married and Perra Koos knew his wife and his two children. He sighed and began to explain again, this time including his ideas about Dragons.

When the men left him, they were solemn yet he sensed an underlying excitement in them. Perra Koos leaned his elbows on the table, rubbed his eyes and yawned. He watched the black shadows under a stool near the fire waver and move. But he took no notice.

Chapter Fourteen

Tilliat had decided to be as diplomatic as she could but she insisted that she and Davin Pearl move out of the Chays' house and use the large hayloft in the barn to sleep in. She pointed out how guilty she felt, taking up room in the small dwelling Ty and Pitzi shared. There was no doubt that Ty at least was relieved to have some time out of Tilliat's presence although she tried (not very hard) to convince her guests to stay in the house.

Tension had built, most of it coming from Ty Chay. She seemed to treat Tilliat as a recalcitrant child while at the same time it was clear that she was afraid of the girl. The four of them had eaten supper and Davin and Tilliat had retired to the barn with Toomay. There was a small stove at the far end used by Pitzi for heating poultices for the animals but which was also perfectly adequate for making the tea Davin couldn't exist without.

A rising wind rattled the trees outside but in here it was warm and cosy.

'How long do we stay here?' Davin asked.

'I don't know Uncle. We've got to Gulat but I have no idea – as usual – what we do now. Ty and Pitzi seem to think Mahzu Vek is the centre of any mischief but they have suggested not one single way of getting near her.'

'And if you *did* get near her, what are you planning to do?'

Tilliat shifted uncomfortably against Toomay's side, unable to come up with an answer. She changed the subject.

'I was talking to Pitzi when Ty was complaining about the crows to you. What was she saying?'

Davin poured more tea into his mug. 'She said she was afraid they were spies. She told me there is a mage in Gulat whose emblem is a crow. She thinks he may have spelled these, to be his eyes and ears here. Ty feels she and Pitzi are distrusted by both the open mage council and Mahzu Vek's secret council.'

'And so they are.' Cloud stalked towards them from the horse's stall. She climbed onto Davin's lap and began a thorough washing.

'Why are they not trusted?' Tilliat asked with some alarm.

'Ty is arrogant and bad tempered. Pitzi is liked well enough but he is completely under Ty's control. Ty is seen as a danger. She is not very strong in magic but she is unpredictable.'

Davin and Tilliat stared at the small grey cat.

'Is there anything to their concern about the crows?'

Toomay wriggled slightly and the cat ignored the question. It was the Shadow that replied.

'Crows safe.'

'You mean they are just – crows – not connected to some mage in Gulat?' Tilliat asked.

The Shadow took its time before answering. 'Crows clever. Think mage worthy of trust.'

'What?' Tilliat sat up straight. 'There's a mage we could contact safely? In Gulat?'

Again there was a long pause. 'Maybe.'

Tilliat huffed out an exasperated breath. 'Who *are* you Shadow? Why are you helping me?'

'Tika asked.'

Tilliat closed her eyes. A woman from a thousand years ago had "asked" the Shadows to help *her*? And she didn't miss the fact that the Shadow hadn't answered her first question. She opened her eyes to see Davin nodding over the cat.

'Bedtime Uncle,' she told him, heaving him to his feet.

The loft was warmer than the floor in front of the fire in the house and Davin was soon snoring. Toomay dozed near the damped down stove and Tilliat lay staring into the dark.

'Shadow?'

'Yes.'

'I would like to see the mage in Gulat.' She sat up. 'The one who uses a crow sigil.'

The darkness became blacker and then she found her feet were steady on a floor.

'Show me.'

She was in a room with a long wooden table down the centre. The table was heaped with papers, maps and books. Books lined three walls floor to ceiling. A man sat at the table, peering closely at a page in an obviously ancient and tattered volume. The man slowly raised his head, turning in his chair until he saw Tilliat. His dark blue eyes glinted in the lamplight.

'Who are you?' he whispered. 'How did you breach my wards?'

Tilliat slid warily onto a chair opposite him. 'I am Tilliat Kranch. Who are you?'

'Tilliat … *You* are the Mage Foretold?'

Tilliat shrugged. 'I've no idea and I still don't know who *you* are.'

The man appeared to be struggling to speak. Finally he cleared his throat and drew in a few deep breaths.

'I am Perra Koos, mage of Gulat. I have no idea how you could have got here or why. Have you?'

Tilliat relaxed suddenly and grinned. The poor man looked stunned out of his wits and she guessed that was not a sensation he was used to feeling.

'I was curious I'm afraid. Someone told me of a mage who used a crow sigil.' She pointed at the heavy gold ring on his left hand, the crow clearly incised on its flat surface.

Perra glanced at the ring. 'It has always been my family's crest.'

'But do you speak to crows?'

'Speak to crows?'

'Yes. With mindspeech.'

Perra Koos looked positively ill.

'They use mindspeech?' he asked faintly.

Tilliat leaned her elbows on the table. 'I'm beginning to suspect that most creatures use it.'

Perra tried to get a grip on his faculties. 'Why are you here? There is another mage here who is seeking you. She believes she can make you work for her.'

Tilliat picked at the scab of a scratch on the back of her hand.

'Hmm. I know. Skala Vek's mother.'

Perra frowned. 'You are named as his murderer. You did know him then?'

'My father hired him to teach me certain arms skills. He brought me from Kelshan.' Grey eyes met dark blue. '*He* was drugging *me* all the way here. My uncle and a – erm – friend can bear witness I speak truth. We did *not* kill him. We lost him, many days ago, before he could kill *me*.'

'You're not an illusion are you?' Perra asked suddenly.

'I don't think so. I'm really here, if that's what you mean.' Tilliat reached to pat his hand. 'Feels real doesn't it?'

'It does indeed,' Perra sighed. 'How do you move yourself – through wards I would expect no one to penetrate? I have never heard of such magic.'

'Ah. Well, I'm not too clear about that, but it seems to work.'

'You said you are travelling with your uncle and a friend. Is your friend another relative?'

Tilliat was somehow aware of layers of wards and shieldings woven through the room and the whole building, but she felt confident about this Perra Koos. She'd made no attempt to reach to his mind but she was sure he meant her no harm. He was waiting for her reply and Tilliat gave him a bright smile. Let him have it all then.

'I am Tilliat Kranch. A trader, Stevro Kranch, raised me as his daughter but I have recently learnt I was born Tilliat A Serissama, daughter of the King and Queen of Vremilia. I was born with a twin brother who is about to rise to the throne. Twins are not allowed to live in Vremilia so I've heard, and I was brought away secretly and given to Stevro Kranch, the man I will always regard as my father.'

She noted Perra Koos's rather grey complexion had become waxy.

'My Uncle is a trader who I trust utterly. My friend is the Dragon Toomay.'

Glancing round the book filled room she saw a silver jug and went to see if there was some sort of liquid within it. Dipping a finger she discovered it was plain water so she filled a goblet and brought it back to the table, pushing it in front of Perra Koos. His hands were shaking and Tilliat held the goblet to allow him to sip a little water. She was relieved to see the waxen sheen on his face fade a little and his hands grow steadier.

'I take no part in the politics of Gulat,' he said eventually. 'I'm not sure what you plan but I would help as I may.'

Tilliat returned to her chair. 'From what I've heard, Mahzu

Vek is a strong mage, but is she strong enough to stir all the troubles across the lands?'

Perra drank more water. 'She is basically a very stupid woman. I can't see that she is powerful enough to cause the chaos that spreads from your city of Kelshan.'

'Then who is behind her?'

Perra frowned. 'No one. She is in charge here without doubt. But...'

'But?'

'She is totally devoted to her god. Besotted might be a more accurate term. Reva, the official patron god of Gulat.' Perra looked confused. 'I have never believed in gods and their supposed governance over humankind.'

'Nor me,' Tilliat agreed. 'There were countless temples in Kelshan and they surely can't all rule our fates.' She chewed her lip. 'What sort of god is Reva? I don't think I've heard that name.'

'He is a god of death and rebirth, but his aspect is dark, threatening.'

'The only one I can think of who'd match him, is a goddess in Kelshan. Varay. I've always suspected she's some sort of memory of the Imperatrix Veranta. She wasn't a pleasant person, according to any of the histories.'

A silence fell while they considered the idea of gods actively involving themselves in human matters. Tilliat stood up.

'I'll have to ask about gods, but I'll visit you again.' She smiled. She really liked this man.

'You haven't told me how you got here, passing my defences when you should have triggered alarms.'

'Perhaps next time,' Tilliat told him. In her thoughts she called Shadows and vanished from Perra Koos's sight and his house.

The mage remained in his chair, trying to think over this whole encounter rationally and calmly. He gave up quite quickly, laid his head on his folded arms on the table, and groaned.

Tilliat blinked and found she was sitting in the Chays' hayloft once more. She peered over the edge and saw Toomay lying near the stove, head on front feet, his eyes gleaming up at her.

'Interesting,' he murmured.

How did he know what she'd been up to? Did he have a link to her mind that she was unaware of?

'What do you know of a god called Reva? Or any others, come to that?'

Toomay yawned. For the first time Tilliat realised just what fearsome teeth a Dragon possessed but Toomay's mouth closed, as did his eyes. She glared down at him then rolled back, wrapping her blankets around her. She deliberately didn't think of Perra Koos, Mahzu Vek, or her brother. Instead, Tilliat closed her eyes tightly and recalled the last trip Stevro had taken her on, seven years ago. She soon fell asleep, a smile curving her mouth.

Tetsura had chafed at the fact that he could not spend all his time with Saima. He understood the reasons why not of course, but it didn't make it any easier to accept. He spent his time going through all the papers Hikmat was sending him, growing ever angrier at Hikmat's attitude towards him. The papers told anyone with half a brain just how deep and devious were Hikmat's claws embedded in nearly every aspect of Vremilian life and business.

Vilad cautioned the boy to stay meek and obedient whenever Hikmat visited him, but Tetsura found it increasingly hard. Tetsura was also growing aware of how isolated he was. He had been told of the hidden community of mages, although not their actual location. Even Vilad and Saima hadn't guessed that Tetsura had practised his new magic and quite easily found the community of heavily shielded mage born.

He felt as though there were spiders inside his skull, creeping through his brain and making new pathways for his thoughts. And for his magic. Tetsura pushed the papers away from him and glared at them. He saw the odd black line round his thumb waver and suddenly it was gone. But the papers on his desk were on fire. Blackness smothered the flames and then the line of dark Shadows settled round his thumb again.

A voice murmured in his mind. 'Control.'

Tetsura was still gaping like a stranded fish. '*I* did that?'

'Yes.' The Shadow's conversations, as Tetsura had discovered, were brief and abrupt but he detected a note of disapproval in that single word.

Tetsura sighed. There was so much to learn, so much to do,

and while he trusted Vilad completely, the old man was in no position to help Tetsura do what he had to do. Tetsura knew he must wrest power from Regent Hikmat. He also knew Hikmat had many men loyal to him, in positions of control not only in this city of Garjetka, but throughout the islands of Vremilia, large and small.

Tetsura had been told Anjit, Commander of the Phoenix Guards, was mage born, but it was impossible to make contact with him. If Tetsura suddenly requested an interview with Commander Anjit it would certainly not escape Hikmat's notice. The Prince had no reason at all to need to speak to the Commander – what reason could there be? But Tetsura's isolation had not gone unnoticed by his faithful Vilad, and with Hikmat's unwitting consent, through Commander Anjit a sergeant was appointed as a new personal liaison officer.

Tetsura was ruefully trying to clean up the rather charred papers and wondering what excuse he could give Hikmat to explain the state of the documents when Vilad entered the study. Vilad held out a piece of paper and Tetsura took it, reading it in some puzzlement. Vilad could use mindpseech and he'd done so with the Prince during the last several days. Vilad grinned and jerked his thumb over his shoulder. The note in Tetsura's hand was signed simply Anjit, and introduced a Sergeant Tag as his liaison officer.

Tetsura shrugged and strolled past Vilad into the main sitting room. A tiny figure stood by the outer door, flaming red hair curling in a tangle from beneath her cap. She was rigidly at attention but Tetsura thought there was more than a hint of disrespect in the startlingly green eyes staring up at him.

'Sergeant Tag?'

'Your Highness.' The small nose twitched. 'Is something burning my Lord?'

'Um, no. Not now. Why don't we take a stroll and you can explain why your Commander thinks a liaison officer is necessary right now?'

Vilad was already opening the door to bow Tetsura out and as the Prince swept regally past he could have sworn the old man was laughing. He strode along the corridor to the great staircase and heard the patter of boots behind him. Outside, he found himself counting. The sergeant took two paces to each one of his, with an occasional hop added in. Tetsura slowed and glanced casually back. Sergeant Tag smiled sweetly although the green eyes were most definitely icy now.

'So. Tell me why I need a liaison officer. Who am I liaising with exactly?'

The smile returned and the eyes thawed. 'Why, to the Commander of the Phoenix Guard my Lord. And of course, as I think you know, I am a friend of Vilad's and Saima's.'

Tetsura slowed down more. Yes, Saima or Vilad had indeed mentioned a Sergeant Tag. He glanced down at her.

'Are you not rather small to be in the Guards?' he asked innocently.

He expected either ice or fire to show in those green eyes but he saw neither.

'I have a certain reputation my Lord, for speed and also for my skill with knives.'

Tetsura studied her more closely. There seemed an unusual number of unobtrusive slit pockets in her uniform jacket and trousers. He wondered how many knives she had about her person.

'Fourteen my Lord. And one or two others I don't admit to.'

They regarded each other solemnly. Fourteen knives? Great stars, why didn't she clink when she moved? Tetsura led the way on to the broad sweep of one of the gravelled paths which encircled the palace, acknowledging various gardeners as he walked.

'You know of my sister?' he asked abruptly.

Sergeant Tag had paused to bend over a rosebush which had small dark blue flowers blossoming all over it.

'Yes my Lord. This is a beautiful colour but it has very little perfume. Why is that?'

'When the gardeners change the colours of many plants they always seem to lose something – size of flowers, too many thorns, or loss of scent. I must admit I prefer the ordinary old ones with all their perfume. What do you know of her?'

Sergeant Tag moved on to where a wicker trellis supported a climbing rose smothered with ragged dusty pink blooms. She stooped to sniff one of them.

'That she is a great mage and is on the mainland, probably in or near the Free City of Gulat. The Commander told me.' She slanted a glance up at Tetsura's face.

The Prince turned slowly, apparently admiring the lawns and flowerbeds spread out around them. Before he could speak, the sergeant did so.

'As far as the Commander knows, there are no spies within the palace my Lord. But I have a suspicious mind and I can't believe the Regent doesn't have *someone* here to watch and listen. It was wise of you to come outside before speaking my Lord, but keep your face lowered – there are those who read what moving lips say even from a considerable distance.'

Tetsura was suddenly exasperated and swung off along a side path towards an orchard of miniature fruit trees.

'Perhaps you could tell me then Sergeant Tag, just how I can even loosen Hikmat's hold on this Kingdom, let alone break it.'

Sergeant Tag trotted silently at his side until the Prince stopped, dropping onto a bench overlooking the orchard. She stood at attention until he glanced up at her and scowled.

'Sit down Sergeant. You're not on guard now.'

'But I am my Lord.' There was a seriousness in her voice which made Tetsura's scowl vanish. 'I am officially your liaison officer but bodyguard may be more accurate.'

She perched on the other end of the bench. 'You thought someone of my size was rather amusing, didn't you my Lord? But I promise you I am far better than most of the Guards would be as bodyguards.'

Tetsura digested that remark. 'You said you are better than most. Who is better than you?'

Sergeant Tag didn't bat an eyelid. 'Only Commander Anjit in fact, sir.'

Tetsura gave an involuntary laugh. 'Somehow that doesn't surprise me.' He sobered. 'Does *he* have any idea what we're going to do? We have a few days over one full turn of the moon. Or so everyone seems to think.'

The sergeant put a hand to her mouth, apparently chewing a finger nail. 'We have people strategically placed my Lord. You see, Hikmat believes he has exterminated the mage born. The Commander deliberately disillusioned him a little and now he is

162

in a considerable panic over the thought of active mage born in the city. That fact is distracting him quite a lot. He has a few in his employ – a very few, who can detect any with talent, who are aware if mindspeech is used near them for example. We know who most of those are.'

'That reminds me,' Tetsura interrupted. 'Did you read my mind – when I was wondering how many knives you had on you?'

'Of course.'

'So you are mage born.'

Green eyes narrowed as Tag stared back at the Prince. 'I have never been mage tested.' Her tone was flat. 'I will not allow it.' She looked away, down at her hands clasped on her knee. 'There are certain things I have talent for.'

Tetsura smiled. 'Like moving very fast and using knives exceptionally well?'

Tag's mouth twitched. 'Just so my Lord. But you must have faith. We do have people in position. We will be able to take out most of Hikmat's "loyal" men at a signal from the Commander. With respect sir, the Commander is in far more danger than you are at the moment.'

Tetsura stood up and started to walk further into the gardens. 'Why is it I have let these things pass me by?' he asked. 'These last two years Hikmat has sent various reports for me to "study" as he puts it. Yet it is only within the last two or three moons that I have seen the webs of deceit and self profit he has spun throughout the Kingdom. I only realised two nights ago what he's done to the tax system. What kind of ruler can I be if I'm so slow to see these things that have been right under my nose? How can the people put up with it all?' Tetsura spoke quietly but there was an edge of bitterness in his voice.

Sergeant Tag trotted at his side, her eyes constantly scanning the gardens around them.

'There is discontent among the people my Lord, but Commander Anjit has been steering that discontent in such a way that most know of Hikmat's treatment of you now. Citizens here are waiting for your Presentation. That is when they will overthrow the Regent and all his toadies.'

In Tag's voice there was anger which she tried to suppress but

163

Tetsura was aware of it, thanks to his burgeoning powers. Under her anger, he sensed hurt, and wondered what Sergeant Tag might have endured at some time during the Regent's rule. He glanced down but could only see the top of her head and red curls flaming out from beneath the grey cap.

'May I ask how old you are Sergeant?'

'I am twenty my Lord. In the army since I was eleven.'

She spoke with no inflection and Tetsura knew he could ask nothing more of a personal nature. He changed the subject. 'I had training with sword and bow but I'm not very good. I hate hunting.'

Sergeant Tag's shoulders loosened and she looked up at him with a grin. 'I'm sure you could hunt if you were hungry enough my Lord, but weapon skills are not necessary requirements for Phoenix Kings now. It is over a thousand years since our people waged war and were led by a king.'

Tetsura nodded. 'King Sato. He took a great army onto the mainland, won several battles then decided all mainlanders were definitely barbarians.'

'And we've had no official contact with them ever since,' Tag finished.

Tetsura changed direction again, leading them towards the ornamental fish pools, but he hadn't missed the slight emphasis on "official" in Tag's last words.

'From that I assume you're going to tell me we *are* in contact?'

Tag laughed. 'Have you ever tried to stop merchant ships finding new markets? It is not generally spoken of I admit, but yes, there are four or five captains who make the journey to Salo Manis. People there keep quiet about visits from Vremilian traders. It is a very profitable business apparently but the trade Commander Anjit is most interested in is of course information.'

Tetsura sat on the sunwarmed stone surrounding the first pool and trailed his hand in the water. Multi coloured fish hurried to nibble at his fingers. Sergeant Tag sat near him, peering at the fish rushing to see what food Tetsura might be offering.

'The Commander has made the journey several times,' she murmured. 'He has a network of informants stretching right across the Kelshan lands to their great city itself.'

'The city where my sister was raised?' Tetsura looked up from the fish to meet Sergeant Tag's gaze.

'He has had news of her for many years my Lord. His contact there was a servant within the girl's home who sent reports of her education and the general manner of her life.'

'But how did he trace her? No one knew of her birth, let alone that she'd been whisked off to the mainland.'

Tag smiled. 'Vilad's sister was the royal midwife my Lord. She went with your sister when you were born. When the baby was given over to a trader, Vilad's sister followed and was employed within the household. She has sent word back to the Commander ever since.'

'How many know of this?'

'Less than a handful,' Tag admitted. 'I have only known about it this last year. Word has spread lately but only among those who are well trusted.'

'I have searched the palace library but I can find no reference to why twin births must be considered such an evil thing.'

Sergeant Tag sat very still. 'It began after Sato's death, gradually, so people didn't really take notice.' She faced Prince Tetsura. 'If twins are mage born, their power is usually far greater. No one knows why. But a coterie of mages decided that nothing should threaten their lesser powers. And so began a policy of declaring twin births anathema.'

Chapter Fifteen

Mahzu Vek knelt on the hard stone floor of her private shrine in the cellar of her house. The dark candles on the altar were burnt halfway down their length. She didn't feel the cold striking up through her thighs or the ache of her knees. She'd come here soon after returning from her visit to Perra Koos and now it was nearing dawn. Her god had refused to answer her pleas for advice for a long time now. But when she'd nearly reached the decision to abandon her attempts he had finally chosen to speak to her.

Reva was vaguely intrigued by this human female who pestered him. She reminded him of someone but he couldn't remember who. To be honest, he hadn't tried very hard: he found humans tiresomely insignificant and unrewarding creatures. But her persistence in calling his name now resulted in his attention. That attention pressed down on Mahzu Vek like the weight of a mountain and her body leaned forward, shaking helplessly under the strain. Reva recalled human frailty and withdrew a little so at least the woman could breathe more easily.

Her mind was awash with ecstasy – that her god realised she was worthy of speaking with him filled her with a joy such as she'd never otherwise experienced. Reva found it difficult to slow his own mental processes to a degree that he could understand the human's words and where *she* could understand him.

'Why do you keep calling me?'

His thought banged painfully inside Mahzu Vek's skull.

'Oh my dearest lord, I call for your advice and assistance to further your cause in spreading your darkness across the land.'

The god nearly left her then. What was she babbling about?

'The lands are already beginning to burn Lord Reva. It has begun, in the very city of Kelshan itself and it spreads quickly.'

The god paused. Kelshan. He did remember *that* name, and yes, he remembered a city. The shards of personalities that formed the god Reva, bound by a remnant of an alien creature, resonated with tangled memories. Rage fuelled those memories but outwardly Reva remained calm as he spoke to this creature.

'There are Imperators there,' he said.

Mahzu brought her hands up to hold her head while the god's voice roared inside her.

'There have been no Imperators for centuries my lord. Forgive my frailty but could you speak a little softer?'

The entity that was Reva snarled with silent contempt but an idea was beginning to germinate within his strange mind.

'Tell me of the Imperators' city,' he whispered.

The whisper boomed in Mahzu's head but it was more bearable than previously and she lowered her hands.

'I know little of Kelshan great one. I have been beseeching your aid in finding a mage, a girl who was foretold in an ancient prophecy.'

Reva reined in his fury. *How* did one communicate with such primitives?

'What prophecy?' he asked.

'The one that the great mage Theeka made when she restored the rule of the Imperator Jemin. She told of a girl who would come and once more face evil which sought to rule the world. We believe the girl is near this city right now, and I need to find her.'

Reva could barely bring himself to continue speaking with this – thing – he was so angry. Somehow he kept to a whisper.

'Why do you want her?'

'Oh my great lord, if she is truly so powerful, she can work for me. For us. And help bring your rule to the entire land of .'

'You will go to the city the other one came from. I will be with you.'

'But… But great one, how shall I get there?' Mahzu was near to gibbering in panic.

'You question your god, woman?' Reva's whisper sent chills through Mahzu's whole body. 'Did I not say I would be with you? What can stand against ME?'

'I will make the arrangements to travel at once great Reva. But I am concerned to leave the girl loose in this region.'

Mahzu trembled at her own temerity in continuing to press her point with this immortal presence, but she felt she had to.

A long silence fell but Mahzu knew the god was still here. On the altar the candle flames had flattened and she felt the thick heaviness of the air in the small chamber.

'This female. I may seek her out, but she offers no threat to me,' whispered the god at last.

The pressure was suddenly gone and Mahzu Vek slumped forward, her thoughts whirling. She hauled herself upright, leaning a hand on the wall as she waited for her knees to steady enough to allow her to walk. Reaching for the door latch, she wondered, slightly hysterically, where the gods went when they weren't talking to their worshippers. In spite of her exhaustion, her weakness, Mahzu Vek left the shrine and clambered, with difficulty, up the steep stairs, right up to her study on the third floor. She sank into the nearest chair and closed her eyes. The great god Reva had said he would be with her and that he would also look for Tilliat Kranch. Her tiredness was nothing compared to her sense of anticipation and jubilation.

Perra Koos also sat in his study, his body rigid with tension. Every mage of any stature in Gulat must have felt the awesome pressure squeezing the very air down towards the earth. It had a foulness to it, an evil taint, which made his blood chill in his veins. But now it was gone. As Perra Koos relaxed, he heard a terrified cry from below, somewhere on his private stairs. He hurried to the door and down the first flight. A frail figure huddled on the landing, arms over its head and wails of fear issuing from it. Perra wrapped his arms round the old man and half helped, half carried him back up to the study.

'Hush Tani, hush.'

Perra settled the old man in a chair by the hearth and turned to put fresh logs on the embers. Tani grabbed at Perra's arm, his mouth a round hole of distress. Perra knelt at his side, holding the bony body close, feeling the violent tremors rattling through the old man. It took a long time until Perra was able to ease Tani back into the chair but even then Perra's hand was still gripped fiercely.

'Now hush dear old friend. Was it a dream that brought you here?'

Perra kept his voice calm and soft and tried to hold Tani's gaze. But the old man's faded blue eyes flickered in all directions, not meeting Perra's.

'He was here. He was here. He was here.' Tani's rusty voice repeated the words over and over.

Perra took Tani's bearded chin gently with his free hand and attempted again to calm him. 'Who was here Tani? I felt a great weight in the air but surely it was but a mage, using the death magic perhaps? He's probably frightened the wits from himself. Be calm my dear.'

Tani mumbled something and Perra squeezed his hand.

'What has disturbed you so?'

'The dark one. The evil one.' Tani began repeating his words again.

Perra Koos frowned. Tani was a powerful mage but had fallen into madness long, long ago. He hadn't worked magic since then. Perra had given him a home here, remembering the Tani who had been his first teacher and that man's brilliance. No one knew what had splintered Tani's mind and no one else had apparently cared. Perra Koos found him in a hovel in the slums, by the southern gate, and brought him back here.

Very occasionally, Tani was lucid, and Perra grieved even more for the magnificent mind that once had been. None of Tani's countless notebooks or journals had survived: he'd destroyed all the texts and books in his quarters, leaving nothing to show of his many years work on the theories of magic. Perra Koos remembered the kindness Tani had shown to the frightened boy he'd been, just coming to terms with an unsuspected mage talent.

Now Perra watched as tears welled over the old man's lower lids and trickled down his wrinkled face into his beard. Tani leaned forward.

'It was him again. I thought he was gone for good.'

Perra let his brow rest against Tani's.

'Who is he Tani? If I know, perhaps I can get rid of him.'

Tani whimpered. 'The dark one. Don't you touch him boy. Don't touch Reva.'

Perra continued to hold the other man, rubbing his back gently while his thoughts raced. What could Tani mean? If only he

169

knew exactly what the old mage had been working on when the madness descended upon him. The girl, Tilliat, had spoken of gods, had asked about Reva. Could there truly be something in it – that gods *did* take action in human affairs? Perra realised Tani had slipped into a light sleep. Carefully, he eased him back into the chair and laid a blanket over the fragile body. The old man's hands twitched and his mouth moved as if he was talking, although he made no sound. Perra leaned against the high shelf above the hearth, staring down at the pitiful wreckage of a once brilliant man. He sighed and sent a thought to Cook. She was already up and enjoying her first solitary cup of tea.

Perra asked her to have breakfast brought to his study and told her Tani was with him. As Tani grew ever older and physically more frail, he rarely left his own room, but he had occasionally wandered off into the city. Most of Perra's household then spent a great deal of time searching for Tani and fetching him home, confused and frightened. Perra withdrew from Cook's mind, knowing she'd bring the food herself, with the honey and cinnamon porridge which always seemed to comfort Tani after one of his disturbed times.

Perra sat at the worktable and pulled one of his notebooks towards him. Keeping an eye on Tani who slept but restlessly, he began to scribble down the sensations of earlier. He added thoughts and ideas as they randomly occurred to him. By the time there was a soft scratching at the door, he'd filled several pages but found again and again he had written the word "gods" and underlined it heavily. He smiled as Cook came quietly in, settling a laden tray on the end of the table. She went to bend over Tani, smoothing the wisps of white hair away from his forehead.

'Poor old thing,' she whispered to Perra, then she pointed at the tray and her expression became stern. 'All of that is to be eaten. And do try to get something into this lamb. Do you want me to stay and see if he'll eat?'

Perra gave one of his rare smiles and shook his head. 'Thank you, but I'll do my best with him.'

'You'd better,' said Cook and left them with a toss of her grey head.

Perra realised he was hungry, uncovered the dishes Cook had

brought and tucked into his breakfast. He'd eaten his fill when Tani jerked awake, nearly falling out of the chair. Perra uncovered the bowl of porridge and the scent of cinnamon filled the air. Perra took the bowl and moved to sit on a low stool by Tani's chair.

'Look my dear. Cook's made your favourite. Come now, see if you can please her and finish it all. We can't disappoint her.'

He spooned some of the porridge into the old man's mouth and smiled as Tani's eyes closed in pleasure. He managed to feed Tani half the bowlful before he refused any more. Tani sighed and looked straight at Perra Koos. Perra kept still. Tani would rarely meet anyone's gaze directly and if he did, he usually made a lucid if brief comment. A trembling hand reached to touch Perra's cheek.

'The Pathmaker might help. I cannot dear boy. He destroyed my mind. I've often wished he'd destroyed my body entirely. I am such a burden to you.'

Perra knew better than to reply. Any words from him now would send Tani crashing back into mindless oblivion. Tani's hand began to tremble again and his gaze flicked away from Perra, skittering over the fire, the bowl in Perra's hand, anywhere but into Perra's eyes.

'The dark one is bad. Stay away boy.' Tani started the repetitive litany again and Perra sighed.

Tani was still mumbling the same words when Cook returned for the tray. She rested a hand on Perra's shoulder, watching the old man wringing his hands.

'So sad,' she said. 'What upset him do you think? Did he have the bad dream lots of us seem to have had last night?'

'What did you dream Cook?'

She shrugged. 'Felt like the house fell down on us and we were all crushed underneath. One of those mage students playing silly games again I'll wager.'

'No it wasn't I'm afraid. I will be redrawing the wards today Cook and adding some extra protection.'

Cook pursed her lips. 'I'll take Tani down to the kitchen with me. If he gets upset I'll send him back to his quarters with Juka. She's a good girl and he seems to like her company.'

By the time the midday bells rang across Gulat, Perra Koos

171

was back in his study trying to ignore a thudding headache. The magical work he'd done after a sleepless and tense night had left his skull throbbing. He slept for a brief time but was woken by the Captain of his house guards. Apparently, there were five mages in a state of some agitation, demanding an interview with him. Perra hurriedly washed his face, put on a fresh tunic and went down to the reception rooms.

The five mages, three men and two women, were all members of the public mage council. All were mages worthy of respect, skilled in their various disciplines. All looked weary and worried and obviously expected Perra Koos to answer their questions. The visitors dismissed offers of refreshments and deluged him with questions and demands. It seemed all mages had experienced the same deadly pressure bearing down on them but none could fathom its cause. Perra heard that three others of their number had tried to trace back along the magic's path. One was dead, the other two unconscious. Perra's expression remained impassive but he was alarmed by that piece of news.

One of the men, Ket Vos, finally sat down. 'Perra, I'm not even sure it was magic. If it was, it was of a kind I've never come across. It had a sickness to it, a feeling that if you touched it, you would become contaminated too. I'm sure that is what brought disaster on the three fools who attempted to backtrack it.'

Privately Perra was inclined to agree with that, but he wanted these mages calm, not flying into further panic. He thought he'd succeeded when Nami Char, one of the women, suddenly spoke up. 'We all believe Mahzu Vek has either discovered some source of energy or power which could be controlling her rather than the other way about.'

Her words fell into a long silence. Perra rubbed his eyes: they felt gritty from lack of sleep. He paced around the edges of the room, feeling five pairs of eyes on him at every step. He made his decision.

'Someone suggested to me there was something to Mahzu Vek's obsession with Reva.'

One of the men waved a dismissive hand but Perra continued.

'Mahzu visited me yesterday – (Was it *really* only yesterday?) – and asked for my help to find the girl Tilliat Kranch. She believes she is the Mage Foretold in that old prophecy.'

Nami Char's brother Taleb frowned, then nodded. 'Vek named this girl as the killer of her son Skala, didn't she? She isn't seeking her for revenge then. If Vek thinks she is the Mage Foretold, she wants her under her control.'

The door opened and a young girl stood there, looking a little uncertain. Tani stood beside her gripping her hand tightly.

'I'm sorry Master,' the girl began. 'But he insisted we come to see you.'

'It's all right Juka.' Perra went towards the door. 'Come in old friend. I have visitors as you can see and they will welcome you.' He glanced back and dared the mages to make mock of Tani.

But Tani seemed not to notice the others. He tried desperately to keep his gaze on Perra but his eyes wouldn't focus steadily.

'Vek killed her own child. She and her son – snakes, poisonous. The girl. Save that girl Perra. Oh keep her safe. Reva hasn't seen her yet.'

Tani's words rang clearly and then the confusion filled his face again. He looked down at the girl beside him and began repeating: 'Snakes. Poisonous.'

Juka tugged his hand gently and pulled him away, along the corridor, and Perra slowly shut the door. He studied the five concerned faces staring intently at him. He was going to need help, a lot of help, and he knew these five, collectively, were not of Mahzu Vek's ilk. None of them lived in even half the luxury he did. The opulence with which Perra Koos surrounded himself he knew was a gesture of defiance at the world, from a boy who had struggled out of deepest poverty, cruelty and fear.

The five before him had no greed for wealth or importance: their work was life for each of them. Two of them Perra knew, had possibly the most brilliant minds now working in Gulat. Perra Koos sat down facing them, took a deep breath, and told them all he knew.

Tilliat Kranch slept through the night, unaware she was protected by Shadows. Their anger was as huge as Reva's but Shadows' anger was cold and clear while Reva's was hot and muddled. Davin Pearl was woken by the noise of Ty and Pitzi Chay stumbling out of their house, gasping for air and clutching their heads against pain. Toomay was undisturbed, aware Tilliat was safe and Uncle untouched. The grey cat Cloud had screeched and fled. The horse had kicked out one wall of his stall, the donkeys were panicking and the hens hysterical.

'There is a small problem Uncle, but it does not affect you, me or Tilliat,' Toomay reassured Davin when he'd climbed down from the loft.

The barn door banged open and Davin saw the sky faintly touched with dawn behind the figures of Ty and Pitzi. The trader hurried to help them, unable to comprehend what the trouble was. The Chays sank onto the floor near the small stove, groaning. Davin stared helplessly, shrugged, and went to the stall where the horse was in a state of sweating distress. The wall between horse and donkeys was splintered apart and Davin reached through, trying to calm all three animals.

The horse steadied at the presence of a human although his eyes rolled and his skin shuddered with his fear. Davin had no idea how much time passed while he spoke softly, soothingly, to the horse and donkeys but suddenly, whatever it was, it seemed over. The horse shook himself and nosed at his feed trough and the donkeys abandoned their position close by the splintered wall and snuffled at their own trough.

Davin glanced out at the Chays and saw them sitting up, their faces pale but relaxed, not contorted with pain. By the time the Shadows decided to allow Tilliat to wake, Davin was in the house with Ty and Pitzi. Toomay explained what she'd missed and she demanded a full explanation from the Shadows. Given their abbreviated manner of communicating, that proved to take longer than Tilliat hoped. Toomay kept his eyes closed during that conversation but was alarmed to find a very irritated girl standing in front of him, hands on her hips, and glaring.

His eyes flashed different colours and he tried to work out why she should be cross with *him.*

'If you know why the Shadows are apparently immune to whatever magic was worked last night, I expect you to tell me,' she demanded.

Toomay pushed himself up and back onto his haunches and wished Thorn was here.

'I don't really know Tilliat, truly I don't. They are not *affected*

174

by that magic but they cannot *overcome* it. I think.'

Tilliat relaxed a little and stroked Toomay's face. He blinked, obviously still worried.

'I'm sorry Toomay but I am getting very tired of not knowing what's happening or why.' She frowned. 'I think I'll have to visit Perra Koos in Gulat again. The Shadows said the power was concentrated there. They also said it *is* connected to Reva but they wouldn't say who, or what, he is. Do you know of gods Toomay? Please?'

Toomay's eyes flashed again as he decided how he should answer. But this human girl was his friend wasn't she? He had chosen to accompany her, regardless of the danger to himself, into these wild human lands.

'There was a hunter god, long ago. We didn't like him much. And a goddess who fussed about the land. We haven't seen or heard from them for a long, long time. We do see the old god of death sometimes. He comes to our Realm when he wants a rest.'

This was the longest speech Toomay had ever made to her and Tilliat understood it indicated how deep his commitment to her actually was.

'I thought Reva was the god of death?' she asked, continuing to stroke the Dragon's face.

'Not the same.'

Tilliat felt Toomay's frustration in his mind tone. 'Reva seems wrong, all darkness. Simert, the old god, he was a cheerful creature. I've only met him twice.'

'And how would we get to meet him?'

'Well you'd just call him. I think.'

'Might as well try then.'

Tilliat moved a little away from the Dragon, just in case, and tilted her head on one side. Surely this must count as the silliest idea she'd yet had? To summon the god of death? Suppose he just decided to whisk her off, wherever he took dead people?

'Shadow?'

'Yes.'

'Is this Simert a danger to me?'

'No. Like Simert.'

Well. Tilliat wasn't entirely sure that someone the Shadows apparently liked meant that person would be trustworthy but she dismissed the doubts and drew a breath.

'Simert.' She called the name quite softly. She waited a couple of heartbeats and opened her mouth to call again when a cone of a smoky substance swirled on the floor between her and Toomay.

The cone, wide at the base and rising to a tapered point higher than her head, thickened then dispersed. A stout man in rather dirty and stained boots, trousers and tunic stood glaring at her.

'Why did you call? You're not dead. Do you have any idea how rushed off my feet I am at present, with all this foolish fighting?'

The man turned away from Tilliat who was gaping helplessly at him, and came face to face with Toomay. The man frowned, then a beaming smile split his bearded face. He reached to touch Toomay's cheek, then frowned again, looking back at Tilliat. He looked between the two several times then slowly nodded.

'So. It is the time,' he said. 'Forgive my shortness to you child but I *am* very busy.'

Tilliat cleared her throat and hoped her voice would work.

'I'm sorry to interrupt you sir, but I wondered if you knew about Reva?'

'Reva?' Simert tugged his beard. 'Don't know of him.'

The Shadow's whisper murmured through the barn. 'Of the Splintered Kingdom.'

'What?' Simert looked appalled. 'I thought that was all destroyed?'

He tugged his beard harder and squinted in concentrated thought. 'Tika foretold this of course, but I don't recall her saying there would be such an obvious link to the time of her trials with this evil.'

'My brother is soon to be King of Vremilia and he has great problems of his own there. But it seems I have to do something about the problems here.' Tilliat blurted.

'Tilliat is my friend and I will be with her,' Toomay interrupted firmly.

The god of death dropped a kiss on the Dragon's nose. 'Of course you will. And the Shadows will be most helpful too I'm sure.'

'I think that Reva is in Gulat,' Tilliat began.

'No. Gone.'

'Do you know the mage Perra Koos sir? He offered to help me.'

Simert shook his head. 'Never heard of him. Sorry. Now look, call me if you really think I could help but I can't do much I'm afraid.'

The Shadow spoke as Simert raised his hands, obviously in preparation for his departure.

'Tani.'

Simert paused. 'Tani? I lost track of him years and years ago. He's still alive then? He never came through my gates but I thought he might have gone elsewhere.'

'Mind broken. Reva.'

'*What?*' Simert was about to say more when he turned his head as if listening. 'Sorry. Got to go. So busy.'

He raised his hands, muttered something, and was gone.

Chapter Sixteen

The grey cat tottered into the barn and lay, pathetically limp at Tilliat's booted feet. She bent to lift the cat and studied her in concern. The emerald eyes were hazy and the grey fur was damp and dishevelled.

'What happened to you little one?' Tilliat asked.

'That evil was too much.' Cloud's mind voice was faint: she was plainly exhausted.

'Shadow, can you protect Cloud as you did me, if we encounter that magic again?'

'Could.'

'Well *will* you please?'

There was a silence. 'Cannot protect all.' There was definitely a touch of sulkiness to the words.

Tilliat's temper began to rise again. 'If you are at my command, then I say you are to protect Cloud, and Uncle Davin, and Toomay if necessary.'

Toomay snorted, eyes sparkling with amusement. 'Shadows cannot do their magic on Dragons.'

Tilliat laughed. 'Shadow, Cloud is very small. I expect I will carry her if she insists on travelling with us. So you *will* guard her against whatever causes hurt.'

'Guard.'

After that one word, Tilliat was aware of a space in her mind and assumed the Shadows had withdrawn. Probably to enjoy a private sulk she thought. She glanced at her thumb and thought the line of Shadows nestled below the silver ring looked thicker and darker.

'We'd better go and see how Pitzi and Chay are faring,' she said.

She held the cat carefully in the crook of her arm and made for the door. When she paused there, Toomay came and peered over her head. Rain pelted down and the trees whipped in a gusty wind. Tilliat pulled her jacket over the cat, ducked her head and ran for the house door. Toomay squeezed in behind Tilliat and rain droplets glittered like gems all over his scaled shoulders. Tilliat waited until Toomay had paced into the kitchen and his tail cleared the door before she shut it against the downpour.

Pitzi was cooking at the hearth stove while Ty and Davin sat at the table, clasping mugs of tea. All three looked across at Tilliat. Ty and Pitzi were very pale but seemed fit enough.

Ty frowned. 'You suffered no distress then?'

Tilliat smiled innocently. 'It seems not.' She sat next to Davin, still nursing the cat. 'I wondered what you could tell me about the mage you think has a connection to crows?'

Ty's frown deepened. 'Koos. That's who you mean. Keeps himself to himself. Thinks he's so much better than everyone else. His house drips with decadence – silk hangings, jewelled mirrors, carpets beyond price.'

Pitzi put a large platter of fried potatoes on the table and a basket of bread.

'I heard he was a boy from the worst slums years ago,' he said mildly. 'From a family of scholars who sank into disgrace and poverty before he was born.'

Tilliat remembered Perra Koos telling her the crow emblem had always been his family's crest. She chewed on a chunk of bread while she thought. Perra Koos came from the slums. Tilliat knew how bad life had been for those in the slums of Kelshan so she could guess how extreme the differences were in his early life and now. And crows were scavengers. Perhaps he had been a scavenger and remembered seeing crows squabble over scraps in slum alleys. When his life changed, maybe he'd seen the irony in choosing a crow as his emblem.

'Thinks he's better than all of us,' Ty repeated scornfully.

Again, Pitzi tried to modify his wife's harsh judgement. 'He took in that old mage, and he's cared for him all these years. It must be forty years, from what I've heard, that he's had Tani in his house.'

Tilliat was alerted to the name Pitzi spoke. Wasn't that the name the Shadows had spoken to the god Simert?

'That old madman,' Ty scoffed. 'He was as stuck up as Koos. Took Koos as his apprentice when he'd never before had any

179

student under his care. Word was that he took that gutter urchin as a servant, not a real student.'

Pitzi smiled ruefully. 'You have such a poor opinion of all of us my dear. Perra Koos turned out to be a competent mage, didn't he?'

'And am I not proved right time and time again?' Ty retorted.

Tilliat kept her gaze on the crust in her hand. What an unpleasant woman Ty was. She reminded Tilliat of one of the senior librarians in the Citadel archives in Kelshan. That woman always behaved as though every scroll, parchment and book were her personal property, and she begrudged anyone wanting to look at any of them.

Pitzi and Davin had finished their breakfast and Pitzi announced his intention of cleaning out the animals before repairing the wall the horse had smashed down. Davin offered his help and Tilliat left the house with them, having no desire to stay in Ty's company. The rain had eased slightly as she splashed through puddles in the yard but once inside, Tilliat spun to stare back at Toomay. He'd sent a thought to her mind which stunned her like a blow.

'Why haven't you made Cloud better yet?' the Dragon asked.

'Can I?'

Long silver lashes fluttered almost coyly over Toomay's eyes. 'Why not try?'

Tilliat saw that Davin Pearl and Pitzi had cleaned the stalls and were starting on fixing the shattered wall. She climbed up into the loft and settled Cloud on a blanket. The cat gave a faint cry of protest when she was moved away from the warmth of Tilliat's body. Tilliat sat cross-legged beside Cloud, rested a hand on the cat's back and closed her eyes. She calmed her thoughts and her breathing then warily sent her mind probing towards the cat's body.

She nearly gasped aloud when she realised she was *inside* the cat somehow. Then she almost recoiled when she saw the cat wasn't just tired: she was badly damaged. Tilliat had no idea how but she could see Cloud's small heart labouring with each beat, how her lungs struggled to expand as they rightly should. For an instant Tilliat panicked. She had no idea how to heal. Then she became aware of Toomay's mental presence, bolstering her strength and confidence.

Cautiously, she let her mind focus on Cloud's heart and imagined the muscles strengthening, the blood flowing more easily through the veins. After a time, Tilliat concentrated on Cloud's lungs and her other organs, all of which appeared to have been affected. Tilliat sensed she had done enough and very carefully drew her awareness out of Cloud's body. She discovered she was trembling, her head throbbed and she felt slightly queasy. Brilliant green eyes stared unblinkingly up at her. Tilliat smoothed a shaky hand over the cat's back.

'Thank you,' Cloud whispered in her mind. 'Sleep now and I will guard you.'

Toomay also spoke, his tone full of pride and affection. 'Cloud is right dear friend. You used more energy than you needed to and you must replace it through sleep.'

Tilliat needed no further urging. She toppled onto her side close to Cloud and managed to drag the blanket over them both before she fell into a deep sleep to the sound of Cloud's rumbling purr against her chest.

Toomay reassured Davin Pearl that Tilliat was well but that she needed to rest right now. He also suggested Davin keep the Chays away from the barn until Tilliat woke of her own accord. Ty had called them in for a midday meal before either she or Pitzi were aware of Tilliat's absence. Davin Pearl explained how very ill Tilliat had been on the journey from Kelshan and that she needed sleep to recuperate her strength. Then he immediately began asking about the state of trade in Gulat and its outlying regions. Davin Pearl had spent a lifetime as a trader, mostly to the southern lands. When the Chays realised the depth of his knowledge and experience of trading, they willingly explained what they knew of the situation in and around Gulat.

The afternoon passed quickly and neither Pitzi nor Ty made any comment on Tilliat's absence. When Pitzi stood up to go to settle the animals for the night, Davin was about to go with him, but Tilliat came into the house before the two men could leave. She looked rested and calm. The cat she still carried also looked much better than it had earlier that day.

Later, Tilliat offered to help Pitzi prepare supper and earned a look of scorn from Ty which Tilliat ignored. She noticed increasingly how Ty sniped and cut at virtually every remark Pitzi made, and she wondered at the huge man's patience. He seemed to be an intelligent man and yet he lived with this harridan. She noticed Davin was relieved when she suggested they retreat to their hayloft.

Lifting Cloud to her shoulder, Tilliat opened the door. She glanced back at the Chays.

'Tomorrow perhaps, we could visit the city?'

Ty looked uncertain and glanced at Pitzi. He shrugged.

'I can seen no reason why they can't go,' he said.

'She'll be recognised,' Ty snapped.

'She can wear a shawl over her head. She's small. No mention was made of her height in that description. Who'd think a little thing like her could kill a warrior such as Skala Vek?'

Ty merely sniffed and turned away towards the fire.

'I'd go with them. We need flour and tea anyway,' Pitzi added.

Ty swung back towards her husband. 'And get yourself arrested for being in her company? Do you really think Mahzu Vek hasn't got her tame mages watching the gates?'

Pitzi huffed out a sigh, as near to annoyance as Tilliat had yet seen him. 'Well. I'm going with or without them.'

Davin poked Tilliat discreetly in the ribs and raised his eyebrows towards the door. Taking the hint, she lifted the latch. The rain had stopped and the clouds had cleared. Stars sparkled coldly in the dark sky and Davin shivered, pulling Tilliat across to the barn. Once inside, it felt warmer than in the Chays' house. The smells of hay, horse, donkeys and hens was comforting and Davin checked the small stove to make sure it would burn through the night.

Toomay settled nearby, watching Davin climb up to the loft. The trader glanced back at Tilliat.

'I'll come up in a while Uncle. Don't forget, I slept half the day.'

Davin smiled. 'Toomay told me you healed that cat.'

Tilliat looked down at the cat sprawled in her arms. 'I think I've worked out how to do it, but I need practice. And I'm afraid of having to heal when we could be in danger Uncle.' She smiled up at him. 'Too much to think about all at once. I might go visiting, with the Shadows, as I did before.'

Davin frowned.

'She will be safe Uncle.' Toomay's mind tone was calm, soothing.

Davin sighed. 'I hope so. I feel useless Tilliat. Really out of my depth with all this.' He waved his hand vaguely.

'Not as much as I do I'm sure,' she retorted. 'Anyway, don't worry if you wake and I'm not here. I won't be long and tomorrow we'll go to the city.'

'I'll be glad to leave here,' Davin said, his voice lower. 'Ty makes me very uneasy.'

He didn't notice the quick searching glances Toomay, Tilliat and Cloud all gave him.

Tilliat waited a while until she could hear the soft drone of Davin's snores, then she held Cloud against her cheek.

'Shadow?'

'Yes.'

'Take us to the mage in Gulat.'

Impenetrable blackness surrounded her and Tilliat realised that she had already learnt to accept it. But the cat in her arms made a noise, a mixture of a snarl and a squeak, and dug several claws deep into Tilliat's flesh. She winced but held Cloud more firmly as she felt solidness beneath her feet.

'Let me see,' she thought when the Shadows kept her in darkness.

'Checking,' came the brief reply.

'Checking what?' she thought in some exasperation.

'Others.'

Instantly Tilliat tensed but then the blackness vanished.

'Safe.'

Tilliat discovered she was not in the room where she'd first met Perra Koos. This room was luxuriously furnished, a reception room rather than a place for serious work. She had a brief moment to note Perra Koos stood by the fireplace facing five people grouped in a half circle of chairs, before the mage realised she was there. He gave a wry smile and held a hand out towards her.

'The person we were discussing has arrived, as inexplicably as she did before.'

Five heads swivelled to look where Koos indicated. The two youngest people rose to their feet, studying Tilliat intently. She felt a push against her mind and instinctively she pushed back, hard. The standing woman dropped back into her chair clutching her head, and the man reached to her in concern. Perra Koos raised an eyebrow.

'I would suggest we show our guest courtesy Nami,' he began.

Cloud wriggled and Tilliat bent to set the cat on the floor, her mind racing. The Shadows had said these other people were "safe" and Tilliat sincerely hoped they were right. Straightening, she met Perra's gaze and he nodded.

'Well my friends. This is the young lady I was speaking of – Tilliat Kranch.' His eyes held a question and Tilliat lifted her chin.

'That's right – Tilliat Kranch.'

Koos introduced the older guests: Ket Vos, a stout man about the same age as Perra Koos Tilliat guessed. Then Varden Herl, who looked a little younger than Davin Pearl. He bowed as Perra named him. The woman next to him gave Tilliat a genuine smile.

'I am Li Kassu, Varden's wife.'

Tilliat smiled back and waited for the two younger mages to be named.

'Taleb Char and his twin sister Nami,' Perra obliged.

Two pairs of dark blue eyes stared at Tilliat, brows drawn into identical scowls. Tilliat felt an urge to laugh but decided that might not be the polite thing to do so she inclined her head towards all five mages.

'I hope I'm not interrupting?'

'You are very welcome in my house. Please, join us.'

Perra pulled a chair in to the half circle and waited until Tilliat had sat down.

'We were discussing a worrying event that seemed to affect all mages last night.'

'Yes. I was told of it but it – er – didn't touch me.'

'How did you protect yourself?' asked Ket Vos, his bald head shining pinkly in the lamplight.

'I'm not entirely sure,' Tilliat replied. 'Were you able to shield yourselves from some of it? It was apparently like a great weight pressing down from the sky.'

Vos ran a hand over his head as though checking to see if perhaps hair had returned. 'We were able to mitigate the worst of it I believe, but there are many mages utterly prostrate today within the city who did not have our strength perhaps.'

'What can you tell me of the god, Reva?' Tilliat asked.

Her question was met with puzzled frowns. Varden Herl glanced round the group.

'None of us are believers I don't think.'

Heads were shaken in agreement except for Nami Char who was still clutching hers.

'Mahzu Vek is a great devotee of the cult of Reva, but I always thought that was an affectation – to make her popular with the citizens and so on.' Herl shrugged. 'Why do you ask?'

'I wondered who exactly Reva is, or was. Was he a hero who defended your city, and through legends and tall stories somehow became a god? Who *was* he?'

For the first time one of the Char twins spoke. 'He is the one who controls death and rebirth. The more unpleasant and vicious the death, the better your chance for a good rebirth. And by good rebirth I mean into a position of wealth, power and control. He is a dark presence.' Taleb glanced at his sister before he continued. 'The rituals are fairly ordinary – at least for the general attenders. There are stories of much more sinister rites performed in private, involving pain and blood.'

His sister raised her head to meet Tilliat's eyes. 'There is an inner cabal in the temple of Reva, as there is in Gulat's mage council. And Mahzu Vek is at the centre of both.'

'And who exactly *is* Mahzu Vek? Does she come from this city? Tell me of her.'

Nami Char shook her head. 'We knew her son Skala years ago.' She exchanged another look with her brother. 'We didn't like him, but Mahzu seemed to really loathe him which was evident to us even at eight or nine years old.'

There was silence again. Finally Vos spoke, an uncertain tone in his voice.

'I really don't know where she came from. She's younger than I am, but I suppose I became aware of her when she had just left the Academy. I don't think I ever heard mention of any family. She married Dor Kanut. He was a mage of limited ability but had a considerable fortune. His wealth gave him higher standing in the council than his abilities merited and he moved Mahzu into the first vacancy there.' He frowned. 'That was after the death of Binta I think, wasn't it Perra?'

Perra Koos nodded. 'A sudden fever it was said,' he began but a mindvoice interrupted him.

'Someone approaches.'

Six mages stared, first at the cat who sat haughtily before the fire and stared straight back at them, then they turned to the door. A faint rapping came. Perra stood and called for whoever it was to enter. The door opened only a little and the serving girl, Juka, peeped around its edge.

'I am so sorry to interrupt you sir, but Tani says he will sit here until you see him.' She glanced down to her left then back up at her master.

Perra moved between the chairs and pulled the door wide. A dishevelled figure squatted beside the wall, muttering softly. Tilliat had followed Perra, the name "Tani" echoing in her mind. Perra crouched beside the odd figure.

'Tani, I have guests just now. I promise I will come to you later.'

He stopped speaking as the cat who'd appeared with Tilliat pushed past him and climbed onto Tani's bent knees and up his chest, her purr extraordinarily loud. Perra watched as the old man's mumbling faded away and his head lifted until he stared straight into the cat's emerald eyes, a look of amazed wonder spreading across his face.

Tilliat touched Perra's shoulder. 'I would like to speak with Tani, if he would agree.'

Perra spread his hands helplessly, stood up and moved back into the room. He watched as Tani struggled upright, holding on to the cat, and walked unsteadily towards him.

'It's all right Juka. I'll call you if we need you.'

'Yes sir. Sorry sir.'

Perra gave her a quick smile and then closed the door on her.

Tani walked straight to the chair where Perra had been sitting and, keeping his eyes locked to the cat's began to speak.

'I have such terrible dreams.'

186

He fell silent and Tilliat, who had dropped to her knees beside the old man, touched his hand lightly. 'I have had fearful dreams too. Can you speak of yours?'

Perra held his breath. If he spoke to Tani during one of the poor man's lucid spells, it had the immediate effect of sending him back into his madness.

Tani sighed, his hand moving slowly over the cat's head and back.

'I dream of black Reva. Black in his soul is Reva. If he has a soul, which I doubt. But he came to me offering such wondrous knowledge. I was so foolish, so greedy to *know* all the things he said he would teach me.'

His audience listened in fascination, seeing the tears beginning to course down his face into his beard.

'For half a year I listened and fell deeper into his grasp. And then, one fine summer dawn, I woke and I realised absolutely that it was wrong, all wrong. Every single thing he'd taught me was evil and his hold on me was too great. I remember the sun blazing through that summer day and seeming to illuminate every dark corner of my mind, showing the twisted shapes he'd put there. I was strong that day, knowing that I would renounce all association with him the next time he contacted my mind.'

Cloud sneezed: the beard she was lying on was drenched with tears now, but she stayed as she was, gazing steadily into Tani's face. Tani blinked, for the first time, and his hand quivered on Cloud's back. He drew a tremulous breath.

'He contacted me that night, when clouds sped across the sky making that sunlit day a darkened memory. I told him at once that I wanted no more of him than he leave me be.'

Tani's frail body shuddered and Cloud's purr increased in volume. 'Such rage I had never encountered or dealt with. He held my mind in his grip and squeezed out my memories and my sanity. He is evil beyond compare.'

When Tani remained silent, Tilliat once again touched his hand. '*Who* is Reva? Can you tell me? I really need to know all I can of him.'

'He is a corruption. A mixture of several creatures.'

For a heartbeat Tani looked into Tilliat's eyes rather than Cloud's. 'The histories. The time of the Imperatrix Veranta.

Clues may be there.'

Tani's eyes closed and his chin rested on his chest. Tilliat sent her mind into the old man's and breath hissed through her teeth. His mind was utterly ravaged but she knew she had to try to mend it. After a short time had passed, Perra moved towards Tilliat, concern on his face.

The cat on Tani's knee jumped to the floor and sat, facing the room. Emerald eyes glared up at Perra.

'Do not interfere. She tries to mend your friend.'

The six mages looked as if nothing more could surprise them: a cat using mind speech? A cat who materialised in this room with an unknown girl? Each of them chose, individually, to accept these things for now, and to gibber later, in private.

Li Kassu was the only one of them who heard the note of worry in the cat's tone. She moved to kneel by Cloud and spoke aloud. 'I do not know your name little one, but I think you fear for this Tilliat Kranch. Is she well versed in healing?'

The cat wailed softly. 'I am Cloud. She healed me yesterday but that was the first time she had done any such thing.'

Cloud crouched by Li Kassu's knees. There was no mistaking her concern now. The mages' attention was divided between watching Tilliat and Tani, who had become completely still, and the mental conversation Li Kassu was holding with this grey cat.

'Toomay is worried, but... ' Cloud suddenly twisted and leaped at Tilliat, claws digging into the back and shoulder of the girl's jacket. There was the briefest impression of blackness then Tilliat, Tani and the cat disappeared.

People were on their feet in consternation except for Perra Koos. He sank into the chair Tilliat had used and rubbed his temples. Before he could speak, yet another voice murmured in all their minds.

'Tilliat and your friend and Cloud are safe. We were worried at how deeply she had entered your friend's mind. She will return to you soon, I am sure.'

'And who in the name of the eternal stars was *that*?' Ket Vos glared at Perra, not quite managing to conceal how disturbed he was by these events.

Perra sighed. 'I'm not entirely sure, but I suspect it was one of the Dragonkind. I hadn't reached that part of my story when

Tilliat – um – arrived.'

Li Kassu returned to her seat. 'Perhaps you'd better finish telling us and then we must consider Tani's words.'

Nami Char nodded her agreement. 'That poor old man gave us some interesting hints – particularly about the wars in Kelshan in which the Imperatrix Veranta was killed.' She gave Perra an encouraging smile. 'Carry on with your tale then Perra. I can promise that you have our full attention.'

Chapter Seventeen

In the Phoenix Palace in Garjetka, it was near dawn and Vilad had gone to Tetsura's bedchamber. A short while before he had woken with a feeling that something was wrong and now he went quietly to the Prince's bedside, shielding the small lamp he carried with one hand, lest the light disturb Tetsura's sleep. He bent closer and his alarm grew. The Prince's normally olive skin was grey, waxen, his breathing fast but shallow. Under the lids, his eyes moved constantly but Vilad knew this was no bad dream the boy was enduring.

Very cautiously, Vilad quested towards Tetsura's mind and found he was totally blocked out. He tried again. Nothing. Then he heard the door to the adjacent sitting room click open. He let out a breath in a sigh of relief. Sergeant Tag, fully dressed but with a slim knife in her hand, came noiselessly to the bedside.

'What's wrong with him?' she murmured.

Vilad shrugged. He set the lamp on the night stand and scribbled quickly on the paper Tetsura always kept there.

'I found him like this. I can't reach his mind and he won't rouse.'

Sergeant Tag placed the fingers of her free hand against Tetsura's throat and frowned.

'It is the girl,' she said, her voice a mere breath of sound.

Vilad scribbled again, cursing the fact that the Sergeant resolutely refused to acknowledge that she could use mind speech. Tag glanced at the page Vilad passed to her.

'I thought she'd learnt control – everyone's headaches ceased a few days ago and that is what Addi concluded must have happened.'

Tag held a corner of the paper to the lamp flame and let it burn, moving to drop it onto the tiled floor below the window. 'If he doesn't wake or improve, you must say it's a return of his fever. I'll let the Commander know at once. Let no one else approach him Vilad.'

The old man nodded. He fetched a cushioned stool and set it close to the bed. He glanced over his shoulder but the door was already closed behind Sergeant Tag.

Tetsura was not dreaming. Somehow his mind had tangled with his sister's. It was as if he was watching through her eyes and a tiny part of his mind wondered if she had watched his world here in the same way. At first he hadn't understood what Tilliat was doing but then to his awed wonder, he realised her mind was inside another's head. She was trying to heal someone.

Tetsura was peripherally aware of voices and guessed there were people close to Tilliat who, by the tone of those voices, were badly worried. The tiny piece of his mind which still seemed to be just him, thought suddenly of the Shadows his sister had given him. Cautiously he called them.

'Here.'

'Should I be here?'

'No. Cannot move you.'

'Is Tilliat all right, doing this healing?'

'No. Cannot influence.'

Tetsura felt a definite agitation even in the abbreviated form of communication the Shadows used. He felt no worry at his situation though.

'So what can I do to help her?'

There was a long pause during which he continued to watch what Tilliat was doing to this person's mind.

'Help her.'

'Does she know I'm here?'

Another pause, not quite so prolonged.

'Yes.'

'But how can I help her? I know nothing of healing.'

'Nor does she.'

Tetsura absorbed the Shadows' curt comment and experienced the first twinge of panic.

'Only two days has she found her power.'

The twinge of panic twitched a little harder.

'So what can I do?'

'Strengthen.'

Tetsura resolutely ignored the growing anxiety and turned his full attention to what Tilliat was doing. Strengthen. What did they mean? Suddenly he began to focus. Instead of trying to escape this tangle, he dived deeper. But not into the stranger's mind. Into Tilliat's. He was no longer aware of exactly what she was doing but he could see her own exhaustion.

He willed strength into Tilliat's body and instantly felt both her power surge up again and also the gradual slackening of the ties that bound the two of them. Tetsura had no idea how long this strange coexistence lasted but he heard Tilliat's faintest whisper: 'Thank you brother.'

Then he woke in his own bed, opening his eyes to see Vilad's worried face close above him. He groaned, then rolled from the bed and staggered to his bathing chamber, and was violently, wrenchingly, sick.

In Gulat, in a sheltered part of Perra Koos's high-walled garden, Tilliat lay slumped beside Tani. Toomay had taken a huge risk and flown to her side at the Shadows' request. Now he curled himself around the two humans, immensely relieved that they were both still alive.

The Dragon mindspoke Cloud: 'I think you should fetch this Perra Koos. The weather is too cold for them to lie here.'

'There is a shelter further along the wall,' Cloud replied.

Toomay was pleased. He wasn't sure about going inside this great building but he didn't want Tilliat out of his sight. Cloud stretched and her tail thrashed.

'The house is all shut up. We will have to mindspeak them.'

'Well you do it – they know you.' Toomay's great eyes gleamed in the murky predawn light.

Cloud settled herself between the old man and Tilliat again and began to purr softly.

'They are coming out,' she told Toomay.

The Dragon rattled his wings anxiously and looked back at the house. Bolts clattered and light spilled from an opened doorway. Perra Koos hurried towards the dark shape halfway down his garden, five other humans trotting at his heels. They halted a few paces away, staring at the silvery Dragon lying there, scales glittering in the light of the lantern Koos held high.

Toomay was nervous but he spoke gently to these new humans. 'My name is Toomay. I am friend to Tilliat.' He glanced down at the two figures hidden by his curled body and slowly unwound a little so they were revealed. 'They need to be warmer. I would prefer to stay close. Cloud says there is a shelter?'

Li Kassu was the first to react. 'There is a summer house just round the corner. May we approach and carry them?'

Toomay inclined his long head, reassured by the female's soft tone and polite manner. Nami Char moved alongside Li Kassu when Toomay uncurled fully and rose to his feet. Both women regarded him in silence, aware of his beauty and the size and power of his sturdy body. Nami swallowed then bent to Tilliat.

'She is so small,' she murmured, easing her hands under the girl's still form.

Varden Herl went to Tani and lifted the old man effortlessly. Perra handed the lantern to Li Kassu.

'There should be a fire laid ready, and lamps, in the pavilion,' he said. 'I will fetch blankets and pillows – we never leave any out there in the winter.'

Li nodded and led the way further into the garden while Perra hurried back to the house.

He called Mink, the Under Captain of his house guards and told him, as he gathered blankets and soft cushions from the store cupboard by the kitchen, that he had unexpected guests who would be staying in the pavilion.

'No one, I repeat, no one, comes to the back of the house or into the garden.'

'As you command Master Koos.' Mink stood to attention but then pitched forward when the kitchen door was pushed open. He glared at Cook, who glared right back, lowering the iron pan she held at shoulder level.

Cook switched her glare to Perra. 'And if you have guests, then they will need food. Sir.'

Perra was already turning towards the outer door. 'I'll tell you when food is needed Cook. Oh, and Tani is with us so don't send everyone off hunting for him.'

Perra hurried out into the still dark morning. Cook gave a loud sniff and gripped her pan more firmly.

'You heard the Master. No one in any rooms facing the garden and...'

'I can hear as well as you,' Mink snapped back.

Cook sniffed again. 'Wonder who these mysterious guests are though,' she muttered.

Mink laughed. 'If the Master wants us to know, we will soon enough.' He leaned closer to Cook. 'I'll tell you if I find out first.'

Cook pushed him away. 'Get on with you. It makes for a bit of a change though. I do hope poor old Tani is behaving. I'll make him some cinnamon porridge.'

Mink grinned. 'You'd better wait for Master Koos to say you can take it out to him though.'

Cook retreated into her kitchen and began to slam pots around. Mink marched off to relay the Master's orders to the house guards.

Perra walked swiftly to his summer pavilion, clutching the large bundle of blankets. Looking back to the house he was pleased to see all the shutters remained closed and light showed only from the kitchen section. He stepped onto the front verandah and one of the double doors opened. Vos's head poked out and he held the door wider for Perra to pass inside.

The shutters here were still closed tight but the large central room, where Perra held the occasional, unavoidable social evenings in the good weather, was lit with many lamps. A new fire crackled in the hearth, Li Kassu on her knees before it feeding larger twigs before adding logs. Carpets were rolled and stacked against one wall but someone had pulled a couple clear and spread them roughly near the fire. Two couches had likewise been moved nearer the warmth. Tilliat lay on one, Tani on the other. The Dragon reclined close to Tilliat, the cat crouched on her chest.

Concerned as he was about the state of both Tani and Tilliat Kranch, one question burned in Perra's mind. He waited while Nami and Varden wrapped blankets around the patients and then turned to the Dragon.

'May I ask, Dragon Toomay, how you moved them out of my house? I feared both of them were unconscious, or entranced, and I'm quite sure they could not have moved themselves.'

Toomay's eyes flashed and his wings trembled. 'I did not move them.'

The six mages stared at him and Toomay's eyes glittered even more. The cat raised her head.

'We do have other friends you know.'

As the mages digested that remark, a man suddenly appeared between the two couches. He saw Tilliat, groaned and slumped beside her couch, holding his head. His face was pale and sweaty. Li Kassu, who was closest, reached across and touched his forehead lightly.

'Oh thank you, thank you,' he gasped. 'Travelling like that is utterly, totally, completely, bloody disgusting.'

He looked round at the stunned faces and climbed to his feet.

'My name is Davin Pearl, Tilliat's Uncle. I am a trader of Kelshan.'

He bowed politely then grinned at Toomay.

'I am very glad to see you Uncle. It has been an eventful night.'

'And how *did* you travel here Trader Pearl?' asked Nami quietly.

'I have no idea.' Davin looked vague. 'I am a trader, not a mage. It seems – er – someone decided I should be here, so I am.'

Ket Vos had been studying Davin Pearl closely. He sighed. 'He speaks the truth. He has no mage ability and he has no idea how he travelled here.' His gaze switched to the Dragon and he smiled wryly. 'But you do, do you not, Dragon Toomay?'

Toomay fidgeted uncomfortably and it dawned on the six mages that he was, in fact, a very *young* Dragon. Before he had to reply, Tilliat spoke.

'For stars' sake stop being so formal and polite. I feel terrible.'

Toomay dipped his head to her, his brow against hers. Tilliat cautiously opened her eyes and tried to sit up. She glared at the mages.

'Thank you Toomay, I feel better. Why couldn't one of you have stopped me feeling so bad?'

'We didn't know you were awake,' Li Kassu answered mildly. 'No one had attempted to enter your mind.'

Tilliat scowled but caught sight of Davin Pearl and held her arms out for a hug. Over his shoulder, she saw Tani lying motionless on the other couch. Holding on to Davin, she got shakily to her feet, tottered the few paces to Tani and sat beside him.

'Have you healed him?' asked Perra.

Tilliat sighed. 'I don't know that he'll thank me. I have repaired a great deal – he should be rational. But his mage powers were entirely disrupted, a long time ago I would guess?'

Perra nodded. 'Nearly forty years since he fell into madness.'

'I doubt he will have any powers when he wakes, and his memory may have considerable gaps. But he will be aware, sane. He sleeps now, which is best. I suspect he has not slept properly for probably as many years.'

Tilliat tucked the blankets closer round the old man. She left him and settled on a heap of pillows, leaning against Toomay. She looked pale and tired but she smiled across at Perra.

'I'm starving,' she said hopefully.

Taleb Char gave a snort of laughter and the atmosphere, which had been fraught, began to lighten. Perra pushed himself to his feet.

'I'll go and order – I think it must be breakfast? – for all of us.'

Ket Vos rose too. 'I'll come with you. Perhaps your amazing cook will have a small titbit to spare to tide me over.' He gave his overlarge stomach a fond pat.

Li Kassu pushed two more logs onto the fire, wrapped a blanket round her slender shoulders and curled up in a chair.

'That was a mighty healing you performed Tilliat. You must have begun your training very early?'

'Ah. Well, actually, I have had no training. I healed Cloud yesterday. That was the first time.'

Li's finely arched brows rose nearly to her hairline. 'And you risked your life, attempting such a healing for one you know nothing of?'

Tilliat looked down at her hands, at the silver ring on her thumb. 'I had heard his name mentioned. But I had some help with the healing.' She met Li's eyes and glanced at the other mages. 'I think Perra has told you all that I told him?'

When they all nodded, she drew a deep breath.

196

'I don't understand how, but my brother came. He did none of the actual healing on Tani, but he strengthened *me* somehow.'

'You were dangerously weak.' Toomay's mindtone was full of affection. 'You must learn to use less power for all these things. There is so much within you that you need only a small part for working most things I believe.'

To Tilliat's annoyance, Nami returned to the subject of Tani.

'You say you'd heard of Tani. As far as I know, he spent all his life here in Gulat, or at some house he owns several days journey north east, in the wilderness. How would you hear of him in Kelshan?'

Tilliat's tired mind tried to think of a convincing story but came up blank. It didn't help when she heard the Shadows in her head: 'Not tell.'

'I'm not sure,' she said, trying to look as innocent as she could manage.

'Where have you been staying in Gulat?' That was Varden Herl.

Tilliat waved a hand vaguely. 'Outside the city. In some woods.' Dear stars, she thought, she sounded half witted. 'A couple gave us shelter when we first arrived and Uncle Davin was – um – unwell.'

'So you arrived in Gulat in the same manner you arrived in Perra's house?'

Nami smiled sweetly when she posed that question and Tilliat gritted her teeth. Before she had to hunt for another reply, Perra and Ket Vos returned.

'Cook will ring the bell when the food is ready and I will fetch it for us,' Perra informed them. He looked around. 'Have I missed anything?'

Varden Herl chuckled. 'Not a single thing dear Perra.'

'Can we know *why* you've come here?' asked Taleb.

'Skala Vek said I had to come. I thought I might find news of my father, of Stevro Kranch.'

Davin rested a hand on her shoulder.

'I also hoped I'd find out what all the secrets are that seem to have surrounded me all my life. Some of them I have discovered, but many more remain hidden. I learnt that my father was murdered, not far from this city, although I don't know exactly

197

where. I will also tell you all that I did *not* kill Skala Vek. We were far from him when he died.'

'You asked Tani about Reva. What has a god to do with anything?' That was Nami.

Tilliat shrugged. 'I just feel it's important. Tani said there were clues in history books. I have studied a lot of those in Kelshan, including those telling of the chaos in the reign of the Imperatrix Veranta. Have you any books on those years Perra?'

Perra Koos nodded. 'Several. I can fetch them when I get our food. Do you prefer to come to the house yourself or remain out of sight?'

Tilliat considered. 'You trust your staff I presume?'

'Absolutely. And I have wards around the whole property which no one, other than you of course, has ever breached.'

'Then let's not irritate your poor Cook. Ours at home would have made us suffer for days if we'd asked her to send food to the garden in mid winter.'

Tilliat felt a pang of homesickness remembering Pakal and Jomah. She hoped they were safe in the Traders' Guild Hall. 'I would ask that Toomay could stay here. Unless your servants could cope with meeting one of the Dragonkind?'

There was a teasing note in her voice and Perra cast caution to the winds.

'Why not? They live their days in extreme dullness I'm sure. But I will carry Tani with us – I think he should not waken alone.'

Tilliat stood, and held her hand along Toomay's face. 'Don't worry. I'm sure they'll all love you to pieces.'

Toomay's eyes flashed many colours in alarm and Tilliat laughed, dropping a kiss on his nose. 'That is another odd human saying dear friend. It just means they will be delighted to meet you.'

Toomay calmed himself, watching when Tilliat lifted Cloud against her shoulder, then he followed her behind the mages. They let Perra go a little ahead and heard a woman's voice clucking and fussing over Tani still sleeping in Perra's arms. Li Kassu slowed to walk alongside Tilliat, and Davin walked next to Toomay, the trader's hand lying lightly on the Dragon's back.

Total silence descended when Tilliat entered the back hallway, Toomay almost treading on her heels, his face peering worriedly over her shoulder. Three guards stood against the left wall, mouths open and slack. A short sturdy woman stood by the kitchen door, obviously annoyed by the invasion of five hungry mages into her domain. Her eyes met the Dragon's nervous gaze and Cook's expression melted.

'Oh you poor lamb. Come in with you this instant. You must be frozen to your very scales in that damp old pavilion.'

Toomay's eyes whirred in apprehension. Tilliat was interested to note that Cook had instantly recognised Toomay's youth and nervousness. Also that the woman showed no fear at having a Dragon in her kitchen. Indeed, Cook had already reached to touch Toomay's face, her hand sliding down his neck and giving a gentle tug. Tilliat backed into the kitchen, hiding her amusement from Toomay's mind.

He allowed himself to be drawn into the cavernous room and led towards an immense hearth.

'Now you just settle yourself and see what I've got for you my dove.'

'Does she not know what I am?' Toomay whispered urgently to Tilliat's mind. 'I am not a lamb nor a dove.'

Tilliat suppressed her laughter with considerable difficulty but didn't reply as Cook had returned with a large pottery container.

'Now you just taste one of these and see if they don't warm your heart.'

The woman held out a small round cake on the palm of her hand right beneath Toomay's nose. Very slowly he lipped at the cake then drew it into his mouth. His great eyes closed briefly, long silver lashes fanning over his cheeks. He let his words be heard in the minds of all present.

'That was extraordinarily pleasing.'

Cook smiled in triumph. 'There's not a soul in this world can resist my honey cakes, poppet. Here.' She pulled a stool closer to the Dragon and set half a dozen cakes on the top. 'You take your time and enjoy those. I'll find something else for you I'm sure.'

'May I know your name?' Toomay asked.

Cook blushed. 'I'm just Cook.'

'No, no, no. You are a cook, someone who prepares food I understand. But I would prefer to use a real name for such a skilled and kind person.'

Cook was scarlet by now, twisting a corner of her apron in her fingers.

'My name is Toomay,' he said, inclining his long head politely.

Cook seemed to calm and gain a quiet dignity. She gave a little bow towards the Dragon. 'Then my name is Giffu, and so you must call me, sweet one.'

Tilliat saw Perra Koos look almost guilty for a moment and also that the other mages had followed the odd exchange closely.

'Then I thank you for these magical cakes Giffu. We only very occasionally find honey where I live.'

Tilliat saw another expression flit across Perra's face and edged towards him

'There's no magic in them, my dear. A simple recipe. But I must feed these hungry people.' Giffu half turned away to the long table which stretched the length of the kitchen before adding: 'You can talk in my head while I'm working though, can't you? Can you hear what I'm thinking?'

'Yes, if you permit me to.'

'Oh certainly my lamb. I think it's very nice.'

Toomay delicately took another cake and people began to talk again.

Perra moved to Tilliat and they both spoke at once.

'What worried you just now?' Tilliat asked.

'I may have caused a difficulty,' said Perra.

'What difficulty?'

'Well, I sent four of my guards east, into the mountains. I had a sudden thought that the Dragonkind might actually be living there, hidden away perhaps by magical means. There are reports of people getting sick or disorientated when they try to persist in certain directions.'

Tilliat frowned. 'Is there any way you can call them back?'

'So the Dragons *are* there?'

'Somewhere that way.' Tilliat was vague. 'But their Realm is ringed with wards which cause the sort of problems you've mentioned.'

'I'll send a rider to catch them up. They won't have got too far yet. It's about six days travel I believe until they could reach the area I had in mind.'

When Perra hurried off, Tilliat saw Davin Pearl had drawn up another stool beside Toomay and had helped himself to one of the cakes. She joined them, slipping her arm around Toomay's shoulders.

'So human food is maybe not quite so dreadful?' she asked with a smile.

'These cakes are wonderful. I let Uncle have one as he was hungry.'

There was a hint of regret in Toomay's tone and Tilliat chuckled.

'You should be ashamed of yourself Uncle, taking one of Toomay's very own cakes.'

Davin grinned unrepentantly. 'They truly are delicious. Why don't you try one?' he asked her with a wink. 'I'm sure Cook has lots more in that pot.'

Toomay looked at the trader. 'Her name is Giffu.'

Tilliat wondered why Toomay seemed disturbed about the cook being called "Cook". She knew that Dragons had only one name and found human names difficult to sort out, but there was something else here.

'Come and eat, Tilliat,' Ket Vos called.

She saw the mages were seated at a section of the long table and, with Davin, went to join them. The stout mage pointed at piled dishes.

'Cook has outdone herself with this breakfast feast.'

Faintly, in her mind, Tilliat heard Toomay:

'She has a name. And it is Giffu.'

Chapter Eighteen

The creature named Reva was aware that the human female was calling him. Again. In various parts of this world, Reva had certain interests. This city of Gulat had caught his attention long ago when it was little more than an isolated trading post, and he still returned on occasions although he could no longer remember why he did so.

There was the smallest trace of humanity within his complicated structure but it was indeed infinitesimal. That trace came from a human absorbed into an alien creature thousands of years in the past, and Reva had never managed to analyse that trace to a point where he could understand it. He was impatient with the slowness of human thought, their apparently simple minds and their brief span of existence.

Reva had fragmented memories of many different beings but the strongest was of Yartay, the creature who the mage Tika had destroyed. Yartay had no specific form. Within limits, he could change his amorphous shape and appear as any life form he chose, but he had no real comprehension of how those bodies functioned. Parts of the creature Yartay had survived and had slowly grown.

Most had hidden away in deep dark places and led secret, harmless lives. A few, including Reva, had chosen to observe this world, and, where possible, influence the dominant species until they had converted this world to a place more satisfactory to Yartay's descendents. These few had no contact with each other – they were solitary beings. Reva had discovered other planes of existence, places "Between" as humans called them. But he had been quite unable to breach these places and explore their possibilities.

Over many centuries he had found they were the realms of beings called gods. Perhaps if he could become a god, those others would allow him access to their realms. Reva often forgot he'd made himself a god for these humans. As with his communication with the female recently, their puniness exasperated him. Their thought processes were so slow and their priorities so trivial he could only bear the briefest contact with any of them.

In this woman's mind though, he had seen thoughts of another woman, one who woke a distant memory of hatred. It was one of Yartay's memories but it burned still, like acid, after a thousand years. Reva had inherited this hatred for the mage Tika but he suspected this new female mage he had glimpsed might prove as difficult an opponent to him. He had inherited something else from Yartay: complete and utter insanity.

Mahzu Vek was in turmoil. Why had Reva ordered her to travel to Kelshan City, over eight hundred miles away, when the Mage Foretold was right here? She had spent most of the night trying to decide whether she *should* go or to send one of the mages who were committed, body and soul, to her service. If she stayed here, she would have to avoid the temple precincts and any of those stupid priests.

Finally, when a murky dawn was trying to lighten the sky, Mahzu summoned Keril Dwar. Keril appeared within heartbeats, dressed and ready for the day.

'The god spoke to me,' Mahzu announced at once.

Keril nodded calmly. 'Yes. When it felt as though the sky would press us all flat.'

'Quite so. He told me I must go to the capital but he didn't tell me why. The Mage Foretold is here in Gulat, or very close by I am positive. My instinct is to stay here to deal with her. We *must* have her under our control.'

Keril Dwar sat down. 'Who will you send in your place?'

'I'm not sure.

'It should be a woman,' said Keril. 'Do you think gods know one human from any other? Perhaps they only register male and female. So if Reva decided to seek you out when you're far away, he may just see a woman travelling west and assume it's you.'

Mahzu Vek looked rather astonished that her assistant thought a god could be that easily fooled. And should she *really* try to outwit Reva? Keril met Mahzu's pale blue eyes calmly.

'The choice is surely between only Tedelah Bren and Dilla Wart?'

Mahzu frowned, thinking rapidly. Both those women would obey her instantly she knew, but Tedelah Bren was a ditherer. She was a more powerful mage than Dilla Wart, but decision making was not a strength she could claim. Mahzu had no idea what difficulties either woman might face on such a journey, but she could imagine Tedelah sitting at a fork in the trail for days before choosing which one to take.

Dilla Wart was a few years younger, in her early thirties Mahzu thought, and her lesser mage abilities were made up for by her quicker wits. Yes, Dilla Wart would go.

'Send for Dilla, Keril. And make sure she understands the urgency of her attendance.'

Keril rose and left the room, allowing herself a slight smile as she descended the stairs. She gave orders to the guard on duty by the main door and watched him salute and trot off to organise a runner to Dilla Wart's house. She took her time returning to Mahzu's rooms, savouring the approach of this silly woman's downfall. She found Mahzu staring unseeing by a window, the city below slowly revealing itself in the growing light.

'You will let it be known that I have gone to Druke. Or perhaps it should be Spurtok.'

The two cities she named were also free cities, independent of the countries they bordered or were actually within. Spurtok was over two hundred miles east of Gulat, and like Gulat, within the borders of Praklina. Druke was further south from Gulat, on the boundary between Strale and Chaban. Mahzu grimaced, turning away from the window. She loathed travelling beyond Gulat city limits and the very thought of even pretending to travel away made her feel queasy.

Knowing exactly how Mahzu was feeling, Keril asked innocently if she would move to one of her other properties beyond Gulat.

'No,' Mahzu snapped. 'I will remain here of course.'

'The staff are all trustworthy,' Keril agreed, with just enough hesitation to make Mahzu nervous. Gods but this woman was easier to play than a fish, Keril thought. Four years it had taken

Keril's plans to reach this point and she had begun to wonder how much more of her life she could afford to let slip past on this particular game.

The tramp of booted feet grew louder on the stairs beyond the door. Keril Dwar rose and opened the door before the guard could knock. Keril stepped aside and bent her head in invitation to the woman who stood between two guards to enter.

Dilla Wart had a round plump face above a body that was scarecrow thin. Large brown eyes peered at Keril then searched on for Mahzu Vek. Her short-sightedness had proved nearly lethal when she'd been learning to mix healing draughts at the Academy. She was not strongly talented in mental powers and had spent the last twenty years working for Morkus Fayle.

Mahzu Vek waved her visitor to a chair in front of her huge desk and seated herself behind it.

'I'm sure you've heard there are plots to remove me from my position on the council Dilla dear,' Mahzu began without preamble. 'I intend to put a stop to this nonsense once and for all.'

Keril, standing discreetly by the door, wondered what twisted idea Mahzu had come up with now.

'I asked you here because you can play an important part in this, Dilla.

Dilla Wart nodded but the expression on her round face showed she had not a clue what Mahzu was talking about.

'I will announce that I have important matters to deal with and thus a long journey to Kelshan City, no less.'

Dilla's face now showed utter confusion.

'You will leave in my place, in my carriage, with my guards attending. You will head west for a day as if travelling to Kelshan in truth, but you will then turn south and make for Druke.'

'Druke?' Dilla repeated in a squeak.

'That's right dear. I do have property outside of the city there where you will remain until I recall you.'

'But…'

'But?' Mahzu's tone was incredulous, her eyes like ice. 'You have an objection Dilla?'

'Well, no, of course not Mahzu. It's just that my great uncle

205

Morkus is far from well and …'

'Yes, yes. Well, he's getting fairly old is he not? You must have adequate servants to care for him? So if that's all I shall expect you to get back here before dark this evening. You will, of course, tell no one, I repeat – no one, of this plan. You will need to pack very little – I will supply plenty of clothes although you will certainly *not* be socialising whilst you're away. You will keep within the house and receive only messengers in my livery. If that's all clear, you may return to tell your uncle of your departure on matters most private on my behalf.'

Mahzu pulled a pile of papers towards her, completely ignoring Dilla Wart. Dilla got to her feet, saw Keril already held the door open and trudged from the room.

'Excuse my impertinence,' Keril murmured when she'd closed the door on Dilla. 'But if neither you nor Dilla are going to be on the road to Kelshan for longer than a day, will the lord Reva not be suspicious the very instant he seeks you?'

Mahzu drummed her fingers on her desk. She could not admit, to a servant at that, that Reva had so far never actually sought her out. He had only made contact after *she* had begged and called to him for half the night.

'I very much doubt that the lord Reva will need me for some time Keril. He has many concerns, of which we can have little understanding. I think this may all work out for the best in fact. It will give me a chance to rid us of those who would be rid of me.'

'As always I am awed by your wisdom.'

Mahzu nodded. 'Indeed. Now, I will speak to the personal staff in the hall at the second bell. Inform them Keril.'

Keril bowed and departed, wondering if Dilla Wart would actually leave for Druke on the morrow.

Dilla hurried through the still empty city streets to the house near the Craft District where she lived with her great uncle Morkus Fayle. Letting herself in, she turned and heaved the iron bar down, securing the door.

'It's only me,' she called towards the back of the hallway.

A large man appeared from the shadows. 'Everything all right Dilla? We were worried – you having to rush off to that Vek woman before dawn had scarce arrived.'

Dilla gave him a distracted smile. 'I have to speak to Uncle Morkus. Is he up yet Parch?'

'He went to his workroom just after you left. He were worried about you. Said he'd wait breakfast until you were back.'

Dilla unfastened her cloak as she hurried up the stairs and along the second landing to Morkus's large workroom. She tossed the cloak on top of a wooden chest just inside the door and ignored the fact that the cloak immediately slithered lazily to the floor. An elderly man was watching golden liquid gurgling in a large flask, pipes leading too and from it where it hung above a small brazier. He looked up sharply when Dilla rushed in, his expression one of relief. He went to her and hugged her close.

'Your experiment Uncle. Don't let me interrupt you.'

'Tosh to the experiment. I was only keeping myself busy until you came back. Quick, tell me what that noxious woman wanted with you?' Morkus Fayle tugged her gently to a sagging couch and sat beside her, still holding her hand.

Dilla shook her head. 'I have to return to her before dark tonight. I am to go in her carriage, with her guards, to Druke. Druke, can you believe! I presume she'll be hiding at her house and letting everyone believe she's away. I am to stay in seclusion at some property she owns in Druke.'

Morkus Fayle twisted his grey beard in his agitation. 'No, no, no. You can't go.'

'I told her you were ill and she said that no doubt we had servants to care for you.' Dilla interrupted.

Morkus scowled. 'It is a ruse, to flush out the plotters on the council,' he said. 'But she must have someone in that carriage to convince any observers that she has truly left the city.'

'Druke is so far, Uncle Morkus, and I could be there for a long time.'

Morkus stood, pulling Dilla up with him. 'I will send a message to Perra Koos. And while we await his reply, we shall have breakfast.'

In Perra Koos's kitchen, the pot boys were washing dishes with wary eyes on the group still seated at the table. Tilliat noted that the two boys didn't seem in the least concerned by the presence of a now dozing Dragon close by but were cautious of the mages. Tani still slept on a truckle bed to the side of the fire, checked regularly by   Tilliat, Cook and Juka, one of the maids.

Tilliat had been pressed hard to explain how she was able to move herself from place to place. She trusted this group of mages, felt comfortable with them, in a way she had not with Pauson. But the Shadows insisted: 'No.'

Toomay's head suddenly came up and he stared at the door. The mages turned when Tilliat's attention was drawn to the Dragon. A mere two heartbeats later, Perra's guard, Mink, entered. He brought a sealed scroll to Perra Koos.

'This just arrived sir. Brought by one of Master Fayle's lads.'

Perra took it and broke the seal. 'Wait please, Mink, in case I need to reply.'

'The boy's still waiting sir.'

Perra scanned the message quickly, frowned, then read it more closely.

'Well? Come on Perra, what's the old fellow want?' Varden Herl leaned across his wife to take one last piece of toast.

'He says Vek wants Dilla to pretend to be her and to travel to Druke, leaving Vek hidden here, to root out those who would see the woman overthrown.'

'There must be more to it than that,' objected Ket Vos.

'Dilla is to leave from Vek's house this evening.'

Perra's frown deepened. 'She is to travel west for one day, as if to Kelshan, then turn south for Druke. It makes no sense.' He looked up and saw an abstracted expression on Tilliat's face. 'Tilliat? Is something wrong?'

She gave no answer at first. Toomay did.

'She speaks with – er – friends.' He rattled his wings in discomfort when six pairs of eyes turned to him.

'This would be the mysterious friends who move her around?' Nami asked with a trace of sarcasm.

'Um – yes.'

Tillat blinked. 'Those two are trustworthy? Or are they Vek's?'

'Stars above, no!' That was Ket Vos again. 'Old Morkus never attends council meetings and loathes Mahzu Vek. Dilla is his niece, or granddaughter, or some such. She is not highly gifted in mage talent but helps him with his research. She is a kind girl.'

'I think I'll tell Morkus to come here, with Dilla,' Perra began.

'That's a bad idea,' interrupted Taleb. 'So far, Mahzu has had no suspicions of you Perra. To bring them here openly would alert her at once.'

Perra stared at Tilliat. 'Cook' he called.

'Giffu,' retorted Toomay.

Perra actually blushed. 'Yes of course. Giffu, have you paper I can use for a message?'

'Yes sir. Here.'

She brought him several sheets of good parchment, a quill and a small inkpot.

'Tell him to let Dilla go this evening,' Tilliat spoke suddenly. 'And that he should pack a few things and be prepared to be – um – moved here after she's gone. He should burn your letter. Dilla will also be moved here so he should perhaps bring some of her things. And he must not be alarmed,' she added as an afterthought.

'Who *are* these friends?' asked Li Kassu.

'I'm sorry, but they really don't want me to talk of them.' Tilliat smiled at the woman to take any rudeness from her words.

The guard, Mink, lit a taper from one of the many lamps and held it while Perra extracted a stick of wax from his belt pouch. He pressed his ring into the melted wax, sealed the parchment and handed it to Mink.

'Send one of our men with the boy, but with a plain cloak to conceal his livery.'

'At once sir.' Mink saluted and marched away.

'It looks as though this house has become some sort of base and we a group of conspirators after all.' Ket Vos grinned. He seemed to be enjoying himself hugely. 'Are you prepared for a siege, Perra?'

Perra regarded the stout mage with a glint in his dark blue eyes, but whether the glint indicated annoyance or amusement, Tilliat couldn't decide. She jumped in before Perra could form an answer, just in case.

'It appears we will need to stay here for a while. At least, Toomay, Uncle Davin and myself. Are you sure we won't be an inconvenience?'

'There are rooms close to the kitchen.' He sighed. 'I imagine you'd prefer to be close to Dragon Toomay?' When Tilliat nodded Perra continued. 'There are several guest rooms above which I will have prepared for the rest of you.'

Li Kassu smiled. 'And will we be your very first guests Perra? Do admit you have never entertained *staying* guests before.'

Perra raised his hands in helpless surrender. 'There is a stairway from one of the pantries up to my own quarters. That's where my workroom and library are, which I guess we'll be using. Will you notify your households that you will be away for a while, preferably without alarming them, or divulging exactly where you are? I think using mind speech might be unwise just now so do help yourselves to paper and ink.'

The day passed swiftly. Perra's unexpected guests sorted themselves into their rooms and let their households know they were safe but busy. Finally, as the afternoon tipped towards evening, the sky darkening from light grey to sullen sludge, they settled in Perra's library, books and scrolls piled in front of them.

Perra had busied himself retrieving the books mentioning 's Imperator wars. He'd also found three large fragile scrolls which held accounts of legends, myths and the beliefs of various peoples in the Gulat region. These he gave to Li Kassu, knowing of her deep interest in those subjects. After one glance, a scowl failed to make her face any less beautiful.

'Years I have searched for these Perra Koos, and you have all three scrolls here in your library.'

Perra stammered some excuses like a nervous boy and Li allowed a smile to reappear. The thought occurred to her, as she carefully unrolled the first scroll. Perra Koos had a reputation for aloofness, for making no friendships. Was he still so conscious of his disreputable origins that he'd isolated himself rather than face a possible snubbing from those of so-called superior status? Li promised herself she would give this unexpected insight some serious thought. But not now. Now, she confronted the scroll with some apprehension. The parchment was brittle with age, the ink was much faded in places and the writing was miniscule.

Taleb and Nami Char had their heads buried behind the

massive worn leather of thick volumes, one occasionally muttering to the other. Varden Herl held a book in one hand while with the other hand he attempted to spread out an intricately marked map. Ket Vos snored unobtrusively in an armchair in a corner of the room. Perra Koos looked round his now crowded library and rather yearned for his old solitude. He was about to go downstairs to check on Tilliat, who was sitting with old Tani, when a man appeared, very nearly in Li Kassu's lap.

Various bundles and satchels cascaded round the startled mages then the new arrival struggled upright. Morkus Fayle's hair and beard were thoroughly dishevelled and there was a certain wildness in his eyes. But he beamed at Perra and the others as he offered a polite bow.

'Absolutely astonishing Perra. Which of you discovered such a wonderful spell? No wonder you told me not to be alarmed. Apart from the suddenness of the departure, it was tremendously exhilarating.'

Nami Char regarded the elderly Morkus coolly. 'None of us brought you here. Have you no hint of how it was managed?'

'None at all, none at all. Fascinating though.'

'We have a couple of other guests.' Perra thought it best to speak plainly at once. 'One is of the Dragonkind, named Toomay. There is also a trader from the city of Kelshan, Davin Pearl, and a young woman …'

'The Mage Foretold,' Morkus interrupted, beaming even more.

Perra stared at him. 'Tilliat Kranch, I was about to say.'

Morkus waved his hands about and paced round the large table, the other mages swivelling to keep their eyes on him. He leaned over Li Kassu's shoulder and jabbed a none too clean finger towards the scroll in front of her.

'Lucky man Perra. That looks like an original. I have a book with fragments of his histories but I do have a little gem of a book too.'

He squatted suddenly, rummaging amongst the various possessions which had arrived with him. He pulled a worn leather-bound volume from a satchel.

'The Books of Prophecy of Z'B'Rak the Obscure,' he announced in triumph.

'Prophecies!' Taleb Char groaned. 'We all know why he was

211

called Obscure Morkus. Like all prophets, he made up riddles so people waste their entire lives trying to make some sense out of sheer nonsense.'

Morkus resumed his pacing. Perra noticed the old man had aged considerably since last he'd seen him, and he limped quite badly on his right leg.

'No, no, no.' Morkus glared at Taleb. 'Z'B'Rak was once renowned for his study of mental illnesses and injuries. That is why his prophecies were much respected – because first he was a scholar of great integrity.'

'I didn't know that,' Taleb frowned.

'Hah! Standards in schools generally and the Academy in particular have fallen abysmally in the last fifty years – as I have often remarked. You would have learned of Z'B'Rak before that time as a matter of course.'

'Well let's have a look at that book then,' said Varden. 'But does he really speak of the Mage Foretold? I thought that prophecy was from a mage called Zara through some crazy priestess, and only recently at that?'

'*Zehara* was the mage,' Morkus replied scornfully. 'And that prophecy was made only twenty or so years ago. It was clearly based on these prophecies.' He shook the book at Taleb Char.

Taleb glared at the old man and whipped the book out of his hand. He, Nami and Li Kassu immediately bent close to study the onionskin thin pages. Morkus grinned and moved closer to the crammed shelves, scrutinising each book as he worked his way down the room. Silence descended. Perra shook his head and left, closing the door gently.

Going down the narrow back stairs he tried to work out just how his life had been turned upside down in the space of less than two days. Exiting from the dried food storeroom, he saw a group had gathered round Tani's truckle bed. As he drew closer, Cook caught his sleeve.

'Mistress Tilliat says Tani is waking. The poor dear's slept so very long sir.'

Maids, the two pot boys and three guards were all watching with interest. Tilliat sat on the bed, holding Tani's hand. Dragon Toomay lay close by, his chin resting on her shoulder. The grey cat crouched on Tani's chest, her purr loud to Perra's ears.

Tani's eyelids fluttered and he muttered something unintelligible. Then his eyes opened and he was staring into Cloud's face. His gaze moved up to the Dragon and his eyes widened. Finally he looked at Tilliat, who gave him a shy smile.

'You slept well Master Tani. Do you feel any better?'

Tani closed his eyes but his hand tightened on Tilliat's.

'Much better dear child. The dark dreams have gone – I can feel all that darkness has blown right out of my head.'

'You have no mage powers left, I'm afraid,' Tilliat began but Tani opened his eyes again.

'And for that, I thank you child. I know who are, and even with no power, I will do all I can to help you defeat the curse of Reva's presence in this poor world.'

Chapter Nineteen

In the capital city of the Isles of Vremilia, the Crown Prince Tetsura was recovering from his strange experience in his sister's mind. He felt physically exhausted and his mind was like a squeezed-out sponge, limp and empty. He'd tried to explain what had happened to both Vilad and Sergeant Tag but his explanations seemed only to confuse them. Regent Hikmat had hurried to the Prince's apartments after receiving word that Tetsura would be unable to meet him to discuss the papers he'd been set to study, due to illness. Hikmat was sure it was some petty revenge for the beatings he'd given the Prince.

Consequently he was taken aback to find Tetsura languishing in bed, pale, with dark shadows ringing his grey eyes.

'I will send a physician to you,' he said in some alarm.

'I'm sure I'll be well tomorrow – perhaps I ate something that disagreed with me. There is surely no need to bother a physician.'

Hikmat frowned, studying the boy carefully. 'Very well.' He turned to Vilad. 'You will send word at once if he is sick again or seems to worsen. I will have a physician here in heartbeats.'

Vilad nodded, bowing deeply. Hikmat moved to the door.

'I have meetings this morning – matters of state that I cannot postpone. I shall visit you around the fourth bell, but do not hesitate to summon me should you fear he is not progressing.'

The last was said with a glare at Vilad who bowed yet again and stayed bent double until the outer door of the Prince's apartment clicked shut. Vilad straightened with a grin, which faded when he saw Tetsura's eyes were closed again.

The bedroom door reopened and Sergeant Tag approached the bed. Tetsura moved slightly and winced, his hand resting on the covers over his sore stomach..

'I know you're there Sergeant, but I haven't the energy to look.'

Sergeant Tag grinned. 'Wait until you've had a night of

drinking. I'm sure you'll feel much worse than you do now.'

Tetsura's eyes flew open. 'Don't you dare threaten me Sergeant.' He managed a wan smile.

'You should sleep now,' Tag told him. 'If you feel better later, a short walk in the fresh air would be good for you.'

Tetsura nodded. 'I'm sure I'll be fit for that.'

'Stay with him Vilad,' Tag barely breathed the words. 'I'll be close by.'

Tetsura slept dreamlessly until the pealing of the third bell when the sun was at its height. Unknown to him, Sergeant Tag had managed to get Saima into the Palace. Saima had worked a healing on the Prince, relieving the worst of his aches. She was afraid to heal him fully lest Hikmat's few mageborn spies sensed her use of power.

When Tetsura woke, he was surprised to find he felt completely well. His belly still had a certain tenderness but he could think of food without blanching. Vilad allowed him only bread and honeyed juice before accompanying him down to the gardens. Sergeant Tag took Vilad's position at the outer doors and trotted quietly two paces behind Tetsura's left shoulder.

'Remember the Regent is visiting you later so you cannot stay too long,' Tag remarked as they approached the five willows which sheltered the little house. 'Saima is already inside.'

Tag slowed to lean against one of the gnarled tree trunks, letting Tetsura stride on to the hidden house.

While Sergeant Tag waited, she considered what Commander Anjit had told her earlier. He had been summoned by the Regent twice yesterday. Anjit was delighted to tell Tag that Hikmat was much disturbed by the reports of unregistered mageborn infiltrating the city. Anjit was not so delighted to have to inform the Sergeant that there was another group who he had only just had information on: dissatisfied merchants, traders and apprentices.

They had joined forces, and they planned nothing less than the overthrow of Hikmat and his ruling council. Merchants and traders were suffering under ever increasing taxation, and thus paying less to their workers and apprentices. Anjit had known there was widespread irritation – not just on the main island but throughout the archipelago. He had not known the irritation had

215

boiled up to eruption point, nor realised that it was all so well organised.

Tag turned her thoughts to the girl, Tetsura's twin sister, and wondered what was happening to her so far away on the . It was hard for Tag to consider the subject of twins. Commander Anjit was the only person she knew who, although brought up apart from his twin sister, had known her and had spent whole summers with her throughout their childhood.

Tag had been born a twin. Her father was dead, killed three months before his wife gave birth, drowned in a great storm off Kalama Island. Half a year later, Tag's mother died and, with no relatives in the small fishing village, a neighbour's wife who was childless, took in the two tiny girls. Tag remembered, although she tried hard not to, the hardships of those years, mitigated always by the joy of her sister's presence.

The neighbour's wife was not kind but nor was she deliberately cruel. Unlike her husband. Tag was ten when he came home one night, dragged his wife from bed and beat her to death. Then he'd turned his attention to the two little girls. When Tag woke, with her left arm broken and a great, hurting lump on the side of her head, he had fled. Her sister's body lay, like an abandoned rag doll, across the woman's corpse.

Other villagers eventually came and removed the now mute child and set her arm and nursed her back to health. But no one could get a sound from her and they soon lost interest. Tag passed her eleventh birthday stowed away on a trading ship travelling to several other islands, listening and waiting. She found the man on the Isle of Crabs and she murdered him there.

Then there seemed no purpose left and she drifted from ship to ship, usually hiding away or occasionally working her passage, until she reached the great island of Vremil. The guards were recruiting in the Traders' Square near the docks and Tag lined up with others, waiting to see the officer. When Tag reached his desk, he gave a shout of laughter which slowly died away when he met her eyes. That officer had been killed in a skirmish with pirates a couple of years later, but Tag often wished she could ask him what he had seen in her eyes that made his laughter cease and for him to take her on.

Her voice sounded unfamiliar to her ears when she answered

216

his questions, only shrugging when he asked her name. When the officer assigned the new recruits their beds in the barrack dormitory, he called her Tag, because, he said, she was the tag at the end of the line. She may have been small but she moved fast and she learned fast.

Tag gave herself a furious mental shake. Enough! She was bodyguard to the Crown Prince. This was not the time or the place for daydreaming.

Commander Anjit was at that moment in Regent Hikmat's office. Hikmat was more rattled than Anjit had ever previously seen him. The Commander had just conveyed the information that it appeared a large section of the trading communities were preparing to rise in open rebellion.

'But surely there is a leader among them Commander. You must have names. If you do, arrest them immediately. And recall some of the regiments – those from the nearest Isles obviously.'

'There are many boats coming here from the whole kingdom sir, but very few will agree to sail again before the Presentation now, fearing they might be delayed and then miss the celebrations. Unless of course any of the mageborn who you keep in your service can somehow communicate to the various regiment captains? As for names, I know the highest ranked merchants as well as you do sir – Bars, Minoak, Renlo, to name but three. But if I take them under arrest and they are *not* involved, it will cause more unrest than ever sir.'

Hikmat hurled the quill he'd been shredding onto his desk and rose. He glared at Anjit.

'Then what *are* you going to do Commander?'

'Watch and wait sir,' replied Anjit calmly.

Hikmat regarded him with scepticism. 'And if you watch and wait too long Commander?'

'My men are well trained. There are no armsmen among the merchant groups, save for a handful of house guards. They are not usually known for their weapons skill, organisation, or discipline sir. They will be a rabble, and my men can deal with any rabble sir.'

'I hope your faith in them is well founded Commander. We will *all* be in serious trouble if you are wrong. Keep me

217

appraised of the situation, and do not fail to inform me if there is any worrying development.'

Anjit saluted and marched from Hikmat's presence. He headed for the Officers' Halls where he had called a meeting for all his captains and under captains other than those on duty. The Officers' Halls were attached to the west wing of the Phoenix Palace although there was no access from the Halls into the Palace. Anjit walked out, turned left and rounded the corner. Straight lay the parade ground and beyond, the main barracks, training areas and dormitories.

Only the paired sentries were in sight but when Anjit pushed open the door at the entrance he heard the murmur of voices from within the smaller Hall which ceased as he entered.

'Relax,' he said, walking to the raised bench at the end of the room. Officers who had snapped to attention sank back onto chairs and waited for the Commander to speak. Looking over the dozen or so officers, Anjit was glad to note Captain Ras was absent. The few others missing also happened to be of Ras's ilk – from wealthy families and in the guards because of the fun and prestige the uniform might bring them.

'You know, I'm sure, that the Regent is deeply concerned at the news of unknown mageborn within the city. It has also come to my attention that there is the serious possibility of an uprising in the Merchant District.'

'No surprise there,' came a rumbling mutter from someone in Anjit's audience.

He shrugged. 'Probably not but let's not get political at the moment. Of the two, I believe the unrest among the merchants and general workers is far more serious than having a few mageborn enter Garjetka.'

'Can we be sure the mageborn offer no threat to the Prince?'

That was Captain Jia, a woman nearing retirement but still as sharp as her sword and Anjit's second in command.

Anjit chose his words with care. 'I am as positive as I can be, from certain informants, that mageborn offer no danger to the Prince. The Phoenix Kings are all mageborn, after all. It is the Regent who has purged the Kingdom of such people during his time ruling on behalf of Prince Tetsura. So it is the workers and apprentices I want us to concentrate on.'

He allowed a brief pause, watching his officers absorb his remarks. 'Have any of you any reliable links to the Merchant District?'

'You mean other than those Ras and Korban have?' asked Under Captain Lenti.

There were chuckles, and Anjit gave a slight nod of acknowledgement.

'My wife knows some of the apprentices sir, through our boy, Jek. He's apprenticed to Tolima Tah, the goldsmith. Tah has been fair to Jek and kept his wages steady, but most of the master craftsmen have laid boys off. And some of the girls are working in the streets after they've worked a full day for a Master – girls who need every coin they can get for their families.'

'If your wife or your boy speak of these things, listen very closely please Lenti.'

The burly guardsman nodded slowly and Anjit studied the other faces. 'Anyone else?'

He caught the flicker of fingers against a sleeve and understood that Captain Berran would speak to him privately.

'I will visit some of the leading merchants and try to find one who will tell me honestly how far their plans might have gone. I want you to tell the guards in each of your squads to keep their ears and eyes open, on and off duty, and not to get too heavy-handed with any troublemakers in the taverns and bars just at the moment. Report directly to me or Captain Jia anything at all that you think may be relevant. Dismissed.'

People began to leave in two and threes.

'Captain Jia,' Anjit called. 'A word in my office if you please. I will be there shortly.'

The woman saluted, and carried on from the Hall. Captain Berran was dawdling behind the other officers and he now knelt, refastening the ties on his boot. He gave a quick glance towards the door then stood again.

'Commander, Ras is in it up to his neck. He hates you, even worse since you ordered him flogged for killing that lass. From hints he's let drop, boasted about in fact, he's been promised your position when this is all over.'

Anjit grimaced. 'Whatever "this" may be Berran. Keep up the pretence of being one of his admirers as you've been doing.' He grinned suddenly at Berran's look of disgust. 'I know it's tedious but...

'Someone's got to do it. Yes I know sir, thank you very much.'

Anjit waited, to give Berran time to catch up with the others before he left the Halls and crossed to the barracks. He ran up the stone staircase which led to the administration offices and headed for his own rooms in the northern corner of the building. Captain Jia was waiting outside his door, by the window, watching a new batch of recruits struggling through an obstacle course in the first field beyond the barracks.

'They get worse every year,' she observed, turning to follow Anjit into his office.

Anjit laughed. 'You say that every year Jia.'

'Yes, but this time I really mean it. Have you *seen* them?'

'We were all raw recruits once upon a time.'

Jia snorted. 'Even you were never that bad.' She smiled suddenly, which made the long scar across her face twist unevenly. 'You were clumsy but not utterly hopeless.'

Anjit dropped into his battered leather chair and scowled at Jia seating herself opposite.

'I was never clumsy, and you know it. That is a vile slander.'

'Enough of these pleasantries. What do you need me to do?'

Anjit paused before replying. 'I need you and your squad to watch my back, and Sergeant Tag's,' he said softly.

Jia puffed out a breath. 'That I can do, I promise you. You are sure about the mageborn being no risk to the throne – remember Pauson's fanaticism?'

'I'm sure.' He hesitated. 'They will do all in their power to protect Tetsura.'

Jia simply nodded. 'I know you were mageborn Anjit, but I think you have no powers?'

They had never spoken on this subject before and it came as an odd relief to Anjit. He held Jia in great respect, admiration and affection, and had been close to confiding the matter of his birth many times over the years.

'No,' he agreed, his gaze locked to her hazel eyes. 'I have no powers, but my twin sister does.'

He realised it was an incredibly stupid thing to admit, but this was Jia, who had pushed him through his early struggles in the Phoenix Guards. If he couldn't trust her completely, then he could trust no one. Jia sat perfectly still, she always did, it was part of her being, as was the wide swordcut across her face. Her voice was the faintest murmur.

'Is *he* a twin? I confess I've always wondered.'

When Anjit simply nodded, Jia got to her feet.

'I'll get my squad prepared,' she said. 'I trust you won't be aware of any of them following you, but someone will be close from now on.' She opened the door. 'And be *very* careful, of Ras in particular. He's stupid but that doesn't mean he's not very dangerous.'

Anjit sat considering which merchant or trader he could approach without making matters any worse. He'd always got on relatively well with Minoak, the head of the fabric trade. Bars, who dealt in various luxury foods gathered from many islands, was a loathsome creature. Anjit found it impossible to be polite to him and avoided him on every occasion. Finally he decided on Poxton Dens of the Jewellers' Guild.

He wrote a carefully worded note and sealed it with a plain stamp. He left his rooms, to go into the administrative area where he called for a runner. A young girl appeared within heartbeats and he handed her the rolled note, telling her where and to whom it was to be delivered. He fished a small silver coin from his pocket.

'You must remove your badge for this child. I do not wish it to be known the message has come from here.'

The girl gave him a cheeky grin, unfastening the brass badge from her tunic and handing it to the chief scribe. 'That'll be extra sir.' Her eyes were fixed on the coin Anjit was casually flipping.

'I know, saucy brat.' The coin flipped higher, landed in an outstretched hand and vanished somewhere about the child's person. The girl spun on a sandaled heel and was gone.

The scribe put the badge carefully in her drawer. 'They are so proud of their badges Commander. That's why they want extra if they have to remove them to take messages.'

'I know, I know,' Anjit laughed. 'I will be back before the fourth bell. If I'm needed urgently, I will be at the Whistling Bird.'

The scribe nodded. 'Good food there Commander. You should eat something – you'll miss the noon meal here.'

'Yes mother.' Anjit chuckled again when the scribe blushed and scowled.

'You fuss about the guards looking after their health and disregard your advice for yourself. Sir.'

Anjit made for the stairs without replying. He thought of the scribe's words as he left the Palace precincts. It was true he supposed. He made sure the guards had good food, clean accommodation and first rate care if they were sick or injured. He plunged into the crowded street leading down to the very heart of the city. Narrow alleys wove between high stone walls behind which lived the wealthy in reclusive splendour.

The streets were busier than usual due to the influx of visitors already here for the Prince's Presentation. The boarding houses had been fully booked for half a year, as were the taverns and the pilgrim lodgings at every temple. It was with some relief that Anjit ducked through an archway into the relative peace of an ornamental garden, one of several Queen had caused to be made throughout the city for the enjoyment of all.

The arch was part of a building which presented a blank face towering over the street but was set with intricately carved balconies facing over the gardens. Two screened alcoves to either side held aviaries with richly plumaged birds – the whistling birds giving the place its name. Anjit removed his cap as he entered the wide doorway. A beautiful girl bowed then offered him a soft white towel damply scented with warm rosewater. Anjit took the towel, wiped his face and hands then passed it back.

The girl bowed again and waved him on to the stairs behind her. At the top of the stairs a slender man greeted him.

'Commander Anjit! It is delightful to see you again. We have missed you of late but understand how busy you must be.'

'Extraordinarily busy Umar, but today I can enjoy one of your wonderful meals. I may have a guest so I would ask for your discretion and a private dining room.'

Umar nodded his understanding and led Anjit along a corridor, past many closed doors on the right hand side until he opened one and bowed Anjit within. The room was dim, lattice screens of stone across the front allowed air to circulate and guests to look out at the sweep of velvet grass edged with delicate blossom trees punctuated with dark straight evergreens. Small flowers in clay boxes lined the window shelf, the breeze wafting a gentle perfume into the room.

Umar lifted a bottle from a silver ewer, ice clinking as he did so. He poured a glass of pale gold liquid and set it on the round table below the window where Anjit had seated himself.

'Thank you Umar. I will wait until my guest arrives then I leave the selection of food to you as usual.'

'You are most complimentary Commander. I will choose only the best for you.' Umar's face was impassive but his dark eyes sparkled. 'And may I beg you *not* to eat *all* the nuts there before you have your meal sir?'

Anjit immediately reached for the bowl and took a handful. 'Just a few Umar, I promise.'

Alone, Anjit gazed unseeing at the cool greens beyond the window, ordering his thoughts and deciding how best to approach the coming conversation. Provided his guest chose to attend, that is. But very little time passed in fact, before there came a faint rap at the door, which then swung open revealing Umar's purple silk clad arm. The man who entered was as tall as Anjit and as broadly built. He wore trousers and jacket of plain dark green, a white shirt, and a broad leather belt the same chestnut brown as his highly polished boots.

Anjit got to his feet. 'I am grateful you could spare the time to meet me Poxton. Please, join me.' He indicated the chair opposite his own.

Poxton Dens, head of the Jewellers' Guild, took his seat. 'I will not play the spy for you Anjit, friends though we are.'

Anjit sat too. 'I'm not asking you to, I need to know what's going on. In general if you prefer, in particular would be helpful.'

Dens rubbed a hand over his clean shaven face and on through his dark hair. He sighed and Anjit noted new lines of tiredness and worry round Poxton's eyes.

'It is mostly down to Renlo, as you must know.'

'I've heard that your Guild is maintaining the wages for apprentices while others are cutting down or dismissing workers.'

'I can understand it though Anjit. Some of the smaller businesses are really struggling under the bloody Regent's taxes.

I sympathise with the rebels Anjit. I'm not sure that their planned violence is the right way to bring about change.'

The door opened to admit Umar and two girls, bearing trays of food. They arranged the platters quickly and silently on the table and departed.

'From your words,' Anjit said slowly, 'I take it that the – resentment – is against the Regent, not the Throne?'

Poxton Dens began to fill a plate from the various dishes arrayed between them.

'Of course not. The Prince is probably unaware of what's going on. There is gossip – that his magepowers have not appeared and Hikmat has been beating him.'

He raised an eyebrow in question.

'Gossip sometimes holds the truth.'

'So.' Dens wiped long delicate fingers on a napkin and looked Anjit in the eye. 'I can assure you no one blames the young Prince. Most people regret they have seen so little of him. His parents would both visit different shops and wander the gardens, chatting to anyone at all. The ordinary people understood that was not a good idea when he was a small boy perhaps, but he could have come out of the Palace sometimes in the last four or five years. They know it is Hikmat's orders – it probably never occurred to the Prince himself, but the Phoenix Throne is respected and mostly loved, by the majority of Vremilians.

'Anjit, this is delicious, do try some or I'll eat it all.'

He pushed a dish across to Anjit who spooned some of the vegetables onto his plate.

'Would it be wise for the boy to appear in the city now – so close to his Presentation?'

Dens thought for a while. 'I think it would make a clear point Anjit. Perhaps I should issue an invitation, asking the Prince to come and select his own gift prior to the Presentation. Do you think such an invitation would get past our deeply hated Regent?'

Anjit didn't pause to consider his reply. 'Send it to me Poxton. I will make sure he receives it.'

For the first time, the leader of the Jewellers' Guild smiled. 'I will suggest four days from now. And I believe you, or someone with the Prince's best interests at heart, should hint to him that it would be very well received if he – loitered – shall we say?

Talked with some ordinary citizens and so on?'

'It will be as you say. This meeting with me – will Renlo and the others hear of it?'

'Of course. I will tell them myself – some of it anyway. And Commander, if you support the Prince, you and your guards have nothing to fear. If you support the Regent, I can do nothing to save any of you.'

Chapter Twenty

While Commander Anjit was talking with Poxton Dens, Saima was deep underground. The mage community had taken refuge in the long-abandoned and forgotten catacombs. Several hundred families had come here for shelter over the last eighteen years, the later arrivals escaping Regent Hikmat's purges. The first families to move here however, had been fleeing from the Mage Pauson's wrath. It had been he who had reinstigated the killing of one of any set of twins born to mage or untalented family alike.

The mage community here lived a fairly normal existence albeit deep below the surface of Vremilia. They had to rely on the few of their kind who lived in the outside world – such as Addi and Saima – for news: mindspeech could not penetrate such a huge solidity of rock.

It took Saima half a bell to reach the outer edges of the community. She was tired from the long downward sloping walk for so long but someone would refresh her energy before she began the even more arduous upward journey back again later. They knew she was coming of course and already she felt the soreness in her legs lessening before she caught sight of them as someone sent her healing strength.

Many more people than usual had gathered to meet her. A woman in her forties, about Saima's own age, was the first to hurry forward to hug the visitor. The others crowded round, already begging for news.

'Let the poor woman get her breath and some tea inside her.' The woman who'd greeted Saima kept an arm about her waist, pulling her gently towards a group of stone benches. Someone rushed up with a tray. They waited with ill concealed impatience for Saima to drink one bowlful, then the questions came from all sides:

'What's happening Saima?'

'Has the Mage Foretold been found yet?'

'Has Hikmat fallen?'

'Has the Prince found his power?'

Saima held out her bowl for more tea and raised her other hand for quiet.

'There is much to tell you. Let me tell it all then you can question me if I haven't been clear. Firstly, the Mage Foretold is on the…'

She got no further. Gasps and cries of – 'Pauson! Has Pauson caught her?' – interrupted her immediately.

Saima sighed. 'I said let me tell you,' she scolded. 'No. Pauson *tried* to get her but she rejected him. She was raised in Kelshan City, the capital of Kelshanite lands, but she was born here. She is the twin of Prince Tetsura. He is finding his mage power but it is as candlelight compared to the sun of hers. She has visited him, her physical body was actually here, although briefly. Such is her power.'

A great sigh of relief echoed through the endless caverns and many people were weeping with joy. The Mage Foretold was in the world, and she was theirs.

In Gulat, Perra Koos sat in his empty library, his unexpected guests finally having retired to their beds. The arrival of Dilla Wart had been traumatic for the poor girl. Perra dreaded to think how much more distressed she might have been had Morkus Fayle not been present to reassure her. Even with Li Kassu's considerable skills it took some time to calm Dilla to coherence. Perra looked at the piles of books, maps, scraps of paper, discarded quills and inkpots, in chaotic disorder on his worktable, and sighed.

It felt strange to him, having other mages in his house. Yes, he had many servants but, by his own orders, they left him to his own devices. Now, he had to consider things like sociable mealtimes, polite conversation. He pushed himself to his feet. He'd try and sleep for a while but there wasn't long until dawn – yet again. Perhaps he should check on Tani and Tilliat Kranch. He was suddenly afflicted with a jaw cracking yawn and made for his bedroom. Everything could wait. He did need some sleep.

Down in Perra Koos's kitchen his old tutor Tani sat on the truckle bed by the fire. He'd declined either the use of a small room close by or to be helped up to his own quarters. He was fascinated by the Dragon Toomay and by the fact that the cat, Cloud, used mindspeech and seemed to have a high intelligence.

Tilliat sat on some pillows, leaning against Toomay's side and Davin Pearl snored gently in Cook's rocking chair. Beside Tani sat the god Simert. Tilliat had called him, hoping he'd not be annoyed, remembering he'd spoken of Tani with affection. When he'd appeared, he'd simply enfolded Tani in his arms then seated himself next to the old man. He spoke softly to Tani whose eyes sparkled with the all too ready tears.

Tilliat watched in fascination while the god of death murmured to Tani, who nodded and began to frown. She made no attempt to try to hear what was said, just observed the two. Simert was a shortish, stout man of apparently middle years, the sort you might see in any marketplace anywhere. Indeed, his boots looked worn and his jerkin was wrongly fastened as though in haste, and it was definitely grubby. But then there was a sudden tilt of his head as though he'd heard something beyond their hearing, and Tilliat knew he was about to vanish. Sure enough, Simert rose, bending to press a kiss to Tani's forehead. He nodded at Tilliat.

'We will meet again child, but sadly I am busier than usual at present. There is much violence in the western lands now.' And he was gone.

'He is such a kind creature,' said Tani. 'In all my years of madness, I never thought to call him. He would have taken me, had I but asked.'

'Perhaps you are meant to be here now,' Tilliat suggested.

'But I can be of no help – my powers are gone. No, child, I do not blame you in the least – indeed I am grateful, so grateful. You must believe me.'

Tilliat stretched her legs towards the gently glowing fire. 'You said he was a kind creature. What did you mean Tani? What sort of creatures *are* the gods?'

'A bowl of tea would help me think.' Tani gave her a sly smile and Tilliat hauled herself up to swing the kettle over the fire.

'They are not of this place I think,' Tani began. 'Do you know anything of the Sapphrean lands, on the other side of this world?

There are people there who came from way past the stars. The mage Tika knew them and counted them her friends. The monstrous beasts that appeared in Kelshan and which Tika finally cast down, also came from some distant world.

'I believe those we call gods are strangers here too, with powers we do not, perhaps *cannot*, understand.'

'We think the same,' Toomay's mind voice was thoughtful.

'But Simert *looks* like we do.' Tilliat handed Tani a bowl of honeyed tea and returned to lean against Toomay.

Tani blew on his tea, sipped cautiously then smacked his lips in satisfaction.

'Do you know any gods Toomay?' he asked.

'We knew two or three but we do not worship individual creatures like humans seem to. We believe that the land is, that the stars are, and infinity promises all answers.'

'Tilliat?'

She shrugged. 'There were many temples in Kelshan. Gods and goddesses for everyone or so it seemed. I never went to any of their ceremonies but certain celebrations took over the whole city. Great processions for the god of the sea at the start of the year and the fishing season, more at midwinter for the return of the sun god, and so on and on. The Imperatrix Veranta outlawed all the temples I think?'

Tani nodded. 'She did and, like the present Vremilian Regent so I've heard, she tried to rid her land of the mageborn.'

'And how have you heard what might be happening in Vremilia Tani? I thought there was no contact between them and these lands for many years.'

The old man chuckled and held out his empty bowl to her. She groaned but rose to refill it for him.

'You should know child, living in a city on the coast, a city of traders. There are always small ships slipping in and out, with no questions asked. The same applies on the east coast. The port of Druke has the advantage over your city by being a free trade city, so no one asks any questions of any ship entering the harbour. For those with an interest in odd snippets of information it provides a wealth of odds and ends. I spent several years there, long ago.'

The door creaked open, revealing the guard under captain,

Mink.

'I've had word from some sniffers,' he said. 'I'm not sure if I should wake Master Koos.'

Tilliat looked blank.

'Sniffers are people who tell tales and sniff out secrets,' Tani murmured helpfully.

'Oh. Well. I think poor Master Koos needs his sleep. Perhaps you could tell us?'

Mink came further into the kitchen. 'Well Mistress, Mahzu Vek is pretending to have left Gulat, but she only took four house guards and two drivers. She takes more guards than that just travelling across the city usually, so no one believes she was inside her carriage when it left. One of my most reliable sniffers says there's a lot of activity amongst her house guards within her compound. I've sent two men to see if they can find out more. They *are* Master Koos's guards but they never wear his livery, so they can be used for this sort of work.'

Tilliat waited for Tani to respond.

The old man scowled. 'It sounds as if she's going to make a move against her opponents, Mink. Send to warn a couple, such as Anat Fursh – fool that he is, or Festa Murk; they can alert any others. Leave Master Koos to sleep until dawn unless the situation changes quickly.'

Tilliat noted Mink's wry smile as he left the kitchen. He must find it disconcerting that an old man, who had been crazy as a trapped squirrel for years, was now calmly giving sensible orders. When the door closed, Tani glanced at Tilliat.

'Can you tell if Perra's wards are still active around this house? The poor boy was so tired I doubt he checked them.'

Could she, Tilliat wondered with some alarm but was saved by Toomay.

'The wards are still intact Tani.'

To Tilliat's mind alone, Toomay added: 'It is very simple. Look in *my* mind and I'll show you.'

Tilliat saw a gold and silver tracery cobwebbing the whole house. She blinked and the slender lines disappeared. She heard a snigger.

'Can break easy.' The Shadow sounded quite gleeful.

Toomay's chin bumped down on her shoulder and she caught

a twinge of nervousness from his mind. She knew he could hear some of the Shadows' communication and actually see them better than she could, but he was very wary of them. Which gave her yet more to think of.

'You should rest,' Tani told her. 'Take whatever chance you can to restore your strength.'

Inexplicably, Tilliat's eyes closed and her head drooped forward. Tani looked hard at the Dragon, who seemed just a touch smug. He snorted.

'She'll be furious if you let her find out you "helped" her sleep.'

Toomay's eyes flashed briefly then calmed when he decided that was probably a human's idea of humour once again.

It was another dark day. Heavy clouds hung low over the city with no hint of where the sun might be. Perra Koos went to the kitchen when he woke. Cook studied him. He was always pale but he had bruises under his eyes which suggested he needed much more sleep. She berated him soundly while serving breakfasts and sending maids scurrying up to the guest rooms with laden trays.

While Tilliat and Perra ate, Tani told of Mink's report earlier. Perra swallowed a mouthful of egg.

'The trouble is, Mahzu Vek virtually commands the City guards, not just her own. Some of us have well trained men but no more than twenty or thirty each I would guess. Mahzu has always insisted on twice that number for her own houseguards and there must be over five hundred permanent City guards besides the volunteer militias.'

'We have to decide where the greatest immediate danger lies,' Tilliat said thoughtfully. She pushed herself up from the table. 'I have to think. When Uncle Davin wakes could you ask him to find me in your garden please?' She smiled. 'I think better when I walk.'

Perra returned her smile. 'Of course – don't get cold out there.'

Tilliat pulled her fleece lined jacket on and headed for the door, watched by Tani and Toomay. She touched Toomay's shoulder as she passed. 'It is too chilly for you my dear. It is quite safe behind these high walls.'

Toomay's eyes sparkled at her then he turned his attention back to Tani and Giffu who were apparently arguing about a recipe for summer porridge.

After the warmth of the kitchen, the air was chill in the garden. Tilliat followed a path of stone slabs along the left of the door. Grey clouds shrouded the sky and drops of water clung to twigs and branches. She wondered how much further north Gulat was compared to Kelshan. She estimated that outside Kelshan by now, the orchards would be in blossom, new crops greening the fields and farm animals dropping their young. She paused to examine a climbing vine plant but could see only a slight fattening at the tips of tendrils suggesting buds might eventually appear.

Tilliat shivered and huddled her jacket closer around her. Following the path she noticed that while there were climbing plants against the high, iron spiked walls, the area in front of them was turned earth through which the tips of green spears emerged. It was a fairly large garden but the trees were towards the centre, surrounding the brick-built pavilion she had first woken in. Perra Koos clearly took security very seriously indeed.

Tilliat was on her third circuit when Davin Pearl joined her. The clouds parted overhead and a weak beam of pale sunlight tried to brighten the garden. Although Tilliat knew this house was deep in the large city of Gulat, the towering walls defended against noise as well as intruders. There was a faint rumble of wagons and carts, an occasional shout above a steady murmur of many people, but it all sounded far away.

Davin Pearl strolled quietly beside Tilliat, content to wait until she decided to talk. Eventually she led them off the outer path, in towards the carefully grouped trees. She climbed the shallow steps under the overhanging roof of the pavilion and turned, surveying the garden.

'I have had a long talk with Tani, Uncle. A very interesting talk in fact, although he kept saying he had forgotten so many things he could be of little help. Besides his mage powers, he has lost all confidence in himself. He feels guilty for what he calls his "weakness" in not withstanding the power of this god, Reva.'

She sighed. 'The Shadows say there is a likelihood of an

232

uprising in Vremilia. I think my brother will have to work with those who are discontented with the Regent's rule and sort out his Kingdom for himself.'

Tilliat sank down to sit on the top step. Davin Pearl lowered himself to sit beside her, still silent.

'I know little of what's happening in Kelshan, Uncle. The Shadows seem – I don't know – angry? Or perhaps confused is a better word. But I *do* know they feel rage, dreadful rage, regarding the god Reva.'

'Do these Shadows *know* what's happening in the west?' Davin asked.

Tilliat grunted. 'I'm fairly sure they do but they are disinclined to say anything helpful.'

Davin nodded. 'And here in Gulat? What will you do with all these mages in such a confusion?'

Tilliat's eyes sparkled with brief amusement. 'A true "muddle of mages" eh Uncle? I think they must work on their own to bring down Skala Vek's mother, who seems to be the root of the problem here.'

'But is that god – Reva? – is *he* here too and working with her?'

Tilliat got to her feet and pulled Davin Pearl up with her. They began walking again, Davin remembering how Tilliat used to pace round and round when she was wrestling with some knotty problem in her school work. It seemed long ago but was scarcely a full season since he'd watched her so, at home in Kelshan city.

'I don't believe so. From what Perra Koos and his friends have said of Mahzu Vek, she seems over endowed with self importance rather than with mage powers. If there *is* a god around I can't imagine why he would work with her. Clearly Tani was far more powerful. When he decided the god was of a nasty turn of mind and rejected him, Reva was annoyed. He left Tani a wreck of a man which seems a petty revenge for someone as presumably powerful as a god.

'I suspect Reva would not make contact with any other humans, but Perra said Mahzu Vek constantly worships Reva. Perhaps Reva found her prayers irritating enough that he bothered to contact her? But if she is as weak as they say, he wouldn't find her mind as attractive as Tani's was perhaps.'

They walked in silence for a time, Tilliat deep in thought again. Davin Pearl cleared his throat.

'So what, exactly, are *we* going to do next?'

Tilliat hooked her arm around Davin's and grinned up at him.

'I'm going to write to Tetsura and hope the Shadows will agree to take the letter to him. They don't seem in the best of moods right now.' She frowned.

'They aren't the easiest of creatures to talk to. And I'll also write to Master Belk but I need to speak with Perra Koos and his mages first.'

The sky had darkened once again and rain began to spatter down. Tilliat tugged Davin faster towards the back door of the house.

'What a pity all this couldn't have waited until summer,' said Davin dolefully as they shut the door behind them.

Tilliat laughed. 'What a pity it had to happen at all.'

They hung their jackets in the hallway and moved to enter the kitchen. Davin Pearl had his hand on the latch.

'Mahzu is a Kelshan name isn't it? Or very like to one. The names of these mages here are strange to me, but Mahzu seems familiar.'

Tilliat scowled. 'You're right, but I don't think who Mahzu is or where she or her ancestors came from, makes any difference. But thank you,' she smiled sweetly as she went through the door in front of him. 'Thank you so much Uncle Davin for giving me something else to think of.'

Davin laughed. 'An uncle can do no less.'

In the middle of the afternoon Tilliat was called up to Perra's study. The room appeared overcrowded with seven mages hunched over the long work table, books precariously balanced on the floor beside various chairs. The eighth mage, and their host Perra Koos, was slumped in a chair by the fire, his eyes closed. Tilliat stood beside him.

'You wanted to see me?' she asked softly, unsure if he was actually asleep.

Dark blue eyes looked up at her and he straightened in his chair with a sigh.

'Indeed,' he agreed. He indicated the mages huddled round the table. 'They wondered how many mages you have in Kelshan, in the city in particular, and of what calibre they might be.'

Tilliat sat on a footstool close to Perra's chair. 'I have no idea. I never had any dealings with mages, not even healers. Jomah always treated any illnesses I had and they weren't many. She set my arm once when I broke it falling off the stable roof.' Tilliat stretched her left arm out and twisted it back and forth. 'It healed well and very quickly.'

'Hmm.' Perra studied Tilliat closely. 'And who is Jomah?'

Tilliat shrugged. 'Jomah is our housekeeper. She's always been with us. She married Pakal – he was papa's best wagon driver until he had an accident – when I was very small.'

'Does Jomah have family in Kelshan city?'

Tilliat thought. 'Well no. Pakal has a sister who is married to a farmer a day or two south of the city. They visit a few times a year, when they bring livestock in for sale.' She scowled in concentration then her face cleared. 'Jomah started to speak of a brother, years ago this was, but papa started telling a funny story and I never heard her mention family again.'

Perra Koos nodded thoughtfully. 'I wonder if she came with you.'

Tilliat stared at him. 'You mean from Vremilia? When I was newborn?' She looked horrified. 'But she may have family still there! All these years, she's been exiled?'

Perra leaned forward to pat her hand. 'If she did come from Vremilia she must have freely chosen to be with you. You must just hope she is safe if civil war is indeed raging in your land.'

Tilliat looked stricken, then drew in a deep breath. She explained her idea to write to both her brother in Vremilia and to Master Trader Belk in Kelshan city. 'I would like your help in deciding exactly what I should say.'

'And these letters will reach their destination how exactly?' Perra asked, an eyebrow lifting in query.

'Ah. Yes. Well I'm hoping the – erm – friends who moved me here, and Morkus Fayle and his niece, might oblige.'

'Surely they will?'

'Hmm,' was Tilliat's only reply.

They joined the mages at the work table and debate raged over the wording of the two letters. The one for Tetsura was relatively straightforward: they advised him to join forces with whoever was opposed to the Regent. The letter to Master Trader Pirus Belk was a knottier proposition.

All of Perra Koos's group felt it was absolutely necessary to ascertain just how many mages were in Kelshan, specifically in the Traders Hall. Then to learn of their strength. Tilliat looked uncomfortable at this point and all faces turned to her, waiting for an explanation.

'I'm not sure how long my – um – friends might wait for a reply.'

Taleb Char snorted and threw his pen on the table, but it was his sister who spoke.

'We really ought to know who these friends of yours are you know.'

'They asked me not to speak of them,' Tilliat began.

'That's all very well,' Nami interrupted. 'But are you completely sure they are trustworthy?'

Tilliat considered Toomay's unease about the Shadows. She concentrated.

'Shadows, can I trust you?' she asked in her mind.

There seemed to be a rather long pause before the Shadows replied. 'Yes.'

'Would you lie to me?'

Another pause. 'Not often.'

Tilliat gritted her teeth, unaware that the mages were watching her changing expressions with deep interest. 'What does that mean?'

But although she waited there was no answer. She blinked and realised she was the focus of attention.

'I do believe I can trust them.' She chose her words carefully. 'The great mage Tika asked them to help me.'

The silence following those words was profound. Li Kassu tilted her head.

'You mean the mage who flew with Dragons and defeated the evil so long ago?' she asked.

Tilliat nodded, not risking further speech.

'Then you *are* the Mage Foretold,' Taleb Char said softly.

236

'And the danger for all of us is not merely civil unrest or uprisings. It is something far worse once more.'

Tilliat found she couldn't look at any of them so picked up a pen and paper. 'Shall we start on the letters? Then, I'm afraid, I will be leaving.'

There was a stir of consternation.

'Tani says I must go north, beyond his estate – if it is still his? He wasn't sure if it still belonged to him since his madness?'

Perra Koos nodded. 'I took it over and pay for its maintenance on his behalf.'

'Well, he says there are people further north who may know how to deal with Reva. He says Reva is the most potent of evils and I must destroy it.'

Chapter Twenty-One

The Crown Prince of Vremilia sat on the small balcony outside his bedroom and watched the dawn's first lightening of the sky. He had slept very little and eventually abandoned his bed to sit out here. There was so little time left until the day of his Presentation to the people he would rule from the Phoenix Throne. Tetsura felt frustration churn through his blood. He had seen Saima only twice. There had been no information given him through either Vilad and his mageborn contacts or from Sergeant Tag.

It would be a while before Vilad came to him yet, and he scowled disconsolately over the balcony railings. Tetsura had learned much faster than Saima or Vilad had realised and he found it easy to shield his mind from any probe. He rose and wandered back into his bedroom, running a finger down the statue of the golden Dragon, then he frowned.

A leather scroll case lay on top of his rumpled bedcovers. His thumb tingled, or rather the thin line of black Shadow around his thumb.

'How did that get here?' he murmured.

'Sister's Shadows,' Shadow replied.

Tetsura snatched up the scroll case eagerly. It was sealed with a wax seal on which was imprinted the outline of a bird. His hand trembled when he broke the seal and tipped out a roll of parchment. Quickly he flattened the long sheet on his knee and began to read. The greeting warmed him at once: "My dear brother," written in a small, neat hand.

Tetsura read it through rapidly then again more slowly. At the bottom were seven signatures in different hands and beneath those a line that touched him deeply: "My love to you brother and good luck in what is to come. Tilliat Kranch." He brushed his finger lightly over those words, a grin on his face. Reluctantly he rerolled the parchment and slid it into the case.

He pulled off the light robe he wore and dressed in loose trousers, tunic and sandals. He heard the outer door of his suite click and felt Vilad's mind touch his lightly. Going through to the reception room he beamed at the old man and held out the scroll case to him. Vilad put a tray on a low table and while he extracted the message and read it, Tetsura poured himself a large bowl of mint tea, with which he always began his day.

Vilad returned the scroll case, a huge smile splitting his face. 'Sergeant Tag is on her way,' he said to the Prince's mind. 'And she says she can't use mindspeech.' He snorted.

Sergeant Tag arrived a very few heartbeats later and was given the message to read in her turn. She held the case towards Tetsura. 'Hide that case somewhere. I must take this to show the Commander.' She began to fold the parchment to Tetsura's alarm.

'I want that back as soon as he's seen it,' he ordered sharply.

Tag tilted her head in surprise, but nodded. 'I won't be long.'

Vilad laid a gentle hand on Tetsura's shoulder. 'How wonderful to have a letter from your sister.'

Tetsura's eyes unexpectedly filled with tears. 'It is, Vilad. It is truly wonderful.' He was struck by a sudden thought. 'And later this morning I am to visit the Guild of Jewellers. Why did I never think of going into the city before Vilad? And meeting people the way I meet the gardeners here?'

Vilad just looked at him and Tetsura knew that everything in his life, and everything missing from it, was down to the Regent Hikmat. 'Your breakfast will be here soon, then we shall dress you suitably for your outing. I believe Commander Anjit is to escort you personally.'

'But you are coming too, Vilad – I insist.' Tetsura spoke aloud, and firmly.

Commander Anjit was bowed into Tetsura's presence by Vilad. Sergeant Tag snapped to attention behind the Prince, who was standing near the window. Anjit appraised the boy in a swift glance: he had rarely been in his company before and never without the Regent.

He saw a boy on the very edge of manhood, slightly taller than average and of a slender build. In the sunshine from the window, his shoulder length black hair was shot with red and gold lights. He was dressed far less ostentatiously than Commander Anjit had feared he might be, in sea blue trousers and tunic. The Phoenix insignia embroidered above his heart gave the only splash of colour with the golden bird and its crimson tail feathers.

Tetsura also wore a narrow gold band around his brow. Anjit met the Prince's grey eyes and saw wariness in their depths. He gave a nod of approval.

'You have been invited to the Guild of Jewellers, Your Highness, so we should be on our way. If there is anywhere else you might wish to visit, you have only to say.'

Tetsura's brows shot up. 'Really?' he began, then bit back further comment. The time was short until his Presentation and he feared Sergeant Tag's suspicion of the Regent's spies within the Palace could well be more likely now.

Commander Anjit marched at Tetsura's side, Vilad and Sergeant Tag directly behind. They descended three floors to the corridor leading to the stableyards. The Phoenix Palace was a vast complex of buildings, a small village above, yet within, the huge city of Garjetka. Tetsura frowned when he saw Guards at attention beside a small two horse carriage.

'I thought we would be walking,' he objected.

Commander Anjit touched his elbow, urging him on. A Guard opened the door emblazoned with the Phoenix crest and waited as the Prince entered the carriage, followed by Anjit and Vilad. Sergeant Tag vanished but Tetsura knew she would be close by.

The carriage moved forward and swung round the side of the Palace, Guards marching to either side.

'We can walk later if you wish but the Regent insisted on some show of state,' Commander Anjit murmured beneath the sound of hooves, booted feet and the creak of the carriage. 'He was *not* pleased that you had accepted this invitation without his knowledge.'

'Good.'

A pair of gates were drawn open, and they were out. Tetsura looked out of the window, marvelling how four years could have passed without his ever leaving the Palace.

People in the streets slowly realised what the Guards were escorting and gradually word spread that a royal carriage was moving through the city. By the time the carriage stopped outside the arched porticoes of the Jewellers' Hall there was a large crowd waving and calling Tetsura's name and blessings on his coming Presentation.

'Just wave back,' Commander Anjit advised. 'And smile.'

Tetsura grinned at him. 'That won't be hard. I can't believe they're pleased to see me.'

So Tetsura waved and smiled at the people held back by the Guards several paces from his carriage, and made his way to the entrance of the Hall. Several men and women were waiting for him and one stepped forward with a bow.

'I am Poxton Dens, Your Highness, Master Jeweller. You are most welcome in our Hall.'

If Tetsura had considered the matter, Poxton Dens didn't look as he might have imagined a jeweller to look. He was a sturdily built man, slightly taller than the Prince and in fact resembled more a farmer or a builder. Dens introduced the various people with him and Tetsura nodded politely before he was ushered inside.

There followed a tour of the many small workshops, storerooms where gold and silver bars were stacked, and trays of colourful gems winked and glittered. Tetsura was finally led upstairs to a large gallery where finished work was displayed for sale. Trays of food and tall goblets of wine were offered. There were quite a number of people there and Tetsura was unsure if they were all workers in the jewellery trade or here as guests.

Commander Anjit was deep in conversation with a slender woman of middle years when Poxton Dens approached the Prince.

'Your Highness, we would very much like to offer you your choice of a Presentation gift. If there is anything you would perhaps prefer to be made especially, it will take time. Have you seen anything you might like?'

'That is very generous of you Master Dens. There are many beautiful pieces of work in the Palace. I'm afraid I am not too knowledgeable about such things. I have two pieces I believe are valuable in my rooms, one of which I am enormously fond of.'

Poxton Dens was listening with interest.

'One is a statue of a Phoenix and I believe it was my father's.

The other was a gift for the first anniversary of my birth and has always stood close to my bed.' He smiled suddenly. 'It is a Dragon, also made of gold like the Phoenix but I love it. Each scale is marked so finely and she has the kindest face.'

Poxton Dens returned the Prince's smile. 'She?'

Colour touched Tetsura's cheeks. 'I've always been convinced it is a female Dragon,' he said firmly.

'I am glad you like her so greatly. I remember my father and uncle working on her.'

Tetsura stared at him in astonishment. Poxton nodded.

'It was commissioned by old Sarral Peach, the governor of the outer Isle of Vash. He was related to your mother I believe.'

'Was he?' Tetsura was surprised again.

Feeling they were edging to perhaps difficult areas, Dens went back to his earlier offer. 'Perhaps you would leave the choice of gift to me then, Your Highness?'

Tetsura glanced around then stepped slightly closer to the Master Jeweller, turning his face away from the room.

'I would like you to make something, three somethings in fact.' He reached inside his tunic and withdrew a folded paper. 'I've drawn what I'd like you to make – not very well I'm afraid. They are drawn the size I would like them made but perhaps you'd let me know if it is possible.'

He slid the paper into Poxton's hand and the jeweller discreetly pocketed it without examining it. 'I will be in touch promptly Your Highness.'

'Oh for stars sake! Please just call me Tetsura. No one calls me "your highness" in the Palace except...' He bit his lip. He stared directly into Poxton Dens' eyes. 'I will rule here soon, and I swear to you Master Dens, things will change.'

Commander Anjit joined them. 'It is time we left, Your Highness.'

Poxton Dens chuckled briefly then bowed. 'We are deeply honoured Tetsura, by your presence here today. I will attend to the matter you mentioned and would like to assure you of our total loyalty to the Phoenix Throne.'

Anjit had stiffened when Dens called the Prince by his name but said nothing. Vilad materialised at Tetsura's elbow and they made their farewells. Back in the carriage, Tetsura waved again at the even larger crowd.

'You said we could walk,' he pointed out.

'Where do you want to walk, Your Highness?'

'Somewhere near the docks? I heard of a tavern, the Sea Slug? And perhaps the flower market district.' Tetsura was pleased to note that Commander Anjit looked distinctly bemused. 'And I prefer *not* to be called "your highness" by any who would be my friends.'

Anjit met Tetsura's gaze. 'I am proud and honoured if you will count me a friend. I swear I consider myself always a friend to you and to the Phoenix Kingdom.'

The carriage rolled on after Anjit called an order to the driver and Tetsura saw the streets were narrowing. He could smell fish, spices, and cooking oil as they wound lower through the city. They passed a public bath house, its frontage swathed in a creeper covered in cream blossoms whose perfume fleetingly filled the carriage.

'I can't remember being in the city,' said Tetsura. 'The Regent took me on visits to other Isles and to the Summer Palace until I was fourteen, but I don't recall coming into these streets.'

Commander Anjit snorted. 'If you insist on visiting the Sea Slug, I don't imagine the Regent even knows such a place exists.' He peered out of the window. 'If you are sure about this, we'll have to walk from here.'

In Gulat, Tilliat was making preparations to travel north to Tani's estates. The Char twins had a small manor just beyond Gulat's walls and had agreed to lend horses for the trip. Two days had passed since Tilliat's mysterious friends had taken messages to Vremilia and to Kelshan. They expected no answer from Tetsura but were hoping to have some response from the Traders' Hall in Kelshan.

Tilliat was none too sure the Shadows would actually retrieve any message from Kelshan. She had specified that the Master Trader, Pirus Belk, *must* have a reply ready, on his desk, by nightfall three days after receiving her message. The Shadows had made it very clear they were unaccustomed to being mere conveyors of letters and they were not happy with her request.

Their truncated form of communication made any attempt on

Tilliat's part to explain her request deeply frustrating. The mages in Perra Koos's house were surprised by Tilliat's short temper for most of one day, and discreet questioning of the Dragon Toomay was met by innocently sparkling eyes and a plea of complete ignorance.

Nightfall in Kelshan corresponded to near dawn in Gulat. Tilliat had fallen asleep late in the small room near the kitchen, Cloud curled behind her knees. A scroll case landed on her head, hard, as though dropped from near the ceiling. Cloud shot under the bed, wailing in fury and Tilliat sat up, hoping her heartbeat might slow to a normal pace quite soon.

Toomay's mind touched hers. 'You are well?'

'Yes, I think so. I'll be with you in a moment.'

Pulling on her trousers, she shrugged into her shirt, grabbed the scroll case and padded barefoot across the hall to the kitchen. Tani was awake, sipping a bowl of tea, and Toomay was lying gracefully beside the hearth.

'Aha, your mysterious friends have brought a reply then.'

Tilliat rubbed her temple. 'Yes. They dropped it on my head, just to make sure I didn't miss it.'

'Well, what do your traders say? Come on, open it.'

Tilliat broke the seal on the end of the case, frowning when she realised there was no mark on the wax. She slid the rolled parchment out and spread it on her knees. Tani watched her scan quickly down through an apparently long message, her frown deepening until she reached the bottom. Then she gasped and her skin paled. Toomay pushed up onto his haunches, eyes whirring in alarm.

'What's wrong?' he asked in her mind even as Tani said the same aloud.

'The signatures,' she whispered. 'There are traders and mages who have signed but the main one, the one who has written this paper, is Jomah.'

Both Tani and Toomay were puzzled: they knew no Jomah. But Tilliat was reading again, more closely, and offered no explanation.

Eventually Toomay murmured in her mind: 'Is it helpful news? Is your home safe?'

Tilliat sighed, passed the document to Tani and went to pour

244

herself a bowl of tea.

'It is helpful to a certain extent. I don't know about our house; Jomah is at the refuge in the Traders' Hall.'

She sat on the floor beside Toomay, sipping her tea. 'Apparently Jomah – Jomah! – is a powerful mage and has been accepted as such by other mages in Kelshan and the Traders' Council. Master Koos had his suspicions about her when I told him she healed my arm.' She glanced across at Tani who had just finished his reading.

'At least they are warned, child. If Reva is going to act against Kelshan, for stars know what reason, they can be as prepared as possible. And they can be on the watch for any such attack as we suffered here and perhaps be able to shield themselves – the mages I mean – as mages here were taken unawares.'

Just then a door opened and Giffu the cook bustled in to the kitchen. She smiled, stroking the side of Toomay's face. 'There now, tell me you've not been sitting here all night with no sleep.'

'Oh no Giffu,' Toomay replied earnestly. 'We were asleep until only a short while ago.'

'So I should hope, my lamb. Now, where are those girls? Breakfasts need to be readied and not one of those scamps out of their beds yet.'

But even as she spoke, four girls and two boys hurried in and began their various chores.

'I shall hunt,' Toomay announced.

Tilliat let him out of the back of the house. 'Do be careful,' she urged him.

'No one will see *me*.' The Dragon's eyes sparkled at her. 'It is a very simple magic.'

Tilliat watched him pace forward on to the wet grass, then he began to rise. She blinked but somehow, he was gone.

'Showing off. Very young,' muttered a sniffy sounding voice in Tilliat's head.

'Shadow, thank you *so* much for bringing the message from Kelshan, it was extraordinarily kind of you.'

'Yes.'

Tilliat swallowed her irritation and decided to continue with the flattery. 'It was indeed,' she agreed. 'Erm – did you happen to learn much of any fighting there, or through the Kelshan lands?

Only I haven't been aware of your presence these three days.'

There was silence but Tilliat could feel the Shadows were still there.

'You safe here.'

Tilliat waited.

'Always know. If danger, we here.'

Tilliat abandoned her attempt at getting anything resembling information from the Shadows and returned to the kitchen. She found Perra Koos seated at the table, reading the message from Kelshan. She was about to join him when Tani caught her arm as she passed him. He held out another rolled paper.

'It was stuck inside the case Tilliat.'

He turned it so she could see a blob of green wax sealing it and her name, written just above it. For a moment she could only stare at it, then broke the seal with her thumb nail and unrolled the paper. Tilliat raised her gaze to Tani's faded blue eyes.

'I must show this to Uncle Davin before anyone else, Tani. I'll go and wake him.'

She saw Perra Koos watching her and tried to smile. 'Explain to Master Koos. I won't be long.' And she hurried from the kitchen.

Perra and Tani were halfway through their breakfasts when Tilliat returned with Davin Pearl. Both looked pale, as Perra noted at once. He stretched his hand towards her and drew her to a chair beside him.

'Tani says there was another letter my dear. Can you tell us what it says, or perhaps it is personal, from your devoted Jomah?' His tone was gentle and Tilliat knew that if she said it was private he would not pressure her to reveal its contents.

Her fingers tightened on the paper, then relaxed. 'It *is* from Jomah,' she said softly. 'She must have written it and put it with the other paper without others knowing.'

'Who *is* this Jomah?' asked Tani.

'I always thought she was just our housekeeper. She had the name per Kranch, which means she and her husband Pakal belonged to our family. Not like slaves or anything,' she added hastily. 'It means they must be accorded the respect due to the Kranch name and honoured as such by others. But now I have to believe she came with me from Vremilia and has watched over me ever since.'

'Then she has shown enormous devotion to you Tilliat. Is that not something to warm your heart? My poor dear student Perra here has shown no less devotion to me for these many years of my madness and I know I can never repay his kindness, except by loving him with all my heart.'

The tears in Tilliat's eyes did not fall. She gave the old man a slightly shaky smile and reached for the pot of tea in front of Perra Koos. He had watched the exchange between this girl and old Tani and he merely smiled when she glanced at him. He tapped the long parchment he'd been studying, ignoring the paper in Tilliat's hand. Before he could speak, Giffu put plates before Tilliat and Davin Pearl, laden with eggs, slices of meat and spiced vegetables.

'Make sure you eat all of that, child. You could do with more flesh on your bones.' She returned to the huge stove and clattered pans in a renewed bout of frying.

Davin slid his arm round Tilliat's waist and gave a gentle squeeze.

'She's right. Eat up.'

'This message from Kelshan suggests they are in trouble, from without *and* within,' said Perra. 'It says only that the Master Trader to whom you said we should direct our message, is dead. It does not say how he died but there is a suggestion of trouble in the Traders' Council.'

Tilliat swallowed a mouthful of food, nodding at Perra's comment. 'This is a personal message, from Jomah.' She lifted the smaller paper then replaced it beside her. 'But she says Pirus Belk betrayed me. She stresses that it was *me* personally, who was betrayed. She doesn't give much detail, but I suspect she killed him.'

Davin Pearl shook his head, scarcely able to believe the words Tilliat had shown him. Tilliat drew a breath.

'I think the council, Traders and mages both, understand what we tried to explain of Reva. Well, the mages probably do anyway. Clearly the city is in chaos. They report fighting all around the Traders' Hall and some of the other Guild Halls. But it sounds unorganised. When we left, the streets were dangerous

247

– gangs roaming everywhere, people being beaten up just for being in the way. It sounds as if it is more of the same but much more violent.'

She touched her letter again. 'Jomah has managed to get word out to many of the citizens and the other Guilds but she was hampered by Pirus Belk refusing to let anyone in or out of Traders' Hall.'

'Just before we left, I spoke with him,' Davin Pearl put in. 'He said a lot of the small principalities would close their borders like clam shells until they saw which way the wind blew. He seems to have sealed off Traders' Hall in the same way but it was always agreed that the Hall would be a rallying point during any unrest, as well as a secure haven in its depths.'

There was a flurry at the door which a kitchen boy hurried to open and Toomay hustled in, making straight for Tilliat.

'Are you well?' he asked, keeping his words for her mind only. 'You are upset.' His eyes flickered with deeper colours of agitation.

Tilliat leaned towards him. 'I am well my friend. Just a little – bothered.'

Toomay sat back on his haunches, ignoring the crunching of a stool beneath him.

'You're sure?' he insisted.

'I am. Truly.'

The Dragon's eyes calmed to a silvery blue and he settled more comfortably, his chin on the end of the table.

'We will discuss this news with the others, but I fear we're all on our own now. Kelshan must fight for itself and so must we.' Perra spread his hands, palms up. 'There are none of us who can farspeak right across the lands, nor across the sea. So we will need to rely on your rather secretive "friends" if we need to communicate with Kelshan or Vremilia. I have no idea how, or even if, *they* can contact *us*.'

Tilliat grimaced. 'My friends found it rather demeaning I think, being asked to take messages. I'd prefer not to risk – offending – them again any time soon.'

Chapter Twenty-Two

The rest of the day was busy. Perra Koos sent armsmen, in plain cloaks with no house badge displayed, to many councillors and merchant guildsmen. The messages were succinct. If the recipient was tired of Mahzu Vek's increasing stranglehold on all aspects of life within Gulat, then they should contact Perra Koos. He and his mage friends had worded the message with great care.

Li Kassu had wanted all of their names on the documents but Perra insisted they remain hidden for now and allowed only his own signature and seal. He pointed out that some of the people to whom the messages would be delivered, were of doubtful allegiance. Their replies must be carefully scrutinised because there would surely be a few who would pretend to be against Mahzu Vek in the hopes of discovering more of Perra Koos's plans for her overthrow.

Koos and his fellow mages had been amused when Mink, captain of the house armsmen, had reported the departure of Mahzu Vek for Kelshan city. It seemed that absolutely no one in the city believed it for a moment. But Mink did have an interesting snippet of news of his own.

Mahzu Vek's closest assistant, Keril Dwar, had been seen slipping into an upper room at the Dirty Fox tavern, not far from Mahzu Vek's house. She had been going there every two or three days for quite a long while. Nothing unusual in that perhaps. Maybe she met a lover there. But she took fairly extreme precautions coming and going from the tavern – heavily swathed in a hooded and veiled cloak in good weather as well as foul.

Taleb Char grunted at that piece of information. 'Perhaps she's meeting a married man who wants their liaison kept secret.'

Mink had grinned. 'She meets someone who lives in the tavern, not someone who just hires a room occasionally.'

'Someone who works there?' suggested Ket Vos.

Mink shook his head. 'I've had a word with the owner.

Known him for years. A man has been living there for over two years, and Shel's never seen his face. He seems to be a cripple of some sort – has never left the room as far as Shel knows. They leave food outside his door and he takes it in to his room, then leaves the plates back outside the door. Keril Dwar made the arrangements for him to live there and she brought him, in a closed carriage.'

'Well thank you Mink. It's interesting but I'm not sure where it leads us.'

Mink saluted and turned to leave Perra's workroom.

'But continue to keep an eye on her,' Perra added.

Mink nodded and closed the door quietly behind him.

'This Keril Dwar got close to Vek quite quickly, didn't she?' Varden Herl asked thoughtfully. 'Perhaps she is plotting against the woman for her own reasons.'

'I would guess you're right,' his wife, Li Kassu agreed. 'I've spoken to her a few times but although there is no doubt about her intelligence, she made it clear she wanted no overtures of friendship from me.'

Nami Char shifted in her chair. 'I've spoken to her on occasion too. Would it be worth trying to talk to her now? She must have an idea of whatever Mahzu Vek is up to.'

Ket Vos shrugged. 'By all means, if the opportunity arises, but we have more important matters to work on. When can we expect any response from those you've contacted Perra?'

Perra Koos frowned. 'Any time I should think, I didn't demand replies by any specific time.'

Tilliat was not present at this meeting. She was with Davin Pearl and Tani, preparing their packs for their journey north. Tani had furnished maps of his old estate and the lands further north of it, which he'd rescued from Perra's files. Giffu had fussed about the sparsity of their clothing and remedied their lack of trousers, shirts and underclothes from some mysterious store. Toomay watched the activity with interest. He felt so sorry for humans: what trouble they had with their need of clothing to keep them warm, cool or dry!

Tani's old estate was five days ride from Gulat so they would take supplies only for that time. Perra Koos was to give them a letter for the steward of the estate who would then supply them for travelling for at least a moon's full turn. While Tilliat chatted with Tani, Davin Pearl said very little. He was going over and over the letter Jomah had added to the scroll case in Kelshan.

Jomah explained that as soon as Tilliat left Traders' Hall, she had used her long-unused mage powers to try to follow Tilliat's mind. She had quickly become alarmed at not being able to find a trace of the girl but only a few days later, Pakal had become ill. He suffered torments of pain for two days before he died.

It was obvious to Jomah's mage sight that Pakal had been poisoned but it was a poison she did not recognise, nor did any of the healers or mageborn who she asked for help. Jomah did not grieve: she was enraged. Clearly *someone* had their suspicions of either her or Pakal being more than mere housekeeper and retired wagon driver.

She revealed her full mage strength to the few mages in the haven beneath Traders' Hall, and, combining their powers, they searched the minds of all in the building. Not one person was aware of their minds being tested but it was evident at once that Pirus Belk was the one who had arranged Pakal's death.

Four mages accompanied Jomah to visit the Master Trader unannounced. They also took two of the Traders' Council – Elim Konti and Jer Fasink. Davin knew both of those and guessed Jomah had tested their minds and found them trustworthy. Davin bit back a groan. He would have sworn any oath that Pirus Belk was a good man and worthy of trust, but he had been, so clearly, not.

Giffu thrust a steaming bowl of tea into his hands. She peered closer into his face.

'Are you ill, Master Pearl? You don't look too happy?'

Davin managed a smile. 'I was just thinking how much we'll miss your marvellous cooking, Giffu.'

Giffu flushed with pleasure. 'I'll pack a few honey cakes, never fear, but you make sure that sweet Dragon gets his share, Master Pearl.'

Davin's smile became genuine now. 'You are most kind, and yes, I'm sure I'll save him one or two.'

Giffu laughed and flapped her hands at him. 'You'll share them properly or you shall have no more.'

An armsman put his head round the door. 'Several messages for the master, cook.' He brandished a handful of rolled and sealed papers.

'Her name is Giffu.' Toomay's words rang in their heads.

The armsman appeared a trifle flustered but he nodded politely to the Dragon.

'Well they're no use to us, you foolish man. Take them up to the library.'

The armsman retreated and Tilliat looked at Tani. 'If Master Koos plans to hold a meeting here, Tani, I think it might be best if it was in that hut in the garden.'

Tani chuckled. 'That "hut" is a pavilion my dear child, but I take your point. A narrow hallway to reach the garden through the house, and armsmen patrolling round the building.'

Tilliat nodded. 'I hope we can leave early tomorrow. I'd prefer to be out of the way before any strangers arrive.'

Tani studied Toomay who was apparently dozing. 'I know you're listening.' He prodded the Dragon with his toe. 'You can seem to vanish, can you not?'

Toomay's eyes opened. 'For a short time, yes. Long enough to get beyond this place of Gulat.'

'And you will be inconspicuous enough in a hooded cloak,' Tani continued to Tilliat. 'Nami Char will walk with you, will she not? Or is her brother escorting you?'

Tilliat laughed. 'There was quite an argument. She won.'

Another door opened and Perra Koos came across to where Tani sat with Tilliat and Davin. Cloud climbed from Tani's lap to Davin's and gave Perra an emerald glare.

'A letter from a couple named Chay. I don't know them and sent no message to them. The Chars were rather dubious about them. But their letter says they know of you. Why would they write to *me*?'

Tilliat chewed her lip and Cloud spat before circling into a ball on Davin's knee. Perra looked puzzled. Tilliat explained briefly how the Chays knew her.

'May I see what they wrote?' she asked.

Perra handed the letter to her at once. Tilliat read it and grunted.

'It says "we" think, and "we" believe, but it is written in only one hand. I would wager Ty wrote this and signed her husband's name as well. I doubt he knows anything of it.' She handed the letter back and met Perra's dark blue eyes. 'Pitzi seemed a kind man but he is completely dominated by Ty. And she is a bitter woman, bears a grudge against the world and always belittles Pitzi. I would be very wary of her.'

'Thank you.' Perra nodded. 'I will keep that in mind.'

'Pitzi is a nice man,' Toomay remarked. 'The woman is not strong in power. She has a slight talent for healing and somehow she has bound the man to her. I do not know how.'

Silence followed those comments then Perra got to his feet. 'I shall tell the others. We are apparently eating in the dining room tonight, so let's feed you up before you leave, Tilliat.' He smiled. 'Giffu's orders.'

Tilliat returned his smile. She liked this man. She was fairly sure he had been deeply shocked by her first appearance, then by her partial healing of Tani's mind. He had also been surprised by the five mages who had descended on him in panic and promptly taken up residence in his house. She'd learned more than Perra might have guessed from both Tani and Giffu the cook, and felt she understood how he had earned his reputation for aloofness.

After a meal on which Giffu and her kitchen staff surpassed themselves, Tilliat and Davin Pearl made their farewells to most of the mages. Nami Char would be leaving with them early tomorrow but the rest would still be in their beds. Tilliat retired to the small room she'd been given, with Cloud, and tried to sleep. Her thoughts were too busy however, with the forthcoming journey even further to the north. When she managed to force her thoughts from that subject, she found Tetsura filling her mind. She no longer felt the fear which had been linked to him, and she was reasonably confident that he had found allies at least.

Finally Tilliat's mind spiralled back to Kelshan city and to what could be happening to Jomah within Traders' Hall. She mourned the loss of Pakal and tried to stem the sudden flood of tears. Cloud crept from her position in the crook of Tilliat's knees and squirmed close to her chest, purring steadily and ceaselessly.

'You were fond of him?' The cat's mind voice was gentle.

'He was always there,' Tilliat thought in reply. 'As solid and firm as the house itself.'

'Then you must remember all his goodness then farewell him in your heart. If he is safe in your heart you can find him whenever you choose.'

So Tilliat lay, curled round the grey cat, and remembered Pakal. And, eventually, she slept.

Long before dawn Tilliat and Davin Pearl were working their way through one of Giffu's magnificent breakfasts. Nami Char joined them before they'd finished and stared at the huge plateful Giffu placed in front of her with some astonishment.

'You've eaten this much?' she asked Tilliat.

'Mmm.' Tilliat leaned back, patting her stomach. 'Delicious. It will be five days from your house to Tani's before we might get fed again like this.'

Nami looked doubtful but began to eat. Her long dark hair was tied in a single braid down her back and she wore a thick green shirt tucked into grey trousers. Close to, Tilliat saw Nami's eyes were dark blue but, unlike Perra's, hers had a hint of green at their edges.

'How far is it to your house?' Davin enquired.

'We are near the west gate of the city here, so it is perhaps two miles to our manor. Not far really.'

Both Tilliat and Davin were grateful that Giffu had produced boots for them: the riding boots they had worn from Kelshan had proved most unsuitable for walking. Davin pushed himself up from the table.

'Well I think we should make a start – if you've finished?' He raised a brow at Nami Char.

She seemed surprised that she had in fact eaten everything on her plate. She'd brought her cloak down to the kitchen and when she raised her arms to swing it round her shoulders, Tilliat realised the woman had several weapons on her belt. Businesslike knives, she thought, probably easier to use than a sword.

Cloaked and laden with several packs, they had said goodbye to Giffu and Tani when the door to the stairs banged open. Taleb Char stood there, a huge grin on his face.

'I'm coming too.' He strode across the kitchen to join the others. 'Did you not hear the hammering on poor Perra's front door? At least ten of those we sent word to. They've just turned up.' He chuckled, looking much younger. 'And they seem intent on becoming Perra's guests. They're all carrying fairly large bags anyway.'

Giffu sprang into action, pulling a cord which rang a bell in the staff rooms, and stoking her stove to greater effort.

'Let's go then.' Tilliat gave a tearful Tani one last hug and reached for the door. She found Mink and three other armsmen waiting for them.

'Master Koos said we're to see you safe to the Char manor.'

They all watched when Toomay squeezed past and paced out into the still dark garden. Davin cleared his throat. 'Lead on then,' he said as cheerfully as he could manage.

Cloud rode in a small pack Tilliat had slung across her chest. They left the house and followed Mink along a fairly wide street in which loomed other buildings with blank walls and heavy gates. They met no one until they neared the huge city gates. The gates were open and a few people were entering, pushing handcarts and carrying large bundles.

'Folk coming to set up stalls in one or other of the market squares,' Mink explained quietly then he raised his voice to hail a group of armsmen in grey and black uniforms.

'City militia,' Taleb muttered, moving alongside Tilliat.

'Not on duty?' one of the uniformed men asked, indicating Mink's unadorned cloak.

'No. Day off. Going to look at some early foals at Mistress Char's manor.'

Nami Char had pushed her hood back a little and to Tilliat's disbelief, Nami fluttered her lashes and actually simpered a little.

Taleb nudged Tilliat onwards and, with Davin and two of Perra Koos's armsmen, they walked through the gate. Tilliat was impressed with the thickness of the city walls. The Citadel in Kelshan city she had thought well built, but this gate in Gulat's walls took thirty paces to pass through.

The morning was still more dark than light but Tilliat found they were in another sort of city. This one had narrow streets and lanes, and houses and shacks built haphazardly, wherever anyone had found some space. There were still very few people about and Taleb picked up the pace, hurrying through twisting ways until they came out onto what Tilliat would have termed a road. The sky was at last showing signs of dawn to Tilliat's right. Taleb slowed, glancing back over his shoulder. Tilliat followed his gaze and saw three figures striding towards them. She recognised the broad shoulders of Mink beside the slighter shape of Nami Char, and following them, the armsman guarding their backs.

Tilliat looked up to the sky. 'Are you safe Toomay?' she thought.

'I am high above you, friend Tilliat. I will see you soon.'

The group walked steadily on with little conversation. More people appeared on the road and a few horsedrawn carts. Most called a good morning and Mink made the replies. After about a mile, they turned off the road onto a narrower track. Tilliat heard Nami Char let out a gusty sigh of relief when they reached a stone wall, about head high, and an iron barred gate. Taleb gave a low three note whistle and two men emerged from a small building beyond the gate.

'Morning to you, Master Char,' one of them called cheerfully. 'And to you Mistress.'

'Hello captain,' both twins replied, while the man unbarred the gate.

'At least it isn't raining for your walk from the city.'

'No,' agreed Taleb. 'But it's cold enough to change to worse than rain again.'

They walked on, listening to the man laughing behind them. Rounding a small group of evergreen trees, a building came into view. It looked a solidly constructed, large farmhouse, similar to those outside Kelshan, Tilliat thought. As they drew closer, she saw that the house was more fortified than it appeared at first glance. There were iron slats set across the lower windows making a pleasant diamond pattern, but Tilliat guessed they would be strong enough to deter most intruders. Walls joined the house on both sides, probably enclosing a large yard she thought, but definitely improving the defences of the place. A shallow flight of steps led to a door, narrower than might have been expected, which was opened by an elderly man as they reached it.

He bowed them in then closed the door, sliding an inner metal gate across the wood of the door. Yes, thought Tilliat, it really looks as if they live in constant expectation of raiders.

Taleb was speaking urgently to the man while Nami led them further into the house. It was now light enough to see through the windows that there was indeed a large enclosed area behind the house, bound on all four sides by buildings. Nami called a name and a younger man appeared.

'These are four of Master Koos's armsmen. They will look at the new foals please. And ask Thias to prepare eight horses for us. Four saddled and four to take packs.'

The man vanished at once. Tilliat saw him crossing the open area to where several horses had their heads out over their stable doors, watching his approach with interest.

'Why don't you just sit for a while?' Nami asked sweetly. 'I promise it won't be long until the horses are ready.'

She made for the door but Tilliat stood in her way. '*Four* horses saddled?' she asked, her tone as sweet as Nami's had been.

'Mmm. We thought we'd join you.' Nami slid round Tilliat and left her speechless.

Davin sat on a couch by the window and grinned at the expression on Tilliat's face.

'It would be good to have company surely, Tilliat. And they know Toomay. And they are mages.'

'Yes, but how strong are their powers? Can they be trusted? We go into danger for sure, Uncle Davin.'

A voice in her head murmured: 'Very strong. Trust. Great danger.'

'Oh.' The Shadows surprised Tilliat. They had been very quiet since the message delivery dispute. 'They will have to know about *you* if they travel with us.'

A long silence.

Tilliat waited. 'You said they can be trusted.'

'Tell later.'

Davin was watching her. He guessed she was mindspeaking the Shadows or Toomay. Her eyes seemed to lose their focus, he'd noticed, when she used mindspeech. Cloud clawed her way out of her pack and bumped her head against Tilliat's chin.

'You can't worry about *everything*. They may be a great

help.'

Tilliat tilted her head so she could look into the cat's emerald eyes but before she could reply, Nami returned.

'Ready?' she asked, then frowned. 'I didn't know you brought that cat. I hope it won't be a nuisance.'

Cloud spat in Nami's direction and slid back down into the pack beneath Tilliat's cloak. Davin stood up.

'Won't your people here wonder where you're off to?' He followed Nami from the room.

'They're used to us coming and going. We have a small house in Gulat, quite near Perra, where we often spend most of the winter. And we sometimes spend a lot of the summer with our herds, on the grazing lands to the east.'

'This is most definitely *not* summer,' Tilliat commented when icy grains slapped into her face once they were out in the courtyard.

They rode out through several paddocks where other horses trotted alongside the fences to keep pace with the riders, until halted by the next fence. By midday, the sudden brief bursts of icy rain had ceased and the four riders had got onto a narrow track, wide enough for them to go two abreast.

Toomay spiralled down when they made camp that evening and seemed pleased with the welcome he received. Tilliat and Davin were both surprised that the weather seemed to warm over the next four days. They were heading directly north and yet it felt far less cold than in Gulat. Davin Pearl was relieved – he hadn't enjoyed the prospect of camping at night in freezing conditions.

On the fifth afternoon they rode round the side of a low hill and saw Tani's house. The Char twins frowned. They had never ridden here before but they were shocked to see what a sprawling, unprotected scatter of buildings made up Tani's estate. Riding towards the buildings, they saw several people working in fields and gardens near the main building. None of them seemed surprised or alarmed at the sudden appearance of four strangers.

A woman emerged from the main house and stood waiting for them. She smiled as they dismounted, handing off the reins and leading ropes to several small children who materialised round their feet.

'Welcome to The Roost. Please come in and enjoy baths and food before you ride on.'

'The Roost?' Taleb Char asked, letting the others enter the house ahead of him.

'That was the name Master Tani gave this place. I never knew him alas, but Master Perra insisted it remain the same, even after the poor old man fell into madness. My name is Tara Syen. I am the steward here.'

'And you were expecting us,' Nami remarked, turning in the hall to face the woman.

'Yes indeed. Master Perra asked a crow to bring word of your arrival. You are Taleb and Nami Char, Davin Pearl and Tilliat Kranch, the Mage Foretold.' She bowed to Tilliat then indicated they go on through the hallway.

They found themselves in a large airy room which was half kitchen and half comfortable living room.

'Would you prefer to bathe first, or eat?' Tara Syen asked.

Tilliat sent the lightest mindtouch to the woman then immediately pulled back, but not before Tara's smile had deepened.

'Yes, I am mageborn,' she answered the unspoken question. 'My talent is for growing things and for healing.'

Nami Char and Davin Pearl chose to soak in hot baths before they ate, leaving Tilliat and Taleb to start eating. The cook was introduced as Tara Syen's husband, Laris, and he served them fresh bread and soup to keep them going whilst he got on with making something more substantial.

They had been aware of voices outside, adults calling and children's higher-pitched chatter and laughter, when Tilliat became aware that silence had fallen. Tara was bringing them a large pot of tea but she froze staring over her shoulder to the window. Tilliat choked on breadcrumbs and made for the outer door. A long silvery face was pressed against the window, huge eyes sparkling with mischief. Tilliat gave Tara an apologetic smile.

'This is Dragon Toomay. He is a dear friend and travels with us,' she explained.

Toomay paused beside her and she gave him a hug, then he

259

paced carefully in to the kitchen. Tara's husband dropped a pan from nerveless fingers. Toomay studied the man with interest.

'I wonder, do you make honey cakes like our dearest friend, Giffu?' His mind voice was gentle, but hopeful, and Laris closed his mouth, retrieved the pan and smiled.

'I certainly do. And cinnamon buns.' He reached for a large pottery jar then sighed.

Tilliat followed his gaze and struggled to hide her smile. Children crowded the doorway, staring at the Dragon, settled comfortably in their kitchen. She cleared her throat.

'Go and sit with him. He'll love to meet you, I'm sure.'

'I've never seen human children,' Toomay murmured to Tilliat alone. 'They are most extraordinarily small aren't they?'

Chapter Twenty-Three

Tetsura had enjoyed his time outside the Phoenix Palace enormously. Two days later he still chuckled each time he thought of his appearance in the Sea Slug. The first person to be aware of his presence was Saima, and she had laughed, and laughed, and laughed. She had come forward and bowed low before him, her shoulders shaking with mirth. She introduced her husband and Tetsura was surprised at Deng's short, plump shape and unremarkable looks. Very quickly he was aware of the real devotion between the two.

The regular patrons sat dumbfounded at finding themselves in the same room as their Crown Prince. Tetsura had decided he and his entourage would have their midday meal there and serving girls dashed madly back and forth. Commander Anjit also thoroughly enjoyed himself, although he kept his expression suitably impassive. He particularly enjoyed the moment when Prince Tetsura had turned to him, his face stricken.

'I've no coin,' he'd hissed. 'Will you lend me some, Anjit?'

'Certainly Your Highness. I am yours to command.'

Tetsura's eyes narrowed. 'I will repay you of course.'

'Of course you will.'

They had wandered through the flower district after leaving the Sea Slug and Tetsura chatted happily to anyone who wished to talk to him. He'd been aware of course, of Commander Anjit and the handpicked Phoenix Guards of his escort, keeping a very close eye on everything around them. But Tetsura did not know how high he'd risen not only in the Commander's estimation, but also in all those ordinary people he'd come in contact with that day.

Tetsura knew that although his servant Vilad had been so very proud of his Prince, he was also extremely worried about Regent Hikmat's reaction. It was not long in coming. That very same evening, Tetsura had been summoned to the Regent's presence.

It was only then that it dawned on Tetsura that the Regent lived in the suite of rooms previously used by the Kings of Vremilia. Tetsura castigated himself for his wilful blindness over so many years.

When he entered the Regent's rooms he was kept standing in front of the seated Hikmat. But Tetsura kept a tight hold on his emotions and showed only boyish enthusiasm as he described his outing. He felt Hikmat's fury, which the Regent failed to conceal completely under an attitude of condescension. Hikmat informed the Prince that there would be a rehearsal tomorrow afternoon so that Tetsura would know exactly how the new Ceremony of Presentation would unfold in the Great Hall of Phoenix Kings.

The Prince looked thoughtful. 'The afternoon you say? I should be back by then.'

'Back? Back from where?' Hikmat almost spat the words, his hands clenching on the arms of his chair and his brows drawing down.

'I accepted an invitation from Master Retan Minoak, sir. As I have visited the Jewellers' Guild, I felt I shouldn't show interest in one Guild over any other. Was that not correct sir?'

It was a visible effort for Hikmat to control himself, and for one moment, Tetsura thought the Regent might actually rise and strike him. There were four Guards standing to attention by the doorway. Tetsura was aware, with his awakened mage sense, that they had become alert, realising as the Prince did, how angry Hikmat had become.

But the moment passed. Hikmat gave a curt nod and lifted some papers from the table at his side. He waved a dismissal.

'Make sure you are not late tomorrow boy.'

Tetsura gave the most minimal bow he dared to the Regent, and left his presence.

In his apartments again, Tetsura stared out over the city. He heard someone at the outer door, then Vilad joined him on the small balcony. Vilad touched the Prince's arm and tilted his head towards the reception room. Tetsura went through and found Sergeant Tag.

'You suggested a stroll in the gardens Your Highness.'

Tetsura knew he'd suggested no such thing but he agreed with alacrity. As ever Tetsura led the way, Vilad and Sergeant Tag a pace behind on each side of him.

'Heard the Regent isn't too happy with you,' Tag muttered once they were outside.

Tetsura snorted. 'News travels fast.'

Tag squinted a quick glance up at him. 'There were Guards present.'

'Aaah.' Tetsura stopped to examine a flowering vine covering an archway. 'He seemed more agitated than I've ever seen him.'

Tag stepped closer, peering at the flowers. 'He's more rattled than he's been since you were born, Your Highness. Everyone knows the Crowning takes place one moon's turn after the Presentation. It has only now occurred to our revered Regent that you might not be quite so easy to control as he has so confidently believed.'

They wandered on towards Tetsura's favourite herb gardens and hot houses.

'The Commander has made contact with the merchants who were planning trouble. He has persuaded them to act under his orders. There is a small group within the Guards who have been plotting the downfall of Commander Anjit.'

'*What*?' Tetsura interrupted in alarm.

Tag pointed to a tiny rose that had entwined itself among the bigger blossoms of the vine.

'They are idiots. Don't worry. The plotters are the stupid sons of wealthy families. They only joined the Guards to show off their uniforms and throw their weight about. They will be taken care of.'

'When will the action against Hikmat begin?'

Tag strolled on without giving an answer until they were nearing the first hot house.

'Your Presentation will be in five days time. The day after will find a great many citizens slow to be about their usual work, and thus far fewer on the streets.'

Five days. Five days and Hikmat would fall. Tetsura frowned. Would Hikmat be taken prisoner or be killed? If he was taken prisoner, what sentence would Tetsura pass on the man? So far, the Prince had only considered his own freedom from Hikmat's power over him. It suddenly dawned on him just how drastically his life was about to change.

263

He must give serious thought to who he could trust as advisors, as governors, as officers of the Palace. He foresaw many long days of thinking, discussions, and of hard work. But he looked forward to it with determination, eagerness and pride.

Tilliat, Davin, Nami and Taleb stayed one night at The Roost and were well supplied when they set off the next morning. Most of the people who worked on the estate, and all of the children, waved them off. Toomay drifted to the height of the main house, then dived, fast, over the children, who shrieked with delight. Tilliat laughed. Toomay slowed and moved more steadily a little ahead of the horses His mind tone had a hint of embarrassment.

'They enjoyed it friend Tilliat. They like to play, just like Dragon children. I will watch for any trouble.' He climbed higher until he was a speck in the sky.

Nami kicked her horse up beside Tilliat. 'He is very young, isn't he?'

Tilliat glanced at her. 'He told me he is twenty-eight years old, but he won't be considered adult until he is one hundred.'

Nami stared at Tilliat. 'You've met adult Dragons.'

Tilliat shifted in her saddle. 'Yes. Two of them. But I can tell you nothing of that.'

'We're travelling north because of something Tani told you. About Reva?'

'He said there is someone called the Pathmaker, who lives in the north. Tani thinks this person may – *may* – be able to help. It might just be a straw in the wind, but I had a strong feeling he was right.'

Two days from The Roost the wider track petered out and they then rode for four more days following barely discernible trails. Davin took charge of cooking a meal each evening and Nami proved excellent at snaring rabbits. The sixth evening they sat around their small fire, replete from their supper, Toomay reclining behind Tilliat. Up to now, conversation between the four had been general, the Chars broaching no awkward subjects. This night it was Toomay who spoke into the peaceful quiet.

'There are wild humans around. They watch you but I feel no danger from them. They have seen me and I felt an agitation from their minds.' Toomay's eyes whirred briefly then calmed. 'I did not try to speak with them.'

'I'd guess they are the ones Tani told me of,' said Tilliat. 'I think we should just keep riding until they choose to show themselves.'

'And Tani has met them?' asked Taleb.

'Long ago, when he was only young. His parents died when he was a small child and he went to live at The Roost with his father's parents. He inherited the place when they died.' Tilliat leaned forward to poke a twig into the embers.

'Have you noticed the weather is so different?' That was Nami.

Tilliat sighed. 'This whole stretch of land is different. Haven't *you* noticed the leaves are fully out on many trees, and they weren't even in bud in Gulat, which is south of here.'

'Why do we know nothing of this place? We live at no great distance,' Taleb objected.

Tilliat gave him a rueful smile. 'But you've never had any inclination to travel this far north have you? I'll wager you've even felt a slight aversion to the very idea of coming here.'

The twins exchanged startled glances.

'But we've come this far with you,' said Nami. 'I haven't felt any sort of discomfort.'

'No. Whoever the people are ahead, they want us – well, they want *me* – to visit them.'

'Tani didn't tell you that.' Nami's tone was definite.

Davin grunted with amusement. 'Tilliat's – friends – probably did.'

Toomay's eyes flashed, his wings rustling against his back. The Char twins simply stared at Tilliat, obviously waiting for an explanation. Her eyes seemed slightly blurred in the faint firelight, but Taleb leaned forward.

'You're mindspeaking,' he accused her.

Tilliat glared at him.

'They really don't want to be talked about,' she snapped.

The Chars continued to stare at her. She sighed again.

'They are Shadows,' she said simply.

Taleb frowned. 'Shadows?' he repeated. 'Never heard of them.'

Tilliat spoke aloud: 'Shadows, hide me please.' And vanished from sight.

Nami toppled off the log she was perched on but Taleb stretched across and waved his hand where Tilliat had been.

'Hah! You're still there. How did you do that?'

'Shadows, move me to the other side of the fire, but still hidden,' Tilliat thought.

Taleb frowned. 'She's gone.'

'No she hasn't.' Davin Pearl stretched his legs towards the fire and smiled at Tilliat, who had reappeared, seated beside Taleb.

Taleb jumped and glared at Tilliat. 'Very funny I'm sure. Who are they, and what do they look like?'

Toomay spoke in their minds. 'Thorn said Tilliat could trust them completely.'

Little more was said after that and the small company soon settled to sleep.

Toomay watched over them, his mind sweeping the area for some distance around. He sensed nothing other than the small night creatures, hunting and hiding, among the undergrowth. He was more content now they were away from Gulat. While he'd been fascinated by Perra Koos's house, and had grown fond of Tani and Giffu, he had been constantly aware of the violence and turmoil in those countless humans in the city. The discordant mind cries had been difficult to block out.

It was a relief to be in wild lands again. He laid his head on his front feet and closed his eyes. He was surprised by how protective he'd become of this female, Tilliat, and was glad now that he had obeyed the Council of Elders and gone to find her.

Tilliat lay awake, Cloud snoring softly near her face. She knew the others were asleep and Toomay was dozing lightly, but the Shadows were muttering in her mind.

'See.'

Tilliat caught her breath. She was looking over a city, the city she had glimpsed in dreams for so long. It was dark, just past sunset she guessed, and crowds of people thronged in front of her. Suddenly there was a great burst of colour above the crowds: huge shapes of flowers cascading through the sky.

'Brother makes.' The Shadows sounded almost proud.

Tilliat saw a great golden circle appear, held in the claws of a golden bird which had long tail feathers of brilliant scarlet. Something was growing within the circle and Tilliat saw it was a golden Dragon. It was not like Thorn or Toomay. *This* Dragon resembled the ones she had seen in Thorn's mind pictures. Finally the Dragon filled the circle beneath the bird, its wings spread to touch each side.

'I did it sister! I did it!'

And Tilliat knew her brother had performed this magic and the Shadows had let her share the moment. She hoped Tetsura would gain control of his kingdom with as little bloodshed as possible. She sent a thought of congratulation, affection, and a warning to guard his back, hoping the Shadows would let Tetsura hear her.

In Garjetka, Tetsura had followed the new rituals devised by the Regent, Hikmat. He had been borne through the city streets in an open carriage, garlanded with flowers, as were the streets and buildings. He had re entered the Phoenix Palace and dined with the Governors and advisors and councillors, none of whom he knew. Hikmat retained the prime position beneath the Canopy of State and Phoenix Guards in ceremonial uniforms lined the banqueting hall. Tetsura turned to Vilad who stood behind his Prince's chair.

'Take this to Commander Anjit. I will go to the Great Balcony shortly.'

Vilad bowed. He took the folded paper from Tetsura and walked along the side of the table. A touch on the Commander's shoulder and the paper changed hands. Anjit read the paper, looked back up the table and found Tetsura's gaze on him. Anjit nodded and pushed back his chair.

Hikmat was leaning towards the man on his left, deep in conversation, when Commander Anjit and six of the Phoenix Guards snapped to attention behind the Prince. Tetsura rose, gave a formal bow to the dinner guests, and marched from the hall. A silence echoed behind him but he didn't turn, just concentrated ahead, on what he hoped to do.

Guards swung open the doors leading to the room from which the Great Balcony projected. Tetsura paused for a heartbeat.

'Stay close Commander.'

Anjit murmured an order and four Guards stood across the

entrance to the balcony, facing back into the room, a solid wall of gold and scarlet uniforms.

Someone among the crowds below spotted movement on the high balcony. Word spread and faces turned up. Tetsura drew in a great breath and raised his hands, the embroidered sleeves of his Presentation robe falling back to his elbows. Vilad trembled in a corner, awed by the amount of power he felt the boy drawing to himself.

Then the sky burst with light and colour: torrents of rainbow hues, flowers swelling like fireworks. Finally, the huge Phoenix appeared, holding a circle which gradually filled with a great Dragon. Vilad slid to the floor, weeping with joy. Commander Anjit breathed a heartfelt sigh of relief. And the crowds roared their approval.

At the eighth camp from The Roost, Toomay informed the travellers that the ground dropped away sharply only a mile or two further north. Taleb thought for a moment.

'We've been going, very gradually, uphill since we left The Roost. So I'd guess we're considerably higher than the land closer to Gulat.'

'But it feels no colder,' objected Nami. 'And it should do, especially at this time of the year.'

Davin Pearl poured himself a bowl of tea and settled back. 'We agreed the land was different days ago,' he said. 'I'm not worrying about it. At least be thankful we're not wet, or freezing in our bedrolls.'

They'd followed Toomay for the last two days, heading always north, as even the faint animal trails had vanished. After the Dragon told them they were being watched, Tilliat had suggested, firmly, that Taleb, Nami nor she herself, should try to mindsense beyond their immediate vicinity. Taleb now glanced over his shoulder at the darkening land.

'I've felt no mind probing towards us. Have you Tilliat?'

'No I haven't. I've kept my mind shielded lightly, not enough to miss any attempt to touch my thoughts. I would prefer not to let these people know how strong any of us might be.'

'Have these Shadow friends of yours told you anything?' asked Nami.

'No.' Tilliat's annoyance was plain. 'They have been remark-ably quiet. I know they are here, but they are offering no inform-ation at all.'

'But they will help us if danger threatens?'

'I hope so.' Privately, Tilliat wondered if the Shadows *would* help the Chars. She had ordered the Shadows to protect Cloud and Uncle Davin, but they had been reluctant to do even that until she lost her temper with them.

'That's all right then.' Nami sounded satisfied. 'Tell us a trading story Uncle.'

Davin Pearl obliged, amused by the increasing number of nephews and nieces he seemed to be accumulating.

Sure enough, early the next morning, they found themselves on the lip of a cliff. Below, trees stretched endlessly into the distance, spreading out in a huge bowl of land. Mostly they had encountered bushy shrubs, heathers, and the occasional small group of trees clustered together like wives at a market. Toomay flew out over the tops of trees which were level with the clifftop.

'There is a winding path a little further on,' he told the riders. 'It goes under the trees but it leads down to the lower place, I can be sure.'

Tilliat shrugged and nudged her horse on along the clifftop. Toomay drifted alongside then turned and floated a little higher.

'Here is the place.

Tilliat dismounted and Cloud, perched on her shoulder, dug claws in after one alarmed look down.

'Put me back in that bag.' The cat's thought was shrill with panic in Tilliat's head.

Once Cloud was safely stowed away, Tilliat leaned further out, holding on to a bush to steady herself. Taleb joined her.

'It looks fine.'

Tilliat gave him a look of disbelief.

'No, it does. It's just this first drop which the horses will fuss about then it goes down quite gradually.'

Tilliat sent a thought to Toomay. 'Can you persuade the horses to stay calm, like you did in those tunnels?'

'Of course.'

It took a surprisingly short time to convince eight horses to

269

drop the height of a man over the cliff edge onto a short stretch of flat ground. Remounting, Tilliat noticed Nami looked rather pale. She gave Tilliat a shaky smile.

'I don't much like heights, and I thought we'd have bad trouble with the horses.'

Taleb led the way, letting his mount pick its way down the incline. Tilliat watched him gently tug the leading rope and the pack horse followed calmly enough. Nami shrugged and moved after her brother.

'You next,' Davin ordered Tilliat.

She laughed and did as he told her. Uncle Davin was determined always to watch her back.

Taleb and Nami were soon speechless. The lower they went, the bigger the trees. Tilliat and Davin recognised them as being the same as the trees in Thorn's Realm. Twice they heard the sound of water rushing fast close by but didn't see any river. Tiny springs burst across their path and then vanished as abruptly as they'd appeared. It was nearing sunset when at last the ground levelled out and they saw Toomay reclining a short way on.

At last they saw the water they'd heard on their ride. Toomay was staring to the side, up the slope they had just descended. A great fall cascaded down from near the top of the cliff, a narrow line which fell to crash into a pool below Toomay. Water churned and splashed but only a little further on, it smoothed into a widening lake, whose far shore was too distant to make out.

They all dismounted, gazing in awe at the tumbling water falling between the giant trees. Toomay gave a gusting sigh and shivered his wings against his back.

'I do not believe Thorn knows of this place.' His eyelashes flickered when he looked back at the four humans. 'Our Realm is not far from here, but we never fly beyond our lands. Thorn will be glad to know there are heart trees still growing here. If you make a fire, be sure to use only fallen wood.'

Davin cut out a square of turf and collected some large pebbles from the waterside while Tilliat searched for fallen twigs and branches. By unspoken agreement, Nami made no attempt to venture into the trees in search of rabbits and they used only the supplies in the saddle packs to make a meal. Taleb and Nami kept staring towards the enormous trees and the wide avenues beneath them leading in every direction.

'Thorn told us the lands were covered in forests of these trees long, long ago,' Davin told the Chars. 'He thought the ones in his land were the last of their kind.'

A full moon glided over the cliffs, its pale reflection fractured at the bottom of the fall but forming a wavering path further out across the lake.

'It is just so amazing,' Taleb murmured. 'Yet it is so close to Gulat.'

Davin frowned and gave Toomay a suspicious look. 'We've been nine days travelling, Toomay. Time hasn't been involved in anyway – has it?'

'Certainly not.' Toomay's mind voice was offended.

'Sorry,' Davin apologised. 'Is it like that barrier magic then, that deters people from coming here?'

'Something like.'

The Shadows sniggered in Tilliat's head but she ignored them. She was looking over the lake and could have sworn she'd seen some of the slender silvery shapes which she'd presumed were the Shadows themselves when she'd seen them before.

'Who are they Toomay?' She directed her thought to Toomay alone.

'Ancient Ones.' The words were barely a whisper in her mind and the tone was one of great reverence.

Tilliat blinked, and the tenuous shapes were gone. The Char twins were already rolled in their blankets when Tilliat turned back to the fire. Cloud was crouched by Davin's knees. Tilliat stroked a finger down the cat's back.

'Not hunting tonight, little one?'

Emerald eyes glittered in the moonlight. 'I think not here,' Cloud replied. 'This is a strange place.'

'Having regrets about choosing to come with us?' Tilliat teased.

Cloud's long moustache bristled forward as she yawned. 'Certainly not. It is all very interesting after the tedium of the Chay house. But this place *does* feel strange.'

'I know, but it doesn't feel threatening to me – just different.'

Davin pulled his blankets around him and Cloud squirmed under them against the trader's chest.

'Do *you* regret coming, Uncle Davin?' Tilliat asked quietly.

He reached out for her hand. 'It isn't quite what I'd planned for my retirement.'

Tilliat gave a gurgle of laughter and settled back in her blankets.

'But I am glad I'm with you Tilliat. You know I have always cared for you, and for Stevro. I shudder to think what could have happened if I had *not* been with you when Skala Vek made you so ill. I suspect he would have killed you outright rather than go through the pretence of trying to cure your "mystery" illness. And I am grateful to have met Toomay and Thorn. So to answer your question seriously: no, Tilliat. Not for one heartbeat do I regret coming on this journey. Although, I do miss my pipe, and I'm trying very hard not to think of what might lie ahead of us.'

Tilliat gave his hand a firm squeeze and tugged her blankets closer.

'And I cannot tell you how glad I am of your company Uncle Davin.'

Chapter Twenty-Four

For two days, the small company rode along the eastern side of the lake. They caught glimpses of deer at the water's edge early in the mornings but they saw few signs of other animals. There were birds in profusion and all seemed unafraid of the strangers. The grass was lush and green in the open but did not grow far beneath the trees. The sun was sinking westward and they were about to halt for the night. Taleb had been looking out over the lake for some time.

'I'm sure I could catch a couple of those fish we've seen jumping.'

They all looked to Tilliat, who shrugged. 'I see no reason why you shouldn't have a try.'

Tilliat and Davin Pearl rode on with all the horses, leaving Taleb and Nami to try their skills at fishing. Surprisingly the twins caught them up while Tilliat was still attending to the horses and Davin starting a campfire. They each held a very large fish. Taleb looked slightly worried.

'They were so easy to catch. They came straight to the bank when we just waggled our fingers in the water.'

'We know there *must* be people here and yet the birds show no fear. Perhaps no one catches fish, so the poor things don't know to avoid you,' said Tilliat.

Taleb waved a fish at her. 'If you don't want any of the "poor fish" for supper, all the more for us!'

Tilliat grinned. 'I'll be delighted with some of your fish for a change. We ate a lot of fish in Kelshan city.'

'We have fish sometimes in Gulat, but it is very costly.' Nami said, wrapping the fish in leaf parcels and arranging them on stones in the fire.

Tilliat woke next morning and lay quietly. She realised she'd been sleeping more soundly since they'd come down the cliff into this oddly isolated country. She heard Davin Pearl moving around and pushed her blankets back. When would the people Tani had spoken of make their appearance? But Tilliat felt no sense of urgency, although Tani had said all must be resolved by the time of the next full moon.

Later, they were approaching the northern end of the lake, which had been narrowing since they set off that morning. They saw the water moving faster again, channelling through a gap ahead. Once more they heard the rushing roar which had been their introduction to the high waterfall on their first day here.

Taleb, in the lead, drew rein and halted just where water like glass slid down and out of view. The others stopped beside him. Two pillars stood, one on each bank. About manheight, four-sided and pointed at the top, there were inscriptions carved into each face of the pillars. Davin urged his horse closer to the pillar on their side of the water.

'I've seen one like these before.' He frowned in concentration.

Toomay settled beside them. 'There are some like this in our Realm.' He spoke in all their minds.

'What do the carvings say, Toomay?' asked Nami.

Toomay shivered his wings. 'I do not know. We do not make marks on stone or paper or wood, like humans do.'

'Have they always been there, in your Realm?' Tilliat leaned down from her horse to touch the Dragon's face. He seemed very disturbed by these stone pillars.

'They have always been there,' he agreed. 'We respect them, but we do not go close to them.'

Taleb turned his mount away from the water and rode past the pillar, finding he had to bear quite abruptly to the right. The bank on his left sheared away in a mist of water droplets. Toomay rose in the air, flying out over the drop. Tilliat saw the Dragon swerve and tilt, as if buffeted by a sudden wind, and held her breath until his flight steadied.

Only then did she follow Nami down the curving bank. She was watching the ground to be sure her horse's footing was secure. So she was taken by surprise when she found herself far too close to Nami's packhorse, with Davin crowding up behind. Her horse jigged, trying to avoid the one in front and it took a moment for Tilliat to be able to raise her eyes to see what was causing the hold up.

A man and a woman stood quietly in front of Taleb's horse, their eyes fastened on Tilliat. The two strangers bowed, turned and led the way on. Taleb and Nami pulled their horses to the side, letting Tilliat and Davin pass them. Taleb took the leading rope of Tilliat's spare horse and indicated she should go first. She rode after the two strangers, studying them from behind.

Both seemed quite a bit taller than usual, both were dark but the sunlight picked out red glints in the man's loose, shoulderlength hair. The woman's hair was in a braid which reached her lower back. Both wore trousers and tunics of a pale brown shade: Tilliat guessed their clothes were of tanned leather rather than cloth, although amazingly supple. They appeared to carry no weapons other than a long knife, sheathed at their belts, but the woman had a long staff in her left hand which she used to help her walk. Clearly there was something wrong with her right leg. Neither wore either shoes or boots.

Tilliat and her companions followed. The only sounds were birdsong, the creak of saddles and harness, the muffled hoofbeats and occasional snort from one of the horses. They were led away from the open space beside the water and in under the massive trees. All the trees looked the same to Tilliat, but their guides turned this way and that as confidently as she would have travelled Kelshan city's streets.

Once among the trees, the light became diffuse; they could see very little sky overhead so it wasn't easy to judge how long they travelled. Just as Tilliat's stomach gave a growl of hunger, she saw a break in the trees ahead. The woman stopped. The man walked on to a small camp where bedrolls were tidily stacked beside a cold fireplace. The woman looked up at Tilliat and smiled for the first time.

'We will stop here for a while and travel on tomorrow.'

Tilliat saw the woman was considerably older than she'd first thought, and her eyes, a bright sky blue, looked weary and worried. The woman spoke the common tongue but with a strong, lilting accent. Tilliat slid from her horse and began the usual routine of unpacking and unsaddling. Davin joined her and helped rub the horses down. Their male guide came over to them

275

with a leather bucket of water.

'There is a spring just over there if you need more.' He pointed beyond the nearest trees.

Davin Pearl took the bucket. 'Thank you.'

The man nodded. 'Join us when your animals are settled.'

Taleb lifted some of the packs they'd unloaded. 'I don't recognise the accent,' he murmured to Tilliat. 'I still can't understand how any people could live so close to Gulat and we know nothing of them.'

'Nor I, unless they really do hide this area with magic, as the Dragon Realm is hidden.' Tilliat caught his arm. 'I know I am the youngest here, but please let me do the talking?'

Taleb nodded and began to walk across to the strangers. Nami followed with another armful of packs.

'Where's Toomay?' she hissed as she passed Tilliat.

Tilliat looked up but could see no Dragon.

'Toomay?' She directed the thought on a tight beam to his mind alone. 'Are you safe?'

'Yes friend Tilliat. I am near but I would hear what these strange ones say to you before I come there.'

'Very well. Stay safe Toomay.'

She heaved her saddle over her shoulder and walked with Davin across to the camp where a fire now burned and a kettle swung above it.

By the time Tilliat and her friends had sorted out their belongings and sat by the fire, the man was pouring tea into the bowls Davin had retrieved from his pack.

Tilliat smiled. 'Uncle seems to live on tea,' she said, accepting a bowl with thanks.

The woman laughed. 'I'm afraid I too am devoted to my tea. My name is Kufu and I am the spirit speaker of my people. We are called the Yasharitza people.' Blue eyes studied them all. 'We know you already. We have watched you for some time before you entered our land – as you well know.'

Tilliat gazed back at the woman.

'I will come,' Toomay whispered to Tilliat's mind.

She got to her feet, noting there appeared no awareness in the woman's face that mindspeech had just been used. She stepped a little away from the fire and Toomay drifted over the trees. Kufu and the man hissed and also stood, the woman holding her staff as if she depended on its support.

Toomay landed and paced towards Tilliat, his eyes whirring as a sign of his anxiety. Tilliat touched his cheek then turned back to the others, her left arm slipping casually across the Dragon's shoulders. Slowly, the two strangers reseated themselves. Kufu sighed, her gaze at last moving from Toomay to Tilliat.

'I would hear the tale of where you found him and how you tamed him.'

Out of the corner of her eye, Tilliat saw Davin Pearl stiffen.

'*He* found *me*, and saved me and Uncle Davin from death.' She sat down, Toomay settling at her back, his chin on her shoulder.

Kufu glanced at the man beside her, then back to Tilliat.

'This is my grandson, Ryo. I am old and find travelling wearisome. You come from the house of Tani.'

Tilliat sipped her tea. 'Tani told me of you. Did you know he has spent long years in madness?'

Kufu bowed her head.

Toomay spoke, his words clear in all their minds. 'My friend Tilliat healed poor Tani's madness.'

Kufu stared, her face suddenly white. Her grandson dropped his tea bowl and gaped.

'He speaks mind to mind,' Kufu whispered.

Tilliat raised an eyebrow. 'Many do. Do you not?'

Kufu still seemed stunned. 'A very few of us can, only after many years of training. It was a common talent among us when my parents were babes.'

'Tani suggested your people knew something of Reva, the god of Gulat.'

The man Ryo spat onto the ground. Tilliat thought he was the same age as the Chars or perhaps a little older. Now, he snarled across the fire and Tilliat felt Toomay shiver.

'Reva is no god. He is evil. He is not even of this world.'

Kufu laid a hand on his arm. 'We will not discuss this now, when darkness is drawing near. It is best spoken of in bright day, and with the Wise Ones of our people gathered.'

'How far do we travel to meet your people?'

'We will leave early and reach one of our villages in two days time. If you so wish, we can travel on to our lagyer which would take four or five days more. Five Wise Ones have come to the village I am taking you to, but if you prefer to speak with all nine of them, you must go on.'

'Perhaps I can decide once I've met the five. What is your "lagyer"? I do not know this word.'

Ryo began to busy himself preparing food and Davin went to offer assistance. Nami and Taleb stayed by Tilliat. Kufu looked perplexed.

'A lagyer is a very large village.'

'Like the city of Gulat?' Taleb spoke for the first time.

Kufu looked as if she would like to spit, but good manners prevailed. 'Nothing like we've heard of that place.'

'But do none of your people go to Gulat? You clearly *do* leave these lands because we have been watched on our journey here.'

Kufu bit her lip. 'The furthest south we go is as far as the house of Tani. His family have always been known as friends of my people. But it is rare indeed that we have visited there. We go to the setting sun a little further because there are few of your people in those lands.'

'And how far east do you travel?' Nami asked.

Kufu smiled. 'Until we reach the barrier to the next Realm.'

'And you have never tried to breach that barrier?' There was a trace of scepticism in Taleb's words.

Ryo glanced over and made that strange hissing sound again, but it was his grandmother who answered.

'We know who dwell there. Long ago when they first came to this land, my people were – not pleased. The barrier was raised by both of us and we choose to ignore them.'

Taleb obviously thought a change of subject might be advisable. 'And north? You travel north I would guess.' He smiled charmingly. Tilliat recognised a flirtatious look similar to what his sister had employed at Gulat's city gate. 'I've always wondered what might lie in the distant north.'

Nami wore a pained expression but made no comment.

'Our young people go into the north on their spirit searches when they come of age,' was all Kufu would say.

Tilliat decided to rejoin the conversation. 'How do you know

278

of me and that I was so near to your lands?'

'You are foretold.' Kufu seemed surprised that Tilliat should ask. 'We have watched through many winters and we knew the time was close.'

The talk became lighter then, with Davin and Ryo putting pots over the fire while Tilliat and Nami sorted out the bed rolls.

Later, they lay silently around the embers of the fire, the moon gliding above the glade. Toomay lay close against Tilliat's side, and Cloud finally emerged from her pack. On a tight thread of thought, Tilliat spoke, first to the small grey cat.

'Why have you not shown yourself, little one?'

'They have no sympathy for us.'

'Us?' Tilliat was puzzled.

'With any creature other than themselves. They would see me as simply a fur pouch.'

'Well if you decide to appear, I will make it *very* clear they are not to touch you, let alone turn you into a pouch.'

Stroking the cat gently, Tilliat felt tension relax from the small body. 'And what are your thoughts, Toomay?'

'I think they are Halflings.'

'Halflings?'

'I will not speak more of them now, in case I'm wrong. But I fear I am not. I had no idea they lived so close to us.'

'Well both of you should sleep, and know that I will never let harm come to *either* of you.'

Tilliat felt affection flowing towards her from cat and Dragon and waited until she thought they were in fact asleep.

'Shadow?'

'Yes.'

'Do you know these people?'

'Did. Not now.'

'Are we in danger already?'

There was a long pause. 'We protect.'

Tilliat breathed deeply. 'I've been meaning to speak to you about that. I ask that you protect *all* my company now, not just me and Uncle and Cloud.'

The silence was distinctly frosty but eventually she had a reply. 'Protect.'

Well that was some comfort, Tilliat reflected, aware the

Shadows had withdrawn from the conversation. She stared up at stars that only showed now that the full moon's brilliance had drifted further south, and thought of her father, the trader Stevro Kranch.

Had he had any idea of what she might face? Had Jomah? Tilliat thought that yes, Jomah would have guessed, if she hadn't known, that Tilliat would face great trials once her mage talent emerged. She was absolutely sure that Jomah knew she would never try to take her brother's place. After all, it was Jomah who had carried her from the Palace straight after her birth. A jolt shivered through Tilliat's thoughts.

That man who served Tetsura, the man who had chosen muteness, just so that he could remain with the Prince. His eyes were Jomah's eyes. She turned closer to Toomay's side and tightened her arm around Cloud at her chest, and tried to empty her mind and get some sleep.

A little further from the fire Ryo slept, but Kufu was wide awake. All the walking she'd done recently had played havoc with her leg. It had been badly broken and then badly set when Ryo was still an infant. Over the years it had become a constantly worsening irritation to the spirit speaker. Now she was trying to ignore the dull pain and seek the mind of Zahi, the strongest of spirit speakers.

But he must still be too distant from the village as Kufu felt no tingle of touching thoughts. She tried to find a more comfortable position again. Where had that girl child found the Dragon? Kufu was considerably concerned what the reaction might be if the Dragon was with them when they got to the village. She was stunned to learn the Dragon – foul creature! – could use mindspeech. And the girl too.

Perhaps it was proof, in the girl's case at least, that she was truly the Mage Foretold. The Pathmaker had told them ten years ago that prophecy was rising, but he had never said the Mage Foretold would actually come among their people. Kufu was not at all sure she looked forward to being involved in any events that would surely unfold all too soon. She tried yet another position, and longed for painfree sleep.

Next day, Taleb offered two horses for Kufu and Ryo to use. His suggestion was dismissed, despite the fact that Kufu was limping far worse than on the previous day. No one mentioned Tilliat's healing talent and the four companions followed at Kufu's slow pace. Tilliat knew she could at least ease the woman's pain, but obstinately decided against any intervention.

They went on until mid afternoon when they reached another open space amidst the great trees. This one was made because one of the giants had crashed to the ground. It had fallen some years ago, Tilliat guessed: its trunk was dry and the half exposed roots withered and brittle. There was a patch of blackened ground a little way away from the fallen tree where camp fires had been lit. Davin estimated this clearing had been used frequently.

When they were dealing with the horses, Taleb moved beside Tilliat.

'She said two days to get to this village of hers. We could have been there by now if they'd got on the horses.'

'I know. I'm going to ask about that in a while.'

Ryo joined them. 'There is a pool across here – I'll show you.'

When they were gathered round the fire after their meal, and the circle of sky overhead was growing darker, Tilliat raised the subject of horses.

'Are there no horses in your land?'

Kufu shrugged. 'There are a few I think. They are meat and leather.'

Knowing how devoted Nami and Taleb were to the breeding of good horses, Tilliat hoped they'd hold their tongues.

'I cannot help but see that walking pains you Kufu. Surely it would be easier to let a horse carry you and so ease that pain a little?'

'We have legs of our own to walk, and backs to carry burdens.' Kufu's mouth thinned. 'All others than the Yasharitza are food.'

Tilliat couldn't hide her surprise. 'But all the birds here seem tame, unafraid of us. Surely they would hide if they had learned to fear human hunters?'

Kufu still looked stern. 'Flying creatures we do not hunt. We take eggs sometimes, but not the birds. We do not eat the scaled fish but there are many shelled creatures in our rivers, which we can eat.'

'Can?' Tilliat queried.

'Our laws tell us what we can eat and what we must avoid. If the food laws are broken, the sentence is death.'

Taleb swallowed. Had the spies seen him and Nami hauling out two fish? Tilliat was obviously aware of Taleb's train of thought.

'And do your laws apply to us?'

'Of course not. You are not of the Yasharitza.'

Well that's one relief, Tilliat thought, just as Cloud clawed her way up out of the pack which was slung, as usual, across Tilliat's chest. Kufu regarded the cat coolly. Ryo sniffed.

'You have made a pet of that thing?' He sounded disgusted.

Cloud spoke in their minds before Tilliat could open her mouth.

'I travel with my friends.' She surveyed first Ryo, then Kufu, with eyes like shards of emerald ice. She stretched, jumped down and stalked across to Davin Pearl, where she settled on his knees.

There was little more talk before everyone rolled into their blankets for the night. For the first time, Tilliat allowed a tendril of her mind to touch the spirit speaker's thoughts. She was amazed to find very little sign of true mage power in the woman. Kufu was straining to concentrate her thought to someone to the north of them. Very cautiously, Tilliat probed a little deeper, past the calling to someone named Zahi.

She found Kufu's thoughts disorganised, a muddled jumble of Tilliat, Toomay and Cloud. Tilliat sensed a huge agitation around these thoughts. Kufu apparently accepted Tilliat as the Mage Foretold. But Kufu was astonished and horrified by the presence of a Dragon and a cat, both of whom used mindspeech as though it was the most natural thing in the world.

Tilliat felt the constant dull throb of pain as a background to Kufu's continuing call to the person somewhere ahead of them. She carefully withdrew from the woman's mind and stared up at the night sky, deep in her own thoughts.

In the morning, they were set to leave the clearing when Toomay paced close to Tilliat and pressed his brow against hers. He let his words be heard by all.

'I will go to feed, friend Tilliat. I will listen for you, so be sure to summon me should you have any need.' He flickered a glance at the two Yasharitzans.

Tilliat put her arms around his neck. 'Be safe, dear Toomay,' she said aloud. 'I will see you very soon but perhaps it will be for the best if you keep clear of this village we must visit. It seems Dragons are not welcome.'

She didn't care suddenly whether she was offending Kufu and Ryo: after only three days in their company, she was tired of their general attitude. She saw Ryo scowl and cast a quick look at his grandmother. Kufu's face resembled a sour, dried fruit, but she said nothing, simply turned her back on the Dragon, and limped off towards the trees, Ryo at her side.

Davin pulled a face, touching Toomay's cheek lightly when he rode past the Dragon. He held his horse back to let the Chars lead the way and then came alongside Tilliat.

'Are you quite sure about this?' he asked her very quietly.

Tilliat gave a short laugh. 'Not in the least, Uncle. I'm only going along with this to meet the Pathmaker. Tani said the Pathmaker – whoever he or she may be – was of great importance. Unfortunately, he didn't specify in what way the Pathmaker may reveal his importance.'

Davin leaned closer. 'Those two really don't like Dragons.'

'I *had* noticed.'

'If all their people feel the same way, will Toomay be safe out among these trees?'

'Toomay can conceal himself surprisingly well, remember? Even without magic. And if Kufu is a "spirit speaker" and thus holds high rank among the Yasharitza, she is amazingly lacking in any mage talent. You saw how astonished those two were to find Toomay and Cloud, as well as me, can use mindspeech. If the rest of their Wise Ones are as lacking, we haven't too much to worry about.'

'They could still be a bit nasty with knives and things.'

Tilliat snorted. 'I can shield us if we stay fairly close to each other.' She flashed a broad grin. 'At least, I *think* I can.'

'Oh Tilliat Kranch, you are such a comfort to an old trader!'

Laughing, they urged the horses on, to catch up with the others.

Chapter Twenty-Five

They only paused at midday to allow the horses a short break, then continued on. Shortly they arrived at a much larger cleared area which opened down to a river. Whether it was the same river Tilliat and her friends had first encountered or another, they had no way of knowing. They saw a cluster of small huts, laid out in a half circle, the open side towards the water. Smoke rose from stubby stone chimneys.

A group of people stood watching their approach, a few children huddled to one side of the adults. Tilliat slid from the saddle and Davin, Taleb and Nami followed suit. Kufu halted in front of the crowd and spoke for several minutes. She used the Yasharitza tongue and Tilliat was struck by its oddness. There were a lot of guttural sounds but they were made in a singsong lilt, interspersed with a hissing sibilance.

Although the people were listening to Kufu, all eyes were fixed on Tilliat. Without turning to check, she knew Davin Pearl was close to her right shoulder. Nami Char gathered the reins and ropes of all the horses when her brother moved up to Tilliat's left side. Tilliat walked steadily towards Kufu, who turned, just as four elderly men and a woman older and far more frail looking than Kufu, stepped clear of the villagers. Tilliat noted Kufu was looking away but five pairs of brown eyes were focused on her.

'You are welcome to our land, Lady Tilliat.' The oldest of the men spoke in the same strongly accented common tongue as Kufu and Ryo had used to them.

Now why, if the Yasharitzans kept themselves as apart as Kufu stated, would they speak the common tongue so fluently, albeit with a marked accent?

'My name is Zahi,' the man continued. He introduced the other old men, and the woman. The only name that Tilliat really caught was the ancient woman's: Kenza.

Kenza met Tilliat's gaze, her eyes sharp and intelligent in a nest of wrinkled skin.

'Rest yourself Kufu and recover from your travels.' Kenza's voice was far younger than her appearance suggested. 'We will settle our guests.'

She beckoned Tilliat closer. 'This will be your shelter for the time you are here.'

She led them to the nearest hut. 'Your animals can be kept close by. None will harm them.'

Tilliat thought she detected a gleam of mischief in the dark eyes. The woman walked slowly with the aid of a black, carved stick. Tilliat and Davin kept to her pace. Tilliat nodded at Taleb and Nami who were leading the horses closer to the rear of the hut they'd been allocated. The four elderly men were huddled with Kufu but Ryo had vanished amid the dispersing crowd of villagers.

Davin opened a door set between two windows and stood aside for Kenza and Tilliat to enter. A quick glance showed one large room with what Tilliat assumed must be four strange beds. Two were of the usual height but the other two were set above them. Directly opposite the door was a hearth built of river stones, with an oven set into the side.

To the left were large pillows, clearly intended for sitting on, scattered around a low wooden table. There were also four stools near the fire. They saw the windows were empty spaces, solid shutters hanging beside them. Presumably in bad weather or at night, with those shutters closed it would be very dark within but for the fire. Nami came in laden with packs and, after a quick look round, piled them by the strange beds.

Tilliat remained with Kenza who stood leaning on her stick with both hands. Davin was already by the fire, checking if there was water in the large kettle there.

Kenza chuckled. 'There is payva if you prefer.' She frowned. 'Beer I think you'd call it.'

Davin smiled. 'I'll stick with tea thank you.'

Kenza smiled back. 'Very sensible. It can be very potent. I hate the stuff. I will let you settle in. There is water from the river and wood behind the shelter. Food will be brought to you later.'

She stretched a hand to Tilliat, who grasped it automatically.

286

The girl looked down in surprise. Kenza's hand was twisted, the joints swollen and knotted. Quite without thinking, Tilliat's mind focused on that hand. Somehow she knew how to ease the pain throbbing around the knuckles. Kenza's mouth opened, then closed. Her grip on Tilliat tightened for a moment.

'Be very careful child, not all are glad you are here.'

'Trust,' came the Shadows' whisper in Tilliat's head.

Close as she was to Kenza, she saw the old woman's eyes flicker and, still holding her hand, Tilliat spoke as softly as Kenza had.

'You can use mindspeech.'

Kenza gave a quick nod then looked apprehensively out of the door. 'I have never admitted it,' she murmured.

'I will speak with you this way later then Kenza.'

With a last squeeze of her hand, Kenza inclined her head. 'I was explaining that a meal will be brought here, and we will speak with them more fully tomorrow.'

Tilliat turned to find one of the elderly men, whose name completely eluded her, was standing rather close. Kenza moved past.

'Come, Zahi, help me back to the magela – the meeting shelter,' she added at Tilliat's questioning look.

Zahi, reluctantly, it seemed to Tilliat, took Kenza's arm and walked slowly out.

Tilliat wondered just what Kufu had told the four men just now: this one didn't look too pleased, whatever it might have been.

With the light rapidly fading, so did the warmth of the day, a reminder that winter was not so far past. Davin pulled several pillows across in front of the fire and lay back with the inevitable bowl of tea close by. The other three were investigating the strange sleeping arrangements and Davin listened to the bickering, a smile on his lips.

Tilliat had had few real friends of her own age in Kelshan, he realised. She was always taught at home and kept busy with extra tutors. Those like Skala Vek, he remembered sourly, and poured himself more tea to take away the taste of the unpleasant memory.

'No, you sleep on the top,' Nami insisted. 'And I will sleep below. Uncle can sleep on the other top one and Taleb under him. That way, we can leap to your defence if need be in the night.'

Tilliat thought she sounded unnecessarily hopeful. Taleb had been testing the upper bed and now dropped down to the floor, grinning.

'It's an ingenious idea, I must admit, and it's really quite comfortable.'

'It's also quite a way down if you fall out,' Tilliat pointed out.

Cloud poked her head out of her carrying pack. 'I will test it for you,' she announced kindly.

Tilliat put the pack on the top bed and the cat emerged, to stalk from end to end, sniffing fastidiously.

'I'll fetch water for the horses,' said Taleb. 'I don't think they'd like us taking the horses to the river.'

'I will come too.' Cloud jumped to his shoulder.

'Stay very close to any one of us, little one,' Tilliat cautioned. 'There's something wrong here.'

The twins regarded her.

'You stay here with Uncle, I'll go with Taleb too. And I'll make sure the horses are securely tied.' Nami marched out into the twilight with her brother.

'What is it?' Davin asked when Tilliat sank down beside him.

Tilliat shrugged. 'I don't know exactly, but this place feels – uncomfortable.'

'Can't say I'm much impressed with the way they live here. Perhaps this hut is kept just for visitors, although I can't imagine too many of those. The other huts might be cosier but somehow I don't believe they are.'

'I would have expected a bit more noise. We should have heard children yelling before we got here, but it was so quiet. They may have had lookouts watching for us, but even so, it seemed odd.'

Davin lowered his voice. 'Are they all mages?'

'The only one with any talent was Kenza – the old one who led us to this hut. I felt nothing from any of the rest, not even the four men they said are Wise Ones.'

The door opened and three women entered, followed by the Chars. The women carried plain boards laden with various dishes

288

and pots. They arranged the food on the low table and began to leave, but the last turned back.

'The flask holds oil, for the lamps,' she murmured, then followed the other women from the hut.

Tilliat peered at the little stone dishes: they closely resembled the odd dish she'd found in Thorn's caves. Taleb poured some oil in each dish, added a twist of threads from a handful on the table and went to the fire. He found a twig from a log, lit the end and then touched the threads in the dishes. A soft glow grew as the threads caught.

Taleb shook his head. 'I really didn't know this form of lighting was still used anywhere in these lands.'

'How did you know what to do?' Tilliat demanded.

'He studies old objects.' Nami answered for her brother. 'The house in Gulat is stuffed with all sorts of old rubbish.'

Settling on the pillows, they ate the food to the usual accompaniment of Taleb and Nami arguing. Davin fed the cat small pieces of meat from the table. Cloud spoke in their minds.

'Many watched me with Taleb by the water. Their thoughts were bad.'

Davin stroked the grey fur. 'No one will harm you, I promise,' he told her firmly.

'Toomay?' Tilliat sent the thought out, beyond the village.

'I am near.'

'Are there any people out, beyond the village?'

'Men walk softly around the place of buildings. They have weapons ready. I think they are guarding.'

Guarding what, Tilliat wondered? Were they there to stop others *entering* the village? Or to stop her and her companions *leaving*?

Toomay mindspoke her again. 'There is much anger in these men as they walk, but I cannot tell what they are angry about.'

'Toomay, please, *please,* take great care.' Tilliat felt affection flow through the mindlink.

'Of course. Remember I am but a heartbeat from your side, should you need me.'

'And you remember to come only if I do call you, my friend. Now rest, and stay safe.'

Nami stacked the dishes onto the boards the women had used and left them just outside the door. There appeared to be no means of securing the door but Nami piled their saddles against it. She grinned at the watching Tilliat.

'At least that will make a noise if anyone tries to creep in,' she said.

The shutters had been closed for a while and they, at least, had bolts to hold them firmly shut. Tilliat climbed cautiously up to the top bed and settled back with Cloud tucked against her side. Davin climbed up to his bed with a certain amount of grumbling and muttered curses. Tilliat found the bed surprisingly comfortable and obviously the others did: they were soon asleep, judging by Davin Pearl's snores.

She breathed steadily, centering herself as so many of her weapons' tutors had instructed, and let her mind drift out and through the village. Almost immediately, she touched another mind and recognised Kenza.

'It is such a wonderful thing,' Kenza's mindvoice was clear, 'to speak mind to mind once more.'

'Why do your people not do so now? It sounds as if they were able to once.'

'The one you must destroy – no, do not say his name! – he crushed our people. All the mageborn among us, unable to reach for their power, and children born since then are – different. They turn away from tales of our mageborn past and shun any idea of such talents.'

'Then how are you able – ?'

'Able to touch your mind? Stars guard me, I was far away when it happened.'

Tilliat felt a great grief through their linked minds and waited patiently for Kenza to continue.

'I was in the Isles of Vremilia. You must understand child, I am well past a hundred winters now, one of the last of us born with our old gifts.'

Tilliat's private thoughts, shielded from the mindlink, were racing. 'One of the last. Who else among you have the talents?' she asked.

'The Pathmaker. He survived the calamity but even I have not seen him for over ten winters, and he does not answer my calls to his mind.'

'Who exactly are the Yasharitza people?'

There was silence, but Tilliat had learned, long ago, that if she waited patiently, eventually people answered her questions. Sure enough Kenza finally replied.

'We were once a great race. We were wild people, what you would probably call uncivilised. We chose to retreat after we had met and disagreed with the other peoples of these lands. Thus we hid ourselves in the north.'

Tilliat waited a heartbeat. 'What does the name Yasharitza mean?

Kenza's mindvoice faded to the merest breath. 'It means Halfling. In the last twenty five generations or so, we have changed, physically and mentally. There are very few now who are born true Yasharitza, and they live far north. Rarely do we see them.'

'And the Pathmaker?'

The longest silence yet. 'He is true Yasharitza. I visited him, but now my body will not endure such a journey. He alone knows of my ability to mindspeak, but as I said, I have not felt the touch of his mind since ten winters past.'

'Could he be dead?'

'We would have been told.'

But Tilliat sensed doubt mixed with anxiety through the link. She changed the subject.

'What will happen tomorrow?'

'You will come to the magela and will be questioned.'

'Questioned?' Tilliat interrupted sharply.

'I'm sorry. I don't know why they want to question you. I am so old, I am discounted as an effective Wise One now although they make me attend their meetings. I suspect they have no one else to make up the Nine. The law says there must be Nine.'

'You should rest.' Tilliat decided she had enough to consider for now. 'I will see you tomorrow.'

She lay for a while, then called Shadows.

'Heard.' The faint whisper sounded thoughtful. 'Look for Pathmaker one.'

'What do you mean?'

'Some of us. Gone now.'

'Tell me exactly what you find out.'

Tilliat realised her head ached slightly and wondered if that was due to mindspeaking Kenza.

'Yes.'

She grunted, turned on her side to curl around Cloud, and slept.

The same three women brought food early in the morning. There was a porridge, palatable but of a flavour unrecognised by any of Tilliat's company. There were bowls of dried fruit, and of nuts, a pile of gritty, flat bread, and a small dish of a bitter tasting cheese. Davin only risked a taste of the porridge then retreated to the fire and a pot of tea.

Taleb went out, with Cloud on his shoulder, to check the horses. His expression was grim when he came back.

'One horse is gone. The rope was cut.'

Nami shot outside to see which horse had gone. To Tilliat horses were still just horses: she had learnt to recognise the one she usually rode only because it had faint speckles of white on its face and shoulders. To Taleb and Nami each horse was an individual.

Davin Pearl frowned. 'I think you should wait until we're in this meeting before you ask about the horse, Tilliat. Do it when there are plenty to hear you.'

Tilliat nodded. Nami returned, her expression thunderous.

'I'll speak of it later.' Tilliat explained Davin's advice and the Chars exchanged a look and grunted their assent, even as Ryo appeared in the doorway.

'The Wise Ones and the village council are ready for you.'

Tilliat reached a hand to Davin Pearl and heaved him to his feet. Cloud remained clinging firmly around Taleb's neck and the four followed Ryo from the hut. There were few people in sight until they reached the biggest hut, the magela, in the centre of the half circle of buildings. Here were most of the villagers, squatting on the ground a short distance from the door.

Tilliat repressed a shiver. The faces turned towards them were either blank or showing a sullen anger. She could see no children. Ryo opened the door and stood aside. Tilliat, Davin on her right and the Chars at her back, walked in. The window spaces in here were high up, near the pitched roof, and morning sunlight poked down onto a raised platform at the northern end of the building. Seated on piles of furs were the five Wise Ones. Kufu sat to one side, on the ground, not the platform. Nine middle aged men sat some way in front of the Wise Ones, not turning as Tilliat and her friends entered.

'Always a bunch of old men in charge – have you noticed that?' Nami Char muttered behind her.

Tilliat gave a snort which she changed to a cough as they approached the platform. Kufu raised a hand.

'You may sit there.' She indicated a place opposite her.

Without a word, Tilliat crossed between the two groups and sat, her back firmly against the wall, her companions following her example.

One of the men on the platform – Zahi? – raised both hands and made complicated gestures in front of his face. Kenza was seated at the end nearest Tilliat but she was keeping her gaze on her hands, or perhaps she was asleep. The man in the middle opened his mouth, but Tilliat got in first.

'I have to ask the Wise Ones and the village council, if they could explain the um, disappearance of one of our horses?'

Zahi was plainly displeased that she dared speak first. 'Horses are meat and leather,' he snapped but Tilliat interrupted before he could start his own speech.

'So you might believe. But you see, Kufu,' she inclined her head graciously in Kufu's direction. 'Kufu assured us that we, and our animals, would be secure within this village.'

There was a disturbance without. Ryo entered, flustered and angry. He approached the gathering and spoke in the Yasharitza tongue. Kenza raised her head.

'We will speak the language our guests understand,' she commanded.

Ryo paled, bowed and began again. 'The horse has been found: butchered. Three village men lie dead beside it. They bear no marks upon their bodies.'

A hissing arose and Tilliat's skin rose in goosebumps. It was Kenza again who seemed to take control.

'If our guests allow, perhaps we can wait to deal with this. The horse is dead. The men are dead. There is no urgency now.

293

We can investigate later.'

Ryo looked as though he would dearly like to argue but he bowed, with bad grace, and left the magela. Instantly Zahi spoke up, forestalling Tilliat.

'You are here because you claim to be the Mage Foretold. We believe this is probably true. Therefore, as you have chosen to reveal yourself in the lands of the Yasharitza, you will reinstate our supremacy through the outer lands, bringing all people under our control. You will be held in high honour and great esteem once you have accomplished this.'

All heads nodded in solemn agreement except for Kenza, Tilliat, and her friends. Zahi looked at Tilliat expectantly. Did he really think she would be overwhelmed with joy and gratitude by his proposal? Tilliat realised she had been deliberately seated lower than the so-called Wise Ones to emphasise their superiority, so she got to her feet. Now, her eyes were level with Zahi's.

She stared from face to face slowly, probing lightly with her mind for any indication of power among the four men. When she met Kenza's gaze she kept her face just as expressionless as when she regarded the men, but she could feel Kenza's apprehension. Tilliat looked back at Zahi and folded her arms.

'Firstly, I do *not* claim to be anything other than Tilliat Kranch, trader's daughter of Kelshan city. I have no control over what you or anyone else may name me. Secondly, why in the name of the stars, would I help you – what? – invade all the other lands, nations, principalities beyond your borders? And thirdly, you speak of honour and esteem, yet you allowed the theft of one of my animals: butchered, according to Ryo. Now why should I either believe a word you've spoken or agree to your absurd demands?'

A low wail began behind Tilliat and she glanced back. Cloud was crouched on Taleb's shoulder, her eyes blazing green fire and her fluffed tail thrashing. The four men on the platform and the nine on the ground, all showed a sneering disgust at the cat's behaviour. Tilliat reached back and lifted Cloud into her arms, where the crooning wail persisted.

The Wise Ones leaned towards each other, muttering rapidly in their own tongue. Kenza remained utterly still, all too plainly disregarded by the four men. Zahi addressed Tilliat again.

'You will do as we say. You are in our power and we *insist* on your obedience and cooperation.'

Unseen, Davin Pearl rolled his eyes. Oh very good, he thought. *Just* how to antagonise Tilliat Kranch. Tilliat drew breath. She spoke very calmly and clearly.

'I think not. My friends and I will leave this village and we will continue northwards. There is one I must speak with – the Pathmaker. I thank you for the two meals you provided us, but the butchered horse amply repays any debt we might owe for food and shelter.'

Her friends were also on their feet as the nine council men leapt up, hands already holding long knives. Tilliat glared at them and the knives fell to the floor, their owners waving their hands in confused pain. Tilliat strode around them and Taleb jumped ahead to open the door. A wall of people stood, blocking their path.

'No!' An angry shout came from behind her. Tilliat looked back to see Zahi standing. 'There is a debt for the three men you've killed!'

Tilliat smiled but the grey eyes were stormy. 'And how did I kill them when your men were watching our shelter all night?'

She turned back to the crowd outside. 'I really think you should let us pass before I lose my temper.'

The nearest people read something in her eyes for, after an instant's hesitation, they pressed back, leaving a corridor through which Tilliat led her friends. They had just reached their hut when a murmur began behind them.

'Don't look round,' Tilliat ordered. 'Nami and Taleb – get the horses ready as fast as you can. Uncle and I will get the gear.'

'We can both use power,' Taleb told her. 'But I'm not sure what to do against a crowd like that.'

'Don't worry, you won't have to do anything. Hurry with the horses.'

Nami was already running to the back of the hut, awkwardly carrying three saddles, Taleb close behind with other harness. Davin and Tilliat gathered the rest of their packs and bundles. Tilliat mindspoke Kenza.

'Will you be safe Kenza? I will speak with you again, but for now, farewell.'

'Stars guide you, child. I wish I was strong enough to travel with you. I had not realised things were as bad as has been revealed this day. I offer my apologies child, and my love.'

'Just stay safe for now, Kenza.'

Tying her bedroll behind her saddle and helping redistribute packs between the three spare horses, Tilliat called Toomay in her mind.

'Keep your distance my friend. We will meet north of this place. Warn us if there are people ahead.'

She swung up into her saddle and turned her horse towards the water.

'We'll follow the river until we're clear of this area,' she called to Taleb.

He nodded, urging Davin to stay close to Tilliat.

They reached the riverbank and began to walk the horses downstream, the village some distance back to their right. Tilliat had hastily buttoned Cloud inside her jacket and it was Cloud who warned her now. Tilliat saw a mob of villagers, men and women, and, to her horror, children too. They were running towards the riders, brandishing knives and sticks. It was all the more unnerving because they were silent. Tilliat held the leading rein out to Davin.

'Keep going, no matter what.'

Davin grabbed the rein and tugged her mount on. Tilliat raised her hands and half turned in the saddle.

'You will leave us be,' she called clearly. 'And you will not follow.'

Her words had no effect, but a wall of flame erupted just ahead of the mob. Fire crackled and now yells and screams came from the other side of the fire. Tilliat slumped, clutching her horse's mane.

'Get us out of here Uncle. Fast would be good.'

Chapter Twenty-Six

Two days after Prince Tetsura A Serissama's Presentation to his people, he was in the Palace garden, in the tiny cabin sheltered by willow trees. He would never admit it but he was actually hiding. Yesterday morning, Commander Anjit had taken control of both the military and the civilian militia. Tetsura still didn't know the full details, but it had happened with an amazing lack of fuss or disruption. The Regent Hikmat had been removed from the Royal apartments and now resided in one of the dungeon cells far beneath the Phoenix Palace.

So many people had been clamouring for audiences with Tetsura, he had chosen what he termed a tactical retreat. Sergeant Tag had sniggered and repeated her belief that he was hiding. Tetsura sat, looking glum. He had tried to appoint Vilad to the post of Palace Steward and had been aghast at Vilad's reaction. The old man had dropped to his knees and banged his head on the floor. Tetsura tried to mindspeak the distraught man but could make little out of the grief and distress swirling in his mind.

He was still trying to calm Vilad when Sergeant Tag arrived. She hoisted the poor man off the floor and dumped him in a chair, bending to scowl into his face.

'I believe His Highness wants to show his affection for you by promoting you to the highest post in the Palace administration, silly man. If you don't want the post, then tell the poor boy.'

Vilad tried to steady his breathing and looked across at the Prince, his face drenched with tears. He mindspoke the Prince.

'Please, Your Highness, I have never wanted more than to be beside you, to serve you with my life. If you make me Palace Steward, I will have an office.' He waved a hand wildly, indicating somewhere distant in the Palace. 'I would never see you, my Prince, and I have watched over you since the moment of your birth. Please Your Highness, don't send me away.'

Tetsura went to his knees by the chair, folding the old man in his arms. 'I am sorry my thoughtless words so distressed you, my dear Vilad. If you wish, you will remain my body servant, but above all others who serve me personally. No one shall mock you or disobey you and you will be with me always.'

Vilad's arms went round the Prince and his tense body relaxed in his relief.

Sergeant Tag, leaning casually against the door, watched and listened with deep interest.

The rest of yesterday had been a chaotic blur of messengers, letters, pleas for audiences. Tetsura knew that Commander Anjit was extremely occupied with neutralising the discontents within the Phoenix Guards and ensuring calm was maintained throughout Garjetka. So today, Tetsura had escaped into the garden.

Tag straightened, staring through the waving strands of willow branches. 'You have a visitor.'

Tetsura groaned and Sergeant Tag grinned. 'You won't mind this one I think.'

She wandered away and Tetsura heard a murmured conversation. But he'd already sensed who was seeking him and he relaxed, smiling as Saima slipped into the ornamental cabin. Saima bowed gracefully and sank onto cushions opposite the Prince. Long fingers, bare of ornament, lowered the scarf from her hair. She gave Tetsura a smile full of sympathy.

'Vilad suggested you might like my company.'

'He was right, Lady Saima.'

Her blue eyes crinkled and Tetsura saw the faint lines etched at their corners.

'I am no lady, Your Highness, just Saima. I must thank you for the great honour you showed my husband and myself when you visited our humble establishment. You have no idea how custom has increased.'

Tetsura gave a shout of laughter. 'You thought it was a huge joke and your poor husband nearly fainted with shock.'

'The thing that shocked Deng most was the fact that you insisted on paying for everyone's meals.' Saima looked innocent but there was mischief in her tone.

'I'm sure you know I had to borrow coin from Commander Anjit, but I repaid him as soon as we returned here.'

Saima grew more serious. 'The streets are peaceful, Your Highness. There are perhaps more militia out among the citizens, but there have been no more brawls than might be expected when people overdrink. I know the Commander has scarcely slept since your Presentation. He has been meeting the Merchant Guilds. I'm sure you know too, that many were on the verge of rising against the Regent, but I hope you understand they have never been against the Phoenix Throne or you yourself.'

Tetsura nodded. 'That has been made very plain. But what I don't understand is, how to be a king.'

Saima reached to stroke the Prince's cheek with the back of her fingers. 'Vilad thought I might be able to help, not that I know much of royal protocol, but perhaps more generally. He also suggested I could arrange new robes to be made.'

She chuckled at Tetsura's expression. 'You will *have* to have something spectacular for your Crowning – you must admit that. Otherwise I thought you could tell me what sort of clothes you prefer and we could get several sets made up, in different colours or materials and so on.'

'Tunics and trousers,' Tetsura said promptly. 'I really don't like robes very much.'

Saima raised an exquisitely arched brow. 'Like them or not, it *will* be robes for the ceremony.'

Tetsura sighed. 'I would be relieved to leave it to you and Vilad. But there are so many people I know I should meet – but I know nothing of precedence. I don't even know *where* I should hold any meetings or audiences. It is only now that I realise how Hikmat has completely isolated me from any idea how to govern. I have never attended any meetings, I don't even know the names of the governors of the Isles, or the Palace administrators.'

There was real anger underlying Tetsura's tone now. 'I don't blame just Hikmat for excluding me, but I am furious with my own neglect. I should have asked questions, made him let me attend some meetings at least.'

'And what would have happened, do you think, if you had made a nuisance of yourself, demanding to know how things were being run?'

Tetsura blinked at Saima's sharpness.

'Hikmat could have kept you even more closely confined. He

only need say you were frail, sickly, and you could even have died. Just like your father did.'

A considerable silence followed Saima's words. The Prince gave another sigh.

'I suppose you're right, but I don't know how to make amends. There is until the next full moon for me to try to grasp the essentials of kingship.'

Saima interrupted him. 'You have mage powers, Your Highness. You can see the hearts of those who wish to serve the Phoenix Throne. You can judge any around you. Many official positions have disappeared during the Regent's time. He took most titles for himself.'

'I didn't even know that.'

'Yes,' continued Saima. 'He dealt with all matters of finance and law so there is no Treasurer or Justicar. We can make a list of the places to which you need to appoint someone quickly and I'm sure the Commander can give you more advice. But he will not be available for a few more days yet I think. You could make a start though.'

Saima was pleased to see the boy definitely looked a little brighter than when she'd arrived. 'You did so well at your Presentation,' she told him. 'The sky pictures were magnificent.'

She'd thought he would be pleased with her praise and was surprised by his sudden sadness. His grey eyes met hers.

'I wish my sister could have been here,' he whispered. 'She saw, though. I'm not sure how, but she saw. I fear she is close to danger now, and I cannot help her.'

A shiver iced down Saima's spine. Stars, but what power must the girl have if she could reach this far to witness her brother's achievement?

'You have the Isles of Vremilia, the Kingdom of the Phoenix, to consider, Your Highness. If she knows of your triumph, I'm sure she will rejoice for you. If she faces danger, you are too far to help her I fear.'

Tetsura had told no one of the time he had helped Tilliat heal someone's mind and he didn't speak of it now. He forced a smile.

'You are right, of course. Shall we make a start on that list?'

'Why not call Sergeant Tag? She's sure to know some names

to suggest.;

Tetsura rose and peered out towards the willows. Sergeant Tag was strolling around the perimeter but changed direction when she saw him raise his hand. Tetsura scowled. Sergeant Tag denied she had mage powers. He'd get to the bottom of that nonsense soon enough, he decided.

Davin Pearl was sick with worry. He had climbed behind Tilliat to hold her in her saddle but she remained slumped forward and he couldn't tell if she was even conscious. Nami Char caught up with him, trailing the spare horses. She bent to peer at Tilliat's face.

'I think she used too much power, Uncle. She has yet to learn to control it properly.'

Davin took some comfort from Nami's words. He glanced behind.

'Where is Taleb?'

'He's held back a bit, just to make sure no one follows us.'

The ground was good riding beside the river and Nami urged the horses to keep a steady pace. Davin was greatly relieved in the middle of the afternoon, when he saw Toomay lying on the lush grass ahead of them. They drew rein and Davin eased Tilliat down to Nami.

'She will sleep until dawn,' Toomay bespoke Davin and Nami.

Lowering Tilliat to the bedroll Davin hastily spread beside the Dragon, Nami touched Toomay's neck.

'She drew too much power we thought? Is that what's happened?'

'It is indeed. Sleep will restore her and there are no people following or anywhere close by.'

'That's one relief then.' Nami went to deal with the horses.

'Will it be all right to make a fire, Toomay?' asked Davin.

Toomay's great eyes sparkled. 'I'm sure it will,' he replied solemnly. 'You must make sure you remain feeling human Uncle.'

Davin laughed. He set about removing a piece of turf and finding his kettle amongst their hurriedly packed possessions.

The sun had dropped below the mighty trees, and the campfire was burning well by the time Taleb cantered up.

'No sign of any followers,' he told them, then stared at Tilliat's still form with concern.

'She sleeps,' Nami explained. 'Used too much power.'

Taleb settled beside the fire, accepting a bowl of tea from Davin. He grinned.

'That was the most effective illusion I've ever seen.'

Toomay shifted his wings. 'It would have been an excellent illusion,' he agreed. 'Except it wasn't.'

Three heads swivelled towards the Dragon in alarm.

'The forest,' Davin began.

'No, no, Uncle, the forest is safe. I – modified – that fire, just a little.'

'How?' demanded Taleb.

Toomay's eyes whirred with uncertainty. 'Well, I turned it from real to an illusion. Only the grass was a little – singed. But those people huddle in their buildings now, wailing to their Wise Ones.'

'Where's Cloud?' Nami chose to ask.

'Still with Tilliat,' Davin replied.

'How did the village men die – the ones that took our horse?' Taleb stared hard at Toomay.

Toomay's wings rattled again and he was definitely uncomfortable with the question. 'I do not know.'

Later, Toomay assured them there was no need for anyone to keep watch: he would alert them in plenty of time if there was any hint of trouble.

Tilliat woke next morning, clear headed and refreshed, and found herself nose to nose with a small grey cat. Cloud's moustache bristled forward as she yawned.

'I'm sure there are mice nearby. I shall hunt my breakfast,' she announced in Tilliat's mind.

'Don't wander too far, little friend.'

Cloud moved away, in fits and starts, shaking her paws free of the detestable moisture clinging to the grasses.

'And you are well Toomay? I was worried that you might meet hunters.'

'I am well. You must really control how you use power, friend Tilliat – you used far too much.'

'It worked though, didn't it? I got the idea from my brother.'

'Well, yes, it worked, but it was real fire you called.'

'*What?*' Tilliat shot up in a tangle of blankets.

'Hush now. I corrected it.'

Tilliat's mind raced. The Dragon had "corrected" her use of power? Just how much magic, power, call it what you will, could these Dragons do?

Toomay's long silver lashes fluttered. 'Have the Shadows spoken of what you must do?' he asked. 'I have a very strong presentiment of darkness ahead.'

'No. They've told me nothing. Toomay, much as I appreciate your presence, I fear for you. Would it not be best if you returned to your Realm? From what Kufu said of a barrier to the east, I'd guessed it was your Realm she spoke of. So it can't be too far and you would be safe.'

Toomay's eyes flashed and whirred. 'I have chosen,' he said. 'My place is with you. You are right though, our Realm is close – a day's fast flight perhaps.' He paused. 'I can reach Thorn's mind. He is moving north too, so we can keep in mind contact. He says he will come if need arises.'

Before Tilliat could react, she heard Davin Pearl stirring awake. The trader's questions as to how she was feeling, woke the Chars, and Toomay took the opportunity to pace to the river for a long drink.

For three days they kept a good pace, following the river northwards. Ahead, the land rose in ever higher peaks and at midday of the fourth day, the river swung sharply east. Taleb studied the water. It flowed fast but he couldn't judge how deep it might be. Taleb led them on for a while, until he found what he'd been hoping for.

The river broadened and slowed its previous rush. After a brief argument with his sister, he dismounted, unsaddled his horse and tied a rope around his waist. Remounting, he urged the animal down the bank and into the water. Nami stood on the bank, the other end of the rope tied to her saddle, watching her brother move across the river.

The water stayed about halfway up the horse's legs until they were a third of the way across. Then suddenly the animal floundered. Tilliat grabbed Davin's arm in alarm, but, with a considerable amount of thrashing from the horse, it resumed its footing. The water now reached its chest but it didn't need to fight a strong current. Slowly, Taleb coaxed the horse on and reached the opposite bank.

Nami immediately organised the unsaddling of all the horses, wrapping all their gear in three large sheets of oilskin she'd dug triumphantly from one of the packs. Tilliat didn't much enjoy the crossing, but was relieved to at least get to the other side without disgracing herself by falling off. She concentrated on imagining the glee on the twins' faces if she *did* fall, and that seemed to keep her glued to the horse's bare back.

Toomay had flown on during the morning and now he bespoke Tilliat.

'Continue north. There are fewer heart trees, but many more of the trees you know. Also many streams coming from the hills.'

Tilliat relayed Toomay's report and after resaddling, they finally left the river, moving into the forest. The heart trees thinned, as Toomay had said, and the riders saw evergreens such as they recognised. A few birches appeared, still bare of leaves, and Davin scowled as a chill wind picked up, blowing into their faces.

The ground was rising but not in a steady incline. It rose and fell, revealing gullies leading nowhere and occasional sheer rock faces, as if half a hill had just dropped away. Tiny streams rushed down from hidden heights, hurrying to join the river the riders had crossed. Rounding a heap of tumbled boulders, each the size of the huts in the village, they were all glad to find Toomay settled in a sheltered corner.

They had a routine by now and camp was quickly made. Davin Pearl listened to the wind chattering through the bushes a short distance away, and was grateful for the warmth of their fire. The four companions had grown used to the milder temperatures of the deep valley of the Yasharitzans and found the increasing cold a worrying prospect. They were all concerned for Toomay but the Dragon dismissed their anxiety.

The sixth day from the village saw them riding through a sudden flurry of snow. They rode bundled up in most of the spare clothing from their packs. Despite Toomay's assurances that he was well, Tilliat was increasingly concerned for the effect the cold might have on the Dragon. Taleb called a halt when he found a flat area beneath an overhang of rock. There was room for the seven horses as well as a Dragon and four people. At least they were out of the continuing wind, which was getting all of them down.

Davin Pearl made a fire against the rear of the shelter, hoping the rock would reflect the heat a little more. Darkness fell early and Tilliat was silent, huddled against the rock, hands clasped round a bowl of broth. Finally, Nami realised Toomay was absent. She looked at Tilliat in dawning horror.

'Where is he? Can you mindspeak him?'

Tilliat's eyes seemed huge, magnified by unshed tears. 'I've tried. I've been trying since long before we stopped here. He does not answer.'

Taleb and Davin both looked appalled and guilty that neither had spared a thought for the young Dragon for half the day. Davin was on his feet, peering helplessly out into the darkness.

'Uncle, come back. You'll freeze out there.'

Davin reluctantly returned to the fire. 'Where could he be? I can't believe he'd just vanish without telling us.'

'He wouldn't, unless… '

'Unless what?' The Chars spoke in unison.

Tilliat shook her head. 'Either something awful happened very quickly, or,' she bit her lip. 'He said the Dragon Realm is only one day's fast flight away. He may have thought to visit Thorn.'

'Thorn?' asked Nami.

'The eldest of the Dragons.'

'Can't your Shadow things tell you what's happened?'

Tilliat groaned. 'I have called them for nearly as long as I've been calling Toomay, and they do not answer either.'

She looked down at her hand. The silver ring on her thumb twinkled in the faint firelight and the others could see a very thin, black line beneath the silver.

'*That's* one of the Shadows?' Taleb asked dubiously.

Tilliat stared into the fire, her eyes unfocused. In her mind, she called yet again.

'Shadows, are you there?'

'Yes.'

Her companions watched in some alarm when her body went rigid.

'Where, in all the hells, have you been?'

'Busy.'

'Busy how?'

'Crazed thing close by. Protect.'

'They say there's been another – episode – like in Gulat.' Tilliat spoke aloud.

Taleb frowned. 'Do you mean when it felt as if a great weight pressed down?'

'I think so. They say they've been protecting us from the effects. They protected Uncle and me last time. Wait. I need to ask them more.'

Taleb, Nami and Davin, waited, wrapped in their blankets, watching Tilliat.

'Why did Reva do this again, and why here?'

'Not here. Village.'

'What do you *mean*? You said you'd protected us – we are far from that village.'

'Most dead there.'

'*What?*' The word came out in a loud squeak. 'What about Kenza? Is she still alive?'

'Yes. Two other Wise Ones.' The Shadow sniggered, clearly unimpressed by the title "Wise Ones". 'Few others.'

'Did you kill the three who took our horse?'

'Of course.'

'Is Kenza well?'

There was a pause. 'Others angry with her. Blame her.' The Shadow sounded scornful.

'Can you get her out of there if there is need?'

'Could.'

'Well, for now, leave her but if she's in greater danger, move her please.'

'Where?'

'To us, I suppose.'

'Too old for coldness.'

'Well I'll think of something else once she's safe,' Tilliat snapped. 'Where is Toomay?'

'Here tomorrow.'

'Thank you.'

Tilliat explained what the Shadows had told her to the others and all three grew thoughtful.

'I wonder how those Shadows kill?' asked Taleb eventually.

'I'd rather not ask.' Tilliat told him.

'Ryo said there were no marks on the men who stole the horse.'

'Taleb, I am *not* asking. I *really* don't want to know.'

Taleb opened his mouth then saw the glares directed at him and shrugged. Wrapping himself tighter in his blankets, he lay down.

'Let's hope the snow today has just been a last throw of winter's dice,' he said, rolling onto his side.

They were all awake at dawn, glad to see a clear sky again. There were still patches of yesterday's snow scattered about but they were rapidly diminishing. The sun was still behind the looming peaks to their right when Taleb led them away from their camp. Tilliat had Cloud in her pack, slung across her chest under her jacket.

The cat mindspoke her. 'Is Toomay near do you think?'

'I'm not going to call him, Cloud. There must have been a very strong reason for him to leave us as he did. He will return and he will tell us in his own time.'

Cloud purred softly from somewhere below Tilliat's chin. 'That would be best,' she agreed. 'I suspect he is distressed.'

'Did you know why he went?' Tilliat asked in surprise.

'I had the faintest hint something was greatly wrong. Then he was gone.'

At midday, they made a brief halt and were thankful to be able to shed a few of their layers of clothing. They were riding along a trail that seemed to lead directly north, although there was no indication it was a regularly used route. Tilliat called to Taleb to find a suitable place to stop for the night much earlier than usual.

The sun was still above the mountains to the west when Taleb led the way down to a shallow dip just off the trail. A tiny stream formed a pool in one of the rocks before overflowing and bustling on out of view. There was grass enough for the horses to graze a

307

little, to supplement their grain and, being enclosed, there was respite from the wind. The wind had continued, at least no longer numbingly cold, but annoying just the same.

There was a huddle of bushes along one side, some showing hints of green but others brittle and dead. Davin Pearl had made sure there was kindling in their packs, but he had worried, the last few days, that there was such a lack of trees up here. At least tonight they needn't worry about running out of fuel.

Nami took a handful of snares and climbed back up out of the hollow. They would all appreciate fresh meat if she could find it. In fact, Nami couldn't quite believe her luck. She'd wandered on a short distance, peering down the sides of the ridge, and suddenly saw movement. She crept closer and found, not one single rabbit, but an entire clan of them. Nami got close enough so that when the rabbits saw her and froze, she was able to bag four of them for the pot.

The most enticing smells were rising from the pots over the fire when there was a flurry of wings and Toomay landed in the hollow. The horses, who had grown accustomed to the Dragon's presence, snorted and fidgeted in momentary alarm, but soon calmed. Toomay paced to Tilliat, pressing his brow to hers. He mindspoke them all.

'I regret leaving in such haste, my friends. I sensed something to the east.' His eyes whirred and although his tone sounded steady there was distress and agitation beneath.

'Thorn joined me and we searched. We found Kezia.'

Tilliat closed her eyes for a heartbeat.

'We found Kezia's body,' Toomay corrected himself. 'Her wings were ripped and torn – she would not have been able to fly. Her head had been cut off, but we were unable to find it.'

Chapter Twenty-Seven

In Gulat, Mahzu Vek was confused, and because she was very rarely confused, she was also extremely angry. She had summoned the members of both councils and a significant number of those members had proffered various excuses for their inability to attend. Her assistant, Keril Dwar, had scrutinised the various messages and had drawn an interesting conclusion.

Mahzu Vek was far too irritated to have noticed the clear distinction between those few who had agreed to attend and the many who had declined. Keril decided not to draw Mahzu Vek's notice to this division. Instead, she thought hard about what it might imply, while keeping a fraction of her attention on Vek's rambling diatribe.

To add to Mahzu Vek's vexation, she had received news that Della Wart, who she had sent to Druke, posing as Vek, had disappeared on the way. Mahzu could not understand how a woman with few mage talents, short sighted, and, in her personal opinion, dim witted, could vanish from a closed carriage surrounded by a large escort of loyal guards.

Keril Dwar realised the rant had ended and assumed an attentive expression.

'Rewrite the messages to those who dare refuse me their presence. Make sure you stress how very inadvisable it will be to offer refusals a second time.'

Keril gathered the heap of papers. 'Shall I deliver at least some of them?' she asked idly. 'I have errands to do – items you asked to be replenished.'

'If you want to waste your time, you can. We have plenty of runners but as long as you are not too long. I have a great deal to do.'

A servant crept into the study to pile fresh logs beside the fire. Mahzu gave Keril a pointed glance.

'I shall be downstairs. Report to me there, when you return, and make sure you are swift.'

She swept from the room and Keril Dwar saw the servant's shoulders relax.

Keril hurried along the corridor from Mahzu Vek's study to the tiny cupboard of a room that was her office. She quickly wrote to the councillors who had declined the meeting and sealed them with Mahzu Vek's seal. Snatching her cloak from the door hook, she ran down to the hall. She called for runners and gave them most of the messages to be delivered. The three boys raced off, followed by Keril Dwar at only a slightly less rapid pace.

She visited several small shops and left with a bagful of packages, looking carefully about for any sign that she might be watched. Keril took a fast but circuitous route through the crowded central streets before cutting through a narrow lane to emerge on Bell Street. Outside the high blank walls she looked up at the house's forbidding exterior.

For a heartbeat, she wavered, but then climbed the steps and lifted the heavy iron knocker, shaped like a large feather. The door opened at once, a broad shouldered, uniformed man looking down at her.

'I have come to see Master Koos, if you please. If you would tell him Keril Dwar begs a moment of his time?'

The man stood aside and Keril moved past him into a narrow hall. Four other guards were there, watching her carefully.

'If you would wait here, my lady, I will see if Master Koos is available.'

The guard, Mink, indicated a wooden bench against the left wall and Keril sat, as calmly as she could manage. Her heart was thumping now. *Was* this the right course? She had her own plans, worked out so meticulously over these four long years. But perhaps Perra Koos would bring about her wish and she could avoid so much risk to herself. Not *for* herself, she thought. For Arvan.

The door at the end of the hall opened and the guard beckoned to her.

'The master is extremely busy,' said Mink conversationally, leading Keril through ever larger passages. 'He said he would see you now, although he hasn't a great deal of time to spare.'

They mounted the broad staircase up to the reception room

Keril had been in before when she accompanied Mahzu Vek here.

Mink opened the door. 'Keril Dwar, master.'

The door closed behind her and Keril found herself facing Perra Koos. He stood by the fireplace and had apparently been chatting with Li Kassu, who sat at ease on a couch to the side. Keril was disconcerted to find the woman with Perra Koos: she had thought, hoped, she might speak to him alone.

'Mistress Dwar, please seat yourself. I believe you have met Lady Li?'

Li Kassu smiled. 'We have spoken once or twice.'

Keril hesitated. Perra Koos sat in the chair by the fire, where he'd sat before, Keril remembered. She realised both of them were studying her closely and her nervousness increased.

'Are you here on Mahzu Vek's behalf?' asked Li Kassu gently.

'No.' The reply was startled out of Keril more sharply than she'd intended. 'I mean, I am here of my own accord.' She drew a deep breath, her hands clenched on the straps of the bag of parcels.

Li Kassu looked concerned. 'Forgive my bluntness child, but has it anything to do with the Dirty Fox?'

Keril blanched and Li Kassu slid along the couch to place a hand over Keril's fists. Keril looked into the woman's beautiful face.

'How do you know about the tavern? *What* do you know?' Keril whispered.

'Now, now, child. We are not trying to threaten you with anything.' Perra Koos spread his hands towards her. 'You asked to see me and we thought perhaps there was a problem, with your – friend – in the tavern.'

Keril sat straight and looked first at the woman beside her, then at the man across the room.

'The friend in the Dirty Fox is my husband. He was Mahzu Vek's assistant before me. We had married, but she had never met me – I don't think she even realised we *had* married. We had rooms right across the city, in Apple Lane. Arvan – my husband – occasionally stayed at the Vek house at night. It is when she often worked on experimental things, he told me.'

She paused, looking from one to the other again. 'Things to

do with the god Reva, he said.'

Perra Koos nodded.

Keril took another breath. 'Some of her guards brought him home. He was barely conscious. He had burns on his face, his chest and his legs, not on his hands. I nursed him, of course, but we soon ran out of coin for healers or medicines. He has spoken only once. He said: "It is the blackest evil." Sometimes he seems to be there, inside his own head again, but mostly not. He looks at me blankly.'

Keril's fists whitened and her eyes were wide. 'He killed our daughter while I was out trying to find work. She was nearing her third birthday. That is when he spoke. When I came home and – found her, – Arvan said those words, and then he wept. He weeps often since then, but he is afraid to go out, afraid to let anyone see him. I managed to get work in Vek's house. I was educated well until my parents died in the summer plague when I was fourteen, so Vek decided I would be suitable to assist her. I asked her once if she had had no other assistant. She said there had been a man, a couple of years before, but he had been a fool. He had been burned and she had dismissed him.'

Keril gave a shuddering sigh. 'I have never spoken of this to anyone. I moved Arvan to the Fox as it cost less coin than our rent in Apple Lane, and I have a room in Vek's house. The Fox is far closer too, so I can visit him.'

Both her listeners were looking distressed now and Keril gave a shaky laugh.

'I thought I was so careful, visiting Arvan, but obviously not careful enough. But he wasn't the reason I came to see you. Not directly.'

'Then tell me, child, what is the reason?'

'Mahzu Vek has no control at all over what she does, calling to this god. I have no mage talent. I suspect that Arvan is so damaged because he *did* have a small gift. I have listened, when she's in her sacred room, as she calls it – a cellar, far below ground. She calls and calls the god. He has only answered once since I have been working there, and he nearly killed her I think. I felt tired, and sick, and dizzy, but she looked like Arvan does. Eyes blank, not really aware of anything around her. It lasted for several days.'

Keril straightened her shoulders and raised her chin. 'I was going to kill her, to avenge Arvan and our daughter. But in recent days, I've wondered if you have planned to – remove her from power here in Gulat? She is much agitated about this mage of prophecy, but I know, for certain, she ordered the death of her son Skala, herself. Then she poisoned the assassins.'

She saw Li Kassu and Perra Koos were completely shocked.

'I came to you Master Koos, because I believe you are the strongest mage in Gulat, you have formed a group around you, and you know more, by far, about this mage Mahzu Vek seeks. One more thing I will tell you. When she called the god, *he* was interested in this mage also. I do not know why.'

Keril frowned. 'And finally, Mahzu Vek keeps servants watching for rainbows. I have no idea why. She mutters about the god coming when there is a rainbow. I did ask if there were rainbows when he came at night but she ignored my question. From what I remember from my lessons, I understood rainbows appear when the sun shines through raindrops? When I mentioned that, Vek was cross, the most angry she has yet been with me. So I let it drop. Is any of this news to you, or of interest?'

'It is.' Perra rubbed a hand over his face. 'Can I offer you refreshment?'

'No, no.' Keril stood up. 'I am doing errands for Vek, I cannot be long. I will have to run all the way back.'

'Tell us quickly then, do you know why she called the meeting of both councils?' asked Li Kassu.

Keril had her hand on the door latch. 'I suspect she intends to kill all those who are not her creatures. You know her house guards are mostly thugs and villains. They have no qualms over *any* of her orders. I must go.'

Perra Koos hurried after her as she fled down the stairs.

'If you have need child, send to me, or just come here. And we will take in your husband too.'

Keril faltered on the last step, looking up at the man she'd thought imperious and aloof. Now she saw an elderly man, tired and worried, but with genuine compassion in his dark blue eyes. She pulled a folded paper from her pocket and laid it on the stair.

'I nearly forgot – she sent you another summons to her

meeting.'

Then Keril Dwar dashed down the hallways, startling the guards by the door, and was bowed out by Captain Mink.

Perra went slowly back to Li Kassu and sank into his chair.

'Worry upon worry,' he sighed.

'I do wonder how young Tilliat is getting on,' said Li Kassu. 'Everything seems to come back to her.'

'Because she is who she is,' agreed Perra. 'That poor woman though – did you know her husband – this Arvan? He must have worked for Vek, what – five or six years ago?'

'Who has any knowledge of her household?' retorted Li Kassu. 'I only know Keril Dwar because she accompanies Vek to meetings and so on.'

'If Arvan was damaged by Reva, then he must be like Tani was, locked inside his own head.'

'If there is anything left of a man called Arvan.'

They sat in silence until Mink tapped the door. He brought the folded paper Keril had left on the stairs. Perra read it and passed it to Li Kassu.

'No doubt we will all have a gentle reminder.' Perra Koos rose. 'We had better tell the others what Keril Dwar had to say.'

Li Kassu followed him from the room. She laughed and Perra turned back, brows raised.

'It would seem the Char twins did travel on with Tilliat and her Uncle. They would have been back here days ago otherwise. I wonder how Davin Pearl copes with their bickering?'

Tilliat and her companions continued riding north. Toomay stayed with them but was very subdued. The weather remained clear and fresh, with frosts at night. They were ten days out of the Yasharitzan village and the Char twins were behaving as though this was merely one of their summer holiday trips. Davin Pearl said nothing, but he knew Tilliat was worried about what might lie ahead.

His own thoughts swung between what might be happening in Kelshan and concern for Tilliat. She looked fitter than she had since they'd left Kelshan city, but her eyes held anxiety in their grey depths, which Davin saw clearly even if the Chars did not. The trader was also concerned about the young Dragon. Davin had never seen Kezia but he knew she had been only young too, and her death, as described by Toomay, filled him with horror. Who, or what, could visit such violence on a Dragon?

They had just begun travelling on the eleventh morning, when Tilliat's horse jinked and shook its head in protest at her sudden clutching of the reins. Davin stopped immediately, reaching to grab the rein and seeing in a glance that Tilliat's eyes looked blurred. Toomay came arrowing back towards them, landing next to Tilliat.

'She speaks with the Shadows, Uncle. Do not fear.' Toomay settled to wait, his great eyes calming to a silvery blue from their kaleidoscopic whirr of worry.

Tilliat blinked. She looked slightly surprised to find Davin and Toomay so close.

'The Shadows say we should halt at midday. They say the Pathmaker is near. They were gone before I could ask if he will come to us.'

Taleb and Nami had caught up in time to hear Tilliat's words. Nami scanned the country around them.

'I've seen no sign that any people live or travel in these lands. I thought you said Kenza told you this Pathmaker is very old?'

Tilliat shrugged. 'Won't be long until we find out.'

They rode on through the morning, still following an apparently clear path northwards. Tilliat was thoughtful and took no part in the Chars' chatter with Davin Pearl. The trader too was nonplussed that there should be such a good road and yet no one used it, or ever had.

They had descended again and there were stands of evergreens along the sides of the track. Davin pointed out a lesser trail, leading down to the west. Taleb went to investigate and called up to the others that there was a good place to camp there. Nami and Davin looked to Tilliat for her decision. She chewed her lip.

'I think we have to go a little further on and camp to the east side. Just a feeling.'

Nami grinned and called Taleb to rejoin them. Not long after this, Tilliat pointed to the right and they all left the path that was almost a road, and rode down behind her. They found more birch trees forming a barrier against the evergreens below a line of rockfaces leading east. The rock wall was pocked with holes but

315

when Taleb climbed up for a closer look, he shook his head.

'We could perhaps squeeze in some of these, and I do mean squeeze, but they don't appear to be used by anything.'

'Anything – like what?' Davin asked suspiciously.

Taleb jumped down and dusted his hands on his trousers. He grinned at the trader and waved airily around them. 'Mountain cats. Bears rousing from their winter sleep.' He chortled at Davin's apprehensive glance upwards. Nami punched his arm, hard.

'Don't be mean. I've seen no sign of cats or bear,' she soothed Davin. 'Only rabbits and small deer and goats.'

Toomay had vanished briefly but now landed close to them. He laid a deer carefully by Davin's feet and backed away, to recline on a ledge of rock about head high to Taleb. Davin set to work butchering the carcase and Cloud daintily accepted her share. The cat then scrabbled up the rock to settle on Toomay's back.

The meat cooking over the fire, the four lounged on their blankets. Nami glanced at Tilliat.

'Nothing from those Shadows I suppose?'

'I think they are here but they are definitely not willing to talk to me right now.'

'Really helpful then?'

Tilliat laughed and Davin was glad to hear it. She was surely too young to deal with this – whatever this turned out to be.

Davin had just decided the meat should be ready when Toomay shivered his wings against his sides. He spoke in all their minds.

'Beware.'

The Dragon moved smoothly down from the ledge, nearly toppling Cloud who hissed in indignation. Toomay settled on Tilliat's left. Davin abandoned the food and scrambled to her right, the Chars closing up on each side. A few pebbles rattled down and all eyes turned to the rock wall. Something seemed to move in one of the larger holes much higher up.

A yellow mist drifted down, to settle across the fire from Tilliat. Slowly, the mist evaporated and a small figure stood there, cloaked and leaning on a staff. The hood of the cloak fell back and the companions simply stared. The head was a hairless oval, with eyes slanted up at the outer corners. The eyes themselves were a vivid leaf green. The skin was a patchy grey and deeply wrinkled. Two ears, larger than a human's and of a different shape, lay close against the bare skull.

He had a short straight nose but his lower jaw protruded and at first, Tilliat thought it was his teeth showing slightly. He smiled and she saw there were tusks growing up, one on each side of his mouth, just long enough to overlap his upper lip. Tilliat cleared her throat.

'If you are the Pathmaker, be welcome at our fire.' She managed to sound quite calm.

The smile broadened. 'And if I am not the Pathmaker?' He tilted his head to one side, an almost birdlike movement. He raised his staff slightly. 'I should not joke.'

He moved, very slowly, towards the fire and lowered himself to the ground, laying the staff beside him. Cautiously, Tilliat sat opposite him, her companions staying close.

'Can we offer you food or drink?' Tilliat asked courteously.

'I eat very little now,' was the reply. 'But please, eat your meal lest it spoil.'

Tilliat noticed the man's nostrils flared slightly, as Toomay's did at the smell of cooked meat. Davin offered a bowl of tea and the Pathmaker took it with both hands. They saw the grey skin was loose on bony fingers and the nails were much thickened, almost like claws.

'Kenza said you could tell me much that might help me. I know nothing of Reva – only that he is some kind of creature with great powers.'

'Dear Kenza. I do not journey to the villages now.'

Tilliat frowned. 'Are there many villages? Like the one where we met Kenza?'

'There were. But the people changed. Reva damaged many, soon after we came here.'

'Where did you come from?' Nami asked, then glanced guiltily at Tilliat. 'Sorry.'

The Pathmaker smiled again. 'We came from a land across the sea, at the time of the Imperator Jemin of Kelshan.'

Tilliat gave a start.

The Pathmaker nodded. 'The great mage Tika, requested of

him a portion of land. This was all once Kelshan land.' He sighed. 'There was always doubt that we would endure.'

'Why did you leave your land across the sea?' Nami asked carefully.

The Pathmaker laughed aloud. 'You have sharp friends my child.' He grew serious. 'There was instability in the people. No. Let me speak only truth. There was insanity in the people.' He regarded Toomay sadly. 'There was a Dragon Lord, once upon a time, a kindly, caring Lord. His name was Mim and his dearest love was for a Dragon called Ashta. They were devoted to each other.

'Then came a Dragon Lady. She was named Gremara. The tales concerning her have grown tangled down the years, but the consistent thread is of her insanity. She had children and the Dragon Lord saw they were evil, even from their births. He made up his mind to kill them himself, but Gremara learned of his plan. She fled here with three of the children. The Dragon Lord destroyed four children and then fell into despair for many years.

'He never knew Gremara came here, I don't believe. The mage Tika was as a sister to Mim: they endured much together, at the rising of their powers. That is why she asked that this land be given to Gremara, her children and those humans who followed her.'

Tilliat and her friends sat spellbound. Toomay and Cloud also listened closely. The Pathmaker sipped from his bowl of tea.

'Children were born here, some of whom inherited the physical marks of the Dragon Lord. Some inherited only the madness. Fewer and fewer down all these generations bear the Dragon signs, but this creature Reva found a hold in the minds of the mad ones. All I am able to tell you, child, is a very little of how the mage Tika nearly destroyed the one who came before Reva.'

The old man studied them for a heartbeat, then sighed. He lifted his staff and used it to haul himself upright, then let it drop. He fumbled at the clasp at his throat and unclipped it. He had an expression of ineffable sadness as he pushed the cloak clear of his shoulders. He was barely as tall as Tilliat, but he stood straight. He wore a strange jerkin over dark trousers tucked into boots of soft leather. Then he stretched his arms out to the sides and behind him spread great fans: huge wings of deepest blue feathers, tipped with green.

Toomay was the one who moved. He paced around the fire and stood before the Pathmaker. Tilliat and her friends saw enormous tears rolling down the Dragon's long, beautiful face. He took one more pace forward and touched his brow to the man's, then turned and resumed his position beside Tilliat.

Tilliat rested her arm across Toomay's shoulders and looked back at the Pathmaker. The great wings were furled now against his back and he lowered himself to sit on the ground again. Even in the fading light, Tilliat saw tracks glittering on his cheeks, and found she was quite unable to think of anything to say.

'Is there more tea perhaps?' The mundane remark from the Pathmaker relieved the tension among them, and Davin Pearl hastened to oblige.

'I am descended from the Dragon Lord. I was spared the madness. I was called Pathmaker because, from my earliest days, I wished only to find the path back across the sea, to our homeland.'

His voice sank to a whisper. 'I have never managed to understand how those first of my kind flew across so much water. I cannot see how it was accomplished. I have little of what you would call mage talents, other than that of mindpseech, so I cannot use power to travel so far. I will die soon, here in the land that has been our exile. There are only two others like me, and none of us has bred children. It is time for us to be gone from the world.'

He gazed across the fire into Tilliat's eyes.

'Forgive me. I am truly old. Let me rest for a while, then we will talk of more important things.'

Chapter Twenty-Eight

When the old man had pulled his cloak over himself, he lay down, his back to the fire, the tips of those glorious wings just visible by his feet. Cloud stepped daintily over legs and knees and sat for a moment, staring down at the Pathmaker. She crouched, then squirmed her way beside his arm where it was bent, pillowing his head.

Softly, Taleb and Nami murmured to each other, still picking at pieces of roast deer meat. Davin leaned close to Tilliat. 'He isn't what you expected, is he?'

'He certainly isn't. I vaguely remember something about the mage Tika in one of those many old books I used to read. She had many Dragon friends. I know one was Fenj, and another name was Mim, I'm sure. I assumed it was the name of a Dragon.'

Davin lowered his voice even further. 'Is he human?'

'He said his people bred children when they came here. I would guess he means there were people here – hunting clans most likely. So there must be a link with humans. Perhaps one day, one of us will write about this journey,' she smiled.

The four settled in their blankets, dozing lightly in case the Pathmaker woke and chose to talk. But it was halfway to dawn when Tilliat heard the faintest movement. She sat up. The old man was stirring the embers of the fire. Tilliat set about making tea without a word.

When it was ready, she moved quietly round to sit next to the Pathmaker. Close to, he seemed even older in the faint starlight, the flames from the fire making dark shadows in the multitude of lines and wrinkles. He drank half the bowl of tea before speaking.

'You understand why we are called Yasharitza now?'

'Halflings. Half Dragon, half human.'

The Pathmaker sighed. 'The two others like me are old, older even than I am. One is very close to going beyond and the other will not choose to live without her.'

'Are they living near here?'

'They are not far,' he admitted. 'I care for them now, since they have become too frail to care for themselves.' He looked across the fire at the three recumbent shapes, then at the Dragon. Toomay's head was resting on his front feet, but the glitter of his eyes showed he was awake.

The Pathmaker lifted an edge of his cloak and revealed Cloud, curled in a ball. He touched her spine gently.

'Creatures such as this were deeply revered among us. It is long and long since I have seen one.'

'They were?' Tilliat wondered what more surprises lay ahead.

The Pathmaker nodded. 'The great mage Tika always travelled with such a one as this, and the Dragon Lord Mim had many in his company.'

Tilliat considered the many times she'd had to retrieve Cloud from various difficulties and wondered why the mage Tika had taken a cat travelling. Cloud stretched then recurled herself even tighter. She spoke in Tilliat's mind, her tone decidedly superior.

'We can get in very small places you know, and most humans ignore us. So we hear all kinds of interesting talk.'

The Pathmaker choked on his tea. When he'd regained his breath, he accepted a fresh bowlful gratefully.

'There are so many things in this world, child, it would take many lifetimes to understand even half of them. And look.'

He pointed up at the stars. 'There are worlds up there too. And some creatures have learnt to travel between the stars, distances unimaginable.'

Tilliat stared at him. Worlds out in the stars? People travelling between them? Was the Pathmaker's mind broken? His green eyes turned from the sky to meet Tilliat's gaze.

'Reva's ancestor was a creature from such a place.'

Tilliat took a deep breath, her thoughts reeling. If this old man spoke the truth, then how was she, a girl of just eighteen, supposed to destroy such a creature?

'I spoke to a god once, not long ago,' she said wildly. 'The god of death apparently.'

The Pathmaker gave her a huge smile. 'Did you? He was a

kind creature. You say you saw him? I had no idea he was still around.'

Tilliat rolled her eyes helplessly. 'You're only confusing me, I'm afraid,' she said. 'Could you just tell me what you know of Reva, please?'

The Pathmaker studied her. He laid a hand along her cheek, in just the way she offered comfort to Toomay.

'Alas, you are so young for this task. But if it helps, the mage Tika was even younger than you are at the time of her battle.'

Tilliat gave him the faintest glimmer of a smile. 'That isn't much comfort really.'

The Pathmaker smiled back. 'No. I suppose not. Well then. Reva's ancestor was called Yartay. We refer to Yartay as "he" although no one knows if "he" was male or female.'

'But Reva *is* male,' objected Tilliat.

'Are you sure? Never mind now. Yartay came from far distant stars and somehow became entangled with this world. He was a shapeless creature, but he could take on the look of others, so at times he was seen as human. His world was so different from ours: his sustenance, even the air he breathed, was different, and he could not adjust to life here. He had enormous powers but no one knows whether his power was part of him, or of the strange craft he travelled in.'

Fascinated in spite of only half believing his words, Tilliat listened closely.

'Tika used mage fire to destroy Yartay and his craft. You have Shadows with you?' The Pathmaker's tone hardened. He waited for Tilliat's nod. 'Shadows took Tika within the craft and she used fire. The craft was destroyed and it was thought Yartay too was finished. In those days, he was also known as the Crazed One, or the Broken One.'

The Pathmaker sank into silence, his domed skull bowed to his chest. Tilliat waited, wondering if he'd fallen asleep, as the very old sometimes did. But his head lifted and his strange eyes fastened on her.

'Fragments of the thing called Yartay were flung far and wide. Most were too small to be of any danger. But some fragments found their way to others and somehow they united. We know that there are at least two others who are nearing Reva's size and

322

capacity of mind to wreak devastation.'

'Two others?' Tilliat asked faintly.

'Indeed. The trouble is, they keep moving and we are unsure of their position. They should be destroyed now, while it is easier – perhaps.'

'But if they move around, how will I find Reva?'

The sky was growing lighter, the stars fading from view. The old man looked weary.

'Reva does indeed move from place to place but, he has what I call, his *nest*. A place where he retreats to, for years at a time. We can have no idea what he does then, if he sleeps, or thinks, – no idea at all. But he *could* be destroyed there, more easily than when he's – active.'

'He's active now though. He caused trouble in Gulat, and in the Yasharitza village. You say he goes off to his nest for years at a time – does that mean he also roams about for years at a time?'

'Think, child. The unrest in all these lands. How long has it been going on?'

Tilliat frowned. 'Most of my life I suppose. It's got much worse in the last five or six years.'

'Exactly. So unless Reva changes the patterns of his behaviour, he *should* retreat to his nest anytime now.'

Tilliat opened her mouth to point out that if that was the case, they could expect peace for several years, so why, exactly, did *she* have to find him. She decided that would be a cowardly and pointless question and closed her mouth without asking it.

The Pathmaker struggled to his feet, leaning heavily on his staff. Cloud sat up straight, tail curled neatly over her front paws, and yawned.

'I must make sure my friends are well and prepare food for them. I will return here before dark.' He hesitated. 'I wonder, would it be possible to take this small Cloud with me? My friends would love her to visit.'

'You may carry me,' Cloud agreed.

Tilliat lifted the cat into the Pathmaker's arms.

'May the stars guide your path and guard your heart,' The Pathmaker whispered.

Tilliat took a step back as the golden mist engulfed the strange figure. When the mist cleared, the Pathmaker was gone too.

323

Tilliat stood there, her thoughts utterly confused. Toomay bespoke her.

'Sleep, friend Tilliat. I will tell the others to leave you for a while.'

Tilliat fetched her blankets and lay down a little way from the fire. Toomay moved over to her, curling himself around her. With her mind spinning, Tilliat thought she wouldn't possibly sleep, but, within heartbeats, she did.

When she woke, it was after midday and Davin Pearl was sitting cross-legged by the fire, puffing blissfully on a pipe.

Tilliat sat up. 'I thought you lost your pipe ages ago, Uncle.'

Davin smiled. 'That Taleb had this in one of his packs. Toomay told us you were to sleep, so Nami ordered all the packs to be sorted out and organised. My word, that girl likes organising. Anyway, there were two pipes *and* a pouch of fruit leaf. One of the pipes was cracked, but this is excellent.'

Tilliat stretched, rose and joined Davin. 'Where are Taleb and Nami now?'

Davin snorted. 'After the "organising", Taleb stalked off *that* way, and Nami went *that* way.' He waved his pipe in opposite directions. He watched Tilliat pour some tea from his ever steaming kettle. 'Toomay said you spoke with the Pathmaker while we slept. Any help?'

'Not much. He took Cloud to visit his two friends.' She frowned. 'He says they are very old and weak, but he's not exactly young. I wonder how he manages? And I got the feeling the three of them keep themselves hidden away from the rest of the Yasharitzans.'

'They seemed so strange in that village.' Davin repeated the comment all of them had made in the days since they'd left it behind them.

'I'm going to ask him, when he comes back.'

Taleb and Nami Char returned to camp at dusk, Nami carrying two rabbits although there was still plenty of deer meat left. She also pulled a few small onions from her pockets. Her brother brought nothing but ignored her anyway.

'I climbed quite a way up there,' he jerked a thumb at the wall of rock. 'There was one place which gave a clear view south. I saw no hint of people, no smoke from any sort of fire, although I

324

could see the smoke from *this* fire plainly.'

'So you think there are no villages here?' asked Davin.

'I've seen no sign of people,' Nami remarked. 'But that path we've been following, isn't a path.' She grinned. 'I scraped away quite a large patch of dirt just up there. There are enormous cut slabs of stone, under the earth. It must have been a mighty road once.'

The sun sank behind the peaks and the Pathmaker did not appear. Tilliat was beginning to wonder if he *was* coming back as the evening darkened. Toomay alerted them so they were prepared for the sight of the mist and then the odd figure of the Pathmaker. Tilliat jumped up in alarm when the man swayed where he stood. She caught his arm and led him close to the fire.

'Uncle has just made fresh tea. Sit down and I'll get you some.'

Cloud leapt from his arms and moved to Toomay. Her mindvoice whispered through their heads. 'I will show you. Let me put the pictures in your minds.'

It seemed as if they were in a cave; a very comfortable cave, with a fireplace and chimney, shelves full of books, a curtained doorway and couches, strewn with brightly coloured covers. On one of the couches lay a figure. The same hairless, domed head as the Pathmaker and, as the figure turned that head, they saw the eyes were the white of blindness.

'You are back! Did you speak with her?'

The voice although faint was female, the wings like a great blanket of pale blue with black tipped feathers.

Tilliat and her friends had thought the Pathmaker old, but this Halfling was ancient. As she stretched out her arm in welcome, they could see the firelight through the fragile skin of the skeletal hand. Another figure came into view, frail as a winter twig. Tilliat realised they were watching this from Cloud's view when the Pathmaker put the cat onto the couch beside the female. The Halfling touched her and wept and crooned and sang to the small grey cat. Cloud looked towards the other Halfling, a male, his eyes the palest blue, his wings, half flared, honey coloured their whole length.

The four watching Cloud's mindpictures had frozen as they absorbed what they were seeing. The tea apparently revived the

325

Pathmaker. He straightened his back and offered a smile.

'Cloud shows you my friends. The blind one is named Zamina, and the other is Siyamak. Those two were friends from babyhood and when Zamina lost her sight soon after she was full grown, Siyamak took care of her. They were both my teachers. So long ago now. When troubles beset the Yasharitza and they feared for their safety, I brought them away. We have lived together in several places, but each time we have moved on because people in the villages said we were too near them.'

He shrugged. 'They say *we* are evil and bring misfortune upon their villages. This place where we live now will be our last home.'

'But how can you live out here?' Nami burst out. 'Forgive me, but you are old. How can you hunt, grow food crops, gather wood for your fire? And you surely must need a lot of such supplies to see you though the northern winters.'

The Pathmaker gave a delighted chuckle. 'Indeed so, clever child. There are a few who know of us and help me. They make sure we are well provided for.'

'Who are they?' Nami demanded instantly. 'I have seen no sign at all – not old sign or new sign – that *anyone* moves in this region.'

He studied her, his leaf green eyes noting the flush of indignation on her cheeks. 'It is not my place to speak of them. They are not Yasharitza. They have lived hidden through these lands since long before we came here. I understand that it is a rare thing that they give their trust to such as I – indeed to any – so never will I betray that trust.'

He hesitated and met Tilliat's eyes. 'They gave aid to the mage Tika.'

A tense silence fell and it was left to the Pathmaker to break it. 'Zamina is a dreamwalker.' He saw that the brother and sister both looked interested, while Tilliat and her uncle looked blank. 'A dreamwalker travels in dreams. They see what is happening in other dreaming minds and remember when they wake. Sometimes they can communicate directly with another dreamwalker. Zamina has no mindspeech although Siyamak does. But Zamina has dream travelled far, and she has seen the place I call Reva's nest.'

'Is it far?' Tilliat asked, her heart banging against her ribs.

'Two days of travel at the speed your animals move. No more. I have travelled these lands – when I was much younger of course – but I do not remember the place I have seen in Zamina's mind. I can put the picture in your minds, if you permit me?'

Tilliat didn't allow herself to think, just gave a jerky nod. Another picture formed in her mind, There were trees, covering a valley floor and creeping up the sloping sides. A line ran through the trees, just like the line of the path they had been following all these days. It led to a tumbled circle of buildings. The fallen blocks were huge, judging their size against the height of the trees, yet were cast down as though they were a child's toys.

Tilliat's stomach lurched. There was a sensation of sinking down, through an immeasurable depth of earth. She had a glimpse of a vast hall, circular, with a mosaic floor, then she hauled her mind free of the picture. She found herself sitting on the ground, shivering violently while sweat dripped into her eyes. The Pathmaker was beside her, gripping her hand.

'You see what you must face, child, and that was simply *seeing* the nest, without Reva's presence there.'

Davin pushed the inevitable bowl of tea under Tilliat's nose and the steam rose to wreath her face. She gulped some down, still returning the tight hold of the Pathmaker's hand.

'Reva has corrupted most of your people.' Her throat felt raw, as though she'd been screaming aloud. 'You have to tell me all of it.'

The Pathmaker nodded slowly. 'Truly, I am not sure what help that information may be to you, but I will speak. We will be gone from this world soon. Perhaps at least one other should know of us.'

He sat back, gathering his thoughts. 'When Gremara came here, the three children she brought were the youngest. We are born as any human, without wings. When we reach fourteen or so, we suffer much pain. Swellings appear down each side of our spines. It takes about a year, and we become very weak, which makes it even more perilous when the time comes for the wings to emerge.

'Of the three children Gremara brought, only one developed wings. The other two did not, but found they were strong in mage powers. Reva was stirring then, at least, that is what Siyamak and I surmise, from what records we managed to retrieve. It was *his* power that strengthened Gremara's wingless children – of that I am convinced.'

Davin had draped a blanket over Tilliat's shoulders. Now, calmer, she pushed it off and leaned towards the Pathmaker, listening intently.

'The wingless ones bred many children, who, in turn, were also without wings. Those of us who are winged all descend from Karn, the son of Gremara and perhaps the Dragon Lord Mim.'

'But you must also come from local people, who were already here?'

The Pathmaker nodded. 'Sometimes a winged one showed the signs of madness and was then killed. Even Karn had a tendency to ungovernable rages but he was aware of this in himself and would go far away to avoid contact with any whilst the fit lasted. Gremara's rages were terrible. She would kill any in her way, and it got worse with time.'

The old man's head bowed for a moment. 'Karn killed her and was torn apart by his brother and sister. We – Zamina, Siyamak and I – believe it was the human blood which diluted the madness of Gremara's line. As the generations passed, fewer and fewer were born who grew wings and we believe that is right. This is *not* our land, we are *wrong* somehow, and thus we should end. I often wonder if there are others like us, still in the lands from whence we came.

'The ones who were born human seemed placid compared to the volatility of the Halflings, but again, over many years, it becomes plain that the calmness hid a sullen, sour temperament. Those are the ones whose minds were touched by Reva. His mind quested out and found a fertile place to root within the Yasharitza.'

The Pathmaker sighed. 'The name was given to us when a human met Gremara soon after she reached here. You see, Gremara not only had feathered wings. She had a scaled body. Yasharitza means lizard.'

Tilliat was processing the Pathmaker's words, sorting them into a pattern she might grasp.

'Those in the village,' she began. 'They seemed – blank,

empty. Was that Reva's doing?'

'Yes. Sometimes they seem almost normal, then, as you describe. We believe Reva uses them, that he can watch what they watch. Even then, he still can't understand any of this world – Yasharitzan or human. There is no place in *his* mind to comprehend ours.'

'And yet... '

'And yet.' The Pathmaker nodded again. 'The mage Tika spoke with Yartay, several times.'

'Mahzu Vek,' Nami interrupted. 'Mahzu Vek has spoken to Reva. It nearly killed her we guessed. Several mages in Gulat died.'

Now the Pathmaker was nodding vigorously. 'Reva is from another world. His mind is so different. The stories say that Yartay's speech was too rapid to understand. He could not recognise any life on this world as having intelligence.'

'I think I know what you mean.' Tilliat scowled. 'You've shown me the place you believe Reva may return to, but he isn't there now. I can't believe I'm just supposed to sit and wait for him, am I?'

'We are sure you must be close by. Reva seems to be aware of you in some way. He has made a connection in his twisted mind between you and the mage Tika. Oh yes, his mind is as crazed as Gremara's was. We do not know from whence that power derives: it is unlike any we know or have heard of. Zamina dreamwalks. She has become aware of Reva trying to track her on several occasions in recent years and has fled back to her body at once. When she dreamwalks, her mind is wide open and so extremely vulnerable to attack.'

Davin Pearl had brewed fresh tea and passed a bowl to the Pathmaker.

'You live utterly secluded here, yet you know who Tilliat is.' The trader's tone held a note of suspicion.

'We heard of the mage Tika's prophecy long ago according to the oldest of our records, yet it is only lately that we have heard the time is now when the prophecy is to be fulfilled.'

'And you heard – how?' Davin stared down his nose at the Pathmaker, who smiled wryly.

'From those who help me protect Zamina and Siyamak, and

keep us supplied.' His smile faded. 'Somehow their minds seem to – repel – Reva. He passes over them, unaware of their existence. They have a name for themselves which I do not know. We three call them the Ancient Ones, because they have been here longer than any.'

The silver ring on Tilliat's left thumb burned icy cold as the Pathmaker pronounced their name and she clenched her fingers over it.

'Shadow?' she called in her mind.

'Yes.' The reply was faint, scarcely audible.

'Are these Ancient Ones the same as the ones Thorn spoke of?'

'Yes.'

'So they are real?'

'No.'

The silence in her head told her the Shadow would answer no more now.

The Pathmaker was watching her, his head tilted in that odd birdlike gesture.

'You spoke with Shadows.'

'Yes I did. What do you know of Shadows?'

'Nothing at all.'

But Tilliat thought his reply came too quickly to be truthful. She glanced at Nami and saw scepticism in her expression. She chose not to pursue the subject.

'You say your friend – the dreamwalker – travels far. Has she news of what is happening in my land?'

'Zamina has seen much trouble – burnings and killings. Mostly much further west. The worst is close by your city of Kelshan she says. She has touched several dreamers there and learned quite a lot.'

He hesitated, then shrugged.

'She has found thoughts of you in many of the dreaming minds. Zamina has also dreamed to your brother, but she left him swiftly as he roused at the touch of her mind. It seems that he too is a dreamwalker.'

Chapter Twenty-Nine

Tetsura still had not confronted Hikmat. He reasoned there was no urgency about the matter. The ex Regent had, after all, controlled the eighteen years of Tetsura's life: what difference could a full turn of the moon make now? After his initial panic at the realisation of his rise towards Kingship, Tetsura had consulted the list Saima and Sergeant Tag had compiled and steadily worked his way through it. Some of those he met with had been nervous or hostile, but the Prince found Saima was correct. He *could* see if the man or woman in front of him was true of heart, whose concern was truly for the prosperity of his Guild, his workers and the Phoenix Kingdom.

Those openly suspicious when they first met the Crown Prince, left the encounter reassured that the boy was willing to listen at least. He had fretted that he had been unable to make any more visits outside the Palace, but Saima had consoled him when she swore that all Crown Princes customarily stayed within the Palace between their Presentation and their Crowning. She ignored Sergeant Tag's raised brow and grin, and, fortunately, Tetsura hadn't seen them.

Commander Anjit sealed the offices and over half the scribes and secretaries had vanished. The few remaining at their posts greeted the Commander with great relief. They had tried, over the years, to mitigate the endless pilfering and illegal deals rife amongst Hikmat's officials. Commander Anjit left them to make some sense of the chaos in the offices and sent a message to the Prince advising him to take heed of the remaining staff in the recruiting of new officials. Tetsura had plunged into work, delighted to at last begin to learn what made the wheels of government turn.

Several days after his change of circumstances, meetings were postponed. The Prince had a slight fever, no more, and would resume his meetings tomorrow. Vilad reported to Saima that the

Prince had slept, but he had been very restless. Vilad knew the boy was dreaming, but had been unable to reach his mind. In the morning Tetsura seemed weak, and was pale and exhausted. Saima and Vilad concluded it was the turmoil of recent days, including his great display of magical power, that had caught up with him.

'Let him rest for the day Vilad,' Saima advised. 'He is resilient. He'll be fine tomorrow.'

Neither Saima nor Vilad yet recognised just how strongly Prince Tetsura could shield his mind. Sergeant Tag was of a far more suspicious nature. She waited until Vilad left the Prince's apartment and then wandered through to find Tetsura sitting on his balcony. She leaned against the wall and followed his gaze over the city out to the brilliantly blue waters of the harbour.

'Was it your sister?' she asked casually, not turning to look at him.

After a few moments, he chose to reply. 'Yes. She called fire. Far too much for what she needed.'

Tag kept quiet and waited.

'She thought she was making an illusion, like my display at the Presentation. But she called *real* fire.' He got to his feet and rested his hands on the stone rim of the balcony. 'I tried to change it to illusion but something else did.'

He frowned, unseeing, at the view before him.

Tag waited a heartbeat. 'What could have done that?

Tetsura looked straight into the Sergeant's eyes. 'A Dragon did that.' His tone was flat.

Even Sergeant Tag couldn't hold onto her neutral expression. 'A Dragon?' she repeated.

Tetsura smiled, a mixture of awe and pride. 'A Dragon who loves her, who would die for her.'

Tag cleared her throat, just to be sure her voice would work.

'If she has a Dragon on her side, I should think she'll be fine.'

'No.' Tetsura shook his head. 'Whatever she has to face, it must be completed by the same time as my Crowning. And she is afraid, even with the Dragon beside her.'

Tag shivered suddenly. 'I've been reading in my spare time,' she began.

'*Really?* Not practising with your multitude of knives?'

'I heard about your sister's visit here and you said she saw the display you performed.'

Tetsura couldn't help interrupting again. 'Some of what you "heard" was only mentioned in mindspeech with Vilad. He has told some of the mageborn in the city. You really will have to be truthful about your talents soon you know.' He watched her face become an immobile mask for a heartbeat then, ignoring his comment, she continued what she'd been saying.

'I've looked at some of the oldest records – of when King Sato went to the mainland. From things I've heard,' she glared at his grin, 'there are some odd coincidences. And I've never much believed in coincidence.'

'What coincidences?'

'About a catastrophe in the lands on the other side of the world.'

Tetsura frowned. 'The Night Lands? I learned something about them from a tutor, I think.'

'Well, there was a mage, a woman. She destroyed a dangerous threat to the whole world. A large part of one of the lands was flooded, although few people lived there so there wasn't serious loss of lives fortunately. But she prophesied that the danger would return.'

Tetsura chewed his lip. Sergeant Tag's information rang in his mind with the clarity of truth.

'And that is what my sister must confront,' he said heavily, dropping back into his chair.

Sergeant Tag slid down the wall to sit on her haunches.

'The mage I read about – there was no name – she had Dragons with her. So I was interested and checked a few other books. Dragons once lived here in Vremilia. Did you know that? Well, the Dragons here seemed quite happy to share these islands with people, but some of the mages said they were too dangerous. They were hunted and destroyed, or else they left. Oddly – another coincidence for you – it was around that time when twin births were pronounced anathema.'

They both remained silent for some time then Tetsura rubbed his forehead.

'Would you have those books sent to me, please, Sergeant, I would read it for myself.'

333

Tag pushed herself to her feet and was on her way out when Tetsura spoke softly behind her.

'Were you a twin, Sergeant?'

Her small, lithe body went rigid and she stood utterly still. Tetsura saw her head duck in a jerky nod.

'Perhaps one day you will tell me your name, and your twin's.'

She looked over her shoulder at the Crown Prince of the Phoenix Kingdom, her eyes enormous in her parchment white face.

'I don't remember.' And she fled.

The books were delivered by a steward of the archives, who seemed reluctant to let them out of his hands. After Tetsura had repeatedly promised he would handle the books with the utmost care, the steward unwillingly departed. Vilad was glad to see the Prince browsing through some old books and left him to himself.

Tetsura had craftily left the refurbishing of the King's Apartment to his manservant and Saima, declaring they had far better taste than he had. He told them only to leave a bedroom and a workroom empty, for him to arrange later, when he actually moved in.

Sergeant Tag was noticeable by her absence throughout the rest of that day, and the Prince retired to bed early, a very great deal on his mind.

Throughout the day, the Pathmaker told Tilliat everything he knew of the old tales of the defeat of Yartay, which in truth, wasn't a great amount. Nami and Taleb had wandered off when the old man began to repeat himself. The Pathmaker drew Tilliat away from Davin Pearl.

'Are the Shadows here?' he whispered.

Tilliat considered. She wasn't aware of them in her mind, but that was no guarantee that they weren't present.

'I can't say,' she admitted. She pointed to the black line around the silver ring on her thumb. 'They are always there but they don't usually talk to me unless I call them.'

'Be *very* careful. They were first used to kill.'

Tilliat looked aghast.

'I know only a little of Shadows. They have never spoken to

me but they once hated my kind.' He took both Tilliat's hands in his own. 'Zamina tells of Reva causing havoc in your city of Kelshan. Strange creatures, monstrous in appearance, have been seen in the streets and lands about. This is what happened before. The mage Tika was inside the city then and clearly Yartay attacked because of her presence.'

'But I'm not there.' Tilliat began in alarm.

The Pathmaker gave her hands a little shake. 'No, and Reva will realise that in a short time. But you *were* in Gulat.'

'I must ask the Shadows to warn them.' She paused. 'He will follow our trail, at least to the village, won't he?'

The old man nodded, pity and sorrow on his face.

'Then Kenza must go to Gulat, with the Shadows. *You* must go to your friends and protect them as you can. There is no time to lose now, is there?'

The Pathmaker didn't reply, just gazed at her. Impulsively she stepped closer, releasing his hands.

'Stay safe, Pathmaker. We will leave at once. The trail is almost too obvious, we can travel safely enough at night.'

The Pathmaker drew her close and his wings unfurled, enfolding them both. Within the confines of his feathered wings, he murmured softly, his lips close to Tilliat's ear.

'The Dragon Lord Mim and the Mage Tika both wore pendants, the size and shape of a small egg. Do you know anything of such objects child?'

Tilliat drew back slightly, her eyes searching his face. 'What were they?'

'Of great importance we suspect but when Lord Mim died, the pendant was never found. It has long been sought.'

Tilliat shook her head: too many things colliding in her mind for clear thought. She managed a faint smile and stepped away from the Pathmaker.

Toomay and Davin watched as the great wings quivered for a heartbeat, then folded against the Pathmaker's back. Davin closed the space between them, holding out his hand.

'I am glad to have met you, Pathmaker.'

The Pathmaker clasped Davin's hand against his chest, his wings flickering briefly again. Toomay joined them, his mindvoice heard by them all.

'I too am glad to have met you. I shall tell Thorn of you and the tale you have told us of your history. I believe you will be remembered in our own stories now.'

Tears slid down the wrinkled face. 'You do me much honour, Dragon child. I am proud to have met you all and I would prefer to leave you now, rather than watch you go.'

He moved back, his eyes fastened on Tilliat. 'May the stars guide your path and guard your heart and give you courage to do what must be done. Never doubt yourself child, that will only help Reva. Our hearts go with you.'

The now familiar golden mist spun around the Pathmaker, and he was gone from their sight.

Nami and Taleb had returned in time to witness the Pathmaker's departure and hear Tilliat say they would travel on at once. Without a word, they began to ready the horses. Tilliat burrowed in her pack and found some writing implements and scraps of parchment. She hastily scribbled on one of the scraps while the camp was struck around her. She read through what she'd written, shrugged and tossed the papers, ink and pen back in her pack.

She closed her eyes, the better to concentrate.

'Shadow.'

'Yes.'

'I ask you to take this message to Perra Koos in Gulat. And also to take Kenza, from the village.'

The silence in Tilliat's mind had more than a touch of sulkiness to it, but the folded parchment in her hand disappeared. She hoisted her pack over her shoulder and climbed onto her horse. Toomay drifted ahead of them as they rode on. Tilliat wondered, if this had once been a proper, stonepaved road long ago, as Nami insisted it was, *who* had built it. She was curious about the tumbled ruin Zamina's mindpicture had shown them.

Had this road been laid just for some great person to reach his palace in comfort? Or were the ruins those of a town? Looking at the country around them, the rising peaks, the forested lower slopes, the bleak gullies, she couldn't imagine this could ever have been farmland, busy with people. There was an air of long emptiness about the land.

Lost in thought, Tilliat barely noticed night had fallen. The half moon rode low in the sky, clouds chasing across its face. Nami trotted up alongside Tilliat.

'How long do you want to ride tonight?' she asked. 'The moon won't be up for long, but those clouds suggest the weather could change. We've been lucky since we came into the Yasharitzan lands.'

'The horses are fit for a while yet aren't they?'

'Oh yes, but I hope we can find somewhere with reasonable grazing when we reach wherever we're going. We're getting low on grain.'

Tilliat glanced across at the woman.

'There's time for you and Taleb to turn back. If you ride fast you can do it in far less time than we've taken getting here.'

'Certainly not,' Nami retorted. Her teeth gleamed a flash of light in the darkness as she grinned. 'We haven't had so much fun in years.'

'It might get a bit less enjoyable,' Tilliat began.

'We know that.' Nami sounded completely serious now. 'We're staying. No matter what.'

Tilliat felt a glow of relief mixed with guilt. She suspected four people were not going to frighten Reva too much; in fact, those four stood every chance of being annihilated with ease. But she was immensely grateful that Nami and Taleb, with their practical commonsense, were willing to stand with her and Davin Pearl.

Cloud was snug in her travelling pack and Tilliat touched the top of the grey head.

'Are you sorry you came on this journey?' Tilliat mindspoke her.

'Of course not. It is a great relief to be away from the Chays' farm. Once you've beaten this Reva, we'll all be renowned. Songs and tales will echo across all the lands. And *I* will be Queen of all Cats.'

Tilliat tried, unsuccessfully, to stifle a hoot of laughter. Cloud's head sank lower into her pack in an injured silence.

They halted when the moon set and rolled into their blankets for a brief rest. Tilliat was fairly sure that none of them actually slept much. Davin was up first, lighting a fire on the bare surface of the trail. Dawn was close when the four mounted up and rode on.

Toomay flew ahead and only returned when the riders halted again at midday. He landed a little way from them and paced steadily to Tilliat.

'I have seen the place the Pathmaker showed us.' His wings shivered against his back and his eyes whirred, the speed and changing tints alerting the humans to just how agitated he was.

Tilliat slipped her arms about his neck and laid her cheek against his.

'You don't like the place?'

'No.' Toomay's mindtone was emphatic. 'It feels very wrong. The air is wrong. Nothing grows for many paces around the fallen stones.'

'Did you find anywhere nearby, where we can camp and wait out of sight of the place?'

'I did. There is a place through the trees, higher, above that place. There is water and grass for your animals and you can look down and watch the lower ground.'

Toomay's eyes were slowing their wild spin as he grew calmer. Tilliat stayed leaning against the Dragon until she felt the tension leave him.

'How long will it take us to reach there?' she asked.

'If you move a little faster, you could be there before dark.'

'Then that is what we'll do. Stay close with us: you bring comfort with your presence, my friend.'

Toomay's neck stretched a little higher and his eyes stayed a calm, silvery blue.

'I will stay near, do not worry friend Tilliat.'

He lifted into the air and flew slowly on. Tilliat scrambled onto her horse while Taleb kicked out the tiny fire and scattered the embers. The twins flanked her, following Davin Pearl along the trail.

'You forget how young he is, in Dragon terms,' said Taleb quietly.

'I've tried to persuade him to return to their Realm,' Tilliat agreed. 'Seeing Kezia's body has unsettled him greatly. I don't think he was very fond of her, but she was the same age as him.'

Nami nodded. 'It's always a shock when someone your own age dies so young.'

Tilliat gave her a quick glance but said nothing. They were all tired and it was beginning to drizzle when they saw Toomay on the trail ahead. He turned off the wider track and moved carefully in among some still bare birch trees. Davin followed with Tilliat close behind. Nami leading two of the spare horses came next and finally Taleb, with the third extra mount.

The increasing cloud and the approaching night made it even darker when they rode from birch trees into a stand of evergreens, but at least it sheltered them from the rain. Toomay stopped and Davin dismounted, leading his horse level with the Dragon. They saw the gleam of Davin's teeth when he turned back to the other three.

'Toomay's the smartest Dragon I know – it's a good place to stop for sure.'

Tilliat caught up and peered out from under the needle covered branches. The ground continued to slope quite sharply up from where she stood, but slabs of rock had slid down from much higher, not that long ago judging by the trees, smashed like kindling, round about. The slabs were large and had come to rest against each other, forming roomy shelters. A stream splashed down the further side of the rocks, and grass had taken advantage of the opened space to grow thick and green.

'The spaces under the rocks are sound. I made sure when I found this place.'

'You have certainly done well, Toomay.' Nami touched his scaled shoulder as she pulled her horses past and on to investigate the shelter.

There was room for all seven horses under just one tilted slab, and for Toomay and four people under another.

'Let's just get something to eat and then rest properly,' Davin suggested, already pulling out his battered old kettle. 'We can explore and settle in tomorrow.'

Taleb darted back under the trees and soon brought back a good collection of firewood. They lit their fire near the entrance just as the rain began to beat down heavily. Tilliat's small company were grateful to be somewhere dry and warm. They spread their bed rolls towards the rear of their stone shelter and very soon, all were asleep.

The rainstorm passed eventually and by the time people were

stirring the sky was clear again. Nami and Taleb went to the horses and retrieved most of the gear which had been left where it was unloaded last night. Davin remained by the fire, nursing his precious tea bowl and his pipe. Tilliat wandered out to poke into the several other cavelike spaces provided by the fallen slabs.

Some were small, some as large as the two they'd chosen at random yesterday evening. Some extended in a narrow corridor of an aperture. It was in one of these that she discovered the supplies. She stared at them thoughtfully for a while before venturing closer. Tilliat came out of the cavern and stood for a moment, gazing over their camping place.

Nami had hobbled the horses, turned them loose and they were steadily cropping the new grass. Taleb was nowhere in sight but she could see Toomay in the depths of the cavern they'd slept in. Nami was walking towards the fire, smiling at Tilliat, when their paths met. Nami chattered about their good fortune in finding this place but Tilliat was silent. They sat behind the fire and it was only then that Tilliat spoke.

She glanced at Toomay then back outside. 'Who left us all the supplies I wonder?'

Toomay pushed up onto his haunches. 'Supplies?' His mind-voice spoke at the same time as Davin and Nami spoke the same word aloud.

Tilliat nodded. 'In another one of these cave things, just along there.'

Nami was gone before Davin could get to his feet, but he trotted after her. Tilliat turned back to Toomay and waited.

'It must be the Ancient Ones the Pathmaker told of.'

'Yes, I rather think it must,' Tilliat agreed. 'But who, in the name of the stars, *are* they?'

In Gulat, Perra Koos and the five mages staying in his house, were all in the kitchen with Tani. The old man had been fretful ever since Tilliat Kranch and her friends had departed. Perra and his guests had fallen into the habit of spending part of the evenings sitting with Tani. It seemed to comfort him and he usually nodded off to sleep, when the mages would tiptoe back up to Perra's library.

Ket Vos had just been making everyone laugh with a tale

against himself, set years back, when he believed he was the most handsome man in Gulat – if not the entire world. A folded square of parchment dropped on Tani's head and into his lap, almost immediately followed by a frail female figure.

She was astonishingly calm although as pale as snow, and Perra leapt to his feet to steady her on hers. Catching her arm and staring down into her face, he realised she was frighteningly old, her hands swollen and twisted with the joint disease.

'My name is Kenza. I am of the Yasharitza. I believe Tilliat Kranch arranged my – visit – here.'

Her voice was faint but clear but as she finished speaking, she began to tremble violently. Cook rushed up the kitchen as Li Kassu put an arm round the woman, helping her into the chair Tani had vacated in alarm. The men backed away to give Cook, Li Kassu and Perra Koos a chance to check the unexpected arrival for injuries.

Cook produced a bowl which everyone assumed was her standby remedy for everything: tea. But when the newcomer took a mouthful from the bowl kindly held by Li Kassu, her brown eyes watered, she wheezed and colour flooded the ashen cheeks. Li Kassu hid a smile, Perra Koos scowled at his Cook.

'It was just a drop of my cordial,' Cook told him defensively.

Li Kassu raised an enquiring brow at the woman, who nodded and accepted a further sip.

'You must tell me the makings for your cordial.' Kenza's voice was stronger.

None of them recognised the lilt that accented the common tongue the old woman used. As his unexpected guest seemed not to be in imminent danger of collapse or worse, Perra took the paper from Tani and unfolded it. He read it, shook his head, read it again and passed it to the others to read.

Kenza's trembling had ceased and she was taking a great interest in her surroundings and the people she found herself among. Perra perched on a stool beside her.

'Did you read the message?' he asked.

'What message?'

Perra gestured to the paper changing hands among his mage guests. 'From Tilliat. She says Reva–' Kenza flinched at the name. 'She says Reva is attacking Kelshan city, believing her to be there.' Perra continued.

Kenza watched him then her eyes closed briefly.

'He will track her back here.'

Perra nodded. 'First here, then into your land. Her message says she has found his lair. Someone called the Pathmaker told her of it.'

Kenza pushed herself forward. 'Truly? He still lives? That gladdens my heart.'

'Well I'm pleased to hear it. But here in Gulat we have a mage who has been busily calling Reva for several years. We believe she has told him of Tilliat Kranch, so we're as sure as we can be of anything, that he will return here first.'

Kenza tapped misshapen fingers on her knee. 'Are there mages among you of sufficient power to shield?' she asked. 'You will not be able to fight him but you may be able to hide.'

Perra's usually pale complexion greyed further. 'Those of us who have never trusted Mahzu Vek have retreated to our houses, which are well warded.' He indicated the group listening to their conversation. 'This house is very strong and these colleagues have been staying here for some time. I have considerable talent for warding – '

'But I arrived here, did I not?' Kenza pointed out.

Perra regarded her warily. 'You did indeed.'

'Have you a cellar? Large enough for all your people? Reva cannot move through earth, rock or water. A cellar needs only its roof shielded. You *may* survive if you have such a place.'

Chapter Thirty

Toomay later reported that he'd seen deer a few miles west and indeed, he brought one back with him for the companions' supper. Inside their shelter, the air was clear: with the fire near the entrance, a funnel of air from somewhere towards the back kept the smoke out. Taleb returned, grimly silent until after they'd eaten.

'You went to look at the ruined place?' Tilliat asked him.

Taleb stretched his legs out in front of him and nodded. 'It is as Toomay said. The ground is bare for a great distance around. It feels bad. I'm not sure if it's warded; I didn't want to test it too much,' he admitted. 'I felt odd there – queasy and disorientated.'

'That is how our barrier works.' Toomay mindspoke them. 'But I don't see how Reva might use something such as we use.'

'How is your barrier made, Toomay?' asked Tilliat.

The Dragon fidgeted briefly. 'It is to do with time, and also a very small discomfort spell.'

Nami rolled her eyes. Tilliat smiled.

'Is there a way to stop its effects?'

Toomay's eyes began to whirr. 'I am not sure, friend Tilliat.'

Tilliat reached up to touch his jaw. She sat leaning against his side, as had become usual, and she sensed he was holding something back. She chose not to press him, instead asking Taleb what else he'd managed to notice on his scouting trip.

'The road stops there. I really can't tell if it was a huge house or a town, but there is no road beyond it. If it was one person's house, it was like Tani's house – the Roost – on a much bigger scale. Many buildings all linked, surrounding a single building in the middle. It was definitely a circular construction. Most of that you can see from just beyond here. I felt too strange to look closely when I walked nearer to it.'

'We have to get closer somehow – we're not going to be much danger if we all feel sick when we get there and face Reva.'

343

Toomay twitched slightly as Tilliat spoke and she hoped he would soon tell her whatever was bothering him.

'Is Thorn well Toomay?' she asked, spreading her bed roll between the rock wall and the Dragon's side.

'I believe so.'

Tilliat paused to stare at him in some concern.

'He has not mindspoken me for a day or two, but I am sure all is well.'

The Dragon was quite obviously far from sure of any such thing, but Tilliat merely nodded and settled to sleep, keeping a tight shield round her thoughts.

They were all disturbed during the night by the sounds of wolves howling to the west. Nami rolled out of her blankets and to her feet, but Toomay bespoke them.

'Never fear. They hunt to the south. They are not close by and they will not bother you or your animals.'

Nami cast a dubious look at the Dragon. 'And you're sure of that?'

'Oh yes. I met them when I sought meat. They never venture this way because of the bad place. They don't like the Yasharitza much either, so they rarely hunt in those lands.'

Four pairs of eyes regarded him. Toomay's long lashes fluttered briefly.

'The lady of the wolf pack showed me her children, they are just out of the den. It was most kind of her.'

His comments were received in silence and the four humans chose to try to sleep again and put all thoughts of a Dragon cooing over baby wolves right out of their minds.

They woke to a sky filled with cloud and the temperature had dropped again. Davin Pearl and Taleb went into the evergreen trees and brought several loads of wood back to stack in another of the rock shelters. Davin had already built a sturdy ring of stones around his fire, to make it easier to put various pots and kettles over the heat.

The two men were deep in discussion about using one of the oilskin sheets to block the south facing entrance should the weather turn too bad and blow rain in, or worse.

Nami and Tilliat scrambled over the eastern side of the rockfall. Tilliat, watching her footing, bumped into Nami's back and looked up.

A tree had been knocked askew and left a narrow gap through which there was a clear view down to the floor of the valley, about half a mile away. They moved on to lean against the treetrunk. Tilliat noted absently that the tree was still alive, despite its battering. As Taleb had told them, from this height it was plainly a circular ruined area of tumbled blocks of stone, and the bare land around was also a clearly defined circle.

Tilliat was aware of occasional birdsong, far less than they'd heard in the Yasharitzan lands but she was willing to wager there would be no birds or animals down in that devastated area. She concentrated on the ruins. Would there be any way inside there? But Zamina's dream picture had shown a great hall with a vast patterned floor.

Nami nudged her at the same moment that she heard the scream of a hunting bird. They squinted up and eventually made out a dark speck high against the grey clouds.

'I've been trying to think of how we might be able to overcome a ward that causes the effects Taleb described,' said Nami.

'Me too,' Tilliat agreed. 'But as I had no idea I had mage powers until recently, I don't know how to begin.'

'I chose to study healing, but I've never come across a ward that can produce these symptoms. There are plenty of herbs – plants to stop sickness, confusion, and so on. But if it's cause is mage based, I don't know what to do.'

Tilliat stared down at Reva's nest, so called by the Pathmaker, and wondered why all this had fallen on to her shoulders. She turned away and headed back over the rocks to their camp.

'Who do you think these Ancient Ones are, Tilliat?'

'Another thing I wish I knew. It seems I know less and less with each day that passes.' Tilliat gave a rueful grin over her shoulder which faded when she saw Nami's amazed expression.

Tilliat spun back towards the camp and saw Toomay, standing beside Davin Pearl, his wings fully extended above his back. She followed the Dragon's gaze up to the sky. The speck she and Nami had taken for a hunting bird was rapidly descending and was none other than the Dragon Thorn. Tilliat left Nami standing and raced down to the flat ground. Thorn had landed and paced forward to twine his neck with Toomay's.

As Tilliat skidded to a halt, Thorn pressed his brow to Davin Pearl's. Tilliat was shocked once more by the difference in size between Toomay and Thorn. The black Dragon was easily twice the size of Toomay. Thorn's head swung towards her and he touched her brow with his. Impulsively, Tilliat threw her arms round his neck.

'I'm so glad to see you.' She used mindspeech, allowing Davin and a slightly stunned Nami and Taleb, to hear her words. 'Toomay said he hadn't reached you for a day or two.'

Thorn's mindtone was far deeper and slower than Toomay's when he bespoke them. 'Much has happened, of which I must speak.'

Large drops of rain began to fall and Tilliat urged the great Dragon into their shelter. He was clearly doubtful at first, but after carefully peering within, he moved under the rock. He reclined much further back, against one side and Toomay settled opposite his many times great grandfather, his eyes whirring with excited delight.

Nami put the horses back in their rock stable and was soaked dashing the short distance between the two shelters. Taleb tossed her a dry shirt and she sat next to him, staring at the black Dragon. Tilliat chose to tell Thorn all that had passed since they'd parted. Toomay became excited when she spoke of the Pathmaker and Thorn asked for images to be shown him of the old man.

Cloud had settled cosily on one of Thorn's large front feet and she let him see her mindpictures of Siyamak and Zamina. Silence fell when Tilliat finished speaking and all eyes were on the black Dragon.

'I will ponder on all this you have told me. It is of great interest but I'm not sure what bearing it might have on your situation.'

The huge head turned to study Toomay, then he regarded the four humans, finally focusing on Tilliat Kranch.

'There has been trouble within my Realm.'

Toomay pushed up onto his haunches, his eyes starting to whirr and flash. Thorn gave a gusting sigh which made the flames flatten and stretch out from the fire.

'All the humans within my Realm are dead.'

Tilliat felt her mouth drop open and closed it with an audible snap.

'All?' she asked faintly.

'All,' Thorn repeated. 'There was no warning. I was far to the north, beyond the haven caves you stayed in, within mindreach of Toomay. Suddenly there were many mindscreams from the Kindred and I flew as fast as I could back to the south.'

The Dragon's head dipped then lifted again, watching Tilliat.

'It was Zehara. She had been gone, none knew where, then she was in the settlement we permitted to be built in the Realm. She destroyed them all, and their buildings. Several of the Kin tried to stop her, to speak to her, but she turned on them too. She screamed only nonsense, nothing coherent or explanatory. She killed Bellia and Terak of the Kin as I arrived.'

The great eyes, the colour of shadows on snow, closed for a heartbeat. His voice was a whisper in his listeners' minds.

'It was as though she waited for me. As I approached, she laughed and raised herself as if to strike. I spat fire and she was burnt to ashes. Laughing all the while.'

A keening moan emerged from Toomay and he crept closer to Thorn. Thorn's wing stretched out, over the smaller Dragon, and gathered him close to his side.

'Why?' Tilliat murmured aloud.

'There has been something – uncertain – about Zehara for many years. Since the time of your birth, Tilliat Kranch. It was she who brought you and your nurse to these lands, but of late, that uncertainty I spoke of, had increased until I would call it unpredictability. She voted against our allowing the human mages to stay in our Realm long before that. Their boats came ashore on our eastern boundaries and the humans were sick, weary. They hastened away from the sea, deeper into our Realm.

'Many died, before they reached the heart of our land. That is when a Gather was called and, of the fifteen Elders, eleven agreed the humans could remain.'

'You, Thorn?' Tilliat interrupted. 'Were you one of the eleven?'

There was a pause then the deep mindvoice resumed.

'I was one of the four against. I could not forget that mages like these had taken our islands from us, that I was one of the first hatched here in exile and in all my long life I have not seen our ancestral ledges or the Gather Circles.'

Toomay gave a whimper and Thorn bent his head briefly to the silvery Dragon curled at his side.

'My sister was another of us to be displeased at the decision. She left us and has lived in isolation ever since. But she knows what goes on within the Realm. Her powers were always the greatest of us all. I felt her mind two days ago, and she will join us soon.'

Toomay's head came up and his eyes were calmer.

'I thought Bone was just a story,' he began, and the tight wrought atmosphere in the shelter dissolved with Thorn's rumbling laugh.

'You could have asked me, child. She was hatched four years after me. All those hatched with me, are long gone, and most of those of Bone's year.'

'How many – erm – hatch in the same nest?' Nami sounded a trifle nervous but her curiosity was stronger than her apprehension.

Thorn's eyes gleamed in the increasing gloom. 'My parents hatched three others with me, then five when Bone came from her shell Our mothers lay their eggs in secret caves; we do not build nests.'

As he finished speaking, three globes of light popped into existence, illuminating the shelter. Tilliat turned away to hide her grin at the Chars' amazement. She caught Thorn's eye and felt his amusement at Nami Char's question. She also felt, beneath the amusement a terrible worry in the black Dragon. He mindspoke them all before Tilliat could say anything.

'Forgive me. I have flown far and fast and am weary. I would sleep now and speak with you tomorrow.'

Not waiting for an answer, he curled more firmly round Toomay, his tail wrapping over his front feet, careful not to dislodge Cloud as Tilliat noticed. Two light globes vanished but one remained, and shadows flickered and twisted over the rock walls. Tilliat lay near Davin and met his eyes for a moment. He raised a brow. She smiled and gave a small shake of her head. The trader returned her smile and closed his eyes.

The rain stopped sometime in the night but the ground was treacherous with ice in the morning. Tilliat chose to wait until the sun rose high enough to melt some of it before venturing out after she watched Nami and Taleb slipping and sliding to the horses' shelter. Davin stood beside her.

'Thorn is a very worried Dragon,' he murmured.

'He is indeed Uncle. He didn't mention that ruin down there, but he must have seen it.'

'Will he be any help against this stars' damned Reva?'

'I have no idea Uncle.'

Tilliat risked a pace outside, tapping her foot on the patch of bare stone.

'It's melting quickly. At least it hasn't snowed.' She grinned at Davin Pearl.

'Hush child. Don't tempt the stars.' He retreated back to his fire in mock alarm.

Toomay emerged quietly and followed Tilliat along the line where the sun touched the edge of their camp. Tilliat leaned against a rock and touched Toomay's cheek when he drew close.

'Thorn is very tired,' he told her. 'And upset.'

'And you?' Tilliat asked. 'You knew some of the people.'

Toomay shifted his front feet. 'Not many of them. We were never encouraged to spend much time with the humans. There were two I knew a little.'

Tilliat thought of Pauson and Zeltan. She had no grief to spare for Pauson: a bitter, single-minded, arrogant old fool in her view. But she felt a slight sympathy for Zeltan. He had seemed intelligent, willing to think for himself, until something had changed him. Had Pauson some sort of power over the young man? It was futile even thinking of it now anyway.

Tilliat had a strong sense of time pressing more heavily upon her. She reasoned that Reva would seek out Mahzu Vek all too soon and although she desperately hoped Gulat wouldn't suffer, she also feared that it would. And then the Yasharitza land. Finally Reva would be here, and she would have to face him.

When Thorn emerged blinking, from the shelter, the sun had some warmth in it and Toomay led the black Dragon off to the west in search of meat. Tilliat began to climb up the western slope of rock, watching the dwindling Dragon shapes flying out

349

over the forest.

Taleb scrambled up to sit next to her.

'Following me?'

He looked sheepish. 'We don't think you should wander off alone.'

'We?'

'Yes, and that includes Davin, Toomay and Cloud.'

'Really?' Tilliat was surprised. 'I don't think there's any danger at the moment.'

'We decided we'd rather be sure,' Taleb said firmly.

They sat quietly for a while before Taleb spoke again.

'You have to get inside there somehow, don't you?'

Tilliat swallowed, her throat suddenly dry. 'I think so, yes.'

'We're coming too. And Toomay.'

His dark blue eyes stared into hers, daring her to argue.

Tilliat looked away, tears pricking the back of her eyes. She'd thought the Chars an insufferably arrogant pair on first meeting. In the time since then she'd come to appreciate their steadiness, common sense and humour. She knew that Davin Pearl would stick with her no matter what, but Taleb's statement of their intent to accompany her to whatever she might have to face, touched her deeply.

'Thank you,' she said softly, unable to meet his gaze.

'Tell me about your brother.'

That made her return her gaze to him. 'What do you want me to tell you? I know so little.'

'What's his name? Does he look like you? Is he like you in temper? I know you've actually seen him – Toomay told us. Davin confirmed it. So tell me.'

'His name is Tetsura A Serissama. It was like looking in a mirror when I saw him.' She shrugged. 'That's about all I can say.'

Another silence fell and they stared out over the woodland.

'Which of you was born first? Nami was born eight heartbeats before me and has never, ever, let me forget it.'

Tilliat looked at him, stricken. 'I have no idea,' she said, and burst into tears.

Taleb slid an arm across her shoulders and rested his chin on the top of her head.

'It seems so odd to me. Odd and awful. We've never spent a day apart, and although she is the most annoying person I have ever met, I just can't imagine life without her.'

Tilliat felt curiously comforted sitting with Taleb Char, waiting for the Dragons to return.

'There they are,' said Taleb eventually. He kissed her forehead and stood, pulling her up beside him. He grinned. 'I won't suggest a race down there this time.'

Tilliat grinned back, shoved him hard enough to make him sit down abruptly and sped down the slope to the camp.

The Dragons landed and Thorn paced to a protected corner and reclined in the sunshine. Tilliat bespoke him.

'I hope you fed well, Thorn, and that you are rested?'

'Indeed child. Toomay introduced me to some wolves he has met.'

Tilliat bit the inside of her cheek.

'We met their newest children,' Thorn continued, and Tilliat heard the note of glee in his tone and kept her expression as solemn as possible. Especially when Toomay broke in.

'They have five children, friend Tilliat. They are amazingly small. They tried to catch my tail.'

Tilliat exchanged a long look with Thorn but neither of them said a word. She heard Davin Pearl having a fit of coughing and glimpsed Nami from the corner of her eye. Nami had a hand clamped over her mouth, her eyes sparkling. Thorn closed his eyes and rested his head on his front feet, obviously planning a doze in the warmth to aid digestion. Toomay lay nearby, oblivious of the amusement the humans found in his interest in wolf cubs.

There was a much more relaxed air about the camp and all four humans found Thorn a reassuring presence in their midst, and by unspoken agreement, nothing was said either about the events in Thorn's Realm or of the imminent arrival of Reva. Thorn spent the day basking and dozing, Cloud stretched on his back in full accord with the Dragon's enjoyment. Davin Pearl wandered with Tilliat under the evergreens.

'Those heart trees were magnificent. I wonder why they stop so abruptly?' Davin mused.

'They grew in the Dragon Realm and the Yasharitzan lands

which touch those borders. The Yasharitzans obviously have Dragon blood.' She paused. 'I can't imagine how that happened but those trees must have some meaning for both of them. Or perhaps the trees just like living with Dragons and Halflings. What?'

She looked back at Davin who had stopped.

'You're just making that up. It sounds nonsense anyway.'

She laughed and slid her arm through his. 'Have you got a better idea then?'

They had walked further than they thought and found themselves at the edge of the birch trees. Beyond those lay the road and the start of the ruined place. Tilliat shivered and turned round. Davin patted her hand which rested on his arm.

'Taleb told you we will all be with you?'

Tilliat nodded.

'He's a good lad. I thought they were a pain, both of 'em. But under that superior attitude they showed at Perra's house, they'll be good company in danger.'

Tilliat stopped. 'Suppose something happened to one of them Uncle?' She stared up at Davin.

He looked puzzled. 'Any of us might get hurt child.'

Tilliat continued walking, thinking of Taleb's words earlier.

At the camp, Taleb and Nami were checking each horse and giving them the care and attention they would have received in the Char stables. Davin took a bowl of tea and his pipe and found a patch of sunwarmed rock.

'I'm going to try and sleep for a while,' Tilliat told him. She rubbed her forehead. 'I have a niggling headache and sleep will get rid of it.'

She went inside their shelter and pulled her bed roll towards the rear. Lying down, she watched the entrance for a while but no one intruded. Closing her eyes, she began to centre her thoughts and nearly rocketed out of her skin when whiskers tickled her face. Her eyes flew open and she glared at the small grey cat while waiting for her heart to return to its usual place. Emerald eyes met hers and claws dug into her shirt. Cloud said nothing, just stared.

Tilliat sighed, wrapped an arm over the cat and called Shadows.

'Yes.'

'Take us to the hall we saw in Zamina's dream picture.'

There was no sense of movement, yet when Tilliat cautiously reopened her eyes, she found herself standing in that enormous hall. She stood for a moment, frowning.

'Shadow?'

'Yes.'

'Why don't I feel sick?'

'Protect.'

Tilliat mindspoke Cloud. 'Do you feel well?'

'Of course. Put me down.'

So, Tilliat thought, the Shadows could cancel out one disadvantage at least.

'How is it we can see in here?'

The Shadows declined to reply: Tilliat concluded they didn't know any more than she did. She looked around her. There was a diffuse light, like moonlight, but she could not see the source of it. She was standing on pale stone slabs at the edge of the hall. Peering up, the ceiling vanished in the gloom. Cloud was stalking forward to where a large darker circle showed in the floor.

Tilliat followed her and tensed when the cat set a paw on the outside line of the circle. When three paws had crossed that line, Cloud leapt backwards, hissing and spitting as she landed clear of the circle.

'What was it? What's the matter?'

'Tingles and itches.' Cloud's fur was puffed up about her and she fixed a furious glare at the offending circle.

From a prudent distance, Tilliat studied the strange pattern. Several different coloured blocks formed a swirling mosaic with a larger square of a golden stone in the centre.

'Spiral.'

'What do you mean?'

'Long time past. Travel far.'

Tilliat bit her lip. Trying to converse with the Shadows was just *so* frustrating. Turning her back to the circle, she regarded the curving walls. Moving closer, she thought the hall, if not the whole building, must have been a dome, but of such a size! There were a few domed towers in Kelshan city and she recalled Tetsura's dreams, of looking out over his huge city: domes and needle thin spires had punctuated the view. But none to equal the vastness of this place.

She walked slowly along, following the curve of the wall. There were inscriptions on some of the slabs but in a form of script she had never seen before. Tilliat stopped in front of a door. It was an unfamiliar shape – broad at its base but narrower at the top. Cloud sat neatly at the door and, when Tilliat hesitated, the cat cast her a look of scorn and meowed impatiently. Not at all sure if it was sensible or not, Tilliat reached for a wide metal latch and lifted it open.

Chapter Thirty-One

Cloud trotted through the door when it swung smoothly back. There was no squeak of rusty hinges, Tilliat noted and she also saw there was only the lightest layer of dust on the floor. She paused. She reminded herself that she had mage powers. Now might be a good time to test what she could do perhaps. Before she could do so, the same diffuse light grew and showed her she was in a wide, vaulted passage, the ceiling much lower than in the hall.

Cloud didn't wait for Tilliat, moving steadily ahead down the passage. The light seemed aware of their presence and obligingly brightened as Cloud advanced. Tilliat concentrated. She sent a tendril of her mind out and around, a tendril that would sense any life it happened to brush against. When she was sure she could maintain it, she hurried on to catch up with Cloud.

Just as she did so, the cat stopped and sat down. The darkness in front melted away, revealing another circular space but with eight passages leading from it. The passages were like dark mouths, unlit Tilliat presumed, until someone began to walk in them. The floor of this area was of slabs of green and white stone, set in a zigzag pattern which converged in the very middle on a large black square.

Cloud looked up at Tilliat. 'Which way?' The cat's mindvoice held no concern, as though they were simply out for a stroll around their camp.

'I can't sense any life here. Wait.' Tilliat concentrated harder, sending her mind in a wider and wider sweep of her immediate vicinity. 'No. Nothing.' She shrugged. 'You choose.'

Cloud rose, shook a back leg vigorously, and marched towards the third passage to their left.

Tilliat lost all sense of time as she and Cloud wandered an apparent maze of passages. They passed very few doors and when she'd peered inside, found they were simply small storerooms of some kind. Opening yet another door, expecting nothing different, Tilliat blinked. It had been some sort of sleeping chamber but everything was in chaos.

Furniture overturned, papers scattered like leaves, bedcovers in shreds. Cloud crept forward, her fur bristling again, but when she'd dabbed a paw on a twisted scrap of paper, she sat back and yawned. Tilliat crouched beside her and reached for another scrap and stared as it crumbled to nothing in her fingers. How long had this been lying here? How long did it take for things to collapse like this?

She moved towards a chair tossed onto its side and pressed her hand to a wooden armrest. It disintegrated under her touch in a silent puff of dust. Far more disturbed than she liked to admit, Tilliat withdrew, closing the door gently behind them. Cloud leading the way, they went on but at the very next turning, Cloud stopped.

Drawing level, Tilliat looked down a corridor just like all the others, but as the strange light strengthened, she gasped. Bodies lay sprawled as far as she could see. She ventured a few paces closer. The nearest corpse was female: at least judging by the ornate gown and long hair tangled across the face. Tilliat stood frozen. It was more skeleton than corpse, the flesh long melted away from the bones.

Tilliat saw there was a far smaller figure half hidden under the woman and swallowed, realising it was a child. She took a step back, raising her eyes to look further. Not far past the woman and child was a great sheet of feathers. Tilliat moaned, bent to scoop Cloud into her arms.

'Shadow, take us back.'

In a heartbeat she found herself lying on her bed roll, Cloud sprawled across her chest, wild eyed and spitting. She saw light globes drifting overhead and worried faces staring down at her.

'Ah.'

Tilliat suspected a frosty reception when she'd explained what she'd done, but after her first words there was only fury directed at her. Cloud sensibly removed herself to curl on Thorn's foot. A storm of outrage broke over Tilliat. She sat up, suddenly furious herself.

'Stop,' she ordered.

Somewhat to her surprise, Davin stopped in mid tirade and the Chars closed their mouths, eyeing her warily.

'You all know of the Shadows. I trust them when they tell me they will protect me.'

'We knew the Shadows had taken you,' Davin interrupted. 'But you've been gone so long.'

'I admit I lost track of time, but even so Uncle. *I* trust the Shadows: you must trust *me*.'

Taleb leaned back against the wall. 'We've yelled at you, you've yelled at us, now tell us what you found.'

Tilliat gave him a grateful smile then began to talk. By the time she'd finished she felt unbelievably tired. For the first time the Dragon Thorn mindspoke them.

'The child is exhausted. Let her rest.' Amusement tinged his words. 'She will go nowhere for a while.'

Indeed, he'd barely finished before Tilliat slid back onto her blankets, her eyes already closed. Three people stared hard at Thorn, who looked the epitome of innocence. After the silence had drawn out a little too long, Thorn admitted: 'It was the smallest of compulsions. The child *was* very tired, and she was shocked.'

Davin checked Tilliat and saw she was deeply asleep. He moved closer to the Char twins.

'What good came of that?' he muttered angrily. 'Except for frightening me into premature old age.'

Nami snorted with laughter. 'Not so far to go though, old Uncle.'

Taleb growled. 'Stop it Nami, you're not being funny.' He looked to Davin Pearl. 'What did you make of it all? Those bodies she saw, and the length of time she believes they've been there?'

'How would I know?' Davin snapped. '*I* have no mage powers. I thought you two were respected mages in Gulat.'

Nami grinned. 'We *might* be – one day. We're only at the beginning.'

Davin scowled. 'What do you mean – either you are mages or you're not?'

Taleb explained. 'We showed abilities when we were twelve – the usual age such talents appear. We were sent to the

357

Academy in Gulat until we were seventeen. All you're really taught there is control of your talents, and fairly basic spells, wards and shieldings.'

'You do find out in what particular area your strengths might lie, but then that's it really,' Nami added. 'I've been interested in medicine and healing as long as I can remember, particularly in how the mind works. Taleb is fascinated with time.'

Davin was rather shocked. 'And that is all you learn?'

'We have to do the usual things: read the histories, the classic authors, numbers, physical training for unarmed combat. Armed combat was optional.' Nami beamed at him. 'Quite a good education really.'

Davin was scornful. 'Tilliat studied all those things, as well as trading routes, law and a great deal more combat training.'

Taleb held a hand up to stop a squabble. 'You told us the Shadows moved you *and* Tilliat, outside of Gulat?'

Davin thought then shook his head. 'Toomay did that.'

The Chars gaped at him. 'Toomay?' Taleb asked, faintly.

'Yes. He said it was a – Dragon gateway, that was it.'

'Well, whether it's Toomay or Shadows, I think one of us at least should go into that place with Tilliat again.'

They sat contemplating Taleb's words until Nami yawned. 'Let's sleep on it,' she suggested.

When they'd settled in their blankets, Toomay mindspoke his many times great grandfather.

'Do you know what will happen?'

Thorn looked across at the sleeping Tilliat. 'No child I do not. I admit I am nervous at the knowledge so much depends upon a human female child.'

The next morning the rain was back and Thorn chose to stay in the shelter. Toomay offered to find him some meat, but Thorn declined.

'I ate well yesterday, I need no more today.'

Toomay shifted his weight from one front foot to the other and back.

'You go though Toomay. You are young and enjoy the exercise.'

'I think I will.' Toomay was gone before more might be said.

Tilliat bespoke Thorn. 'Is he going to see those wolves?'

'Probably. He was most enchanted with them.'

'Are wolves not fearful of Dragons?'

'Why would they be?' Thorn was surprised. 'They hunt, as we do, the grass eaters. They are as little brothers to us.'

'What did you think of the Pathmaker?'

Tilliat wasn't sure if Thorn would answer but eventually he did.

'It explains much. The mage Tika spoke of the one the Pathmaker named Mim. She had great affection for him. She also spoke of Gremara but she was troubled by that one. His story feels as true as he knows. I learned to detest the Halflings. We called them abominations. Yet perhaps, the fault was not theirs alone. Now I feel pity for the three who are left.''

'I almost forgot,' Tilliat said suddenly. 'Just as the Pathmaker was leaving, he spoke of necklaces – no – he said pendants.' She scowled in concentration. 'He said the Dragon Lord and the mage Tika both wore one. They were like small eggs. He said, after the Lord Mim's death, his pendant was never found, and they had searched for it ever since. Pathmaker didn't know what it actually was but that it was believed to be of great importance.'

Thorn was again silent for a time. 'I know of what he spoke. The mage Tika indeed wore such a thing.'

A picture filled Tilliat's mind. The dark haired girl with the emerald eyes surrounded by silver. And hanging on a gold chain the object the Pathmaker had described to her. It was caught on the collar of the mage's shirt and appeared to have two halves, one solidly gold, the other a clear honey amber. The picture faded as Thorn heaved a sigh.

'Was the Dragon Lord's the same?' Tilliat asked.

'I have no idea. I was very young remember, although I did ask the young Dragon Farn what it was or what it signified. He said it was very important but he didn't know why. I have discussed it often through all these long years with my sister.' Thorn sighed again. 'Bone believes it is connected with a blood binding.'

Before Tilliat could ask more, she saw Taleb hurrying towards their shelter and asked quickly: 'Can you not take Toomay home?'

Thorn's eyes flashed their shadows on snow colour. 'He has chosen to be with you.'

There was something in his tone Tilliat couldn't decipher.

'I suspect he will remain with you, whatever happens and wherever you go.'

Tilliat blinked. She had a momentary vision of herself, strolling through the streets of Kelshan city, Toomay pacing at her side.

Taleb came into the shelter just then and poured a bowl of tea from Davin's permanently simmering kettle.

'Nami has taken Uncle to look for some more of those onions.' He sipped his tea and grimaced. 'How long has this been stewing?' he asked.

Tilliat glanced at Thorn then took a breath.

'Would you come with me now Taleb?' she asked.

'What do I need to do?'

'Nothing particular. It's best if you close your eyes. Hold my arm.'

Cloud clawed her way up Taleb's trouser leg and he hauled her up under his arm.

'Tell them not to worry, Thorn.'

With Taleb standing close, his hand firmly gripping Tilliat's wrist and his eyes tightly closed, Tilliat called Shadows.

Feeling solid ground underfoot, she looked around. Taleb stood beside her, unusually pale but calm. Cloud wriggled and Taleb opened his eyes. Tilliat was disconcerted: they were not in the great hall but in a corridor. The strange light was appearing, at least, and she watched Taleb's expression while he squinted to find the source of the light. She nudged him.

'Come on. I just followed Cloud before – we might as well do the same this time.'

Taleb dragged his gaze from the ceiling to see Cloud, tail upright, marching down the corridor. Walking after the cat, Tilliat wondered aloud why the Shadows had brought them to a different place. They reached a door on their left and Taleb exclaimed at its odd design. He ran his fingertips over the latch before lifting it open.

'What, in the name of the stars, is this?'

Tilliat squeezed up beside him. Cloud crouched at their feet, giving a low growling wail, her tail lashing. They waited until the light grew brighter, much brighter than Tilliat had yet seen it. Taleb sniffed just when Tilliat noticed an odd smell. It was a metallic scent which made the back of her nose and throat tickle. Cautiously they went a few steps inside.

There were – shapes – against the walls. A crazed carpenter had made tables, chairs, cupboards, and stood them around the room. They had spots of colour scattered on them, each a perfect circle about the size of Cloud's paw. The spots were randomly dotted over the sides and fronts of all the objects and on the floor was a dark smear. Taleb bent to touch it but Tilliat grabbed his jacket.

'No.' She ordered.

When he glanced at her in question, she shrugged.

'Sorry, but I really feel that would be a bad idea.'

'What *is* all this?' Taleb indicated the strange furniture.

Tilliat went no closer but looked carefully at all the haphazard pieces.

'I think it's Reva's work.'

Taleb shook his head but Tilliat continued.

'It's as though someone has seen something we use and then tried to copy it, but with no idea of what it might be used *for*.'

'Yes.'

'What?' Tilliat spoke aloud and waved a hand at Taleb when he looked perplexed. 'Shadow, what do you mean?'

'Yartay.'

'Yartay?' Tilliat whispered, still speaking aloud so that Taleb could at least realise who she was talking to.

'These like Yartay's things.'

'But they're all lopsided and wrong.'

'Reva not see. Remember bits faintly.'

Tilliat scooped Cloud into her arms and caught Taleb's arm. 'Shadow, take us back.'

Both Taleb and Tilliat stumbled, falling to their knees inside their shelter. Only Thorn was present, to Tilliat's secret relief.

'We weren't long this time then?' She mindspoke the Dragon.

'No. Uncle and Nami have not yet returned, nor Toomay. The rain stopped so they will probably have gone further.'

Tilliat considered him. 'Did you see what we saw?'

361

Thorn waited while Cloud settled herself between his front feet.

'The Shadows permitted me to follow with my mind.'

'It wasn't too bad, being moved like that,' Taleb commented.

'Don't tell Uncle that; it made him feel dreadful.'

Taleb was still chuckling when Nami and Davin Pearl returned, damp but cheerful.

'We found quite a lot to add to the stew,' Davin began, then stared hard at Tilliat. 'What? What's happened now?'

Tilliat sighed, regretting momentarily that Davin Pearl had known her for quite so long and quite so well. Taleb launched into a description of their brief visit to the ruined place. Tilliat helpfully busied herself making fresh tea after one glimpse of Davin and Nami's darkening expressions. Nami tore into Taleb before he'd finished and a full blown row seemed inevitable.

Tilliat chose to slip outside, to wait for Toomay's return should anyone ask. She wandered along the rock face, absently glancing into the shelters large and small. Thorn emerged from their particular shelter.

'I think I shall fly for a short while.' His mindtone was thoughtful. 'Those two humans hatched together, so Toomay told me. Were they never taught to behave in a mannerly fashion?'

Tilliat smiled. 'I wouldn't know. If they were, it doesn't seem to have worked, does it. There are more supplies in here.' She pointed to the narrow shelter beside her.

Thorn lowered his head and peered inside. He turned his huge eyes upon her for a heartbeat then lifted gracefully into the air without a word. Tilliat scowled after him.

'You know far more than you let on, old Dragon,' she muttered, and stomped back to see if the Chars had quietened down.

An icy silence held between Taleb and Nami but Davin Pearl was calm enough and enjoying his tea and his pipe. Tilliat dropped down beside him.

'More supplies have appeared Uncle.'

'Do you think those Shadows bring them?' He puffed a cloud of fruit scented smoke.

'Uncle, they told us it was the Ancient Ones, whoever they might be.'

Davin raised a brow at her waspish tone.

'What will you do – about that ruin? I suppose we have to be inside it when the Reva thing turns up?'

Tilliat studied the silver ring on her thumb. 'I wonder why he, or it, is called Reva? Do you think he just happened to hear people in Gulat praying to someone named Reva and he thought it was a good idea to become him?'

The Chars were listening as Tilliat thought aloud.

'Didn't the Pathmaker say what we call Reva was really a remnant of the other creature?' Nami asked.

Taleb nodded. 'That's right. Yartay. That's what the other one was called. I wonder what would happen if you used that name to him, instead of Reva?'

Tilliat gave a mirthless laugh. 'Does anyone really think we will have time for conversation before he squishes us?'

Taleb persisted. 'The Pathmaker said the mage Tika spoke with Yartay.'

'Yes he did, didn't he?'

'Not long.'

Tilliat stiffened, her eyes going blank as she concentrated on the faint voice of the Shadow in her mind.

'Not long? You mean Reva's coming?'

'No. Tika spoke with Yartay. Not long. Burnt him.'

Tilliat shivered. 'How? How did she burn him?'

'Called fire. Through her hands.'

Tilliat thought yes, she could understand why that mage used her hands: so that she could direct the fire on a possibly moving target. But that mage had been able to *see* Yartay. Was Reva a solid creature then?

'Sometimes.'

'Are you sure he will return here? Where is he now?'

A pause. 'Gulat place soon. Have not many nights.'

She knew, from a sort of emptiness in a place in her mind that the Shadow would speak no more for now. She relayed the gist of what she'd learned to the others. Davin climbed to his feet.

'Let's see what supplies we've got this time.' He gave Tilliat a pat on her shoulder when he passed her. 'I think we should get some packs ready – who knows how long we'll be in that hole.'

Nami upended her pack and began sorting out what she

363

thought might be needed. She glanced at Tilliat.

'Will the Dragons come with us?'

Tilliat sighed. 'Toomay will I'm afraid. I hope Thorn will either wait here or go back to his Realm.'

'Your brother – is he safe?'

'I believe he is. When the moon is full again, he will be the Phoenix King.' She gave a wistful smile. 'I wager that will be a magnificent occasion.'

Nami reached for Tilliat's hand and squeezed it. 'Perhaps this Reva business will all be over and the Shadows will take us all to watch.'

Tilliat giggled suddenly, sounding like a young girl who faced nothing more serious than which boy to choose as her partner at a ball.

'I'm not at all sure they'd be agreeable to any such idea.'

Nami began checking a coil of rope dug from the depths of her pack.

'They sound a miserable lot, those Shadows. Wonder if they know what fun is? Did I tell you about the time Taleb glued all the text books shut in the Motivation for Mages class?'

Tilliat gaped at her. 'You're not serious? There is really a class called that?'

'Really. Some of the most tedious we ever sat through.'

'What happened – did Taleb get caught?'

'No, but when the whole class was threatened with *days* of extra homework, we confessed.'

'We?'

Nami glanced up from her rope in some surprise.

'Well of course. We always shared punishments.'

There was a sudden bugling cry from outside. Tilliat dashed out, Nami close on her heels. Davin and Taleb stood holding sacks of the new supplies. They all stared up at the sky. The cry came again and a shape against the pale clouds spiralled slowly down. They watched as a Dragon the size of Thorn drifted to land on the grass. This Dragon was the colour of old parchment and its eyes a pale golden honey. Those eyes studied each of the four humans, finally fastening on Tilliat. A melodious female voice mindspoke them.

'Greetings. My name is Bone.'

She stood, her neck a little longer than Thorn's, her long, scaled face a little more beautiful. Tilliat took a few paces towards her and bowed.

'I am Tilliat Kranch, Lady Bone. I am honoured to call Dragon Thorn my friend and honoured to meet you.'

Laughter pealed through their heads and the Dragon moved closer to Tilliat, lowering her head to look into the girl's face.

'We are called only by our names, child, and I am Bone.' She tilted her head in a gesture which reminded Tilliat of the Pathmaker.

'Thorn and Toomay are flying,' Tilliat began but before she could say more, to her relief, Thorn arrived in a flurry of leathery wings.

Bone turned to him and for a heartbeat they simply stared at each other. Then the newcomer moved, to twine her neck around the black Dragon's. Davin Pearl nudged Taleb, who was staring at the new Dragon in amazement. Taleb followed Davin back to their shelter carrying the supplies. Nami also disappeared and Tilliat found her rearranging their bedrolls and packs to leave more room at the rear of the shelter. Tilliat was surprised when Thorn paced inside, Bone behind him.

Both Dragons reclined gracefully against the rock. Thorn's eyes flashed and sparkled a little more than usual, Tilliat noted, but his mindtone was calm as ever when he spoke.

'My sister knows of you, friend Tilliat. I have told her much of what has passed, but I will speak with her now of the things you told me – of the Pathmaker.'

'Will we disturb you?' Tilliat asked, indicating the muddle of gear on the floor. 'We were preparing our packs for – for the next part of our journey.'

'Of course you won't, child.'

Tilliat turned away, aware, at the very edges of her mind, of a faint tingle which she assumed was the Dragons communicating with each other. She paused when Cloud emerged from under someone's shirt and picked her way daintily back to the Dragons, to sit regarding Bone solemnly. Shaking her head, Tilliat returned to the grassy area stretching across to the trees.

She perched on one of the rocks, broken in the slide she supposed, and looked to the west for Toomay's return. Taleb came to sit next to her.

'She seems quite a bit different from Thorn and Toomay,' he said quietly.

Tilliat smirked. 'She's female.'

Taleb laughed but before he could respond, Tilliat pointed. Toomay landed, pacing towards Tilliat. He wasn't aware of the new arrival it seemed. Tilliat told him of Bone's appearance and that she was now deep in conversation with Thorn. Toomay bounced from one front foot to the other, his faceted eyes whirring with excitement. Hoping to distract him a little, Tilliat asked if he'd seen the wolves. Unfortunately, that seemed to excite him even more.

'Oh I did. I find it difficult to believe quite how small their children are. The human children I've seen were quite small, but these wolves are tiny!'

Tilliat wondered briefly how Toomay might react to the sight of a human baby, glared at Taleb whose stern expression belied the fact that he was desperately suppressing laughter, and slid her arm across Toomay's back. She leaned against him and asked for a full report about his precious wolves.

Chapter Thirty-Two

In Gulat frantic preparations were taking place. Perra Koos had talked with Li Kassu and they had dispatched messengers to those in the Civil Guard who they hoped might be free of Mahzu Vek's influence. They sent urgent instructions that the great catacombs deep beneath Gulat be opened at once and the populace encouraged to move there in the hops of some protection against what was to come.

Li Kassu became distressed to hear how few people took notice of the warnings they were being given. Under Perra's house were cellars, descending three levels. He hadn't even realised they were there when he bought the house and had never been able to discover the reason for such extensive underground storage areas. Now though, he thanked the stars that the cellars were there. All his books and papers were crated and rushed downstairs.

The mages who were his guests decided it made far more sense to stay where they were, having only small basements in their own homes or no cellarage at all. They chose to ignore any possible action from Mahzu Vek and scurried to their homes to collect vital documents and to instruct their households to go into hiding in the catacombs. Mages all across the city were either rushing to Mahzu Vek's compound or to Perra Koos.

There was an air of distraction throughout the streets – not panic yet but a general questioning disturbance.

'Will we know when Reva approaches Gulat?' Ket Vos asked quietly when the mages gathered in the kitchen for a quick meal.

Perra shrugged. 'I have no idea. When he answered Vek's call days ago there was no warning, was there?' A glance at his companions' worried faces confirmed his fears. 'I think we should move down to the cellars by tomorrow at the latest, and stay there. Reva really can't be too far distant now.'

There were hearths on each cellar level, the chimneys

cunningly aligned with chimneys in the house above. The first level down was already stocked with food and some of that was hurried down to the next level, along with firewood, coal, lamp oil and candles. Giffu's kitchen staff were racing up and down with pots, pans and bedding. More mages had turned up on Perra's doorstep and he had taken in every one of them.

Morkus Fayle was fascinated by the lowest level. He prowled the several rooms with a lantern, examining the walls closely and muttering to himself. The Yasharitzan Wise One, Kenza, trailed in his wake, saying nothing, her gnarled fingers tracing indentations along the stone. She stopped, Morkus Fayle having retraced his steps and now beside her.

'Do you know this script Kenza?' he asked.

The Wise One shook her head. 'I have seen it before. I do not think any of my people have deciphered it. All I can tell you is that it is old, *very* old. The Yasharitza found places like this when first we settled in the northern lands.'

Morkus held his lamp high, looking round the small chamber in which they stood.

'This is hewn from the very bedrock. It must have been one of the earliest places in Gulat, with homes built above time after time. I have never seen its like.'

Kenza shivered. 'It is in the bedrock as you say. Pray to the stars it keeps us safe from evil.'

Before Morkus could reply, a deep dull boom reverberated through the chamber, shuddering up through the soles of their feet. Kenza clutched Morkus's arm in alarm.

He patted her twisted fingers. 'Never worry, my dear. I think Perra has closed the entrance above us.'

'But how could we hear it this far down?'

Morkus frowned then shrugged. 'I have a good feeling,' he said firmly. 'This place *will* keep us safe.'

Across the city, Mahzu Vek sat in her study, unmoving, her face blank. Servants had looked in on her then sought Keril Dwar. But she was nowhere to be found, having moved into the Koos house the night before with her stricken husband. Mahzu Vek's chest rose and fell with slow breaths but her body was now an empty shell. Reva had the thought that the woman might still have a small use for him although he was thankful she could no longer *talk* at him.

Tilliat had been left to herself for stretches of time over the last days, her human companions finally aware of how much was to be asked of her. If Toomay was absent then Cloud stayed close, neither Dragon nor cat imposing on Tilliat's thoughts. She was aware that the Shadows were with her too, not speaking, just present. Now, four days after Bone's arrival, Tilliat looked around the fire in their shelter and smiled wryly.

'I really don't think there is much time left. If you are all still determined to come with me, then I think we should go into that place. Not for long, just to make sure none of you suffer any ill effects.'

Davin Pearl swallowed the last of his tea and heaved himself to his feet. 'What are we waiting for?' he demanded, pulling a pack onto his shoulder.

'I too will come,' Toomay announced calmly.

Tilliat's eyes prickled with tears but she refused to let them fall.

'I can make a gateway beside the Shadows,' Toomay added.

'Really?' thought Tilliat. 'Now how could he do that?' But that was a problem for later – if there ever might *be* a later. She glanced at the adult Dragons and felt affection wash through her mind although Thorn's concern also seeped through.

'Stand close to me and shut your eyes.' Tilliat slide one hand round Davin's arm and let her other hand briefly rest on Toomay's cheek. 'Shadows, take us to that hall again.'

Bone shifted uneasily and Thorn rumbled as four humans, a cat and a young Dragon vanished in front of them. The Shadows took them to the circular hall and Cloud demanded to be set down. Toomay appeared beside Tilliat a heartbeat later, his eyes whirring rapidly. Tilliat reached for him and he calmed, peering around the hall where light slowly brightened, and stared at the spiral mosaic on the floor.

'Could use spirals.'

Tilliat frowned, then spoke aloud to let the others know she was communicating with Shadows. 'What do you mean? I know nothing of spirals, so how would I use them?' She waved at the great mosaic circle in the centre of the hall and the Chars and

Davin Pearl moved closer to stare down at it.

The Shadows sounded irritable. 'Told you before. Long ago. Travel with spirals.'

'Do you know how they work?'

'No.'

Tilliat rolled her eyes. 'The Shadows say the pattern in that circle somehow let people travel great distances but they don't actually know how it works.'

Nami stood at the very edge of the huge circle and Toomay paced closer to stand next to her. Taleb and Davin Pearl were investigating the doors set at intervals around the curving wall. Cloud sat by Tilliat's feet watching the Dragon and Nami Char. She looked up at Tilliat.

'Will we find somewhere to hide and then leap on this bad thing?' she asked. 'Do you think it will come to this hall first or that funny room?'

Tilliat squatted beside the cat. 'Would he really go to that room?' she wondered.

Cloud yawned. 'The Shadows said Reva made that room. I don't think he made all this place, so perhaps he'd go there.' She blinked as Toomay turned away from the circle to join Tilliat.

'I feel Cloud is correct,' he said. 'This place could not have been made by a creature such as Tani or Pathmaker described. It was made by humans.'

Davin and Taleb had rejoined them, listening to the talk in their minds. Both men nodded. Davin indicated the walls.

'It was built by a master builder, possibly one using mage powers – the stones fit so precisely. I agree with Toomay that Reva must have simply found this place and perhaps he caused all the damage outside before he decided he could use it himself.'

Tilliat straightened, glancing at Taleb. 'Let's see if we can find that room again and check what's immediately around it.'

'I remember the way.' Cloud stalked towards one of the trapezoidal doors, tail upright, and waited for it to be opened for her.

When Cloud stopped outside another door, identical to every one they'd seen, Taleb lifted the latch and looked back at the others with a grin.

'She's right!' He pushed the door wide and his sister moved

closer to look in. Davin joined them while Toomay gazed over their heads. Tilliat listened to Taleb and Nami murmuring to each other. Davin came to lean on the wall next to Tilliat.

'Looks like a crazy woodworker's frenzy of invention,' he grunted.

'The Shadows think Reva made it all, from memories he inherited from the creature the Mage Tika destroyed. I have no idea what all those circles are.'

'Make ship work.'

Tilliat scowled. 'Ship?'

'How he travelled through the starfields.'

'Oh.' If these things were known, so long ago, Tilliat pondered, *why* were there no accounts recorded and held in the archives in Kelshan?

'Reva.' The Shadows answered Tilliat's unguarded thought.

'The creature can change records?' She frowned in disbelief.

'Influence many. If he chose.'

Tilliat recalled the senior archivist and her reluctance to produce various papers and reports Tilliat had requested. Could this strange being, of whom she had so recently learnt, have been manipulating certain minds over all these countless years?

'These two rooms either side have a door into Reva's room,' Taleb called.

Nami emerged from a doorway further along the corridor. 'This one has a door in the back,' she said. 'But there isn't a door leading sideways.'

Toomay moved warily through the doorway, his wings tight to his sides. This room was completely empty, no piled furniture on the verge of disintegration, no tumbled papers or cloth. Nami was already through the next door, Taleb at her heels. Tilliat glanced back and saw Davin Pearl had taken his position, guarding her back, while Toomay moved ahead of her.

'No one here.'

'I'm quite sure you're right but we still prefer to be cautious.' Tilliat's thought snapped back at the Shadows.

The second room was identical to the first with another door at the further end.

'Oh. Stairs.' Nami sounded surprised. 'I wondered if there was any way upwards. They couldn't have built such a massive

371

place and then only lived on one level. But it's dark in here.'

A globe of light popped into existence above her head. She grinned back at Toomay.

'We've never been able to do that,' Nami remarked. 'You'll have to show us how.'

Toomay huffed but said nothing. Tilliat made no comment either but it had been *her* power that made the light. The two Chars vanished, with the light globe drifting above them. Tilliat and Davin paused at the door, seeing there was a flat square landing with stairs leading upwards, but also down.

'I cannot get through those spaces,' Toomay murmured to Tilliat and Davin.

'I think it best that we just wait here for a while,' Tilliat spoke aloud, meeting Davin's eyes.

Davin nodded towards the floor. 'It has been long since anyone walked in here – look at the dust.'

Tilliat saw the Chars' footprints clearly marked in the thick layer of dust on the steps. She turned away and retraced their route, Davin and Toomay following.

'The Chars will explore I expect, but somehow I know they'll find their way back to us. Come on.'

She led the Dragon and trader back through the room with the deformed furniture, with its red painted dots, and gained the wide corridor beyond. Tilliat let out a breath when the door closed behind them. She looked at Davin Pearl for a long moment then turned her gaze on Toomay. The Dragon stared steadily back at her, his eyes quiet and calm.

'I have made my choice, friend Tilliat. I will stay beside you and Uncle.' His mind tone was gentle but firm.

Tilliat sighed, reaching to trace a fingertip along the line of his cheek. The door to Reva's strange room suddenly opened, making Tilliat and Davin Pearl jump.

The Chars grinned. 'More rooms up the stairs but all gone to dust ages ago,' Taleb reported.

Despite his increased liking for both of the twins, Davin Pearl felt a strong twinge of apprehension. This situation would more than likely prove lethal for all of them but treating it as no more than an escapade did not bode well for any caution in what they all faced.

Toomay's wings lifted a little then folded tight against his back.

'What is it?' Tilliat sent the thought to his mind alone.

'Thorn is high above. He says there is a darkness coming in this direction and it approaches fast.'

'Is he safe? And Bone?'

After a pause, Toomay replied. 'Both he and Bone are climbing higher than I thought possible.' The Dragon's eyes flickered, indicating a growing unease.

'If we assume this thing will arrive in that big hall place,' Davin said abruptly, 'which door is the one closest to this section?'

Nami and Taleb both headed down the corridor without replying.

'It will be here soon Tilliat?' Davin spoke low although the Chars were already out of earshot.

When Tilliat nodded, he gripped her arm. 'We are with you Tilliat. Always.'

'Indeed.' Toomay murmured the word to both humans' minds.

Tilliat's eyes filled with tears and she blinked furiously but the Char twins returned before she could speak.

'The first door round the corner would be the nearest.' Nami announced. 'I think we should try to take this creature from both sides. Taleb and I will hide in the room down there.' She waved vaguely in the direction from which they'd come.

'We?' Tilliat enquired slightly caustically. '*We?*'

Nami had the grace to blush and shrugged. Inside Tilliat's head there was a distinct snigger from the Shadows.

Ignoring them for a moment, Tilliat moved to Nami and hugged her tight before repeating her action to Taleb. She stepped back. 'I can never tell you both what your support means to me. I am glad of your company and will always be grateful to you.'

Taleb laughed. 'Sounds like a farewell to me. You don't think this thing can finish *us* off, do you?'

Nami grinned at her brother's side. 'We'll see you later. We have a few magely tricks worked out, never fear.'

Tilliat watched them hurry back down the passage, a deep

373

foreboding growing in her heart.

'Yartay thing close.' The three words from the Shadows held a mix of emotions: fury, disgust, and a gleeful anticipation among them.

Tilliat swallowed and grabbed Davin's hand, pulling him in the opposite direction to the Chars. She opened a door straight across from what she thought of as 'Reva's room', and urged Davin and Toomay inside.

'Use no power,' the Shadows ordered, as Toomay caused a small globe of light to pop into view.

The Dragon instantly extinguished his globe and Tilliat knew he'd heard the Shadows' command. She saw Davin Pearl held a long knife ready, his face set in determination, before they were plunged into blackness. Toomay's chin touched her left shoulder and she knew how fearful he was, but also as determined as Uncle Davin.

'Yartay thing causes pressure,' the Shadows reported.

'You *are* protecting the Chars as well as us?' Tilliat thought quickly.

There was a moment before the answer came. 'Yes.'

She wondered, crazily, if Shadows had teeth – that reply sounded as if they were gritted. Then: 'Gone. Into room.'

Tilliat's thoughts whirled. Why hadn't she at least thought of *some* sort of plan against Reva? It was all very well to split into two groups, but what might Nami and Taleb be doing? All those days waiting – *why* hadn't they discussed this at all?

'They think *you* plan,' the Shadows informed her helpfully.

'Thank you.' It was Tilliat's turn to grit her teeth.

'Tika used fire.'

'So you told me.' She felt the Shadows suddenly come alert, like dogs scenting their quarry. 'What is it?'

'Others move.'

Tilliat cursed aloud and started to reach towards the door.

'No. Wait.'

There was a brief sensation of something appallingly heavy pressing down and there seemed to be no air to breathe. Cloud squawked and burrowed lower under Tilliat's jacket. Just as suddenly it was gone. The Shadows doing whatever it was they did to protect her, Tilliat hoped.

She put a hand out to touch Toomay and tried to stop any of her thoughts leaking to his mind. Why must it be up to *her* to deal with this terribleness? How could she possibly prevail?

'Do not despair dear friend. You will not fail.' Toomay offered her all his hope.

In Garjetka, Prince Tetsura felt he was slowly, very slowly, learning the basics of how to rule. He'd had only brief visits from Commander Anjit but the men and women he had himself appointed to various government posts were proving most satisfactory and hardworking. Commander Anjit had visited him yesterday evening and informed him, almost casually, that the ex-Regent Hikmat had died. He didn't explain how his death had come about but Tetsura had preferred not to ask for details.

Sergeant Tag was a constant discreet presence, but since she'd admitted to once being one half of twins, there had been a reserve between them. This afternoon Tetsura looked up from the stack of papers on his desk when Vilad appeared in front of him. Vilad bowed and mindspoke his Prince, at the same time offering him a small card.

'Poxton Dens of the Jewellers Guild requesting a private moment.'

Tetsura's expression lightened. 'Show him in Vilad, please.'

Tetsura stood as Poxton Dens entered the study. The head of the Jewellers Guild bowed but Tetsura waved impatiently. 'No need for formalities in private Poxton. Please have a seat.'

The man who still looked more like a farmer than someone as skilled as he was in delicate metalwork, smiled. 'I have brought what you asked of me. If it is not correct or to your complete satisfaction, no matter. I will be pleased to redo it until it is absolutely what you want.'

Tetsura glanced up. 'Thank you Sergeant. If you could leave us for now please?'

Sergeant Tag snapped a salute and departed. Poxton Dens grinned. 'I know the Sergeant is a very small person, but I truly hadn't noticed her.'

'No,' the Prince replied a trifle ruefully. 'She's rather good at being unnoticed.'

Poxton took a small wooden box from an inner pocket and

handed it across the desk. Tetsura opened it slowly and studied the contents. Poxton waited patiently. He hoped he had achieved what the Prince had asked for but, as he'd said, he'd be happy to recraft the objects until they were right.

Tetsura lifted one item from the box and scrutinised it closely. Then another, then a third. Gently replacing them, he shut the box and gave the jeweller a dazzling smile. 'They are just what I'd hoped for.' He hesitated then made up his mind. 'One is for my sister, my twin sister.'

Poxton Dens merely nodded. Tetsura send a tendril of his mind towards the jeweller and found him calm and steady, quite relaxed. He withdrew the thought probe and wished, not for the first time, that Poxton Dens could be persuaded to work as a councillor, or advisor, to the Phoenix Throne. Although Tetsura knew that Poxton had no mage powers, it was almost as though the man had read his thought. He smiled at the Prince.

'I don't know how you can endure being stuck in here all day. I work, and I love my work, but I often leave a piece and go for a wander through the gardens, or have a meal somewhere then return refreshed.'

'I walk in the Palace gardens but of course, everyone knows exactly where I am. And it appears that my signature is needed for so very many things! I do thank you most sincerely for these treasures Poxton, and I would like to let it be known that I consider you to be jeweller appointed to the Phoenix Throne – if you are agreeable.'

For a moment, Poxton looked stunned then he rose quickly to his feet. He bowed deeply to the young Prince. 'You honour me sir. I would be proud to be the royal jeweller.' Poxton moved towards the door, turned to bow once more, and quietly left the Prince's presence.

Tetsura peeped into the box once more, nodded to himself, then tucked the box into a desk drawer just as Sergeant Tag re-entered the room.

'No one waiting to see you,' she announced with a faint smile.

'Stars be thanked for that,' Tetsura replied.

'Your meal has been delivered to the sitting room.' Tag opened the inner door leading to Tetsura's private apartment. Tetsura stretched as he got up. Rolling his shoulders he headed for the door. He'd just drawn level with Sergeant Tag when he gasped, his left hand reaching to grab the door jamb. Colour drained from his face while he struggled to stay upright.

'Sir? Sir? What is it? Are you ill?' Tag slid under his arm and took his weight, furiously calling Vilad with her mind.

The manservant rushed towards them from the sitting room and between them, they heaved Tetsura to the nearest couch. He seemed unconscious by the time Vilad and Tag stood back, staring at him.

Vilad's eyes narrowed at Tag and he mindspoke her directly. 'Don't you dare deny you are mageborn again – you nearly blasted my mind to bits when you called me then.' He turned back to Tetsura and his frown deepened. 'I cannot reach his mind. I have no idea what this could be.'

Sergeant Tag stubbornly spoke aloud rather than using mind-speech. 'Could it be something to do with his sister?'

Vilad's eyebrows shot up his forehead. 'Surely not. Why would you think such a thing?'

Tag took a breath. 'Last time – you remember? Before his Presentation. He seemed ill in the night and was terribly sick when he woke.'

'Go on.' Vilad's mindtone was neutral but Tag prudently moved away slightly.

'He told me he had been helping his sister to heal someone.'

'Helping her *heal*? He knows nothing of healing.'

'Neither did his sister,' Tag snapped back. 'She just plunged in and tried to mend someone's mind but she got sort of – tangled I think. I didn't understand all he said but I didn't want to interrupt him.'

Vilad looked as ill as Tetsura. 'Why did you not tell me? Or Saima? And you think his sister may have called him again?'

Tag shrugged helplessly, moving behind the couch and resting her small hand on Tetsura's shoulder.

'Sister faces battle.'

Tag looked at her hand and saw the thinnest of black lines round her thumb. Were these the Shadows Tetsura had begun to speak of on one occasion in the gardens? She moved her hand away from the Prince but the line remained. 'Are you the Shadows?' she asked faintly.

'Of course.' That voice was definitely tetchy. 'Sister not call. Brother aware though.'

'What are you talking about?' Vilad demanded. 'Shadows? They are merely folk tales.'

Tag glared at the old man. 'Really? Who brought his sister here? You saw her you said. *Shadows* brought her.'

There was silence while they both studied the young man lying unconscious before them. Vilad's mind sounded calmer when he bespoke Tag. 'Saima is on her way. I think we should get a couple of the guards to move His Highness to his bedchamber, he is too tall to be comfortable on this couch.'

Vilad and Saima had finally left, still arguing about what might ail the Prince. Sergeant Tag remained, watching the still figure in the bed. She'd dozed off when Tetsura's voice jerked her awake.

'The box. The box in the office desk.'

Tag got to her feet, gazing down. Tetsura's eyelashes flickered and for a heartbeat, his grey eyes stared straight at the sergeant before closing again. Tag hurried through the rooms to the office. She pulled open four drawers before finding a polished and carved dark wood box. Returning to Tetsura's bedside she hesitated then put the box close to where his hand lay on top of the covers. His eyes half opened, his fingers clamped around the box and he lay still once more.

Chapter Thirty-Three

Tilliat wrenched her jacket open and pulled Cloud away from her body. 'You have to stay here little one.' She barely breathed the words into the cat's ear. 'No,' Tilliat forestalled argument. 'I have come to care for you dear Cloud, but you *must* stay here, very still, very quiet, until this is ended.' She kissed the furry face and let Cloud slide down her legs to the floor. 'Shadows?'

'Yes.'

'Can you make Uncle Davin and Toomay stay here? Unaware?'

'Probably.'

'Where are the Chars?'

There was a longer pause. 'Female in room round corner.'

Tilliat's heart seemed to lurch in her chest and then resumed beating with a hollow thud. 'And the male?'

'Outside creature's room.'

'Doing what?'

'Nothing.'

'What do you mean?'

'Dead.'

Tilliat knew this truncated conversation had taken mere heartbeats but it felt as though time had stopped. She took a steady breath, then another. 'Shadows, take me inside that room.'

'Hide you.'

The blackness intensified and Tilliat heard a muffled curse and a hiss, presumably the Shadows immobilising Davin Pearl and Toomay. Then she realised her feet were not on any sort of floor.

She left herself entirely in the control of the Shadows. She'd no sensible plan before Reva arrived, she certainly had no clear idea of what might happen next other than her imminent death. Tilliat became aware of a hint of light. It felt like she was looking through a gauzy grey veil. She blinked and gradually saw more clearly. She tasted blood. She'd bitten her lip.

379

Reva was beyond anybody's nightmarish imagination. He – she? – was an amorphous thing, stretching across the entire width of the room. She judged it was a similar height to herself, if not taller. Strange protrusions emerged along its length, tapping and twisting over the red painted dots on the misshapen furniture. It was not entirely solid, or at least Tilliat didn't think so. What appeared to be veins and arteries glittered and spun within a covering almost like liquid fog.

Suddenly something horribly resembling a child's head extruded from the mass of grey. The head turned directly towards Tilliat. Her stomach somersaulted when the Shadows blocked her vision and she had the sensation of several jerky movements. The faintest line thinned again in front of Tilliat's eyes and she realised the Shadows held her close to the ceiling in a corner of the room.

The head was looking away from her now, although she'd not seen any facial features apart from a lump that could be considered a nose. Her ears hurt when a high pitched whine filled the room. She screwed up her face against the sound, the Shadows held her too tightly for her to move to block her ears. The whine slowly faded to a lower drone. Tilliat gradually heard words amid the noise. 'Nasty,' was repeated many times but slowly the creature appeared to be calming.

The Shadows' words were the faintest tickle in the back of her head while they slowly lowered her until her feet touched the stone floor.

'Plays with dots. Almost dreaming. Attack him soon.'

Attack, Tilliat thought? Suddenly she was weary beyond belief.

'Fire. Tika used fire.'

Tilliat remembered using fire at the Yasharitzan village. She'd *thought* she was creating an illusion but it had been the real thing. Again, the head shot upwards, out of the grey creature and again, the Shadows whisked Tilliat out of reach. When she was permitted to see once more. she found herself, alarmingly, directly above it.

Strange jagged streams of blue light were cascading across the room towards the door. Towards exactly where Tilliat had been heartbeats earlier. The blue wasn't fire but it was energy of some kind, and Tilliat knew it would be deadly if it touched her. The 'nasty, nasty', chant began again. It sounded almost childish, but that thing beneath her was no child.

Reva turned away, the head vanishing again while the extrusions patted at the red dots. The Shadows moved her once more and set her down against a side wall, the door to her left, Reva to her right. Tilliat began to pull power into herself then nearly cried out as the door flew open.

Nami Char stood there for less than a heartbeat, her face snow white, her eyes blazing and wild. She held a long knife in each hand and screamed something incomprehensible except for her brother's name. Nami started to step forward but the blue streamers speared her in place. Before Tilliat's horrified eyes, Nami Char flared like a torch and fell forward, her body black and smoking.

'Now.' The Shadows urgent whisper pulled Tilliat's gaze away from Nami's corpse, back to the creature Reva.

She raised her hands, palms outward, and called for fire. And fire came, roaring through her whole frame. The high-pitched noise began again but Tilliat barely heard it over the sound of the fire blazing from both her hands towards Reva. But she could smell the stench of burning meat. She was distantly aware of blue streamers coming towards her and knew the Shadows had somehow slowed them: they flickered and faded before they reached her.

Stepping away from the wall, Tilliat stood, her feet apart, hands raised, body shaking with the force of the power screaming through her. Something struck her a glancing blow on her forehead but she ignored the sudden pain and stood firm. She felt hot liquid dripping into her eyes but whether it was blood or sweat she neither knew nor cared.

Her hands were becoming numb although fire still bloomed relentlessly from them. Tilliat never knew how long she stood there; she just knew that was all she could do, so she did it. The flames from her hands winked out. She peered blearily at Reva and saw only drifting ashes. She started to turn and saw Nami, looking so much smaller, lying dead by the door. Tilliat swayed.

A furious roar sounded nearby, mingled with a flood of trader curses, then Toomay and Davin Pearl were staring across Nami

Char's body. Tilliat wanted to speak, to reassure them and to mourn the Char twins, but blackness overcame her utterly.

In the Phoenix Palace in the Isles of Vremilia, Prince Tetsura opened his eyes. Dawn was fingering the sky beyond the window and a lamp burned very low near his bed. Sergeant Tag sat close by and the manservant Vilad sat opposite. Tetsura's fingers ached and, glancing down, he saw he gripped a wooden box tightly enough to have made his hand cramp.

Vilad touched the Prince's arm while he mindspoke the young man. 'Are you well sir? We feared you had a fever, but it was one such as even Saima did not recognise.'

Tetsura glanced at the sergeant but her face was shuttered, only her green eyes betrayed concern. The Prince's face had regained a tiny flush of colour although he was far paler than usual. He pushed himself up into a sitting position and waited to see if he'd fall back again. Slowly he moved his legs over the side of the bed.

'Where are my boots?'

'Here.' Sergeant Tag fetched the soft leather boots and handed them to him.

Vilad intercepted the boots, clasping them to his chest. He shook his head but before he could mindspeak, Tetsura held up a hand. Gently, he took the boots from Vilad and gave him a faint smile. 'Leave me now dear Vilad. There are things I have to do.'

Still shaking his head, Vilad's thoughts shouted urgently in Tetsura's and Tag's minds. 'What do you plan boy? It is but eight days until you are Raised to the Throne—'

'And I will be here. Now, please, leave me.'

Vilad's eyes filled with tears of fear and frustration but he bowed low and left the room.

Sergeant Tag moved to follow him but Tetsura stopped her. 'Wait Sergeant.'

Tag looked back at him. Tetsura pulled on his boots and got to his feet carefully.

'My sister won the battle,' he said. 'She is badly hurt. I must go to her.'

Tag just stared at him. He gave her a faint, very faint, smile. 'We'll travel the same way she did.'

'We?' Tag found her voice. '*We?*'

Tetsura's smile grew. He tucked the wooden box inside his tunic and held his hand out. 'Come on.'

Tag swallowed, scrutinised his expression then sighed. 'What do we do?' she asked, sliding her hand into his.

Tetsura shrugged. 'Shadows?'

Tag flinched then grew still when she heard that voice in her head again.

'Tetsura spoke aloud. 'We need to see my sister. Will you take us to her?'

After a pause, during which Tag and Tetsura's hands tightened their grip, the Shadows replied.

'Take. Close eyes.'

'Why?' Tetsura demanded.

'Open eyes make sick.'

Tag's eyes squeezed shut instantly. She *loathed* being sick.

They found the next few heartbeats both terrifying and exhilarating in equal measure. They also both fell over when their feet settled on solid ground. There were still stars speckling the sky above but a blurred line of gold on the eastern horizon suggested dawn was near. They could hear a river burbling but there was no sense of any human habitation.

'Where are we?' asked Tag.

'Safe place.'

'Where is my sister??'

'Others bring soon.'

Eyes becoming accustomed to the dimness, the Prince and Sergeant Tag could make out trees some distance away. A darker mass suggested they were close to a cliffside.

'Go in.'

'Go in where?' snapped Tag.

There was a derisive snort from the Shadows. 'There. Safe place.'

Turning slowly on the spot, Tag pointed at the cliff. 'In there somehow?'

Tetsura stared in the direction Tag indicated. Both of them caught their breath as an attenuated wisp of silver wavered by one of the trees then vanished.

'Make light.' the Shadows sounded exasperated.

Tetsura concentrated, imagining a lantern in front of him. A faint light glimmered by his face.

'More strong.'

Tetsura visualised a much brighter lamp and flinched back, shielding his eyes from the sudden flare. Tag sniggered and he glared. '*You* try then.'

'No sir. That looks fine to me – as long as you don't stare at it directly.'

Tetsura muttered something then imagined someone walking in front of him, carrying the light towards the tree by the cliff. The light wafted off in the right direction and Tetsura and the sergeant followed. Nearing the tree, they saw the entrance to some sort of crack, or cave, in the rock. Tag caught Tetsura's sleeve and slowed him. She passed him and led the way within, light glinting off a slim blade in her hand.

Tag moved cautiously into a surprisingly wide cave, the river gleaming black along one side. Tetsura's light wobbled ahead, rising up a sloping rock floor. Tetsura drew closer when Tag halted. The light hovered, revealing a roomy cave. They saw what was unmistakeably a fireplace in the further wall. Blankets were heaped near the fire and an assortment of pots and dishes lay jumbled in another corner.

'Who could live here? whispered Tag.

'Ancients. And Thorn.'

Tag looked an enquiry at the Prince. He shrugged and asked: 'Who is Thorn?'

'We like Thorn.'

Tag crossed her eyes and Tetsura laughed. 'When will Tilliat be here?'

'Soon.'

Tag groaned and Tetsura admitted defeat in conversing with the Shadows.

'At least it's not cold enough to need a fire,' Tag commented. 'We'd probably fall in the river trying to find wood to burn now.'

Tetsura didn't reply and she watched him. He was sorting through the tangled blankets and covers, shaking them out and folding them neatly. She joined him.

'These are quite dry,' he said. 'They must have been put here recently.'

Finally Tetsura sat down, his back to the wall beside the hearth. He let his floating light fade away as Sergeant Tag sank down beside him. With the false light gone, they saw dawn light creeping through several long slits in the outer rock wall opposite them.

'Almost like windows.' Tag murmured.

'Tilliat was here,' Tetsura said softly. 'She liked this place.' He studied the walls more closely. 'It has been a safe place for a very long time.'

Tag reached a hand up and stroked the rock beside her. Tetsura saw her nod thoughtfully in the slowly growing light.

'Now. Others come.' There seemed more emotion in the Shadows' mindspeech than they'd previously heard.

Tag was already on her feet, a knife in each hand. Suddenly the large room seemed crowded. An older man, holding a grey cat, a small, limp female figure, and a silvery Dragon with wildly flickering eyes. For two heartbeats there was silence, then the Dragon paced to lie beside the unconscious girl, the grey cat hissed and struggled down from the older man's arms as he sank to his knees with a groan.

Tetsura moved to the girl, kneeling opposite the Dragon, and stared in horror at the burned clothes and blistered skin.

'What is wrong with the old man?' Tag thought to the Shadows.

'Travel makes sick.' The Shadows' reply was ever so slightly sympathetic.

'What can I do?'

'Touch head. Stomach. Uncle feels very bad.'

Tag cursed to herself and almost rolled her eyes again when the Shadows sniggered. She bent to lay the palm of her hand on the man's forehead and thought of a soothing coolness flowing across the blur of pain, which she found she could sense in her own head. The man's eyes opened.

'Oh thank you my dear. Travelling that way is unbelievably foul.'

Tag put her hand on his belly and imagined a smooth, calm steadiness. The man sighed with relief then his gaze jerked to the girl lying motionless between the Dragon and Tetsura. He lurched on his knees, to take position at the girl's head, brushing

385

badly singed hair away from her face.

For the first time, Tag looked on Prince Tetsura's twin sister and her hand found his shoulder, gripping tightly. There was still cloth on parts of her body but they looked to be burnt into her actual skin. Her eyelashes and brows were gone and her face swollen and blistered. Tag saw that Tetsura held one of Tilliat's wrists and had carefully turned her hand up. Tag's stomach twisted. Flesh was seared away from bone.

'How could anyone hope to mend this?' she thought.

'Thorn might.'

Tag looked at Tetsura, at the older man, and finally at the Dragon. The Dragon's eyes held her gaze, they had stopped flickering and shone with an even, gold hue touched with blue. Tetsura's head lifted and he watched the Dragon.

'I am Toomay of the Dragon Kin, friend to Tilliat and Uncle and Cloud.' His mindvoice was young, slightly nervous, but steady. 'Thorn is my many times great grandfather and he mended friend Tilliat once before.'

'I am Tetsura, brother to Tilliat.' His voice trembled then firmed. 'I thank you with all my heart for your care and protection for her. My companion is Tag.'

Toomay regarded the sergeant and bent his head in her direction.

'And I am Cloud.' This was a feminine mindvoice, sounding greatly subdued. The grey cat inched forward by Tetsura's knee. 'Tilliat healed me but I have no ability to do such things.'

Tetsura's free hand settled on the cat's back, stroking her soft fur.

'I am Davin Pearl, trader of Kelshan City.'

'He is Uncle,' chimed three voices insistently, Cloud, Toomay and, somewhat surprisingly, the Shadows.

The trader scowled. 'Just because Tilliat calls me Uncle, they all think that's my name.'

'If that is what my sister calls you, then I would gladly do so too.'

Davin stared at the young man for his first proper look at him in the still weak light. He was probably nearly a head taller than Tilliat, Davin guessed. He had the same dark unruly hair and although Davin couldn't see clearly enough, he would wager the boy had the same grey eyes. His face was uncannily like hers although unmistakeably masculine.

'She called fire.' It was a statement not a question from the young man.

Davin turned his gaze back to Tilliat as he nodded. 'It would seem so. We were not with her.'

Tag's hand tightened further on Tetsura's shoulder while they waited for Davin to continue but it was Toomay who mindspoke.

'She must have asked Shadows to make us unable to move, then they took her to the room where the creature was.' The Dragon shivered, his wings quivering against his back.

Tetsura lifted his hand from Cloud's fur and brushed his fingers along Toomay's jaw. The Dragon's voice whispered in their minds.

'Taleb and Nami died.'

Before Tetsura could ask who those people were, Toomay's head stretched high, eyes sparkling. His mindvoice carried immense relief. 'Thorn. And Bone.'

Heads turned to the entrance. Tag gulped when a massive black Dragon carefully eased himself inside. He stepped up to Toomay and necks twined gracefully if briefly. Thorn leaned forward to touch his forehead to Davin Pearl's then he looked down at the grey cat crouched by Tetsura's knees. A deep voice spoke gently in all their minds.

'I am glad to see you safe Uncle, and you Cloud.' His eyes were bigger than Tetsura's fist but the Prince rose to his feet and bowed low to the Dragon.

'I am Tilliat's brother, Tetsura, from Vremilia. I am honoured and humbled to meet you. I will soon be King on the Phoenix Throne and I would be proud if you could attend my crowning.'

There was a gasp but Tetsura's eyes were locked with the black Dragon's so he didn't know who was apparently shocked by his words. 'I had no idea,' he continued, 'that the Dragon Kin once lived in our Isles, but I have learned much of late. I would welcome the presence of your Kindred should you wish to return.' He paused and glanced down at the burnt body at his feet. 'And if you could do anything to help my sister, my gratitude would last longer than the stars can burn.'

Thorn too gazed downwards to Tilliat's motionless form and

the silence stretched on. At last the old Dragon gusted a huge sigh. 'I will think on your words young man, but mend your sister? I fear she is far beyond my own powers alone to heal.'

Trader Pearl's head suddenly lifted. 'Perra Koos. Or Li Kassu. In Gulat. I'm not sure if Perra can heal but I *know* Li Kassu can.'

Tag was aware of a strange emptiness in the back of her head where the Shadows usually seemed to be, and by the look on Tetsura's face, he felt the same absence. Then two more people appeared, sprawled in a tangle of limbs, behind Davin Pearl.

Davin peered over his shoulder. 'Welcome Perra. How were things in Gulat?'

Perra Koos snorted while he helped Li Kassu climb to her feet beside him. Turning, he saw the massive, black scaled Dragon and then the burnt girl lying so still below Davin. 'Stars forefend!' he whispered. 'The poor child.'

Li Kassu had taken in everything in one penetrating glance. She bowed low to the black Dragon and told him her name, then gently squeezed herself between Davin Pearl and Tetsura. She studied the girl so very badly injured, nodding when she turned a hand and saw the bones exposed in the palm.

'I can start to heal this, but it will take time.' She stared round at the worried faces. 'For a healing such as this, there would be a team of us working together.'

'Who else do you need?' asked Davin. 'The Shadows could bring them.'

Li Kassu shook her head. 'We were still in Perra's cellar. Gulat suffered enormous damage. Among the mages gathered in his home, none were strong healers with whom I have worked before.'

'What help do you need?' Thorn asked.

Li Kassu frowned. 'I would need someone with strong powers to bolster mine should I tire. Someone who can continue healing when I have dealt with the worst of it.'

'I can do that.'

Li Kassu studied the huge Dragon. 'I will also need water, warm water for Tilliat, cold water for me to drink as I proceed. Some sort of gown or clean cloth at least, to wrap her in.'

Davin stood. 'I'll fetch water but I don't know where we'll

get clean clothes. Our packs were lost in that creature's place.' He headed for the cave exit. 'I'll find wood too,' he called back.

'I'll help you.' Tag hurried after the trader.

'No. He can manage.'

Tag stopped, looking at Thorn in some surprise.

'There are many rooms here. The man from Gulat can accompany you. Look along the wall, by the fire.'

Perra Koos shrugged and went where Thorn had suggested, Sergeant Tag at his heels. Perra gave a soft exclamation when he found the fold in the rock wall. Tag opened her mouth to point out how dark it was, and closed it again when Perra conjured a small ball of light above and slightly ahead of them. They saw a flight of steps, uneven but hollowed in the middle, as if countless feet over countless ages had passed over them.

Perra and Tag began to climb. Tag heard Tetsura asking how he might help the healing.

'I presume that lad is Tilliat's brother?' Perra remarked from ahead of Tag. 'And who are you?'

'Sergeant Tag, the Crown Prince's personal guard.'

Perra halted near the top of the steps and regarded Tag. Flaming red hair blazed around her head and ice green eyes stared back at him. He noted the small frame but also the easy way she stood. She was comfortable in her own body and there was a considerable confidence in her stance. Perra tilted his head to one side. 'Personal guard hmm? Knives, or unarmed combat?'

Tag allowed herself a small smile. 'Either, but knives for preference.'

Perra nodded and turned to climb on.

With the aid of his light they found several more rooms of various sizes, some towards the front of the cliff with narrow cracks allowing light to enter. Some of the even smaller rooms were behind the lit rooms and if it were not for Perra's light ball, they would have been in pitchy dark.

It was in one such place they found supplies. They stared silently at sacks and cloth bags and boxes. Tag sank to her knees and reached for a bag. She pulled out a length of soft cloth that smelled of herbs and meadow flowers. Perra took it and drew it further. When its length finally came clear of the bag, a small roll of parchment fell to the floor. Perra began to fold the cloth while

Tag inspected the scroll. Perra saw a feather incised in the blue wax. Tag turned it in her fingers. 'It is named for Tilliat.' She raised a brow.

'Open it then. Obviously Tilliat is unable to read it at the moment.'

Very carefully, Tag slid a knife under the wax seal, easing it away from the parchment. Perra Koos hadn't seen where the knife appeared from but he smiled. 'You've clearly done that before! What is the message?'

Tag frowned. 'It is in the common tongue but I have never seen the letters formed this way.

Perra squatted beside her, both of them squinting to decipher the spidery writing.

'Dearest child, We shall be gone from this world when you read this. And not before time I suspect. The friends who have supplied us these many years, and you in your encampment, believe you will need help for a while when your task is fulfilled. May the stars keep you and guard your heart, and may you find some kindness in your memories of us. Stars bless you child. Pathmaker.'

'Can we be sure these supplies are all safe? Free of poison?' Tag enquired.

Perra nodded. 'I'm quite sure they are. Shall we sort through them or just take them down?'

'Why don't I take the cloth down now, then we can check the rest.' Tag clasped the folded cloth and trotted off.

Perra turned his attention to the mysteriously delivered supplies.

Chapter Thirty-Four

Davin Pearl had brought water, started a fire in the hearth and then joined Perra and Tag upstairs looking through the supplies. 'Thorn said it was Ancients,' he explained. 'They supplied the Pathmaker and his two friends, and us. We don't know who they are. They lived here once though, long ago. The Dragon Bone is outside,' he added. 'Thorn's sister.'

Toomay's eyes sparkled a little. He'd been very subdued until now. Li Kassu sat cross legged beside Tilliat, her breathing slow and deep. Tetsura also sat, head bowed, close by. Toomay mindspoke the others. 'They are linked. Li Kassu is deep within Tilliat, strengthening her heart and lungs where they suffered intense pressure. Tetsura watches and will help if needed. Thorn is ready to send his strength into any of them should it be necessary. And Bone follows all through Thorn's mind.'

Time passed, incredibly slowly to Tag, Davin Pearl and Perra Koos. The mage from Gulat eventually suggested they have a look outside now it was full daylight so the three made their way out past the guardian trees. Judging by the sun's position it was around midday. Davin had brought a sack to collect wood and busied himself along the river bank. Perra and Tag strolled some distance further, studying a panoramic view spread below them.

'Beautiful country,' Tag commented. Then she looked puzzled. 'No farms, no villages.' She turned to Perra.

'This must be the Dragon Realm,' he said. 'Keep going east,' he pointed ahead. 'You'll come to the sea I suspect.' He waved behind them. 'That way leads to the lands of men. The Dragon Kin have warded these lands. If anyone gets to the borders, they get sick, disorientated, confused. All they want to do is leave the area.'

'Useful trick,' Tag agreed.

Perra tugged at his lower lip. 'From what little Tilliat told me, Toomay brought her and Uncle here when they'd been travelling from Kelshan City. Someone tried to poison her and when she got here, a mage cleared the poison from her system. No one's mentioned people living here, have they?'

Tag shook her head. She turned back to the cliff and caught her breath. Perra looked where Tag stared up to a broad ledge. A large Dragon reclined gracefully, staring back down at the two humans with interest. Suddenly, wings lifted and the Dragon, the palest honey coloured ivory, was drifting down towards them. The Dragon glided onto the grass close to the cave entrance and settled gently.

'My name is Bone. I am sister to Thorn. I have seen, through Thorn's mind, what your friend attempts. It is very slow work I fear.'

Being so small, Tag was used to everyone towering over her so she felt no discomfort craning to look up into Bone's long, surprisingly lovely face. Perra Koos however was a touch disconcerted to feel so diminished by Bone's sheer size.

There was amusement in Bone's mindvoice. 'Why do you not sit and enjoy the sunlight for a while? It is very soothing I find.' She rested her head back between her wings and closed her large golden eyes. 'I believe your friend Li Kassu is near the limit of her strength and skill. The child was close to death and twice now, Li Kassu has had to reawaken her heart. The child's body is deeply shocked by the hurts inflicted upon it. Her brother is helping heal the worst burns. Thorn is guarding Li Kassu's strength but she will have to rest, very soon.'

'Is Tilliat out of danger now?' Tag asked. 'Is it safe for the Prince to be healing?'

Bone sounded irritated. 'He is healer born is he not? And he is her brother.'

'Yes, but he doesn't know that and he tried to help her heal someone else. He found it difficult to get free of either her or the hurt one. I don't really know which.'

Bone's head snapped up, her eyes flickering with orange lights. 'He doesn't know? Has he had *any* training?'

'No.'

There was a brief pause and Bone's eyes slowly calmed. 'I have told Thorn to watch the boy more closely.'

Tag was on her feet. 'The Prince is safe though? Thorn will

keep him safe?'

The golden eyes regarded Tag with curiosity. 'Li Kassu sleeps now and so does Tilliat. The girl is not unconscious as before, but she must sleep. The boy speaks with Thorn.'

Tag sat back on the grass beside Perra. 'Tell me what happened in your city?'

Perra grunted. 'Many came to my house to shelter in the cellars. When the creature Reva arrived, there was a great weight pressing down and the air seemed to be squeezed out. My cellars are deep, cut into the bedrock.' He closed his eyes briefly. 'So many died. I have no idea how we can even start to think of rebuilding, reorganising, or if we even should. I'd guess my friends who survived with me, will be struggling with those problems now, but Li Kassu and I were brought here with no warning, so I know no more.'

Davin Pearl joined them, leaving his now filled sack near the cave entrance.

'Are you well Uncle?' asked Perra. 'I have still not heard what you must have faced. Clearly Tilliat used fire, but you seem unhurt?'

Davin scowled. 'Those Shadows did something which meant neither Toomay nor I could see, hear or move, and they took Tilliat to meet Reva. I suspect they finally released us because they were too busy helping shield Tilliat to bother with us. When we got to Reva's room, she was still standing, but collapsed as we arrived.'

'The Char twins?' Perra asked gently.

Davin swallowed, meeting Perra's eyes squarely. 'We don't know what Taleb attempted, but he was killed outside Reva's door. I do not know how. Nami seems to have at least got inside; her body was burnt black. I'm so sorry Master Koos, I don't even know if they had family?'

Perra sighed, rubbing a hand over his face. 'No Uncle, they were the last of their line.'

Tag could sense deep sadness in both men but it was Bone who mindspoke them all.

'Why do you not go inside and make one of your strange foods? You are all tired and hungry and food always helps I find.' The Dragon's eyes flickered slightly when the three humans all suddenly grinned at her.

'Good idea.' Davin extended a hand each to the other two and pulled them up.

'What was that about strange foods?' Tag wanted to know as they made their way inside.

'Dragons eat raw meat,' Davin explained. 'They find the smell of cooked meat quite foul.'

'They seem to like honey cakes I recall,' Perra added. 'Even Dragons have a fondness for honey cakes.'

A short time later, Tag understood the trader's words better. Davin had found plenty of dried foods among the supplies and a stew was soon simmering gently over the fire. Thorn and Toomay both left the cave room, Tag noting the twitching nostrils of both Dragons. Li Kassu lay a short distance from Tilliat, wrapped in a bedroll, and Tetsura still sat watching his sister.

Tag left Perra and Davin Pearl arguing about a recipe for cinnamon porridge and dropped down beside the Prince. She studied Tilliat's motionless form. Her face was still swollen but free of blisters. There was a pale line of scarring from the centre of her forehead across to the outer edge to where the left brow should be. A length of cloth was laid over her body so Tag couldn't tell how much had been healed there. She could see Tilliat's hands swathed loosely in more cloth but couldn't guess whether they'd been fully restored.

She touched Tetsura's arm. He gave a long sigh then turned to Sergeant Tag. 'I saw what she had to face, back in the Palace.'

Tag nodded; she'd guessed that from his words then. 'Is she hurt, internally?' she asked.

'Li Kassu healed a very great deal. I think Tilliat will need a lot of time and peace and rest before she is fully recovered.'

'What about the burns? Her hands were–' Tag stopped, unable to find words for the damage she'd seen.

'Li Kassu did what she could but she was exhausted by then. She may be able to do a little more when she's slept and recovered some of her powers.'

'If we could get her back to Garjetka, perhaps Saima could do more?'

'I asked the Shadows about that. They said they *would* move her but they doubted if she would survive in the state she is now.'

For the first time, Tag realised the grey cat was still close to Tetsura's knee. She could hear a low rumbling purr. Tetsura followed Tag's gaze and lightly touched the cat's back. Cloud looked up, eyes as green as Sergeant Tag's.

'I know nothing of healing. If *only* I did.'

'Shh now,' Tetsura murmured. 'Tilliat knows you are near little Cloud and your presence gives her much comfort.' Cloud wailed softly, scrunching herself lower by Tilliat's arm.

'Sir,' Tag began, 'we cannot stay here indefinitely.'

'I know, I know. I believe we could stay another four days.' Tetsura caught Tag's doubtful glance and sighed again. 'Three?'

'Three at the most I should think,' she said. 'Poor Vilad will be going crazy with worry.'

Tetsura reached to brush a wisp of hair from Tilliat's cheek.

'You look so alike,' Tag murmured. 'Do you know which of you was born first?'

Tetsura gave a rueful smile. 'She was. Vilad told me so. So she should sit on the Phoenix Throne.'

Tag digested that information. 'Does she know? Would she want to take the Throne?' Her mind spun at the ramifications of such a situation.

Tetsura snorted. 'I'm not convinced it's such a great idea for myself. You can be quite sure Tilliat will want to stay here.'

Tag still harboured some qualms on the subject but wisely kept them to herself.

After a surprisingly good meal, Tag and Perra Koos decided to continue their exploration of the upper caves. Perra conjured his ball of light and followed it and Tag back up the uneven stairs. They went through the various rooms they'd seen before when Tag stopped abruptly. 'I thought we took the supplies downstairs?'

'Hmm. So did I.' Perra agreed. 'At least there's no chance they'll starve however long Tilliat and Uncle have to stay here.'

'Why is the trader called Uncle?'

Perra laughed. 'Dragons use only one name. They heard Tilliat refer to the poor man as Uncle so they insist that *is* his name. And now everyone calls him that. And by the way,' he turned to Tag with a frown, 'why do you hide your mage talents so deeply?'

Sergeant Tag stared at him, her face expressionless. 'Surely that's my concern?'

Perra Koos shrugged, watching as she visibly tried to appear relaxed. She folded her arms and leaned against the wall. Suddenly she jerked away from the rock as if it was red hot.

'What is it?' Perra asked, moving closer to the Sergeant.

'I thought – no, I must be imagining things.'

'*What?*' demanded Perra again.

Tag cautiously put her hand against the rock. Her eyes widened. 'Can you hear that?'

Perra shook his head. He made no attempt to probe Tag's mind; he had already discerned she was a strongly gifted mage who for some reason, was unable to admit that fact. Her small hand splayed starfish like against the pale rock. 'It speaks to me.'

'What does?'

'The wall. It remembers the first ones.'

Perra had no idea what Tag spoke of but he nodded, just to keep her talking.

'The first ones are still here somehow. They are the ones who bring supplies.' Tag frowned. 'They regret they cannot help more. I think that means they can't help heal Tilliat.' The frown cleared and she nodded. 'That's right, they can't influence events directly. They couldn't help or protect or heal – although their servants can.'

'Servants?'

Tag's voice sank to a whisper. 'Shadows.' Slowly she withdrew her hand and stepped away from the wall. 'Why couldn't you hear it?'

'Sergeant, you surely know each mage is talented in a different way. Something within you is open to contact by such as these Ancients.' He paused, drew a breath and risked the question. 'Why do you deny your mage gifts child?'

'I am not worthy. My sister would have been so much better, so much stronger, so much *more* than me.'

Perra saw the tears clinging to her lashes and kept silent.

'I killed the man who destroyed us.' The silence stretched too far while Tag struggled to keep the tears from spilling.

'How old were you?' Perra whispered.

'We were ten.'

Perra closed his eyes: the pain in those three words was still far too raw. But he got no more from Sergeant Tag. She marched briskly back down the stairs and left him to wander through a maze of rooms.

Much later, Li Kassu woke, ate some of Davin's stew and settled beside Tilliat once more. Tag lay on a bedroll not far from Tetsura and fell asleep almost at once. Tetsura raised an eyebrow at Thorn who huffed gently.

'The child is much disturbed. Sleep will do her good.' The deep mindvoice sharpened. 'You too should sleep. I am watching the healer and your sister. All is well for now. Rest.'

Davin sat to one side of the hearth with his pipe and bowl of tea and kept his eyes on Li Kassu. Toomay lay along Tilliat's side, Cloud now curled on the Dragon's front feet. Perra took his tea bowl and settled closer to the great black Dragon. 'Do you know what happened upstairs earlier Thorn?' Perra used a tight thread to mindspeak the Dragon alone.

The huge head swung to study the mage. 'No.'

Perra explained what Tag had told him. Thorn listened closely, then asked Perra to let him see into his mind, to hear exactly what Perra recalled. Thorn's eyes, the colour of shadow on snow, began to flicker. 'But the mage Tika felt this. When she was here she spoke to the stones. She said they told her another child would come here and fight a battle such as she, Tika, had just endured.'

Perra was stunned and confused. 'Tika? The mage from long ago?' He could feel Thorn's excitement.

'Indeed.' Thorn sent pictures to Perra's mind of a clear summer's day a thousand years ago. Perra watched enthralled as a silvery blue Dragon spiralled down outside these very caves. A small figure slid from the Dragon's back as a much larger golden Dragon landed, followed by an even bigger scarlet Dragon.

When the pictures faded, Thorn related all he knew or remembered from that distant day in his youth. He left Perra with a very great deal to think about before he finally succumbed to sleep.

It was decided the next day that Tetsura and Sergeant Tag would return to Vremilia the following morning. Tetsura argued for staying longer but was eventually convinced to leave then. Li Kassu had continued to work on Tilliat's hands but could only sustain her power for ever lessening periods. Now, on Tetsura's last night here, everyone seemed to be asleep except for Tag and Toomay, although the Prince suspected Thorn was not quite so soundly asleep as he appeared, nor Cloud.

He touched the side of Tilliat's arm, leaning close as he called to her mind. Her eyelids quivered. He called again, and grey eyes stared up into his.

'I have to leave dear sister. When you are properly fit, please visit me. I will come here as I can. I wish you could attend my Crowning but I will try to remember every single moment to share with you later. I have brought a gift for you, one of three that were specially made to my design. I will give it into Uncle's keeping for now. Mend swiftly my dear Tilliat. I am so proud of you.' Leaning even closer, he touched his lips softly to her forehead.

Moving back, he eased a carved wooden box from within his tunic. Opening it, he lifted one item out, wrapping it carefully in the small square of silk on which it had rested. Closing the box and returning it to his tunic, he raised his eyes to Toomay. 'You will know when Uncle must give her this?' he asked.

Toomay tilted his chin down. 'As you say.'

Rising, Tetsura crossed to Davin Pearl. Davin woke, instantly looking first to Tilliat. 'She rests Uncle. Will you give her this, with my love, when Toomay tells you it is time?'

Davin took the tiny parcel and slid it inside his jacket. 'Of course I will lad.'

Tetsura returned to his place by his sister and sat silently through the rest of the night. The Shadows had been even more reticent than usual but they responded immediately when Tetsura called them at dawn. He and Tag bade thanks and farewell to the others, clasped hands and vanished.

The pair reappeared in the Prince's bedchamber in the Phoenix Palace. They both retained their footing this time although Vilad fell over from pure shock. Tag immediately requested permission to report to Commander Anjit and left Tetsura to calm Vilad. The next few days blurred past: fittings for royal robes, rehearsals for the ceremonies, officials to see and documents and decrees to be signed and sealed.

Tetsura saw little of Sergeant Tag except when he had to move between various areas of the Palace, but he requested her presence late the night before his Crowning. The Prince ordered an exhausted Vilad to go to bed and sat at his desk awaiting Sergeant Tag's arrival. The Palace had fallen nearly silent before the sergeant appeared. She stood in front of the desk, eyes fixed above Tetsura's head.

'You sent for me Your Highness?'

Tetsura waited a heartbeat. 'Please sit down Sergeant.'

Tag reluctantly perched on the very edge of a chair set back from the desk. Tetsura studied her carefully. 'I know you will be close by tomorrow.'

She nodded.

'I would have you join me on the balcony at dusk for the sky magics.'

Tag paled. 'Commander Anjit–' she began.

'I have spoken to the Commander. He knows I wish your company at that time.'

A frown creased Tag's brow. 'Your Highness?'

Tetsura took a deep breath. He too looked slightly pale now. 'I have a gift for you, which must be given then.'

'A gift?' Tag echoed, now totally confused.

Tetsura stood abruptly and began to pace behind his desk. 'Tomorrow I will be the King on the Phoenix Throne, King of Vremilia and the Isles.' He looked down, directly into Sergeant Tag's upturned face. 'I would like you to be my Queen.'

Tag's mouth opened and closed several times before a faint squeak emerged. 'Me? Queen?'

'Yes. I trust you completely Sergeant.' His mouth twitched in a quick grin. 'You'd do much better in a fight than I would too. But while we were with Tilliat, I knew something upset you and I just wanted to make you know that I'd always keep you safe. I would prefer to do that with you by my side. As my Queen.'

Silence settled in the room but a comfortable silence, not strained. Finally Tag blew out a long gusting breath. 'I am greatly honoured Your Highness but I must think before I answer you.' She climbed to her feet to leave.

'One thing Sergeant.' Tag half turned back from the door. 'Will you not trust me with your name?'

Her green eyes were enormous in her still pale face. 'Tomorrow sir. When I answer your other question.' And she slipped from the room quietly.

Tetsura went through to his bedchamber and stared out at the night sky. He could see stars thrown across the dark expanse but no sign of the moon, which would rise again tomorrow – a new moon and a new king. He realised he had made no mention of the love he'd found growing in his heart for Tag. He groaned aloud, and went to bed, where he lay wakeful until dawn.

His mind whirled through the night, from Tilliat to Tag, from the worries of kingship to the possibilities of marriage and – stars forefend! – children. So his last night as Prince of Vremilia was not the restful night he might have hoped for.

Across the sea, deep in the Dragon Realm, Li Kassu had used all the skills she knew and was pleased with her work. Tilliat had not been roused although Davin Pearl had helped Li Kassu in regularly lifting, washing and resettling the girl's slowly healing body. The grey cat Cloud had decided it was safe to leave her position beside Tilliat several times each day, and she could then be found enjoying the sun with Thorn's sister Bone.

Thorn had been of major assistance to Li Kassu, particularly in the repair of Tilliat's hands and her thighs. The burns on her upper legs had been deep, dangerously deep, and Dragon and mage toiled long and hard at the healing. Sometimes Perra Koos wandered outside to chat with Bone, or to help Davin Pearl hunt for dead wood for the fire.

Toomay left Tilliat very briefly to feed on meat hunted by Bone but clearly preferred to stay by his friend. Thorn usually left the cave when Davin began cooking. This evening, Li Kassu, Perra and Davin were drinking tea after their meal when Thorn paced softly into the cave. Davin Pearl smiled at the old Dragon reclining against the rock wall. 'I've lost count of the days we've spent here now Thorn. Has that lad been crowned king yet?'

'It is tomorrow he becomes king Uncle. And I have a mind to witness this crowning myself.'

Toomay's head snapped round to stare at his many times great grandfather. 'It is too far to fly, you said so yourself.'

Thorn huffed. 'There is no such thing as "too far" with Dragon gateways. If you know exactly where you want to go,' he amended quickly. He'd allowed his mindvoice to be heard by all of them since they'd arrived here and now he regarded Li Kassu. 'You must let the child awaken tomorrow at moonrise,' he told her. His gaze moved on to the trader. 'That is when you must give her the gift the boy left with you. Toomay will know when the time arrives.'

'Are you going to Vremilia alone?' asked Perra Koos. 'Will Bone travel with you?'

'No. Bone will stay here to help you if you have need. Another will travel with me though, to witness this crowning.'

'Who?' Toomay sounded hopeful.

'Joseya, from the Elder Council. She arrived here some time ago.'

'When will you leave?' Perra asked. 'And are the Shadows still here? I've noticed there's no sign of them on Tilliat's poor hands.'

'We here.'

Perra stiffened as the whisper tickled at the back of his head.

'We will show.'

Perra had no idea what that might mean but prudently decided to ignore it. There was the distinct sound of a snigger in the back of his head. He ignored that, too.

In Garjetka, the day seemed endless to Tetsura. He was ritually bathed, anointed, robed and garlanded with ropes of pearls, sapphires, rubies and diamonds. He was escorted to various areas of the city, through cheering crowds throwing flowers before him. The actual ceremony of crowning was to take place in a vast building near the Phoenix Palace and as Tetsura mounted the steps to the large white marble dais towards the waiting priests, there was a great gasp from the crowds waiting to witness.

Two great Dragons shimmered into view to one side, one black, one, slightly smaller, pale lemon. The priests hastily backed away in the opposite direction and Tetsura halted, staring up at the two Dragons. A delighted smile spread across his face and he climbed on towards Thorn. He bowed low before the black Dragon.

'I, and my people, are honoured above all by your presence here today Dragon Thorn.' He bowed to the lemon scaled Dragon. 'I do not know your name, but I thank you for coming here to bear witness.'

Thorn and Joseya both dipped their heads in return and settled gracefully on the marble floor.

Into a deep silence, Tetsura knelt before the priests and spoke the vows and promises of kingship. A simple gold crown was lowered upon his head, and Tetsura arose, King of Vremilia.

Chapter Thirty-Five

The King mindspoke Thorn when the ceremonies were ended at last. He invited him and Joseya to the Phoenix Palace where a sumptuous reception and banquet would last for the rest of the afternoon and into the early evening.

'We would prefer to try and find the places our ancestors told of, our old ledges and roosts. We would rejoin you when you make the sky flowers at moonrise.'

Tetsura was hard pressed to conceal a grin, guessing the Dragons would find the smell of the banquet unbearable.

And so that long, long day wore on. Tetsura could somehow sense Sergeant Tag's presence near him throughout but caught not a glimpse of a short person with hair flaming red from under her cap. Commander Anjit and two guards accompanied the King closely while he met ambassadors, governors, guildsmen and yes, representatives of the mageborn. He was delighted to greet Saima, looking stunningly beautiful beside the dumpy figure of a beaming Deng. He met the leaders of many of the guilds, spending some time with Poxton Dens, the Royal Jeweller.

Vilad walked behind his king, nearly bursting out of his pale blue dress robes with pride. Tetsura had hidden his disappointment when Vilad showed no interest in hearing how Tilliat fared. He understood how much Vilad had endured, physically and mentally, to ensure he would be able to stay close to his friend's son. Tetsura understood the mute Vilad had devoted his whole existence to caring for and protecting the young Prince.

But now, Tetsura was the King and must loosen Vilad's hold on him, however loving that hold had been. Commander Anjit had raised the subject only two days earlier. He told Tetsura that Vilad had peremptorily sent away two senior scribes who had brought detailed reports on the reopening of two government departments – Finance and Justice. The reports had been requested personally by Tetsura yet Vilad saw fit to turn the scribes away.

All these thoughts were simmering through the King's head even as he made polite conversation with so very many people. Also, he was wondering if Sergeant Tag would actually show herself later or if she would just disappear, into the city. Tetsura glimpsed Saima again through a gap in the press of guests. She was happy to be his friend and occasional counsellor, but was more than content to stay as landlady of the Sea Slug. (She reported business had greatly increased since Tetsura's visit and perhaps he might like to call again?)

Commander Anjit by the King's shoulder, cleared his throat in discreet warning. Tetsura focused on the man advancing on him, four women fluttering at his heels. He racked his brain for a name – Bar! Master of the luxury traders. The man bowed and gave him an oily smile. He seemed gratified that the King knew his name. He waved a hand, laden with large gaudy rings on every finger. 'May I present my wife Your Majesty. And my three daughters. All unwed as yet,' he added archly.

Stars forefend! Commander Anjit coughed again. 'The Governor of Rashken awaits Your Majesty.'

'Ah yes, of course. Do excuse me Guild Master. A pleasure ladies.'

Tetsura followed Anjit between two large pillars where the crowd was marginally thinner.

'Strange don't you think sir, that people are exactly what they look like?

Tetsura glanced at Anjit who stared ahead. 'Ferrets.' he said succinctly.

Tetsura snorted. 'Where are we going?'

Anjit turned to the King. 'To meet Rashken's Governor. He's in the inner garden – crowds upset him.'

They rounded a corner, Tetsura nodding and smiling to all he passed.

'Those Dragons sir. They were real weren't they? Not some magic?'

Tetsura halted so suddenly his two escorts nearly trod on him. 'They were real. Once upon a time, they lived in these Isles and would have been our friends. Our ancestors chose to control or

404

kill those Dragons – stars know why. So the Dragons left these lands. They could so easily have destroyed every human here but they chose exile, and made a home for themselves on the mainland.'

Tetsura met the eyes of Anjit and the two guards in turn. 'Thorn and his Kindred are welcome here now, by the express command of the Phoenix Throne.'

The three guards snapped salutes. Tetsura nodded, continuing round another corner and down a short flight of steps to a garden. A slender white-haired man awaited the King, robed in a swirl of green and blue robes. He bowed, touching his lips, forehead and heart and spreading his open hand towards Tetsura. The King had never seen such a greeting, but he returned the salute exactly. The man smiled with genuine delight.

'I am Lerash, Your Majesty, and I cannot express the joy I feel at seeing you at last upon the Phoenix Throne. It is so long since I last saw my distant cousin and you sir, are so very like her.' The man's dark grey eyes were filmed with tears while he beamed at Tetsura.

Tetsura was processing Lerash's words and now exclaimed: 'You were related to my mother?'

'Oh yes. We were much of an age and often spent time together until she was ordered to Garjetka to become King Tetso's wife.'

'*Ordered?* I didn't know that.'

Lerash moved further into the garden, past exquisitely tended roses and brilliant flowerbeds, Tetsura beside him.

'We were immediately forbidden from contacting sweet Naila of course, although we *did* receive a very few letters from her. Sent by the most circuitous of ways you understand.'

Tetsura nodded, his head beginning to ache with yet more new things to come to terms with.

'Regent Hikmat, of cursed memory, tried to eliminate our family – we were too well known as mage born for his taste. But many of us found places to hide and, with great care, we survived.'

Tetsura stopped. 'Will you remain here a few days? I would know more of my mother's family.'

Lerash smiled and bowed. 'It would be my enormous pleasure

Your Majesty.

Tetsura indicated the increasing numbers of people spilling into the garden. 'I cannot linger as you can see, but I look forward to speaking with you soon.'

Even as he spoke, horns sounded from various points around the Palace. 'That means a brief respite until the banquet begins, doesn't it?' Tetsura asked the Commander hopefully.

'Indeed sir. We will escort you to your apartments and you will have time for a short rest or a shower if you wish before you make your appearance in the great hall.'

Vilad was waiting and while Tetsura showered, he brushed out the ceremonial robes and laid them out ready to be redonned. Before leaving his rooms, Tetsura collected the small carved wooden box and tucked it safely in a fold of his robes. Vilad put a hand out to remove it, tutting in his strange way while mindspeaking Tetsura. 'That must stay here Majesty, it spoils the lay of the cloth.'

For the first time ever, Tetsura slapped his hand over the hidden box while glaring at Vilad. 'I choose to take it with me Vilad. *Never* do such a thing again.' Tetsura felt guilty seeing Vilad's suddenly stricken expression but hardened his heart and strode to where Commander Anjit and four guards waited. He loved Vilad dearly but the old man *must* understand, and quickly, that Tetsura was no longer a lonely, neglected boy. He was the King.

Across the sea, four people, a small cat and a young Dragon sat inside a large cave room. Toomay had alerted Li Kassu and she had gently roused Tilliat to full awareness for the first time in nine days. Tilliat's head had been lifted and rested in Davin's lap as he sat behind her. Li Kassu and Perra Koos also sat close by in silence. Outside, Bone reclined on the ledge high above the cave entrance, sending the pictures from Thorn's mind into theirs.

They watched the slender boy climbing steps towards Thorn, saw his delighted smile, heard his words of greeting and thanks. Tears slid slowly down Tilliat's cheeks. She saw her brother in such gorgeous robes, the scarlet phoenix embroidered on the front, heard his steady voice repeat the oaths before such a great multitude of people. Then the roar from so many throats when a gold circlet was set on his brow and he rose as a king.

'We help show.' There was no mistaking the pride in the Shadows' tone.

'Thank you, thank you. It was wonderful to see.'

Li Kassu's fingers brushed Tilliat's forehead and the girl slid back into sleep, a smile still on her lips. The warmth from the fire had already dried the tears. Tilliat's skin on the front of her body was still too sensitive to bear more than the lightest touch.

Davin Pearl eased Tilliat's head from his knees and reached to swing the pot of water over the fire. He laughed. 'Just imagine. They'll all be drinking the finest wines now while we'll toast a new king with tea!'

Li Kassu and Perra both smiled at the idea. Cloud stretched then wrapped her tail neatly round her front paws. 'Ty Chay liked that wine stuff. She used to shout at Pitzi and hit him a lot when she drank it.'

Li Kassu exchanged a glance with Perra. 'I wonder if they still live,' she said quietly.

Perra thought of the many people within his own house in Gulat. 'How long will we stay here now?' he asked Li Kassu. 'Could you manage here with Uncle if I returned to Gulat?'

Davin Pearl passed a bowl of tea to Li Kassu, scowling at Perra as he gave him a bowl too. 'You are surely the same age as me Perra Koos. It's most annoying that you call me Uncle.'

'But Uncle is your name.' Toomay's mindvoice was firm.

Davin glared at the Dragon, then at Perra when the mage choked on his first sip of tea. Li Kassu intervened. 'Tilliat is mending better than I dared hope. Davin is perfectly able to give me any assistance I could need. I think it is time you left Perra. Another few days and the child can wake properly, then Davin, Cloud and Toomay can care for her.'

'Tomorrow morning,' said Toomay. 'You must wait tonight.'

Perra shrugged. 'Morning is fine. But will the Shadows agree to take me back?'

'We take.'

Well, that answered that question, Perra thought. Then he wondered if the Shadows would still occupy his head once he was back in Gulat, and would that be a good idea? He flinched slightly when he heard an unmistakeable snigger.

407

The banquet was nearly ended. Tetsura made his first official speech from beneath the canopy of state, thanking all the guests for both attending his crowning and for the many varied gifts they'd brought him. 'Please take your time,' he ended with a smile. 'I have matters to attend to but will rejoin you soon.'

There were cheers and applause; the guests all knew that meant their new king was preparing to create the sky pictures. Commander Anjit stepped aside, waiting for the king to leave the high table while a full escort formed a wall between him and still seated guests. They made their way to the second hall, from which the balcony projected towards the centre of Garjetka.

Once more guards formed a line across the wide doorway leading out to the balcony, ready to face any who attempted to enter the room. Commander Anjit waited close to his men while Tetsura started through to the unlit balcony. A small figure moved in the corner but Tetsura kept his gaze fixed on the darkening sky.

He was aware that Sergeant Tag had moved forward to be level with him, leaving an arms length between them. He waited, his mouth suddenly dry and his heartbeat thudding in his ears. Slowly Tetsura reached into the fold of his robe and drew out the carved box. He took out two small silk wrapped objects. He held out his left hand with one of the items on his palm. Small fingers barely touched his skin as Tag took the gift.

'Whatever your answer, the gift is yours,' murmured Tetsura. He heard a soft hiss of breath, the silk fluttered to the floor.

'It is beautiful sir.'

'I had three made some time ago, while Hikmat was still Regent. One for my sister, one for myself and this white gold one, for you.'

Tag lifted the chain and starlight sparkled on the beautifully wrought Dragon. It was similar to the Dragon in Tetsura's room, unlike Thorn or Toomay. Every scale was perfectly delineated and tiny ruby eyes flashed as the Dragon twisted on its chain.

Tetsura opened the other square of silk and held up a similar Dragon. His was yellow gold with sapphires for eyes. He lifted his hands to fasten the clasp round his neck, never ceasing to watch for the first hint of the new moon. He sensed Tag repeating his gesture, and continued to wait. He was aware when she moved closer although he could barely hear her whisper.

'My name is Editha, and I would ask if you wish a queen or a wife.'

Tetsura bit the inside of his cheek to keep his shout of victory from escaping. 'I would like a wife first, who will become a magnificent queen,' he replied.

'Then my answer is yes, Your Majesty'

Tetsura saw the tiny fingernail of moon rise from the dark waters of the ocean and raised his hands. Lights burst and sprayed across the sky: flowers, birds, wheels of colour, a phoenix and finally, a golden Dragon.

In the heart of the Dragon Realm on the mainland, Tilliat was once again awake. Her wide smile made her cheeks hurt but the smile remained in place. She guessed Thorn was watching this amazing display from somewhere near, but outside, the Phoenix Palace. She was aware of the old Dragon's delight when the golden Dragon at last filled the sky above the Palace. And then it was over.

Toomay's long face dipped down to breath softly over her. 'Uncle has a gift your brother left for you. He had three such things made Thorn said. One for you, one for himself, and one for his female.'

Li Kassu and Perra Koos both chuckled. 'One for his wife Toomay, his queen.'

Toomay's eyes flickered. 'Why do humans have so many different words for the same things?'

But Davin Pearl was holding a small silk wrapped article in front of Tilliat.

'Open it for me Uncle, for I cannot.'

Davin carefully unfolded the silk, stared for a moment, then lifted a buttery gold chain. Swinging and twisting on the chain was an exquisite gold Dragon with eyes of diamond. Tilliat couldn't stop looking at the beautiful thing and eventually Li Kassu propped up some pieces of firewood and hung the chain, with its Dragon, there.

Tilliat lay looking at it for a long time before Li Kassu told her she must sleep again.

'I must get well quickly, so we can visit my brother and inspect his queen,' she managed to murmur before her eyes closed again in healing sleep.

The story continues in 'Echoes of Dreams …

Books in the "Circles of Light" series